ANDROMEDA'S VENGEANCE

BOOK 3 OF ANDROMEDA'S ACCOUNT

L.B. BENSON

EMERALD MOON
PRESS

ALSO BY L.B. BENSON

ANDROMEDA'S ACCOUNT

The Bartered Soul
The City of New Aphros
Andromeda's Vengeance
The Northman's Lullaby

THE WOLVES OF WOODBINE HOLLOW

Sunset Daydreams
Neon Elegies

ANDROMEDA'S VENGEANCE
BOOK 3 OF ANDROMEDA'S ACCOUNT

By
L.B. Benson

Cover design by Hampton Lamoureaux/TS95 Studios www. ts95studios.com

Edited by Aimee Vance
www.aimeevancebooks.com

ISBNs
979-8-9861231-6-5 (eBook)
979-8-9861231-7-2 (Paperback)
979-8-9861231-8-9 (Hardback)

Published by Emerald Moon Press
https://lbtheauthor.com

For all the girls who have enough rage for the rest of us.
Don't waste it.
xo, LB

CONTENT WARNING

Andromeda's Vengeance is an adult fantasy/romance that contains content that might be upsetting for some readers. It is intended for readers over the age of 18.

To view detailed content/trigger warnings, please visit the author's website: https://lbtheauthor.com or scan the QR code below.

PROLOGUE

Nine Years Ago
Grand Castle of Aphros, Selennia

Queen Adelaide stared out the window while the herbs Salome gave her long ago steeped in a mug of boiling water on her desk. *I should have listened to you, old friend. I can only hope your wisdom can help me now,* Adelaide thought, remembering Salome, the former High Priestess of Selennia and her once closest friend. Salome had warned her these days were coming, but no one had taken her words to heart.

How did I let this happen? Adelaide wondered, her heart breaking as she surveyed the scene beyond the castle proper.

The broken bodies of Adelaide's loyal soldiers hung from the walls of the pristine castle. From this distance, their blood looked like rust staining the grey and white stone they were pinned to. The crofts that laid between the castle and the port in Aphros still smoldered in the fading afternoon light, black smoke curling into the air. The screams of her people had already begun to fade, dead or despondent now, and only the shouts of Blackwell's soldiers and the whinnying of horses punctuated the silence. With the Central Temple hidden by the forest, Adelaide had no way of knowing if it had been destroyed yet — if its destruction contributed to the smoke choking the sun — or if they'd simply hauled the priestesses out for execution. She had little hope that the holy women had survived this long, or that they'd escaped in time.

It had taken some time, but Blackwell's brutal followers had finally defeated them.

The siege was over.

The castle lost.

Failure and sorrow weighed heavily on Adelaide as she turned from the window to stir the steeping tisane, eyes sweeping for the last time over the room she'd spent so many days in since becoming queen.

Steam wafted off the mug, curling in the air before disappearing, carrying her last hope with it. Even staring at the poison, Adelaide wasn't afraid to die. Whatever the herbs would do as they eased her toward death would hurt less than the vicious whims of Dargan Blackwell. Even after Adelaide had ignored her words, Salome had left her with this last solace.

This way, Blackwell could never have her.

Without the true queen by his side, he would never receive the Goddess' blessing. He would never be seen as the legitimate ruler of Selennia by its people or the land itself. And, despite what he may think, his god would never tame this island.

The certainty that the Afterlife waited for her — and the hope that Gareth would be there to greet her — was a comfort, but a tear still slipped from her indigo eye at the memory of her lover, lost so many years ago. Gareth was likely stolen from her by the same man who now stole her home, her castle, and her country.

Dargan Blackwell.

Another tear slid down her cheek, this time for her daughter — *Nerissa*. Regret burned in her breast as her heart ached, causing her to close her eyes against the phantom pain. So much was left unsaid between the two of them, and now it was too late.

Adelaide had never told Nerissa the truth. Never seemed to find the right time to confess that she was her mother, not a loving aunt who had taken her in. And now, all she could do was mourn their future together while hoping the last piece of her love story — her daughter and heir — had escaped. Regrets of all sorts flooded Adelaide, rushing from her eyes as she sank beneath the window to cry while the tea on her desk cooled to a temperature she could drink.

She cried for her people, for her country.

She cried for the Goddess, for Her loyal followers.

She cried for Gareth, for Salome, for Nerissa.

She cried for herself. For a future she didn't have. For all the mistakes she'd made.

When the tea was ready, Adelaide began to sip the bitter poison. She didn't know how long it would take to work, but time was running out. Now that the gates stood open to the enemy, it was only a matter of time before her tower would be breached and they would come for her.

In between sips, she finished a letter to her daughter; a coded confession, just in case. When the ink was dry, she folded it into an intricate design and slipped it into a gap in the stones of the wall of her room — a location Nerissa had discovered once as a teen. Adelaide had little hope that her daughter would return to the castle, but on the chance she did, she hoped Nerissa would think to look for the message. Standing back to be certain the parchment was hidden from the naked eye, Adelaide swallowed another sip. Then another larger one.

Steps sounded outside her room, coming from the stairwell at the end of the hallway. At the noise, Adelaide downed the remainder of the liquid, then tossed the mug into the fire raging in her fireplace, her stomach flipping with fear as she palmed a sharp knife and squared her shoulders. She stood in front of her desk with her back to the window, the smoke and fires outside the castle a solemn backdrop for her final stand as the footsteps ended at her doorway and the pounding at the lock began.

Within moments, the thick oak splintered and the door swung wide, allowing Dargan Blackwell and his second in command, Russell Charleston, to step into her chambers. Adelaide didn't flinch as several other men in red and black filed in behind their leaders, flanking the door to prevent her from escaping. Their boots tracked thick mud on the grey stone underfoot. Her limbs tingled and stomach knotted, whether from fear or the herbs beginning to work, she didn't know. But Adelaide maintained a calm expression, a wide smile spreading across her face.

"Come now, Dargan. All this just to woo me?" Adelaide crooned in a singsong voice, the one she knew infuriated the man from across the sea, even as her mouth grew uncomfortably dry. "You'd think by now you would have figured out this is certainly not how to win my heart."

"The time for wooing is over, Adelaide. And I don't give a shit about your heart." Blackwell's voice was cold and full of bitter hatred as he stared at the queen he once sought to wed. "Your people are defeated. Your soldiers are dead. What further need do I have for you? This island is mine."

The Blackwell that stood before her was different from the one who'd originally arrived in Selenna to propose to her so many years ago. Harder. Crueler. But, even then, Adelaide knew he'd only seen her striking beauty and the lack of a man at her side. As the youngest son with three older brothers, he had little hope of inheriting a title or estate from his family. But she'd seen through him from the beginning — he didn't want her. He wanted *power*. He hoped to win her heart and use her love to slowly leech the power of her title so *he* could rule Selennia.

Perhaps if he'd been more convincing, things would have ended differently, but, time and time again over the last twenty years, she had rebuffed him. Now, he was finally taking what he wanted by force.

"My people will never accept you," Adelaide said, her voice thick as she looked at the men while her vision began to cloud. "My people are loyal not only to me but to the Goddess. They will never love your God or your priests. You cannot rule by fear and force alone."

"Ruling with love and gentleness hasn't worked out well for you, has it?" Blackwell sneered. Never willing to do his own dirty work, he turned to the younger man always by his side, jerking his chin toward Adelaide. "Charleston, take her."

Blackwell's words stung, but he wasn't wrong. She'd been foolish enough to think that the people's love would save Selennia. That notion was how she'd gotten here.

Salome and her many warnings had been right in the end. Even after Adelaide's numerous rejections, Blackwell hadn't faded away — his thirst for power was too great. Adelaide had underestimated the machinations he'd already begun to take hold of the small island country.

Peace wouldn't save Selennia like Adelaide had hoped, but she hadn't heeded Salome's warnings to protect Selennia from Blackwell in time. She hadn't stopped Salome from fleeing to New Aphros when her pleas for actions to secure Selennia were ignored. And she'd waited too long to search in earnest for the truth of the ancient priestess-queens' powers until her greatest ally was already across the sea.

More regrets, ones Adelaide would never be able to resolve.

In the time her mind had wandered to her old friend, Charleston crossed the room. For as long as Blackwell had come courting, Charleston was always at his side — ready to do his bidding, no matter how loathsome. "Come on, Addie. Be a good girl and do as he says," he ordered, a sarcastic smile tugging at the corner of his mouth.

As the Commander reached to take her arm, Adelaide stepped into him. "Fuck you, Russell," she whispered, then dragged the knife hidden in her opposite hand down his cheek.

If she'd had her full faculties, she would've aimed for

something more vital than Charleston's ruggedly hand-some face, but in her weakening state she only managed to cause him enough pain to force him to stagger away from her, gripping his cheek where the blade had sliced from the outer edge of his eye to the corner of his mouth. His bellow of pain filled the air as Adelaide looked up to meet Black-well's dark eyes. Her smile was no longer sweet and placating as it had always been. Now her lips curled like a feral creature trapped in its den, waiting to rip out the throat of her enemy, even if she knew she couldn't defeat the contingent of men standing in her doorway.

Two soldiers left their positions to aid Charleston, wrapping his face in cloth as Adelaide faced Blackwell. She wiped Charleston's blood from her blade, staining the silver floral embroidery on her gown a deep scarlet. Now the shimmering leaves matched the soiled foliage of the countryside where her soldiers had bled for her. When the steel shone silver again, she sliced through her palm. A stream of crimson ran down her pale forearm, dripping on the rough stone floors under her bare feet as she recited ancient words to the Goddess. She swayed as she spoke, regretting any doubts she'd had in the Goddess after Gareth's death. Numbness spread through her from the poison as she quickly prayed for her daughter, her people, her country. Her only comfort was that Salome knew her herbs, and she would be dead before she could be used by this man as a symbol to subdue Selennia.

"Pray all you want, Adelaide." Blackwell laughed. "Your Goddess fled your country long ago. She won't help you, just like she hasn't helped any of your temple whores."

The numbness remained as Adelaide prayed, but it was

now accompanied by fear as she worried for her daughter at the temple in Athene, her stomach clenching with nausea and the color draining from her face at the thought that Nerissa might have already perished. Her words changed to a silent prayer of protection for Nerissa, to help her escape so she could one day return to save Selennia.

To do what Adelaide couldn't.

As her strength waned, the knife slipped from her shaking hand. Adelaide reached into her pocket, as though she might have another weapon hidden, but she merely gripped two locks of hair tied with silver ribbon — one black, like a raven's wing, so like her own; the other dark brown, the last thing she had of Gareth's now that his knife had fallen from her weakened fingers. Her knees buckled and she fell to the floor, the fabric of her dark blue gown soaking up the blood she offered in prayer while a sheet of black hair streaked with silver hid her face, staring without focus at the bloody stones under her.

"Go get the bitch," Blackwell ordered on a sigh, as if Adelaide's collapse was a mere inconvenience or another distraction, worry never coloring his tone. Two soldiers stepped from his contingent to grip her under her arms, pulling her along toward her fate as she clutched the remains of her family. Adelaide smiled as she heard a sorrowful howl through the open window before her last breath left her lungs.

PART ONE
HOLD FAST

CHAPTER I

I watch from the shade of the quarterdeck of the *Bartered Soul* as Lyra bounces on her toes, tan fingers gripping the railing as the tropical jungle of Delosia comes into view. The bright island sun brings out the red and gold that glint in her dark, tightly coiled, curls glistening with sea spray as she turns her face to the light, warming her cheeks and highlighting the crescent sigil on her brow.

The call of "Land ho" had reached us below deck, where we were practicing Lyra's elemental control in the surgery. Immediately she'd dropped the hovering ball of seawater into its bowl and rushed to the stairs to watch as we cut through the bay's smooth turquoise waters.

Seeing the delight written in her features, I envy her resilience after the losses we've suffered since our journey together began months ago. Her bright grin is contagious, and I can't help but share in her excitement as the shimmering white sands beckon, even if my own smile is far less enthusiastic and my head and eyes ache from lack of sleep from the recurring nightmares that haunt my nights.

It's been nearly two months since we said our final farewells to Salome at her funeral pyre and almost two weeks since we departed New Aphros laden with supplies provided by the Merchant Council. We took to the seas earlier than anticipated despite the potential for late winter storms.

After the attack by Blackwell's soldiers and priests in the square of New Aphros, we nursed bruised hearts, explored the new power that Delphine had channeled into me upon Salome's death, and made sure that everything was in order for Celeste to take over Salome's former duties as madame. Until our return, Celeste will manage the *Den of Sinful Delights* for Delphine and aid in running the boarding house Lennox bought her. If the threat of Blackwell sending more ships to the west hadn't loomed, we might have mourned a few more weeks, but, as it was, we were eager to set sail for Delosia, and then onward to the tiny island of Nemi for the annual meeting of the pirate captains on the Spring Equinox.

Luckily, the fair weather has held, and both our ships — the *Bartered Soul* and *Andromeda's Vengeance* — have made the voyage with little fanfare. While our crew is fond of the island in the distance, our arrival in Delosia serves several purposes: Lennox hopes to gain aid in our endeavors against Selennia's false king, Dargan Blackwell. In addition, Lennox can inspect the newest ship Erik claimed for him when he retrieved Lyra and Siobhan. The visit also coincides with Lyra's seventeenth birthday, one that will fall on the same night as the full moon. A celebration — possibly the last one for quite some time — is in order.

Across the sea, sailing in tandem with us, is Erik

Varangr, Lennox's former quartermaster and now captain of the *Vengeance,* with my sister priestess Siobhan by his side. Lyra, Delphine, and Delphine's friend Daniel all sail with us on the larger *Bartered Soul.*

Since Daniel joined our group in New Aphros, he's proven himself a worthy addition, providing internal knowledge of the King's religion and the priests' behaviors, as well as a link to the other young men who renounced their new faith in the square and now bunk with our crew.

Delphine has been more of a challenge.

The young priestess' already difficult attitude is heightened by her mourning for Salome, who was both a surrogate mother and a mentor to her. Del's increased alcohol consumption has only served to exacerbate her acerbic personality, much to the chagrin of anyone unfortunate enough to cross her path. I hope the change of scenery the island provides, along with Lyra's gentle friendship, might soothe her. But as I watch Del's pale curls appear through the hatch, grey eyes squinting in the bright light and a scowl on her lips, I can't help but worry for the young woman.

Delphine winces and rubs her temples, likely due to seeking the bottom of a rum bottle last night, as she reaches Lyra's side at the rail, offering a gentle smile in response to Lyra's excited chatter. Their words are carried away on the ocean breeze, not reaching me where I stand at the entrance of the Captain's quarters, but relief fills me at the softness between them. Delphine has someone she can speak with, or at least be comforted by, since she refuses to do anything other than scowl in my direction. Taking a deep breath of the briny air, I turn toward the great cabin to ready for shore.

"Hello, wife," Lennox greets me as I enter our cabin. I smile at his cavalier use of the title since neither of us has officially shared with our crew that we handfasted in private one night under the dark moon.

"Hello, husband," I answer, watching him pack items into a trunk to be hauled ashore. "We'll have to be careful throwing those words around on shore, won't we?" We'll likely both be forced into false personas once again in the months ahead, and I sigh at the thought. I look forward to a day when I'm finally able to just be myself. I can only hope those days will arrive sooner rather than later.

"We will, my pretty priestess. All will be well," he soothes, standing and striding across the room to pull me into an embrace. I rest my cheek against his chest as I stare out the back windows to the bright blue sky beyond.

The stack of books I found waiting for me from Salome still rests on Lennox's carved desk, mostly untouched. I can't quite explain why I haven't delved into the ancient texts, but anxiety ripples through me at the thought of studying them. It's almost like doing so is the final step to solidify my transition from fleeing priestess to returning queen. Of course, I looked through them before in Salome's office in the *Den of Sinful Delights* alongside my mentor, and she'd told me she pored over them after she left Selennia. But tension still skips over my skin when I glance at them as if the power I acquired upon Salome's death has changed my relationship with the very words they hold — it isn't just the history of our homeland within their leather bindings; it's mine as well.

Salome's revelations about my mother, my bloodline, and the history of the Goddess rocked me in New Aphros, opening my eyes to the truth of who I could be. Her injury at the hands of Blackwell's men, and her final sacrifice to gift me the power that should have been my birthright, was the final push needed to set me on the path we all now travel. Though I've continued to practice with the elements, as well as the deadly slicing *glow* I was gifted the night Salome died, I've put off inspecting the texts. But I know I won't be able to do so for much longer.

The farthest I got in the stack was opening the cover of the first book, the one that contains the drawing of the first king and queen of Selennia that Salome showed me in her office — the image of the Goddess and her wolf. When I opened the cover, I found a letter in Salome's swirling script hidden away for my eyes:

Nerissa,

It sounds cliche to write these words, but, if you're reading this, then my prediction has come to fruition and I haven't returned from the Solstice celebration. I'm sorry that I kept my visions from you, and that I asked Siobhan and Delphine to do the same. I know you have endured so many secrets, yet here I present you with another.

I leave you these texts to study. Now that I've gifted my power to you, the balance should be restored — the rightful queen and heir of the Goddess holds the full power she should have possessed these past generations. The power to protect herself and our homeland like the Goddess intended when she gifted it to Her heirs so long ago. I still haven't determined what happened to sever the queen's power, but I have faith that you will know what to do to save Selennia and reclaim your throne.

You have a Channeler, *a* Seer, *and a* Healer *at your side now, not to mention the might of William's crews and connections. Lean into their support and remember what I taught you. Use your emotions. Don't let them stifle you again.*

Adelaide would be so proud of you. You have her kindness and her heart, even if you bury it deep, but you have Gareth's bravery and strength, too. All traits Selennia needs in its Queen. I'll be certain to tell them both about you when we meet in the Afterlife.

Take care of William and the others, and take care of yourself, Nerissa. The Goddess is with you and will stand at your side when you need Her.

All my love,

Salome

"Shall I pack them?" Lennox asks casually when he sees what captured my attention, as though he's ignoring the fact that I've avoided them this entire time. His warm voice pulls me back from my memory of Salome's words, and I nod for him to load the books in the trunk with our other belongings. Perhaps having my feet on solid ground will encourage me to search the texts for meanings Salome may have missed before.

Instead of darkening his hair this voyage, Lennox has allowed the color to return to its natural deep gold. It's longer than I'm used to seeing it, skimming his collar, and light stubble glistens on his cheeks and chin. Instead of revealing my true nature as he does, I cloak the knotwork crown that extends across my forehead, only allowing my crescent sigil to show on my brow like the last time I was here. I'm unsure what reaction the additional mark would attract when we land on the Delosian shores, and I plan to keep it hidden until the right time.

"Yes," I reply. "I think it's time for me to begin studying them."

"I can help you search through them. You don't have to do it alone," he responds, stepping away from me to gently place the books in the trunk amongst our clothing. The weather still isn't as warm as it was when we last visited Delosia, but the closer we've drifted to the island the brighter the sunlight shines and the more temperate the days grow. We won't need our heavier clothing items, leaving linens and the lightest wools to cradle the ancient books in the trunk.

"I know," I answer. This isn't the first time he's reminded me of the fact that I have friends to support me, but I still catch myself retreating inward more in the past weeks. Not necessarily from him, just to sit with my thoughts and come to terms with the choice I've made and the dangers we face, constantly wondering if returning to Selennia to reclaim the throne is the right decision.

Lennox's touch draws my eyes up to his face as he returns to my side and cradles my cheek in one palm. I gaze into his dark green eyes, my heart swelling with the emotions that burn brighter each day we spend together. "Are you all right?" he asks, studying my face as I press my cheek into his caress.

"Yes," I breathe, kissing his palm.

"You're certain?"

I nod, reassuring him and pressing a kiss to his full lips

before crossing the room to add a few extra items to our trunk.

THIS TIME WE DOCK IN THE HARBOR, NOT BOTHERING WITH THE secret bay the pirates usually use when they come to Delosia. We aren't expected, but Lennox's presence isn't unusual here, and since Lyra's grandmother, Marie, is the leader of the island we have no reason to hide our arrival. I follow Lennox down the gangway to the dock, followed by Lyra, Delphine, and Daniel. The young man, dressed in the rough clothing of the other sailors instead of the black habit of the priesthood, has filled out noticeably since the Solstice, and his lash wounds have healed into pink scars to cover his flesh like Lennox's. He walks protectively behind Del and Lyra, looking around curiously at the dockworkers and island residents as they go about their duties. Daniel's relationship with Delphine is still a mystery to me, but the young woman hasn't offered any details to clarify, even if I know he slips into the room she shares with Lyra frequently to help look after his friend.

We stand on the white sand beside the dock while we wait for Erik and Siobhan to leave the deck of *Andromeda's Vengeance*. Once they clear their ship, our group proceeds to Maryanne's tavern in the center of town. Delphine and Daniel marvel at the lush jungle filled with tropical plants that thrive here year-round on our way to the only town on the island. Some of the trees are broken and debris litters the edges of the path, but overall the island looks the same as it did when we left it nearly four months ago. The blooming flowers fill the air with sweet scents and surround me with memories of the hothouses at the Grand Castle in Selennia.

Strolling in a group through the sandy streets, Lyra points out a few sights to Delphine and Daniel, the trio making easy, quiet conversation while Lennox and I walk hand in hand toward Maryanne's. I glance around, looking for signs of the encounter with Blackwell's fleet, but don't notice anything out of the ordinary. Erik and Siobhan walk quietly at the back of the group, so I fall back to stroll alongside them, letting Lennox lead us through the streets.

"Was any damage done by the soldiers, or is this from the storms?" I wonder, gesturing to palm fronds that have fallen along the path.

"The cannon shot did not make it this far inland, and the men in town were surprised by the militia, so I think this was all storm-related," Erik answers as he inspects the buildings and broken trees.

"I'm anxious to see if my shop still stands. I know they ransacked it, but I didn't take inventory or inspect it afterward. We left so quickly for New Aphros," Siobhan says, looking down the sidestreet that leads to where her shop and home were located. She sighs, "My garden is likely ruined, but I suppose I won't need it anymore."

Sadness washes over me at the memory of Siobhan's peaceful garden on the outskirts of town where she grew herbal remedies as well as fruits and vegetables for her neighbors. "Perhaps someone kept up with it while you were gone? Was there no one else who would have tended it?"

"Perhaps," she replies, toying absentmindedly with the

gold torc at her throat, but her tone doesn't seem convinced. Erik wraps a long arm around her and pulls her tight to his side as we walk, offering gentle comfort so at odds with his menacing frame.

"And your grandmother rules here?" Delphine asks Lyra, still looking around at the various businesses on the main street.

"She's their leader, but she isn't like a queen or anything. It's all by vote. She wins each time because she's well-liked and fair. There's an agreement between her and the captains of several pirate vessels who make decisions, helping ensure the residents get the goods they need while skirting excessive taxes. Plus, the pirates know they can dock here without harassment. They usually have a peaceful accord with one another while on the island."

I cut my eyes to Lennox, finding a small smirk twitching at the corner of his mouth at her words. The last time we were here, the accord was almost broken when another captain laid hands on me at Marie's Hallow's Eve masquerade. For a moment that evening, I thought he was going to punch Captain Mario di Micios in the middle of the dance floor.

"Here we are!" Lennox announces, pushing through the bright coral door of Maryanne's little tavern. He holds it open for us to pass through into the dimly lit interior where customers cheerfully sip rum punch and look our way as we enter.

As soon as the door closes behind us, a cheerful voice booms through the room. "Lyra, darling girl what are you... Lennox! Andromeda! Siobhan! You're all back!" Maryanne, the middle-aged bar owner dashes from behind the bar to greet us, pulling each of us into a tight embrace against her full bosom in turn. She pauses at Delphine and Daniel momentarily, but smiles and grabs them too, saying, "Any friends of this lot must be good ones, come here loves! I'm Maryanne, who might you be?"

Daniel can't resist the woman's infectious glee and introduces them while Delphine's face remains impassive at the affection. "I'm Daniel and this is Delphine, Mistress. We're traveling with them from New Aphros."

"Oh, no need for formalities here, Maryanne will suit just fine. Let me get you all something to drink!" Before we can protest or make any requests, Maryanne has already turned toward the bar to pour ladles of rum punch into mugs. She returns to where we have taken seats around a large table, distributing the drinks in two trips before standing next to Lennox with a hand on his shoulder.

"Oh, I like this one," Delphine murmurs once she's tasted her drink. She holds it up to Maryanne in a gesture of appreciation before relaxing into her hardbacked chair to look around the room.

"So, New Aphros? Did you see Salome for the Solstice then?" Maryanne inquires, cheerfully sipping from her own mug. At the mention of Salome and the Solstice, all our faces drop.

"We did. It didn't end well, Maryanne. That's part of why we're here," Lennox murmurs, gently patting the older woman's hand as she studies his face with apprehension. "I need to send a message to Marie to let her know we've arrived."

"Of course, I'll grab you a parchment and quill. Just a moment."

Maryanne disappears into a back room, leaving us all in silence as the rest of the customers carry on with their conversations and dining. The tavern is unchanged from months ago; tables are still tightly packed together and the shutters allow the breeze to blow through, cooling the crowded space. The memory of how relieved I was to feel free in this pub returns at the sight of the men and women laughing together, encouraging me to relax in my seat and take comfort in the familiarity. Although a new young woman carries empty dishes to and fro, the rest of the establishment remains as cozy as if the skirmish with Blackwell's soldiers was a dream. Before long, Maryanne returns with a sheet of parchment, a quill and inkwell, and a stick of wax. Lennox scratches a short note, then seals the letter with the wax, pressing his signet ring into it.

Maryanne calls the new serving girl over and hands her the note. "Take this to Mistress Benoit directly and with haste. Wait for her response and bring it straight back." The girl nods and dashes out of the tavern, not even stopping to remove the apron she wears to keep her dress clean from her duties.

When the girl returns from her errand, everyone is quietly sipping their second mugs of rum punch. All our heads turn to her when she approaches the table. She averts her eyes when Lennox looks up at her but hands him a note with a deep purple wax seal — Marie's color that I remember well from my first visit. He cracks the wax, mossy eyes traveling over the script, then hands it to me to review.

.   .   .

William —

Dinner, tonight. Bring everyone involved. Chastain will be there. —M

"Who is Chastain?" I ask, handing him the note back. He stuffs it in his inner coat pocket before responding.

"Captain Morel, of the *Island Queen*."

"Ah," I reply, having suspected as much, remembering the pirate captain who winters here on the island.

"He's likely to ally with us, but tonight will be important," he adds, finishing his drink.

I nod my understanding and look over our small group. Daniel, Delphine, and Lyra chat quietly across the table while Lennox turns to Erik, explaining the plan for the evening. Siobhan watches the men, then turns toward me, our eyes locking momentarily as we give one another matching tight smiles.

Tonight, the wheels will begin to turn in earnest.

CHAPTER 2

"What do I need to know about Captain Morel? I don't remember much about him from our last visit," I ask Lennox as we stroll toward Marie's home, the sunset painting the sky in pink and orange streaks over the jungle.

"As you may have surmised by Marie's casual reference to him as *Chastain*," Lennox says with a relaxed smile, "he's close with her, and the Delosian people in general. He's native to the island and his family still lives here. Morel's brother sails with him, as do several cousins. They always ensure the best prizes they take at sea benefit the people here first."

"He also has the best gossip on the island, and a wonderful sense of humor," Lyra offers, earning a sharp glance from Delphine as they walk side by side.

"He *is* known to be lighthearted with those who call him a friend, but don't think that makes him any less danger-ous. There's a reason Marie and the militia call for his aid from time to time. He can be ruthless, and is a brutal fighter when crossed," Lennox concludes as we come into view of Marie's.

Marie Benoit's home is as elegant and inviting as it was when we last visited with its welcoming verandah and open shutters allowing the fragrant island breeze to dance through the parlor. We are whisked through the foyer and into the formal dining area as soon as we arrive, where the large dining table decorated in bright orchids and palm fronds is set for our meal. Marie sits at the head of the table beautifully attired in a cobalt linen dress accented by a printed head wrap, regal as any queen. Lennox takes the seat at the other end after I declined the place. The rest of us select open chairs — me to his right, the rest filled in with Erik and Siobhan, Pike, Lyra, Delphine, and Captain Chastain Morel.

I vaguely remember Morel from our last visit, even if I was too distressed at Marie's hints about my heritage to pay close attention to him. He has a dazzling smile which he flashes with ease. His dark eyes and complexion are nearly the same shade of rich, dark brown as Marie's, and his tightly curled hair is nearly black, worn closely cropped to his head. It's hard to determine his age, but I assume that he's similar in years to Lennox and myself, possibly a few years older.

The same butler as before brings refreshments around the table while we become reacquainted in the candlelight, Lyra chattering with Marie and Pike, Siobhan and Erik engrossed in one another, and Delphine downing her drinks faster than a small woman should be able to.

Lennox grazes my hand under the table, his warm touch sending a pleasant shiver over me as I watch him. His gaze drifts around the table to our friends with a small smile on his lips. I already long for the comfort and quiet of our room back at the boarding house after several weeks on the noisy ship, but the meal has yet to begin, and I assume this won't be a short engagement.

"Andromeda," Marie calls from the end of the table, drawing my focus to her. We only exchanged the briefest salutations upon our arrival before being whisked to the dining room, so this is the first time she's directly addressed me. "What did you think of New Aphros? I was sorry to hear about the loss of Salome."

Lennox had pulled Marie to the side once we entered the foyer earlier, explaining how Salome died in the square on Solstice. The older women didn't know one another closely, only by name and in passing through their link with Lennox's mother, but her startled gasp, and the fierceness of the embrace she wrapped Lennox in, was enough to know she recognized the impact of the loss.

I clear my throat slightly before answering. "New Aphros was enlightening. But I think it's time we all start using my real name, don't you? Please, call me Nerissa."

The table grows quiet as I speak, and even Delphine looks up from her wine glass. Although those closest to us know my true name and identity, I rarely use it in public, my alias feeling like a comfortable second skin I've inhabited for so long.

Marie gives a small smile, dipping her chin to me in response, her ebony skin creasing at the corners of her dark eyes. "Very well, *Nerissa*. Can I take that to mean what I think it does? Are you here for more than just Lyra's birthday celebration?"

"That depends. I had hoped we could speak about it privately, but if your men and Captain Morel agree to help me… help *us*… then yes. I believe it does." All eyes travel between me, Marie, and Captain Morel as I sit straight in my chair.

"What is it you are asking me to do?" Morel speaks, his voice deep and accented like those native to Delosia.

"To aid us in overthrowing Selennia's king. The way Erik helped you dispose of his soldiers when they came here," Lennox responds when I look at him to answer. "We plan on taking the request to the annual meeting on Nemi but thought to ask you now before the rest of the captains convene. To ask you to back Nerissa's claim to the throne of Selennia."

Morel nods his head once, a thoughtful expression turning the corners of his lips upward as he considers the request. Marie watches him with a goblet of wine in her fingers.

"Varangr did aid us. But would those soldiers have come here if not looking for you?" Morel asks me, studying my response to his statement. Although his question grates on me, there's nothing hateful or disrespectful in his tone, more like a musing or thinking out loud.

"*That's* a shitty thing to say," Delphine slurs from across the table. I tense as all eyes turn to her, but her only response is to purse her lips and shrug, taking another drink from her freshly refilled wine glass.

Morel laughs deeply in response to Delphine's attitude, his sense of humor in line with Lyra's comments earlier. Thankfully, he's not as offended as I expected, with a wide smile that lights up his handsome face with glee. "The truth is often unpleasant, Miss," Morel says to Delphine with a wink. Surprisingly, she raises her brows and purses her lips in an expression that says she agrees. "But, I think it's a valid point nonetheless. No offense meant to you, Captain. Nor to you, Mistress," he directs to Lennox and me.

"You're not wrong, Captain Morel," I admit. "But, judging by the infiltration by Blackwell's men in New Aphros before I ever arrived, I have no doubt his reach would have extended to the island regardless. Between his search for me and Blackwell's desire for power, no one will be safe from his ambition if we don't defeat him."

"I have no love for Dargan Blackwell, especially after his trespasses this winter," Morel begins, swirling his wine and following the dark liquid with his eyes as it circles his goblet. "But I'll need to speak with my crew before making a commitment. I want to do what's best for the people of Delosia, for my people. Mistress Marie, is this why you invited me tonight?"

Marie turns to Morel, her long silver braids falling over her shoulder as she does. She smiles wide, sipping from her wine glass once before nodding. "Yes, Chastain. I hoped that *Nerissa* would return to take her place in Selennia, even if my daughter-in-law and granddaughter are no longer trapped under Blackwell's rule there. Having a queen in Selennia again will increase trade, which benefits Delosia, *and* would allow some of you who don't wish to live a life on the account any longer to return home." Her last words settle over us, while her dark brown eyes focus on Lennox. His jaw twitches, but he says nothing.

"Very well," Morel nods, sipping his drink. "I shall speak with the crew this week and return my answer to you. If they agree, we will side with you at the council meeting on Nemi at the Equinox." A curt nod from Lennox ends the topic, and the butler files in a few minutes later with the next course, while the gathered guests fall into quiet conversation once again.

Lyra and Pike decide to remain at Marie's after dinner, choosing to spend more time with her when Marie offers spare rooms to them for the night. I could see the eagerness in Siobhan's eyes after Marie mentioned the neighbors near her shop had cleaned up the mess left by the soldiers, so it's no surprise when Erik and Siobhan retreat shortly after the plates are cleared. Delphine agreed to stay with Lyra, preferring her company to mine, but I doubt she will be awake much longer as it is.

Lennox and I left hand in hand after dessert and cordials, bidding farewell to Captain Morel who turns the opposite direction from our boarding house. "Do you think Delphine will behave?" I ask, my arm resting in the crook of Lennox's as our boots crunch on the grit underfoot. The breeze is cool and the temperature is mild as we meander through the dark streets.

Lennox shrugs, answering with a huffed laugh. "Even if she doesn't, Lyra and Marie can handle her. I think her soft spot for Lyra will keep her in line, but Marie has a good sense of humor. Either way, they'll all be fine for the night."

"Do you think Morel's men will agree to back me?" I toy with the seam on the edge of my pocket with my free hand, hoping to dissipate the nervous energy our meal has failed to soothe. The Delosian captain seemed amenable enough, but I know one's placations don't always equate to action, and I'm nervous about our proposal being openly broadcast before the time is right.

"I think so," Lennox says, placing his hand over mine where it rests on his arm, the touch comforting. "Marie has more sway than she and Morel let on at dinner. If she supports your claim, the rest will fall in line. No one wants to be at odds with her in the end; they know it will make trade difficult for them here. But," he pauses, squeezing my hand lightly, "you may have to show them a bit of your power to convince them."

Stunned by his words, I stop and drop Lennox's arm. "I'm not going to threaten them to side with me."

"That's not what I meant." He snags my hand, casually pressing a kiss to my knuckles before entwining our fingers and pulling me to walk with him once more. "I only meant for you to show them what they might ally with. Pirates aren't known for their self-sacrificing nature, but if they see what you can do, it would encourage their loyalty."

"I'll consider it," I concede as we near our lodging. "Perhaps on the full moon."

We arrive at the steps of the boarding house, where the lantern swings gently in the breeze out front, its flame flickering merrily. Laughter floats out of the open doorway promising a busy courtyard beyond. It seems like both a lifetime and no time at all has passed since we stood here last. Except then, the most pressing thing I had to worry about was whether or not I should reveal my true feelings to Lennox. Now, I feel as though I have the weight of the world on my shoulders. Or, at least, the weight of Selennia.

Lennox pauses before leading me up the stairs, looking into my eyes in the glow of the lantern. "You've taken the first step, Nerissa. Trust that the pieces will come together. Let's get settled here for a bit. We can start looking through the texts Salome left, plan Lyra's party, and, once Morel has decided, we'll determine our course of action." He tips my chin up with his index finger, smiling at me with his head cocked. "You're not alone anymore. Don't get lost in your mind." He brushes a soft kiss against my lips before guiding me with a warm, steady hand at my lower back up the stairs and into the boarding house to get lost in one another instead.

CHAPTER 3

"Delphine... *Del*? Are you listening?" My voice is sharper than I intended, but my frustration leaks through as I attempt to capture Del's attention. She snaps her head up to glare at me, eyes sunken from lack of sleep as they've been for the last week.

The first full day after arriving on Delosia was spent settling in at the boarding house. Both Lyra and Delphine are staying on the bottom floor in adjacent rooms, while Lennox and I share the larger suite upstairs that he claimed on our last trip to the island. In the week since then, I've met with both of them and Siobhan to continue our work from the voyage, attempting to hone our powers and test our strengths. Today, we intend to practice for a few hours, then we'll turn our attention to the excitement of preparing for Lyra's birthday and the full moon ceremony this evening.

"What?" Del asks with a frown from where she sits across from me at the small table in my room. The sounds of the birds in the jungle outside the boarding house drift in through the open shutters along the back wall, but I know the lull of birdsong isn't what distracts Delphine.

"We'll perform the ceremony first, then have dinner, then we can enjoy the beach." Lyra patiently repeats my earlier words, studying Delphine. Lyra's full lips tilt downward at the edges just enough to show she's growing frustrated with her friend, too.

"Ceremony, food, sand. What is it you need from me?" Delphine asks, rubbing her temples.

"Your participation," I snipe, tired of Delphine's lack of focus. While Lyra has continued to study and increase her skills, Delphine has come to a point of stasis, as though the loss of Salome has stunted her desire to use her powers at all. I can sympathize with the pain she feels, the need to numb it and to be lost in something other than her grief, but I also know that if she continues to handle it the way she's been doing, especially pushing her friends away, it could end up bringing her more pain in the end.

"Why don't you come with me, Delphine?" Siobhan interrupts, walking behind Delphine's chair to place a gentle hand on her shoulder. Her words are for Delphine, but the look in her eyes, showing she's putting herself between both mine and Del's rising tempers, is for me. "Come help with my garden. We can gather supplies for the decorations to take to Marie's. When Erik and I visited, there were plenty of plants in bloom that would be beautiful to display tonight."

"Fine."

Delphine stands, following Siobhan out and shutting the door while Lyra and I remain in my chambers.

"How is she?" I ask Lyra once they've gone.

Lyra drops into the chair across from me that Delphine abandoned, her slouched posture showing her exhaustion. "Not well. But she wouldn't dare tell *you*. Or admit it to anyone else," she grumbles, her usual sunny disposition faltering. "I try to be there for her, to get her to talk, but she won't." Lyra's cheeks flush with her frustration, tears barely held at bay in her hazel eyes. "She won't talk to Danny either. She just drinks and rages during the day, but I can hear her crying at night when she thinks I'm asleep. I tried to hold her the first night I heard her, but she pushed me away and went up on the decks instead, so I've pretended to be sleeping since."

I lean forward, taking her hand in mine. "You can't soothe everyone's hurts, Lyra, as much as I know you want to. Everyone processes grief differently. I wish she would talk to you, but maybe she needs more time. I can't imagine how hard losing Salome has been for her, but I'm at a loss for how to help her aside from giving her space."

Guilt eats at me, a nagging ache since that night, knowing Delphine blames me for Salome's death, even though I had no idea what she was planning. I too mourn the loss of the woman I grew close with while in New Aphros. If Salome had told me of her visions instead of asking Siobhan and Delphine to keep them secret, perhaps I could have helped discover an alternative to her death in the square of New Aphros. A way I could have taken on her power to boost my own to the level of the former Selennian Priestess-Queens without requiring her sacrifice. But I was never given that chance.

Pushing the knot of guilt and worry down, I plaster a smile across my face for Lyra's sake. It's her birthday, and I want her to have a night of enjoyment before we turn our sights to the seriousness of the meeting on Nemi and then what awaits us in Selennia. At sixteen, she reached the age we would usually have celebrated as her entry to womanhood in Selennia last year, but her birthday was never celebrated openly in the *House of Starlight*.

Celeste kept Lyra carefully secluded, hidden from everyone but those of us who lived there. Her unusual upbringing in the brothel meant Lyra is far more mature in some ways, but was sheltered in others, so Lennox and I want her to have a proper celebration after the years of quietly marking the passing years. I just hope the night will go smoothly after I make my announcement. Lyra's party is the only opportunity to address the islanders en masse, even if I hate to detract from her night.

In the last week, Morel has hinted to Lennox that his crew is hesitant to back an unknown without a show of power, regardless of Marie's enthusiastic support, and I wonder how many other Delosians will feel similarly.

"Now," I start, smiling more broadly despite my gnawing thoughts, "tell me again about the cake you requested Marie's cook to make while we figure out seating." Lyra returns my smile before starting to chatter about cakes and flowers.

CHAPTER 4
LENNOX

"How was your dinner with Morel?" Captain Jackson asks when we step into the street in front of the boarding house.

It's always a pleasure to see Jackson's smiling face and patchwork coat. As usual, his dark brown hair is tied back in a tight club at his nape, and his blue eyes narrow in the bright sunlight, deepening the lines that always bracket them. Without him, I'd never have had the opportunity to lead a mutiny against the captain of the ship I'd been pressed onto after Blackwell's initial invasion. When Jackson and his crew of pirates had approached far from Selennia, it had been enough to distract the captain and quartermaster who had so enjoyed brutalizing me for my rebellious nature. They never expected so many of the others would join me in rising up against them. After escaping and joining Jackson's crew, the outlaw captain became like a father to me, encouraging me to take my own ship and allying with me afterward. Jackson arrived in Delosia last night, having taken an extra week to depart

New Aphros, and is just now catching up with me after settling his crew on the island.

"Successful, for now," I answer, squinting into the bright island sun. "I hope his crew will cooperate, but he's mentioned that some of them are distrustful of Nerissa."

"Of her? Or outsiders, in general?"

"Both. They want to know what the power of a priestess can do, if needed."

"That seems understandable."

I nod. "I've given Morel time to gather his crew and discuss. I assume I'll hear from him in the next day or two with a decision. I wanted to get through tonight — the ceremony and Lyra's party — first before we truly begin planning. We need to sail in a week to reach Nemi by the Equinox."

Jackson gives a noncommittal snort. "If they saw what she did in New Aphros, they'd likely shit themselves."

I chuckle knowing his words are true. Nerissa's power, and Del's for that matter, are unheard of these days outside of ancient stories. If I hadn't seen them standing next to Salome blinding the priests and soldiers lining the walls of the cathedral in New Aphros, watched Delphine wrap them in protective shadows, or witnessed Nerissa slicing men in half with the brilliant power Salome passed to her, I wouldn't believe it myself. Even Siobhan and Lyra, with their respective *Sight* and healing, are wonders to add to our ranks.

"I'm sure Chastain can convince his crew. They trust him," Jackson reassures me, clapping me on the shoulder as we stroll toward the center of town, planning to join Erik outside Maryanne's tavern before meeting with the crews to prepare the bonfire.

I want to believe him, to trust Chastain and his crew will side with us, but doubt has begun to cloud my mind. Worry over Nerissa competes with my confidence in our crews the closer we get to the captains' gathering on Nemi. I can tell she worries too, even if she keeps it to herself. Each day since we left New Aphros she becomes quieter and more withdrawn. I'm not sure if it's the prospect of the meeting with the captains, the idea of returning to our homeland, or the impending battles we face that rattle her, but she's been avoiding my questions, so I've allowed it to drop for now.

Erik's tall frame looms in front of the tavern by the time we arrive, and he steps in line with us as we continue our walk to the docks. "Good morning, Varangr," Jackson greets Erik, glancing across me to the towering Northman.

"Good morning, Jackson. Glad to see you arrived safely," he replies before greeting me, "Captain."

I smile at the title Erik still refers to me by, even if he's now a captain in his own right. "How's Siobhan's shop faring, Erik?"

"Good." He nods. "Better than anticipated. Marie made sure some of her neighbors tended it well in her absence, they even cared for her garden. It is a comfortable home again for us to stay in while we are here."

"Excellent." I smile. Erik and Siobhan have stayed at the apothecary shop for the past week, and he's hidden away with her, busying himself with whatever she needs to set it to rights. Siobhan was dragged from her home by Black-well's men during their invasion this past winter, but Erik retrieved her before she could be taken back to Selennia.

"Is she planning to return to her life here?" I ask as delicately as possible, keeping my eyes trained on the glittering sand under our feet instead of him. Erik has seemed as lost in thought as me lately, and I wonder if he fears Siobhan won't return to sea with us when we depart. She never enjoyed being at sea, her fear of the depths being part of what kept her grounded here on the island instead of at Erik's side for all these years.

"She says she wishes to return home to Selennia, but I can tell it is not an easy decision for her. This was her home for a long time, but she is loyal to Nerissa. She will go where Nerissa does."

"She's loyal to *you*, man." I nudge him with my elbow. He quirks the side of his lips in response, giving me a half smile in return. Since they met, it's been easy to see that Siobhan and Erik were meant to be. Now that she's had a taste of what it feels like to be at his side for more than a few weeks, I can't imagine she would turn away. If we're successful against Blackwell, she can begin a new life on land in Selennia with him, if she wants. And if we're unsuccessful... Well, we'll likely all fall together and end up in whatever Afterlife awaits together, too.

I shake my head to clear the morbid thoughts of failure and the Afterlife. Tonight is the full moon and Lyra's birthday — not a time to be sinking into my worries. Those can wait until our plans are fully underway.

ONCE THE CREWS HAVE GATHERED ON THE BEACH, THEY BEGIN dragging driftwood, gathering fallen limbs, and cutting wood to build the massive beach bonfire. Leaving them to their duties, I'm eager to see the ship Erik captured for us after the raid here this winter, left in the shipwright's hands, and Erik and Jackson accompany me to the shipwright's cabin near the docks.

The older man, Adair, is likely around the age my father would be now had he lived past my childhood. He steps from the threshold of his home to watch as we climb the steep trail from the dock to his door. His craft is visible in all aspects of his home, from the sea creatures carved into the front door to the waves that crash on the trim of his windows as though his love of his work spills over onto whatever he touches. He's spent his life turning wood into art for each ship he modifies — the priestess of the *Bartered Soul*, the wolf that graces *Andromeda's Vengeance*, and the mermaid on the prow of Morel's *Island Queen* are all examples of his craftsmanship. A young man in his early twenties steps from the door, a younger version of the shipwright, to stand with his father.

"Captains! I was wondering when you'd come to see me!" Adair calls, uncrossing his arms and walking the short trip down the path to meet us with an outstretched hand. He shakes each of our hands and then steps back for his son to do the same.

"Good to see you, Adair. Erik told me he left a ship of mine with you the last time he left. I'm here to inspect it," I explain, looking around at the different ships at the docks. None of them resemble one of Blackwell's fleet, but that doesn't mean Adair hasn't already retrofitted it with a new figurehead to make it less conspicuous in my absence.

"Yes, yes, of course," Adair says with a bright smile. "I

took some liberties with it, my boy. I hope you don't mind, I had Jacob do the figurehead. I left the name, but it needed something new to make it worthy of you."

"Let's go see," I reply, a smirk tilting my mouth at the man's enthusiasm. I've seen some of the work Adair's son, Jacob, has done on other ships, proving to be just as talented as his father, and I look forward to seeing what he's prepared for me.

We wind down the pathway behind Adair's home to the private docks where he keeps ships hidden while he works on them. The sun glints off the ocean in the distance, but my focus is on the frigate sitting at anchor in a berth. The flags have been removed, all symbols of Dargan Blackwell scrubbed clean from the vessel, but the figurehead looms: a tentacled Kraken reaching for its prey. Painted on the stern is the *Kraken's Maw*.

"Well done, gentlemen. Well done." I clap Adair on the shoulder, then shake his son's hand. I marvel, looking up at the carving, each suction cup visible on the tentacles. I can almost hear the clicking of the beast's beak as I examine it. "The craftsmanship on the Kraken is astounding. Did you throw all of Blackwell's trappings out?"

"Thank you, Captain Lennox," Jacob replies, looking pleased even if he quickly averts his eyes from me. "And, no. We stored the flags, leftover uniforms, and anything else of value that remained. Just in case."

"Good."

"Dammit, Lennox. My protege wasn't supposed to surpass me so quickly. Look at these beauties you now have in your fleet," Jackson grumbles in jest as he gazes up at the ship.

"Let's just hope they stay in one piece," I mutter under my breath as I walk toward the ship to board it and look around, hoping my words are the jest I intend and not a premonition.

After departing the company of the shipwrights, Erik heads toward the apothecary shop to meet Siobhan, Jackson retreats to the boarding house he frequents, and I stroll toward my own. My quarters here on the island feel like a second home to me — the same one I shared with Nerissa when we came here together the first time, although now we happily share one room instead of pretending to be separate.

Dinner will be by the water tonight; Davey, our cook from the *Bartered Soul*, and Jackson's cook are partnering with Marie's household staff to host the meal on the beach after the priestess' full moon ceremony. Two pigs were slaughtered and already turn on a spit on the beach, the savory scent of fat made my mouth water when I passed by earlier. Entering the open-air courtyard, I look up the stairs towards our quarters, smiling at the thought of Nerissa, wondering how she spent her day.

Bounding up the stairs, I reach the door and open it eagerly. The sight of Nerissa freshly bathed and sitting in a dressing gown on our bed, staring out the window to the verdant jungle beyond, lost in her thoughts, is enough to steal the breath from my lungs. The scent of vanilla and lavender lingers from her cooling bath water. Nerissa's long hair hangs in damp waves down her back, as dark as the ink that spills from the Kraken carved on the prow of our new ship. She turns to face me when the door clicks shut, sapphire eyes studying me as I approach. I bend down to kiss the sigil on her brow, bringing a smile to her face as she closes her eyes.

"A good day, my pretty priestess?"

Nerissa sighs, the sound heavy as she looks back to the window. "A long one. But I think it will be worth it in the end. We need something lighthearted to brighten our spirits, don't you think? I can think of nothing brighter to celebrate than Lyra."

Moving towards the water basin, I pull my sweat-dampened shirt from my body, casting it aside as I dip a washcloth into the water to refresh before redressing for the ceremony. "I agree. Are you ready for tonight?"

"I think so. The full moon ceremony will be mostly the same as before, then dinner to kick off Lyra's celebration. I hope Delphine holds herself together for Lyra's sake. But, to be honest, I can tell we're all distracted." She turns the gold ring around her middle finger as she speaks, the token I gave her the night we handfasted.

"It'll be fine, Nerissa."

"Did you see Morel while you were out?" she asks, glancing up at me and raking her gaze over my bare chest as I sponge myself off.

"Not today, no. He'll be there tonight, but I don't plan on bringing up his crew's commitment until tomorrow. I don't want anything to ruin Lyra's celebration."

She nods in understanding, moving to sit in front of the vanity mirror to comb her hair before deftly braiding it back from her face.

"Will you act as High Priestess tonight?" I question, pulling my clean shirt over my head and tucking it in. I roll up my sleeves, forgoing a coat tonight since the air is warm and we'll be near the fire.

"For the first time officially, yes. I suppose it will be good practice for whatever is to come. I don't want to take away Lyra's spotlight, but it's time for my announcement to be made as well."

With another deep sigh, she looks over toward the stack of texts that await her review before standing and dropping her dressing gown to slip into the cloth of silver priestess robe that once belonged to my mother. Somehow Lyra was able to clean the blood left from the battle in the square of New Aphros from the fabric, and it looks as pristine as the first time I saw Nerissa wear it on the *Bartered Soul*.

Watching her dress, I feel the same as I did the night I saw her in the flickering bonfire of the rites nearly twelve years ago. My chest tightens with emotion and my stomach clenches with need for her. I can't help but step closer, pulling her against me for a kiss, running my hands over her curves, and tracing the gold chain that circles her waist through the silky fabric. She sinks into me, responding immediately as she always does, wrapping her arms around my neck and threading her fingers through my hair as she returns my embrace. With a sigh, her lips part to deepen our kiss. Her breathy sounds of contentment go straight to my cock as she presses her hips against me, forcing me to break away from her with a grin.

She smiles up at me as I give a hoarse chuckle. "Fuck, Nerissa. As you've said before, we'll never make it to a full moon if we start the night like this."

"And as I've told you several times, I would be more than happy to skip it to stay in bed," she teases, poking me in the chest with a slender finger. Her tone is jovial, but she swallows with a tight smile and sorrowful eyes. "But it seems we are both too important now and would be missed."

I nod in agreement, kissing her once more. I know she never truly wanted to start down this path, but we are both steadily walking it. The point of no return is already far behind us. Blackwell has pushed too far for us to simply escape, and she made her choice the day we said farewell to Salome at the pyre.

I'll stand by her side as long as I can stand, and then I'll crawl if I have to. Squeezing her hand in mine, I stroke my thumb over her ring, then help her adjust the circlet on her brow before walking out the door hand in hand to join the others heading to the beach.

CHAPTER 5

L aughter sounds from behind me as I lead the way down the sandy path to the beach, the mood already upbeat for the night ahead. I glance over my shoulder to see Pike clapping Erik and Tom, Erik's quartermaster on *Andromeda's Vengeance*, on their shoulders in the rear of our group, but they're too far behind for me to make out their words.

Behind me, Lyra fans the skirts of her robe around her, letting the ocean breeze catch the lightweight green fabric as she walks arm in arm with Siobhan, Delphine and Daniel trailing them.

Townspeople and sailors visiting the island meander down the streets heading toward the beach for the ceremony, chattering with excitement as the moon illuminates our way, shining brightly overhead in the cloudless night sky. I can't help but notice the different dialects and accents, reminding me of New Aphros and the people milling in the square.

Even though everyone around me seems excited, I can't shake my nerves, feeling resigned to the future ahead.

Although I fully made my claim in New Aphros after Salome's funeral pyre, only those who gathered on that faraway riverbank heard it. Tonight will mark my official announcement to the public of my title as Selennia's Heir and my intention to retake the throne.

The crews of our ships are aware of my true identity, and Jackson and Morel have surely passed the word to theirs, but tonight I will make it known to the island of Delosia, and everyone will bear witness to the power I hold. A stronger variation of that which all the priestesses in our midst control.

Wood for the bonfire waits near the water's edge, stacked, but unlit, just as I requested. People gather in a circle near it but give a wide berth as they await our arrival. The enticing aroma of roasted pork draws some farther down the beach toward the spits, and long trestle tables are set up on the sand, their wooden surfaces hidden under bright-colored tablecloths covered with huge palm fronds where platters of cut fruit and dishes of food await us. Another table bears pitchers of wine alongside casks of ale ready to be tapped. It will be a grand celebration indeed to mark the moon and Lyra's birthday.

The crowd parts as we step onto the beach proper, offering a pathway for us to reach the unlit bonfire. Siobhan, Delphine, Lyra, and I have our sigils visible, shining the same pale silvery-white as the moon overhead. We each wear our ceremonial garments — mine silver with gold embroidery and jewelry, Siobhan's deep gold with midnight sigils decorating the hems, Delphine in darkest black with her golden serpents, and Lyra in healing green and gold. The grim similarity to the night of Winter Solstice, the night everything changed, sends a shiver down my spine despite the warmth of the evening as we take our places around the stacked wood. Our men once again create a circle around us, keeping the crowd back while the four of us stand equidistant from each other.

With a small nod to my sisters, I raise my arms overhead, closing my eyes and concentrating. The warmth of the *glow* surrounds me quickly, dispelling the chill of doubt. Power fills me as my hands heat further and further until I sweep them downward toward the fire. I open my eyes as the crowd gasps and smile at the flames licking at the driftwood with green and blue sparks as the fire grows. This is the first time the people of this island have seen the elemental power of the Goddess demonstrated, as far as I know, and I study their reactions before I begin the full moon chant. As expected, awe and fear dance together in their firelit faces, but I refocus on the moon and my sisters as I chant and commence with the ceremony.

After the songs and offerings are complete, I hold my hands out to halt the crowd's dispersal. Food beckons, but I want to make sure my words are heard directly, not relayed through drunken whispers or rumors in the darkness.

"Friends, I ask for your attention for another moment before we dine and celebrate our dear Lyra," I raise my voice over the whispers of the crowd. Lennox stands at my back, his warmth heating me as much as the fire I look through. The people pause, looking at me with curiosity. Taking another deep breath, I continue, "You may remember me from my last visit when I sailed here with

Captain Lennox from Selennia. Some of you share that island across the sea with me as your homeland, and I hazard a guess that you fled for the same reasons I did." I pause and note who gives grim nods or murmurs in agreement.

"Many of you bravely joined Captain Varangr when he returned to fight alongside Captain Morel and the militia against Dargan Blackwell's forces when they came searching for me. But you may not know *why* they came for me and I want you to hear that reason from my lips." Silence descends on the beach, even the waves seem quieter as they lap on the shore, awaiting my words. I swallow, then allow the cloaking I've held over my full sigil to fall, revealing the knotwork curling across my forehead.

Another round of furious whispers travels through the gathering, some look fearful while others' eyes merely widen.

"I'm Nerissa Faelan, Queen Adelaide's only descendant. The rightful heir to the throne of Selennia. Dargan Blackwell murdered our queen, my sister priestesses, and countless innocents in his quest to steal my throne. To steal *our* home." Lennox slips his hand into mine, squeezing to offer me his strength when my voice trembles. "But, even Selennia wasn't enough to sate his greed. Now he threatens your peace here on Delosia as well. I plan on destroying him before that happens."

A small cheer rises from the crowd at my words, but the hesitation of many proves unanimous support won't come easily.

"I would never demand you follow me. There is no monarchy on this island, and I respect that you're all free to do as you please. But I'm not naive enough to think I can retake my throne without assistance and allies. If you feel compelled to support us please do so. You can join our crews or offer aid in other ways, and in return, I offer you my gratitude. I will not forget Delosia and the kindness you've shown me here on this island when I take my throne."

Another cheer goes up, this time louder as Marie applauds. Captain Morel stands out, a smile curling one side of his mouth as he dips his head to me.

"Now, let's set aside talk of conquest." I wave my hand to the food and tables beyond. "Let's celebrate Lyra on this joyous night. Please, enjoy the feast Mistress Marie has so kindly provided!"

Everyone begins to speak at once, gossip undoubtedly spreading through the ranks of people as they file down the beach to eat, drink, and dance in the moonlight, even as their eyes follow me, flickering away when I meet their gazes.

"You did well, my she-wolf," Lennox whispers against the shell of my ear, sending a pleasant shiver dancing along my skin.

"There's no going back now." I turn into his arms and tuck my cheek against his chest. "Even if I wanted to, there's no stopping it. We are going to war. Whatever losses we suffer going forward will be my fault. I can no longer blame Blackwell for everything."

"Nerissa. Look at me," Lennox orders, forcing my eyes upward with his fingers under my chin. "Is this what's been bothering you these past few weeks?"

My silence is answer enough.

"You can't shoulder the blame for every bad thing that happens. You know that whoever joins us does so of their own accord. You are *not* like Blackwell. You aren't forcing anyone to do anything. You aren't asking us to slaughter villages or burn people alive on your behalf. These doubts prove you will be a *good* queen. If you didn't care about the risk, you wouldn't be."

My breath hitches as I let his words sink in. I want to believe him, to trust that I'll make the right decisions. But even though his words soothe the dread in my heart, they don't erase it. Nevertheless, I smile up at him before he presses a gentle kiss to my lips and runs his thumb over my cheek before we join the party.

***

"Cheers to Lyra! May you have a birthday that's as beautiful as you are!" Daniel toasts, holding his mug of ale high in the air before downing the frothy liquid.

Lyra laughs, drinking wine from a goblet at the center of a long table where she sits between Daniel and Delphine. Lennox and I are farther down the table, next to Marie, Pike, Erik, and Siobhan, letting the younger members of our group celebrate more boisterously than we do. Most of the guests have finished their meals, and couples have begun to drift off to the seclusion of the dunes or head back to town. A few congregate around the bonfire burning close to the water's edge. Those of us still seated raise our glasses at the toast and sip, but the future seems to weigh heavy on us all despite the celebratory mood of the night.

"Captain Lennox," a voice pulls our attention from our

quiet conversation as Captain Morel approaches from where he and his crew ate at a separate table during the meal.

"Morel," Lennox greets, moving to stand from our bench.

"Please, don't trouble yourself with standing," Morel says, holding his hand up to stop Lennox. His dark gaze travels from Lennox to me. "My lady, I wasn't sure how to properly address you, but I wanted you to know that my crew has taken a vote. We spoke earlier this week after dinner at Marie's, but after tonight it's been agreed."

I hold my breath, one hand clenching Lennox's under the table while my other hand toys casually with the stem of my wine goblet. "And what have you decided?"

"The *Island Queen* and its crew are yours. The men hope you and the other priestesses will demonstrate your other abilities, but tales of great power follow you and they wish to side with the rightful Queen of Selennia in this matter." Morel dips his head in respect, then stands waiting for my response.

"Thank you, Captain. I'm honored to have your crew's loyalty. Perhaps after the Equinox my fellow priestesses and I can offer more of a demonstration." My voice is steady, but my heart patters wildly in my chest. Morel's smile is bright in the light of the lanterns spaced out along the tabletop.

"Thank you, Chastain," Marie says, patting Morel's forearm gently.

"Of course, Mistress Marie. Whatever will be best for Delosia," Morel replies, then, with a bow to me, he takes his leave to rejoin his crew. I watch as he grins and wraps his arms around a pretty woman who waits at another table, whirling her in the air before they walk off into the darkness. Once Morel has faded from view I exhale forcefully, relieved at his crew's response.

"That is good news," Erik says from across the table. "Now we only need Trevino and di Micios. I am certain the *Hadriel*'s crew will side with us."

Lennox nods his agreement, wrapping an arm over my shoulders to pull me close as he kisses my hair and whispers, "Let's take a walk."

We pass the few guests who still lounge at the long table, pausing to speak with Lyra. She looks serene as she sits among her friends, and I'm delighted this night was possible for her. Daniel sits next to her, eyes alight from the alcohol now coursing through him as he cuts his eyes toward Tom, the smiling young quartermaster. Lyra stands when she sees us near, smoothing the light fabric of her robe. Delphine silently slipped away earlier, and, even though Lyra smiles broadly and hugs Lennox, then me, her eyes flit over the guests as if she seeks the other young woman's whereabouts.

"Have you had a good evening?" I ask, cocking my head as I observe Lyra and squeeze her hand fondly.

"I have! I've never had a real birthday party before and everyone has been so kind. I think I'm going to go with Grandmama and Uncle Pike now though. I'm feeling a bit drained," she answers with a small smile.

I frown at her words, concern settling over me. The full moon should be energizing for her, not the opposite, but I've noticed that Lyra's gifts sometimes work differently. Her empathy seems to leach more power as she heals or levels moods than the general drain elemental manipulation causes, tiring her out quicker than Siobhan or I. I'm not sure if Delphine's shadows have the same effect, but we haven't been on good enough terms for me to ask and expect a reasonable response. "Did you exert too much energy at the ceremony?"

She shakes her head. "No. I think being around so many people and being so excited for the past week has made me tired. I'm all right!"

Reassured by her answer, I give her a tight hug, then release her to join Marie and Pike who still sit at the end of the table.

Leaving the partygoers nibbling on cake at the tables, Lennox and I approach the fire, shimmering vividly in red and gold. Others step from our path and walk away to give us privacy as we near. We pass to the quieter side of the fire where only the crash of the waves and crackle of the flames speak, and Lennox pulls me into his arms, slanting his mouth across mine in a deep kiss. Finally, alone together, I relax and hold him close, pressing my soft curves against the hard planes of his body.

"We should go for a swim," Lennox urges, the waves splashing close to our feet in the sand.

"Tonight? It seems a bit crowded and chilly for that." I chuckle but tug at his shirt until the front is untucked so I can graze his stomach with my fingertips. His flash of a smile and subtle shudder in response makes me press closer as I run my palm under the fabric to his chest.

"I don't care. I want to feel you against me in the water, under the moon," he says against my neck before nibbling on the place it meets my shoulder, sending goosebumps over my skin and heat to my core.

"You fucking bitch!" An unfamiliar male voice cuts through the celebratory air like a blade, stealing my attention from the pleasant sensation of Lennox's mouth against my skin. The chatter of the partygoers hushes, and we pause, listening for the argument to continue. Any desire spooling in me is doused like water over a flame.

"Fuck you! Go seek entertainment elsewhere," Delphine responds in the dim light near the treeline, the same direction as the original shout.

Lennox and I pull apart with a heavy sigh, silently sharing a worried look before we begin to march through the sands toward the voices, wondering what trouble Delphine might be involved in. As our eyes adjust to the dimness, the moon taking the place of the fire to illuminate the scene, we find Delphine holding an empty glass while a man stands across from her, wearing the contents.

Lennox raises a brow but keeps his voice even. "What's happening here?"

"This bitch threw her drink on me," the man answers, still wiping rum from his eyes.

"You sought company when it wasn't wanted. Leave me be or you'll get worse than that," Delphine answers confidently, if a little slurred, and I note a swirl of dark mist forming between the palm trees at her back.

"Did you accost this woman?" I demand, staring at the man.

"No! I swear it, mistress… I mean, my lady… I mean…" His voice trembles as he looks between me and Lennox, realizing his error. "She was looking at me the whole time after you finished the ceremony. I would never have approached her otherwise, but as soon as we made it over here she pushed me away and threw her drink at me."

"What's your name and who do you sail with?" Lennox asks, looking over the man and then at Delphine. His expression is unreadable, but the sailor shuffles his feet as though he's a scolded child while Delphine simply glares back.

"It's Rogers. I sail under Captain Morel. I would never do anything to cross the captain! Or you, Lennox."

"Del, what happened?" I question, unsure what kind of answer to expect. She stands with her empty glass dangling from her fingers, back against a palm, smirking as if she's watching a performance.

"Maybe I flirted with him, but I decided that I didn't want him after all." She shrugs. "He didn't like my decision, so I made sure I was clear. I could've done worse if you would've preferred?" Del's response drips with sarcasm, and, even though she has the right to reject someone at any point, I furrow my brow wondering if she isn't enjoying this a bit more than she should be.

"Rogers, stay away from her. I'll speak with Morel about this tomorrow," Lennox orders, sending the man back toward the bonfire with fear in his eyes.

"Delphine, are you all right?" I ask, trying to determine if she's putting on a facade or if she needs support.

"I'm fine. I can take care of myself."

"Perhaps you should ease up on the drink and come by the fire with us?" I ask, reaching out to place a soothing hand on her forearm. When Lennox turns his attention from the retreating figure back to us, irritation is plain on his face. Delphine looks between us, then down at my hand on her arm.

"Oh, yes. Maybe I should join you both once again? It *is* a full moon, after all." The venom in her voice and sneer across her pretty face has me pulling my hand from her as if she's a hot kettle and sends me back a step.

"That's not what she meant, Del, and you know it," Lennox snarls, anger rising to counter Delphine's.

"Isn't that your usual solution, Nerissa?" Delphine arches a brow. "To fuck away your troubles? Or did I misunderstand?"

I take another step back, my lips parted in shock. My mind is suddenly blank as I struggle for a reply, not finding the words to respond.

She isn't wrong.

I *have* used physical release as a distraction in the past; even the night I shared a bed with her and Lennox was to take my mind off my worries over Erik's trip to Delosia. But it wasn't to use her. I made it clear that it would go no further than that night, and she agreed. Even though she's likely only lashing out to try to share her pain over the loss of Salome, and the blame she places at my feet for that loss, her words cut deeply.

"That is *enough*, Delphine. You have acted like a petulant brat since we said goodbye to Salome. We're all hurting, you don't have to add to it," Lennox responds when I remain silent.

"Yes, you're *all* hurting, and yet you both have someone to be lost in. Don't you dare judge me for my choice of distraction," she retorts, holding her empty glass aloft.

"You have people who care about you, Delphine," I

finally whisper. "You need to gain control over your love of drink before it consumes you."

"*Who*? Who cares about me?" Delphine's eyes have gone glassy as she holds her hands out and turns in a circle on the sand. "Show me who would care if I remain drunk the rest of my days!"

"I do. You damn fool." Lyra's normally gentle voice stops Delphine mid-twirl as she walks up the beach to stand next to Lennox. Delphine's expression drops along with her eyes, looking toward the sand as she lowers her arms.

"You care about everyone, Lyra," Delphine murmurs, all viciousness erased when she raises her eyes to look at Lennox's niece. "You're too good."

"You know what I mean, Del. And Daniel cares," Lyra says, stepping closer to Delphine, slowly, one small step at a time.

"It's not the same." Delphine watches Lyra out of the corner of her eye, wary but not moving. "You know it's not."

"Delphine, just—" Lyra lifts one hand to cup Delphine's cheek, gently forcing her to meet her gaze. "Just let me in."

For a moment Lennox and I hold our breath. This feels like a moment we shouldn't witness, but any sudden movement might startle the young women so we merely look at each other with brows knitted in concern.

"I—" Delphine whispers, but something shutters behind her stormy eyes and she steps away quickly. "I can't, Lyra."

Turning on her heel, she lifts the hem of her black robe and staggers through the sand back toward the crowd enjoying the bonfire, her pale curls glowing under the white light of the full moon, leaving Lyra standing before us with her jaw clenched.

"Lyra, are you—" Lennox starts.

"She's so damn stubborn!" Lyra blurts, shocking both Lennox and me with her fervor before she throws her hands in the air, then disappears down the beach, leaving us standing alone at the tree line.

CHAPTER 6

"This one's also in the ancient language," Lennox mutters, carefully closing the leather cover and passing the book to me before running a hand through his messy golden hair in frustration. He pulls the next book from the stack Salome left me and opens it.

The morning after Lyra's birthday, I woke ready to start looking through the books, acutely aware that I was running out of time, and ever since we've spent most of our days here in our room. I pull the book from Lennox and open the cover, seeing the old script of Selennia, which Lennox isn't fluent in. That first day, he jotted down anything relevant that caught our attention, while I translated until our heads ached and our eyes burned. Today has been much the same. I feel mildly guilty not spending time with Lyra or Siobhan, but I know we'll all be together for the coming weeks, possibly months, and needed a few days of solitude to regroup after the excitement of the full moon and the sting of Delphine's barbed words.

I close the book, adding it to the stack on my right as

frustration wars in me. So far, the only relevant information we've discovered is the location choices for the temples that dot the coastline of Selennia, which Lennox and I will map once we're back on the ship sailing to Nemi. From what I gather, each temple was strategically placed, not just for worship, but for the island's defense as well.

Living in the Western Temple of Athene, I knew we were close to the port, but never thought much of the location. Now I can see the queens of Selennia's past, my ancestors, selected the building sites to spread the concentration of priestesses around the island to best thwart those who might attack via the sea. Had this information been widely known, had Salome's warning been heeded by my mother, could we have defended ourselves against Blackwell altogether? I haven't seen the state of the temples aside from the destroyed remains of the one at Athene, so I don't know if they might help us upon our return, but Lennox and I tuck the information away for the meeting on the Equinox.

"Finally, something I can read." Lennox sighs in relief, holding the newer text toward me so I can view the writing within. "Wait—" He pauses, flipping through the pages with a furrowed brow. "This is Salome's writing." His green eyes flit across the pages as he turns them. "This is an old journal with all of her notes."

"Well, this would've been nice to have on the top of the pile," I huff, holding out my hand to take the book. "Why wouldn't she have put her letter in this one instead?"

Lennox stands, stretching his long arms overhead and rotating his neck, not bothering to answer my rhetorical question. Two days of studying have made us both tense, and I'm about ready to give up for the day.

"These notes are dated from before she left Selennia. It has theories and questions for her to bring to my mother." I read from the text, flipping through and scanning the looping script, pausing my finger on a line that says, *Ask Adelaide to research Queen Genevieve and Cordelia to confirm my theory.* "I don't know what she thought I would glean from these that she didn't. If she took this many notes and read all of these with no solution or discoveries, how will I?"

"Perhaps she thought you would recognize or remember something from living in the palace? Something Adelaide would have told you that she wouldn't tell anyone else?" Lennox suggests, pouring a glass of wine. The shutters are thrown open and the insects that sing at twilight begin their symphony in the darkening jungle beyond. He brings me a glass, then retakes his seat next to me. "Take a break, Nerissa. We've been at it for days; you have the entire voyage between here and Nemi. Take a night to breathe."

"I wish we'd had more time with Salome to discuss everything." I sit back, rubbing my temples. "Now I possess whatever power I should have had from the beginning — both from the priestesses and my mother's line — but I have no way of knowing what it can do without trial and error. How it might work with the others, how broadly it can affect the elements. Why couldn't Salome have passed her power to me at the beginning and *then* taught me everything instead of allowing her vision to become the truth, leaving me with books full of mysteries to solve on my own?" The frustrated questions that have swirled through my restless nights all fall from my lips as I take a sip of the sweet wine.

"I have no idea, my love," Lennox replies, refilling his wine and approaching me with the decanter. I hold my glass out and he pours a bit so it's full once again, then leans against the table facing me. "I don't know if she *Saw* it too late or if she was too stubborn to risk giving you the majority of her power and leaving her to live out the rest of her days weakened. Whatever her reason, if she didn't tell you in her letter we'll likely never know."

"Or perhaps Delphine knows." I sigh, taking a long drink and closing my eyes. "She *was* Salome's closest confidante. But after the other night, I'm fairly certain she isn't going to welcome me for a chat right now."

"You're worried for her." Lennox's words have me snapping my eyes open and cutting them upward to meet his gaze.

"Aren't *you*? She's been drowning her sorrows in hard drink since we departed New Aphros. Her clothing hangs from her; I don't think she's eaten a full meal in my presence in weeks. Even Lyra can't seem to reach her."

"Delphine is a grown woman. Her choices are her own, and we all deal with loss differently. It will warrant our worry if she hasn't snapped out of it by the time we meet at the Equinox. Until then, I'll let her be. At that point, she'll become a risk to us as we approach Selennia."

I'm shocked by his indifference, but then, his words ring true. He and I have both suffered losses through the years and dealt with them differently — he lashed out with violence which in turn earned his reputation and ship. I retreated inward, closing myself off from anyone who might have offered comfort, keeping me from a friendship with Celeste or being reunited with Lennox earlier. The difference was that neither of us had friends who could see us through until later when the sting of mourning had dulled; we were surrounded by strangers when our grief was fresh. I only wish Delphine would lean on those around her, instead of a bottle.

Am I being selfish? I wonder. If Delphine can't pull herself from this, then she and her shadows and channeling will be of no use to me, or any of us, when we reach Selennia. Any advantage from stealth, spying, or transference of powers will be lost to us.

The wine sours in my mouth as I ponder whether my true worry is over the loss of her talent, or for the woman herself, causing me to place the goblet on the low table at my side instead of drinking the rest of it.

Is this who I have to become? Someone who can't figure out whether they care about a person, or just what they can do for me?

"What are you thinking, my love?" Lennox pulls me back from my moping.

"Nothing," I reply, reaching for the journal again.

"Come with me to the beach," Lennox coaxes, walking around the back of my chair and lifting the dark curtain of my hair from over my shoulder before running his rough fingers down the side of my throat, then tracing along my collarbone. He leans over and whispers against my ear, "We never got that swim after the ceremony, but the moon is still bright. We can enjoy the warmth before we head toward cooler waters again."

The sultry breeze from the jungle wafts through the

shutters as if trying to help Lennox convince me to venture out into the night. He's right. The weather on Delosia will always be warmer than we could ever hope for in Selennia, even if we manage to take the island back by early summer. This may be one of the last few nights of peace we have on land for a while, one of the last few we have before I have more pressing thoughts than swimming in the ocean with my lover or how Delphine is handling herself.

Leaving the journal where it sits, I stand, smoothing the lightweight indigo linen of my skirts and step around my chair to where Lennox waits so that I can wrap my arms around his neck. He returns the embrace, his hands drifting to my backside and pulling me closer as our lips meet. When I lean back, I run my fingers through his golden hair, brushing it from his brow where it hangs. "You're right, Billy," I say, looking into his smiling eyes. "Let's forget everything else tonight, everything except each other."

Lennox gives a wicked grin as he tightens his grip, pulling my hips against his so that I feel his intentions through his breeches before releasing me so we can head to the door. As I wait, holding the door open, he snags the bottle of wine and one of the extra blankets from our bed, folding it messily and tucking it under his arm before swinging the one holding the bottle over my shoulders.

The stroll through the streets is punctuated by the usual sounds of the island — laughter and loud voices from the taverns, singing from the windows of the boarding houses and residences sitting above the shops on the main street, and the night noises of the insects and nocturnal birds in the jungle that lines the pathway to the ocean. The waves break lovingly against the sand, their constant comfort further relaxing me as I kick my boots off to carry while we walk through the tide hand in hand. When it's only the two of us, so far away from our homeland, it's once again easy to imagine secreting away into anonymity to live the rest of our days in quiet peace.

"What would you have done if Blackwell hadn't come?" I ask, staring out into the water, watching the waves illuminated by the white moonlight.

"What do you mean?" Lennox asks, leaving his boots higher up on the beach once we reach a secluded spot far beyond the various tents from sailors' camps.

"Had he not invaded. If you'd never been pressed into servitude, never sailed. What would you have done? What was your dream before all this?"

"I haven't thought about that in a very long time," he answers quietly, taking my boots from my hands and dropping them near his alongside the blanket and bottle of wine. "I had dreamed of moving closer to the mountains, perhaps building a cottage on a coastal cliff so I could hear the ocean."

"Oh? And what would you have done there to make a living?"

"I never really thought that far ahead, Nerissa. I was young and prone to dreaming. I thought perhaps I would return to the temple in Athene once the cottage was built, once I had something to offer, and beg the High Priestess there to tell me who you were. That maybe I could woo you away from your duties like my father did my mother." His smile is shy when he looks into my eyes. "Of course, now that I know who you are, I know that dream would never have come true. You wouldn't have wedded someone who lived in a cottage on a cliff. You would have probably already been back in the castle by the time I had anything to offer you."

"So perhaps it's better that things happened the way they did?" I ask, my chest aching at the sadness in his eyes.

"Never," he whispers. "If I could trade what we have for you to never have suffered the way you have, to save my mother and sister from the things I've seen, then I would. I'm not so selfish as that."

"Perhaps I am," I confide, sliding my palm against his cheek, then running it through his hair. "Knowing what I know now. Having the power I have now. Having you in my life. Perhaps it was all necessary. Perhaps this is all fated and had to come to pass to start things over the way they should be."

"All I know is we can't undo the past, but we can live now." Lennox tilts my chin up so our eyes meet, then brushes a soft kiss against my forehead, my lips, my throat, as I lean into him. "And we can change the future."

"Yes," I murmur against his lips when he kisses me again. "Let's live now."

Slowly, we peel our clothing away, tossing his tunic and breeches and my loose gown to join our discarded boots resting on the sand. Laughter explodes from my chest as he turns and playfully splashes through the waves, diving under and resurfacing with a laugh as he smooths his hair from his eyes. I join more slowly, wading through the salty surf until I'm submerged to my waist before dipping below the surface.

Underwater the sounds of the waves are muted, the ocean soothing the ragged edges of my nerves and buoying my spirits as much as my body. I'd always known water was healing, but I never spent much time thinking about it until so many of my days were spent sailing on, or walking next to, it. Now, the crash of the waves is calming, and I can imagine the peace Lennox would have found in the cliffside cottage he dreamed of, living with the song of the sea as a steady backdrop to his daily life. Of course, as a pirate, he has the sea as his companion, but it rarely comes with peace.

I float in the waves, the gentle tide cradling me as the moon's glow reflects off my skin. For a few quiet moments, I let all my worries slip away, forgetting the past, the future, and the what-could-have-beens. Lennox is nearby, a comforting presence even if he doesn't speak or reach out to me, letting me get lost in my thoughts the way he seems to be.

Finally, I stand, sinking my toes into the dense sand underfoot as the water sluices over my body. Swimming toward me, Lennox surfaces and wraps his arms around my waist, pressing his chest against my back and his lips to my shoulder. One arm stays around my chest, palming my breast while the other explores my abdomen, slipping down between my thighs. Reflexively, I arch my hips against him, rocking my behind against his arousal as he rumbles his pleasure against my neck, peppering my salty skin with kisses. Then, he turns me in his arms, claiming my lips and lifting me from the sea to carry me back to the shore.

Standing me on my feet, Lennox quickly shakes out the blanket, spreading it over the sand to shield us somewhat from its irritation, but he kneels and pulls me down to his side just as swiftly, capturing my lips with urgency as he gently rolls me onto my back. With the newly full moon lighting us, and the breeze rustling through the palms in the jungle beyond, I'm momentarily transported back to the grove outside Athene so many years ago where Lennox and I first laid together under the starry skies for the rites. Except now, we both bear scars, visible and internal, and can look upon one another completely, all masks discarded.

Lennox's rough palms skate over my damp skin, sending heat blooming where he caresses and igniting my core, the warmth so at odds with the gooseflesh from the cool breeze. He lavishes kisses over my breasts, then lower down my belly, licking the salty brine of the sea from my skin. I whimper when he stops just below my navel with a lopsided grin. As if reading my thoughts, he cocks his head to meet my eyes and murmurs against my inner thigh, "We haven't made love in the moonlight since the rites, my pretty priestess."

"I distinctly remember taking the lead that night, Captain. If you don't stop toying with me, I might have to do so again," I tease, arching my back to encourage him to continue his exploration.

"Perhaps I wanted you to. You do look so pretty riding me." His words make my belly clench with need and deepens the ache between my legs, desperate for him to keep touching me. Instead of waiting for him to continue his teasing, I grip his hair and roughly pull him back up my body so I can claim his mouth, our kisses crashing together like the surf and sand. Lennox moans as I tug his hair, sliding his fingers through my slick center before I push him away and onto his back.

"Is this the view you're craving?" I ask, my voice breathy as I straddle him. Automatically, his hands find my hips as I slide against his length, teasing both of us equally with the friction.

"*Fuck*. Yes." His voice is a ragged whisper, eyes reflecting the moonlight as they focus on where our bodies collide, desire clouding their mossy depths.

Resting one palm on his chest, I grip him with the other, stroking him from base to tip as I raise up on my knees over him. Lennox's head slips back to the blanket beneath us as a gasp of pleasure leaves his lips when I slide down over him. My own moan joins his alongside the sounds of the sea as I begin to rock my hips, both hands now pressed against his chest for balance as I dig my fingernails into his tattooed skin.

Wrapping his arms around me, hands splayed across my moonlit back, Lennox sits up and holds me against him as our hips move together and our lips dance. Burying my face into his neck I breathe in the smell of him and grip his shoulders, pulling him closer as I near my release. Moments later, I tumble over the edge with my pleasure, muscles gripping him as he chases his own climax. As our breathing slows, he presses a soft kiss to my brow, then rests his forehead against mine with a smile tugging at his lips.

"I think perhaps we should do this in the moonlight more often. Seems to suit us, don't you think?" His voice is a rough whisper, but humor tinges the words to match his grin.

"I do," I pant, still catching my breath. "Once we return home, it might have to become routine." I return his smile but have to rest my head on his shoulder as I swallow my returning worries.

Once we return home, I can only hope it will be so easy to find solace in one another's arms, let alone time to make love under the moon.

Strolling back toward the jungle path, shoeless, but clothed, we pass the bottle of wine between us when two men suddenly stagger from the treeline laughing and clinging to one another, far more drunk than we are. I smile at their happiness and stifle a giggle when one stumbles over his feet while tucking his shirt in.

"Look at what a mess you've made of me," he teases his companion, pulling him close for a kiss. His voice is familiar and when they pull apart, realizing they're not alone, I recognize Daniel. Embarrassment clouds the young man's face when he sees us, his mouth popping open as though he wishes to speak but can't remember how.

"Tom. Daniel. Nice night, isn't it?" Lennox says with a knowing smile, holding the bottle up as if in a toast.

Tom, the quartermaster of the *Vengeance*, steps into the light and runs a hand through his dark curls, grinning in response. "Evening, Captain. My lady," he greets, dipping his head and grabbing Daniel's hand in his, pulling the younger man close once more. "Hope you're both having as nice a night as we are."

"Oh, I believe we are," Lennox replies with a chuckle and a casual bow. "Goodnight, gentlemen." Then we stroll past, listening to the hushed murmur of their voices and the resulting laughter in our wake.

CHAPTER 7
LENNOX

The warm sunlight trickles through the shutters as the jungle birds' songs rouse me, tangled in the bed linens. A ray of light caresses Nerissa's cheek, reflecting off her raven hair where she sleeps soundly beside me. Aimlessly, I smooth a lock between my fingers, unable to resist touching her even after these months of being able to do so freely.

That she rests soundly is a comfort to me as I release the soft strands, quietly standing from the bed. She's been restless in the night often lately, and I can't help but notice the circles darkening beneath her eyes. Fastening my breeches and pulling a lightweight tunic over my head, my gaze settles on the stack of books and journals on the table.

We've both pored over the texts for days, Nerissa translating when necessary while I grow more irritated that I didn't heed my mother's needling that I should study the old language in my youth. So far, the only thing that has piqued her interest, besides temple locations, is the reference to a previous queen and companion priestess. We also found a curious line of translation that Salome wrote out about the Goddess departing the castle as time went by — the word "departed" underlined multiple times.

Despite the number of texts we've reviewed, we have yet to find any revelations about what happened to the Goddess, or what caused the queens to lose their power and priestess standing. We can only hope that something will be revealed when we reach the Selennian shores, but so many factors play into that step that I can't concentrate on it. Only two days lie between now and our departure from Delosia, which means the hourglass will start running in earnest soon.

"One step at a time," I murmur under my breath as I step into the hallway, pulling the door closed on silent hinges to make my way downstairs for a tray of tea and breakfast without disturbing Nerissa. The courtyard is starting to fill, and I nod to a few of the sailors I recognize while I wait for the serving girl to bring me the tray for our room.

"Sorry for the wait, Captain," she says, dipping into a curtsey as she holds the silver tray up for me.

"No trouble at all," I reply, taking it from her with one hand. Palming the tray, I hand her a coin from my pocket which she accepts with a grin, dipping her head once more then dashing to one of the tables where a man gestures for more tea.

When I make my way back up the stairs and enter our room, Nerissa sits upright in our bed, eyes frantic as she holds the sheet around her chest.

"Nerissa, what's wrong?" I ask, placing the tray on our low table and striding to her side. Her other hand grips her dagger next to the mattress as she settles her breathing. When I drag my eyes back to hers, my heart plummets at the sadness I find. I sit at her side, unwrapping her fingers from the weapon before placing it on the bedside table.

"I woke and you were gone. Again." She looks upward as she takes a deep breath. "I'm foolish. Of course, you just went to get breakfast." But, while her words are casual, the tremble in her voice belies her worries, the opposite reaction I'd hoped for.

"I'll never willingly leave your side again, Nerissa. You know this."

Guilt twists in my chest knowing that she woke remembering the last night we stayed in this very boarding house when she woke to find me gone with only a letter telling her how I felt in hopes she would seek me out at the docks if she felt the same. My gamble had paid off; her feelings were as strong as mine, and reassured us both that she came with me because she *wanted* to, not because she felt obligated. But seeing her this way, thinking of how she must have looked when all she found of me was a slip of parchment, makes me feel like a coward for not being able to confess my love differently then.

"I know," she replies as I press my forehead to hers. "I know. I just... I can't shake this fear of what we're returning to. What it means for us."

"We'll face it together, my love. All of us, together."

With the shimmer of tears fading from her eyes, she finally smiles and nods, her muscles relaxing again as I kiss her cheek.

Later the next day, I leave Nerissa in the foyer of Marie's home so she can confer with the older woman while I meet with Jackson, Erik, and Morel to finalize the next morning's departure plans. We'll rendezvous later this afternoon with Lyra and Delphine for a final meal with Marie to say our goodbyes, but Nerissa insisted that she speak with Marie alone first.

Sauntering through the center of town, I catch snippets of conversation in my wake — the words *Selennia*, *Goddess*, and *Queen*, all drift on the jungle breeze. Most of the island's inhabitants smile pleasantly when I make eye contact, but a ribbon of unease snakes through the town, just like it has since we arrived. The memory of Blackwell's invasion is fresh, and the islanders understand that if we fail in our plans the king across the ocean may come to take payment from them for our attempts to retake the throne and to punish them for any aid they may offer us in that endeavor. Should we be successful, it will mean mutually beneficial, direct trade routes between Selennia, Delosia, and New Aphros. *Legal* trade routes that will benefit everyone here on the small island — more profitable sales, as well as more affordable imports. But, should we fail, it could mean disaster for the fruitful island.

The docks swarm with sailors from the various ships, carrying crates, trunks, and canvas sacks of supplies and belongings for everyone joining us. Some men tip their caps, while others merely step out of my way as I approach the fifth ship waiting at the docks, the *Kraken's Maw*.

"Erik!" I shout, drawing the attention of the tall man standing on the deck. I climb the plank to reach his side as he watches Jacob make final adjustments. "What's been decided?"

"She'll sail with the smallest crew possible, laden with the fewest supplies, as you commanded."

"Very well. We may need her, so I want to keep her armed and ready, but out of the way. It will serve to make our fleet look larger, but we can spare her should it come to that."

The shipwright's son looks pained at the idea of his craftsmanship sinking to the depths, but he hastily resumes his task under my scrutiny.

Erik nods. "Are you ready for Nemi?"

"I think so. Nerissa and I need to have a final discussion about the plans I'll present, but I'm hopeful for the outcome."

"My cousin will agree to join us, I am certain of it. The crew of the *Hadriel* is vicious, and they have no love for Blackwell."

"Your cousin isn't my concern. Trevino and di Micios are the wild cards. Di Micios and I are always at odds it seems, but Trevino may side with me just to spite Mario. Time will tell. Will you and Siobhan join us for dinner at Marie's tonight?" I ask, preferring to worry about the meeting on Nemi after we depart Delosian shores.

"We will. She has packed up almost her entire shop. There is not much left to do before we sail."

"Good. We'll have one last celebration then."

Shaking hands with Erik once more, I descend the plank to meet with Jackson, then Morel. The crew of the *Island Queen* is busy loading ammunition and Morel's flares as I approach.

"Take one case each to the other ships we sail along-side!" Morel shouts to his men before clasping my hand in greeting. "Ah, Lennox! Each ship will have flares for signaling if needed. They proved efficient when Varangr helped us on the beach; hopefully, they'll be again, even if only used as a distraction before your women can do their work. My crew and I still look forward to seeing their power *in full* before we reach Selennia."

The insinuation isn't lost on me, even though Morel maintains a broad smile and casual tone. He and his men still want proof of the extent of the power that we have on our side. Whether it means they will bow out if it isn't shown, or whether it's just curiosity, I can't yet tell.

I nod, slapping him on the back in a friendly gesture. "In good time, Chastain."

Militia members line the beach, their packs waiting to be loaded onto the ship. The frenetic energy of men ready to take to the sea swarms around the docks, trickling out into the shimmering sand surrounding us. Turning to look back at Morel, I say, "Should you need more room for the militia there's space on the *Kraken's Maw*, any extra men or belongings can travel there."

"As you say, Lennox," he answers. "We'll see you at sunrise. The men and I will spend the night on the beach to say goodbye to the island before we sail."

I look over the people of the island waiting to load their things, their friends and lovers gathered by tents and small fires. Children run across the sand laughing as their parents prepare to spend their final night together before bidding farewell to those who will sail off in the morning.

"See you in the morning, then. Rest well."

Hours remain before I'm needed at Marie's. Instead of returning to town, I pass through the makeshift camp along the beach, trading a coin for a bottle of rum from one of the better-stocked tents. I walk past the edge of the camp, through the jungle, and continue until I find an empty bit of sand: a secluded beach cradled between the edges of the forest and the ocean.

The sounds of people vanish behind me as the ocean and the music of the jungle take center stage. I shed my linen coat, remove my boots, and roll my breeches above my knees. Pulling the cork from the bottle with my teeth, I carry the rum with me as I walk into the sea. Cool water caresses my feet and calves while the crash of the waves settles the nerves that have been tingling since stepping onto the docks to view the mass of people now under my responsibility.

Nerissa thinks this is all her doing, that she will be the one solely responsible for the deaths that may await us, but my name and my reputation contribute to this as much as her power and birthright. Without trust in me, these crews and captains wouldn't eagerly join our side, and I worry just as deeply as she does over their fates. Although our prayers to the Goddess are usually said under the moonlight, I tip my face to the sky, the hot island sun warming my cheeks as I squeeze my eyes tight against the brightness, then begin to pray.

The ocean has been my home for nearly a decade now, her waves lulling me to sleep and her storms reminding me of how quickly life can change. While the Goddess of my homeland may be of the moon, her power over the sea is felt at all hours, just like Nerissa's pull over me.

Our fates are seemingly entwined as much as that of the tides and the moonlight.

I pour the rum into the waves in offering before taking a deep drink from the bottle, the spiced liquid burning my tongue and throat as its warmth burns through the chill of worry in my chest. Wading back through the sea I sit on the beach, elbows on my knees as I finish the bottle, then lay back in the sunlight, eyes closed, to listen to the waves crash as they consider my request.

CHAPTER 8

Marie enters the foyer to greet me after I bid farewell to Lennox on the verandah. She's the most relaxed I think I've seen her, wearing a casual swath of vibrantly printed linen with her silver braids hanging loose down her back. I sent word yesterday that I would visit earlier in the day than my companions, but her attire makes me worry that perhaps I've arrived even earlier than anticipated. Marie's broad white smile, crinkling the edges of her eyes, erases that concern quickly though, as she greets me with a bowed head.

"You don't have to do that, Marie," I remind her, embarrassed at the greeting.

"Nonsense. If you're to be respected as Queen of Selennia you must get used to it. From everyone, my dear," Marie chides. "Even dignitaries from other lands."

"As you say," I reply with a smile of my own. "Is now still a good time for you?"

"Of course! Come to my study, we can have tea and talk." Marie gestures for me to follow, leading me down the hallway and toward her office, calling over her shoulder, "Julian, please bring us tea."

"Yes, Mistress Marie," the butler says as we cross through into the tidy space.

The memory of our first meeting in this room — the fear and denial of my identity making me dash from its confines — rears up, followed soon after by heat in my cheeks when my gaze lingers on the full bookshelves that Lennox and I used for a tryst on Hallow's Eve. I quickly avert my eyes and clear my throat, even as Marie smirks at me with twinkling eyes the color of polished wood.

"What is it that brings you to me today on your own? Not that I don't welcome your visit." Marie settles behind her desk, gesturing towards the chairs in front of the carved surface.

"It's simple, really. While I was raised in a castle, trained as a priestess, and now have the knowledge of how to access the power of the Goddess, I was never schooled on how to be a great leader," I explain, taking my seat and picking at a pill on the linen of my dress to hide my emotions. "I find myself, yet again, in need of guidance, even if my lesson must be abbreviated."

"You flatter me, Nerissa," Marie begins, only to be interrupted by the gentle tap on the door. Julian enters with our tea and serves our first cups, then quietly departs the room yet again.

"As I was saying — you flatter me with your compliment, and I'm happy to share what I've learned in my years, both as an inhabitant of Selennia and a leader here on Delosia. You may take the advice and use the pieces you find helpful, but know this, you are already a strong leader. Your willingness to ask such a question proves it to me."

"Anything you might offer would be helpful. I have examples to look to: Lennox has shown how he leads, Salome while I was in New Aphros... and my mother, of course." I whisper the last words, taking a swallow of my tea before continuing. "But she failed in the end. I wish to do better for my people. How have you maintained your position here for these years so smoothly?"

"Ha!" Marie chuckles, dabbing at her lips with a linen napkin. "The early days weren't smooth whatsoever. I've had to learn hard lessons, as you will yourself. As you already have. But, in the end, I learned I had to set my own desires and opinions aside, even if only temporarily. A good leader will consider the opinions and needs of *all* their people, not just their own, or those closest to them. You can't simply be a tyrant and enforce your own wishes, nor can you succumb to the desires of *everyone* who crosses your path. The secret to good leadership is balance."

"Balance?" I furrow my brow considering her words.

My mother was loved, but she seemed to flow along the easier path, at least when it came to the parts of her life I witnessed. I now understand so much happened in secret and that she must have been in turmoil, but in the end, she never made huge strides for change in Selennia. Instead, she favored the way things were done for decades. The way she was taught to behave, unless you count her sending me to the temples at Salome's behest.

Now, I wonder if her reluctance to support Salome's ideas in favor of appeasing antiquated expectations was indeed part of her downfall. In contrast, Blackwell took control and continues to rule by force and fear, an option I know I cannot abide by. The truth of Marie's advice sinks in as I sip more of my tea.

"One must find a balance between innovation and tradition, the needs of the rich and the poor, and their own desires versus what's best for the people they represent. You have now spent your life in many stations and can relate to your people, regardless of their status. Who better to take back the throne of Selennia and usher it into greatness alongside new allies?"

"But how do you know you're making the right choices? Taking the right risks?"

"You never know for certain. But like I told you when we met before, you demand respect, evoke love, and strike fear into those who would wrong you, even more so now with what you can do. You should sail from this island with full confidence in your endeavor, Nerissa." Marie smiles at me, her bearing so similar to Salome's that my heart aches.

"I appreciate your faith, Marie. And your friendship. I promise Selennia won't forget Delosia once I've returned."

"I know it won't. Just remember to heed all the information presented to you, and then follow your instincts; they've kept you safe this long. Let the Goddess keep guiding you."

I RETURN TO THE BOARDING HOUSE AFTER MY TEA WITH MARIE to bathe and change before our evening meal. Even though I had thought to stay until the others arrived, I need time to reflect on Marie's wisdom before I'm swept away at sea, where I'm unlikely to be alone with my thoughts, or otherwise, for quite some time.

Tonight will be our final meal as a group until the equinoctial meeting on Nemi. The voyage should take about two and a half weeks with good wind and no surprise storms, which I've been warned can still occur despite the winter season being nearly over. I'm not sure what to expect from the remote island, which is only used for clandestine meetings and illegal trade, but a thrill of anticipation creeps down my spine as I think about the weeks and months ahead and how much closer to Selennia we'll be.

Dressing quickly, I head down to Lyra's room, hopeful that she and Delphine are still there to walk with me back to Marie's. As I turn the corner, I find Daniel waiting in the hallway, listening at the door.

"Daniel?" I murmur as I approach, causing the young man to whirl in my direction with wide eyes. I haven't seen him since the night Lennox and I ran into him and Tom embracing on the beach, but in the flickering light of the sconces, I note that his cheeks have become ruddy and his dark hair has gold threading through it from the kiss of the island sun.

"My lady!" he fumbles. Clearly, my assumption that he was eavesdropping is correct, and his cheeks flame even redder at being caught. "I, uh, I was…"

"Listening at the door?" I offer with a smile. It doesn't take much to eavesdrop; the sound of the two women's voices is easily heard, even if their words aren't intelligible. "Are they arguing?"

"I can't tell. Del always sounds like she's arguing these

days." Daniel sighs, his shoulders relaxing as he looks at me from the side of his eye. "I came to check if they need me to carry anything for them to the ship, but when I heard them I didn't know whether to knock or to leave."

I stand beside him for a few moments, straining to hear the words through the door without actually pressing my ear against its surface. The tenor of the conversation is assuredly tense but, rather than continue to spy, I exhale and rap my knuckles against the wood.

"*What?*" Del snaps as she yanks the door open to find Daniel and me in the hallway with wide eyes. "Oh. I thought it was a servant."

"Not that you should speak to servants as rudely as that," Lyra retorts, closing the lid of her trunk.

"I was checking to see if either of you need help getting your belongings to the ship," Daniel explains, looking between the two women. Delphine empties the goblet in her hand, then waves toward her own trunk stuffed haphazardly at the end of her messy bed visible through the wide open door of the adjoining room.

"That's all I have. Is it time for your dinner?" she asks, turning to face me.

"It is." I cock my head toward Lyra. "I thought we could all walk together if it suits you."

"Delphine won't be joining us," Lyra replies tartly, crossing her arms over her chest. "Or have you changed your mind?"

"No. I'll stay here as you suggested earlier," Delphine answers, ringing the small bell by the door to summon one of the servants. "I wouldn't want to be an embarrassment to anyone, would I? Danny, would you like to stay?"

"Del, you know that's not what I meant!" Lyra very nearly stamps her foot in frustration at the same time Daniel answers, "Yes, I can do that."

"It's settled then. You two have fun." Delphine holds the door wide, gesturing with the other hand for Lyra and me to depart. I let Lyra storm through in front of me before widening my eyes at Daniel as I follow her out.

This may be the beginning of a very long voyage, I think to myself with a deep sigh as I trail behind Lyra through the boarding house courtyard and into the streets beyond.

CHAPTER 9

"Lyra, is everything all right?" I ask once we've walked in silence for several blocks. It's unusual for her to remain so quiet, and I'm mildly distressed at her lack of conversation.

"No. No, it is not. Del is being selfish and rude and just plain mean," Lyra spouts, crossing her arms over her chest.

"Have you *met* Del?" I ask, hoping the joke will bring a smile to Lyra's face, but she glares at me.

"I can *feel* how upset she is, Nerissa. Why won't she let me comfort her?"

Our steps slow as we turn onto the residential street to Marie's home, slowing more as our conversation deepens to allow us to finish talking before joining our friends and Lyra's family. I try to gather my thoughts, realizing how relatable Delphine's behavior is to my own years ago, even if I chose to bite my tongue rather than use bitter words to keep those who might help me at arm's length.

"Sometimes, Lyra, when someone blames themself for something bad that's happened, they don't think they deserve comfort. Even if there was nothing they could have done to change the outcome. In time, I hope the guilt and pain will lessen their grip on her. Until then, we may have to let her be bitter. Unless her actions directly impact us, there may not be anything we can do."

Her shoulders sag, and I reach across to squeeze her hand as she says, "It's so hard. It hurts me to see her like this after how carefree she was when I met her in New Aphros."

I bite my tongue. Even though I remember Delphine being more lighthearted after Lyra's arrival, I can tell by Lyra's distress that she saw a wholly different side of Del, one perhaps Salome knew too, and a pang of sadness for both of them aches in my chest.

"Let's try to have a pleasant dinner," I encourage, squeezing her hand again. "We can figure out Del once we're underway tomorrow, yes?"

"You're right. I want to have a nice time with everyone. I don't know when I'll get to see Grandmama again. Thank you." Lyra pulls me in for a quick hug, then we walk together up the steps of the verandah and into Marie's.

Lyra peels away from me to find her grandmother once we've made it inside, while I pause in the doorway. My eyes immediately slide to Lennox, standing alongside Siobhan and Erik in the main salon space. His damp hair is combed back from his brow, falling just below his collar, and he's still dressed in the clothing he wore when he departed this morning. Standing just out of eyesight, my heart clenches as I watch Siobhan laugh in response to something he's said while Erik smiles and wraps an arm around her shoulders.

The three of them seem as though they have not a care in the world.

No nerve-wracking proposals to make.

No battles to wage.

I wish I could be more like them. That I could set my worries aside and live in this moment.

"Would you care for a drink?" Julian says from where he stands in the doorway between us. I smile as I snag a glass of wine from his tray, taking a long drink while I linger in the foyer, then enter the salon to join my friends.

"Hello, my pretty priestess," Lennox greets me, pulling me to him and pressing a kiss to my brow. "I thought you'd still be here when I arrived, but Marie said you'd returned to the boarding house." Looking over my shoulder toward the door, he questions, "Did Delphine not join you?"

"No. She and Daniel are finishing packing." When he tilts his head in curiosity I add, "I'll explain later. Let's just have a peaceful dinner for once."

"Since the days ahead don't promise peace, that sounds like the perfect plan," Siobhan murmurs, reaching across the space between us to grip my hand between her freckled fingers. She squeezes lightly, smiling as she clinks her wine goblet against mine. "To a night of peace."

The evening progresses without incident, sharing laughter and the heavily spiced island cuisine I'll miss dearly.

"Do you remember the storm from when we brought you here the first time, Siobhan?" Lennox asks over dessert.

"Great Goddess, how could I forget it?" Siobhan places a hand over her chest. "I'd never experienced such foul weather before, let alone a giant funnel of water! I was certain we were going to die." She shudders as she nibbles on the tarts laid out strategically over the length of the table.

"And then I thought Erik was going to gut me after." Lennox grins wickedly as he swirls whiskey in his glass, looking between Erik, who now blushes, and Siobhan.

"Well, it taught you to knock, didn't it?" Siobhan chuckles, turning nearly as red as Erik.

"What on earth happened?" I can't resist asking, making Erik drop his head into his hands to hide his smile.

"I guess the fear of the storm got everyone's... *passions aroused*, shall we say? I went searching for my quartermaster, as one does in the aftermath of a storm," Lennox scolds, but smiles broadly at Erik and Siobhan. "And these two were in quite a state of undress."

Siobhan giggles into her napkin along with Marie while Lyra hides a smile behind her hand.

"Never had Erik shown such insubordination. What a bad influence you were, Siobhan," Lennox teases, barely holding back laughter.

"Hush," Siobhan retorts, tossing her napkin toward him and leaning her head against Erik's shoulder. "You were just jealous and lonely."

"I did apologize for my reaction to you walking in," Erik adds with a smile. "It was just an inopportune moment."

"Yes, yes, all in the past." Lennox waves it away with a flick of his hand and a sideways smile. "Let's hope we don't run into any storms on the journey to Nemi or else your crew will all be helpless if you two have to see to your *needs* afterward."

At that, Siobhan's smile drops, her eyes becoming fearful. Erik scowls at Lennox and takes her hand in his. "You will be safe, Siobhan. We made it through the storm on the voyage to New Aphros, we will be fine on the way to Nemi."

"Of course. I'm sure all will be well. Hopefully, I would *See* a storm early enough to be prepared," she says, smiling with tight lips. But Lennox looks worried, and the remainder of the evening is notably more somber after her reaction.

Before I realize the time, dinner is over and we all stand on the airy verandah to return to our rooms for our final night on the island.

"I'll be at the docks to see you off in the morning," Marie says in farewell, closing the door behind her as we step down the stairs and into the gritty streets.

Erik and Siobhan turn down the road to the apothecary with a wave, while Lyra walks with us to the boarding house in weighted silence. Entering the courtyard, she worries at her bottom lip, looking toward the hall where her room adjacent to Del's waits. With a deep sigh, she says, "I'll see you in the morning, bright and early."

"Good night, Lyra," Lennox replies with a gentle smile.

"Sleep well." I hug her tight before she turns toward her room, then Lennox and I climb the stairs for the final time this trip.

In our suite, our trunks wait for last-minute additions. I wrap the journals and texts in their ribbon and cradle them in the fabric of my clothing before adding the final layer of goods to the trunk and snapping the lid closed. Lennox is already packed, and the only belongings left out is our attire for the morning: breeches, tunics, boots, and light-weight coats all in similar styles but different cuts for the two of us. Smiling, I trace the buttons on my coat, thinking of the morning I first donned it to race to the docks to catch Lennox. It feels like a lifetime ago, and yet hardly any time has passed.

"Are you ready to truly become a pirate queen, my she-wolf?" Lennox murmurs against my neck, standing behind me and wrapping an arm around my waist. "You'll be the first member of royalty to step onto Nemi for the meeting on the Equinox."

"I'll need some of your bravado to do so, but I think I am," I reply, hoping the anxiety I already feel about facing the remaining captains is hidden. I shouldn't be afraid. If anything, now that I've tested myself in New Aphros and continued to hone my skills, *they* should be the ones afraid of me. But, I still fear for those at my side if we can't garner the strength we need to take on Blackwell's army.

"I think you have plenty of fire in your veins to accomplish the task, my love, bravado or no. Now, let's enjoy our last night on land for a while." Not waiting for an answer, he spins me in his arms and slants his mouth across mine, stealing my breath and muddling any doubt that tries to claim my attention. I cling to him and enthusiastically return his embrace.

GULLS CRY OVERHEAD AS I WAIT FOR OUR CREWS TO FINISH their last-minute preparations, louder than the soft lap of the waves on the pillars of the docks, or the men and women carrying supplies and saying their farewells. Lyra and Siobhan stand with Marie, chatting like they did when I departed these shores before, but this time Marie will be the only one left standing on the white sand when we set sail.

While Celeste is a little piece of me left in New Aphros, Marie is my tie to Delosia, both reminding me of the places that stand with us and the strength of the people who believe in our endeavor. The early morning sun kisses my cheeks, its heat drawing my face upwards to soak it in. Soon enough, the temperatures will drop and the waves will darken as we near Nemi and Selennia, and I'll sorely miss the tropical air. Something almost like regret tugs at my heart, but Lennox's approach brings me back to the task at hand, urging me to say my goodbyes to Marie.

"Keep my Lyra safe, Your Majesty," Marie says, pulling me close for an embrace. "And yourself, too. All of you," she adds with a tightening of her arms before releasing me and turning to Lennox. "I hope to see you again soon, Captain. If not, send your regards with Morel when you send him home." Never do Marie's dark eyes shine with silver as she speaks. Either her confidence is unwavering, or her mettle is so strong she won't allow us to see her doubts.

Choosing to believe it's the former, I stand straighter as I grasp her dark hand in mine. "We'll send word as soon as we can. As soon as Selennia is back under its rightful ruler."

"May the Goddess give you speed and keep you safe." With a final squeeze of my hand, Marie turns away, stepping from the wood of the dock and standing on the white sand, a steady beacon on the shimmering shore.

Soon, the ships weigh anchor and drift to sea — the

Bartered Soul, Andromeda's Vengeance, the *Kraken's Maw,* the *Selkie's Tears,* and the *Island Queen* — sails filling with the warm sea air and sailors' shouts as they carry us east, toward the island of Nemi, and then home and whatever fate awaits.

CHAPTER 10

"I still can't believe I never realized the temples were placed strategically around Selennia for defense purposes. Did you?" I ask Lennox, looking up from the scribbled map splayed open across my lap as I revisit the notes I made on Delosia. His head pops up at my words as if the break in silence surprises him.

I set the map aside and recline in our bed in the captain's quarters, while he sits at his desk, studying another volume. The wall of windows behind him casts his face in shadows and accentuates his sharp cheekbones while he works. In the week since departing Delosia, we've continued to read through the stack of books, as if we may have missed some important scribble or translation. I've attempted to work with Lyra and Delphine, but Lyra has been reserved, and Delphine uncooperative, so for today I stayed in our cabin to avoid the headache of the tension between the two of them.

"It does make sense." He stands from his seat and pulls

a larger map from a stack of papers to bring over to the table, indicating with a tilt of his head for me to join him. "The Northern Point at Airmedan would keep anyone from taking the island from the north, or potentially trapping them between the mountains and the sea if they came from Artemisia. The Eastern and Western Temples would stop those coming in at Athene or Murias, but then they could also sequester those who did manage through the mountains in the Cybelene woods. And of course, the Central Temple and the castle at Aphros would take on anyone from the south."

"Salome was right — the priestesses of the past were ready for battle," I whisper, scanning the map and taking in the locations and topography of the island as he points. "It's a shame that no one kept up with it, that they didn't teach battle magic or defensive training like they did in the past. If Adelaide had placed soldiers at the temples, perhaps even just that would have made a difference when Blackwell invaded."

"I wonder if Blackwell has realized it though," Lennox says, running his fingers through his hair before grabbing a quill and scratching notes on a sheet of parchment from his desk. "He razed the temple at Athene. The cathedral they're building in its place is just a simple structure; there's no wall or battlements to serve as a fortress. We might be able to use that to our advantage if we send ships to each of them."

"Do you think the men on the other ships will be as capable as an army though? The militia from Delosia possibly, but the others?" My brow furrows at the thought of the ragtag men I've observed between the beaches of Delosia and the streets of New Aphros.

"Don't underestimate these crews. Many of them have defeated full companies of Blackwell's soldiers before." He drops a kiss on the top of my head, but it doesn't release my worries. "I think we should consider the temple locations for our strategy, even if Blackwell has destroyed what once stood there."

"And what of my idea? How to get near Blackwell?" I ask, knowing what he'll say. He's already rejected my idea once when it was a mere suggestion, but the closer we get to the meeting, the more firmly I believe it's the best option.

"No. I don't want to put you at risk like that. Not unless we have no other options." He steps away and turns back to his desk, fists clenched at his sides at the suggestion.

"Is it so late already?" I change the subject, letting the idea settle for now. My eyes snag on the darkened windows behind his desk as I watch the tense set of his shoulders. The ship had started to rock more noticeably, but not so bad that I was concerned before now.

"No." His voice drops, even more serious than before, and tension tugs his lips into a frown as he looks through the panes. "It isn't late at all."

Changing course from his desk toward the door, he pulls it open only for it to slam shut in his face. Upon a second attempt, we find the wind whipping over the decks, carrying the sailors' shouts off along with anything light enough to fly away.

With a grim look, Lennox sighs, "Prepare yourself for a storm, my pretty priestess."

"THE CLOUDS ARE GETTING WORSE. ARE YOU CERTAIN THERE'S no way around it?" I ask Lennox again, raising my voice over the wind, although I expect the same answer he's given me several times already.

"I'm certain. I didn't think we would run into a storm this late in the season, but it's not unheard of. We'll have to hope for the best." His brow knits with worry as he stares at the wall of grey and black ahead. Lightning flashes through the building cloud cover, and the rumble of thunder blends with the pounding of my heart. "You should take shelter in the cabin. I'll tell Lyra and Delphine to do the same."

My hair whips violently around my face, stinging my cheeks as it pulls loose from its knot as I nod. I've never experienced foul weather aboard a ship. The thrashing storms in New Aphros were enough to set me on edge, even on solid ground. Now, my stomach flips as I grip the railing next to Lennox. Lennox remains outwardly calm, his voice steady, but I can sense the tension radiating from his clenched jaw. He's likely just as nervous as I am.

Neither Lyra nor Delphine has come above to see what's happening. The sky is visible through the porthole in their room and would show them the impending squall, but the thought of the two young women alone below decks doesn't sit well with me.

"Lyra and Del should both come join me in our cabin. Even if Del is still frustrated with me, we should all be together. I'll go to them," I reply, pleased that I hide my fear with my steady voice.

"Hurry, and return to the cabin immediately." Pressing a

kiss to my forehead, Lennox turns to the helm to guide the helmsman and give orders.

Gripping the railing, I slowly make my way to the stairs that lead below deck. The ship's rocking has become pronounced as the storm winds whip around and the waters grow rougher. Rain pelts my bare skin, stinging anywhere my gown doesn't cover, and the additional water makes it even harder to keep my footing on the increasingly slick planks. By the time I make it to Lyra and Delphine's cabin, I'm panting with the ordeal. Without pause, I push the door open, not bothering to knock.

Del reclines on her bunk, sipping who knows what, while Lyra wears a sheen of sweat as she watches from the porthole. Her face is pallid and I feel bad for her when I recall how seasick she felt on our first few days at sea. Both of them snap their attention to me as I enter the room, stumbling slightly as the ship tosses suddenly to one side.

"Both of you, with me. Now," I order, pushing damp strands of hair off my face. Lyra stands immediately, while Delphine narrows her eyes and opens her mouth as if to protest.

"I want no argument, Del. Not over this. This is *not* the time."

She snaps her mouth shut at my tone, sensing the urgency, and stands on wobbly feet.

Even in the few minutes I was gone, the storm has worsened. We make it up the stairs, rain hammering us as we struggle against the wind. Lennox shouts over the squall at the helm as crewmembers struggle with rigging and sails. Lyra clutches my hand as we head to the great cabin. I drag the door open, fighting the force of the wind trying to slam it shut, then hold it for Lyra to enter and turn to seek Delphine behind us. She stands near the railing, her loose blonde curls wet and whipping wildly around her upturned face. Her eyes are tightly squeezed shut against the rain, almost as if she stands in worship of the violent storm that soaks her.

"Delphine!" I uselessly call out, but the wind and thunder drown out all sound.

"What is she doing?" Lyra shouts to me from the interior of the cabin, fear in her eyes as she gazes through the doorway.

"I have no idea," I answer, sighing deeply before gripping my soaked skirts in my hands to walk back into the storm.

"Delphine! *Del*!" I call over the storm, trying to gain her attention as I trudge back over the deck, to no avail.

As I look around, all I can see is the heavy rain. The other ships we sail with are nowhere to be found in the darkness that surrounds us, and I swallow down the fear that swells in my breast as the winds shift and the ship begins to list to one side. I can't hear Lennox's words, only the sound of his raised voice as I stumble sideways. Glancing back up after regaining my footing I shriek, "*Delphine!*" as I watch her stumble, hitting the railing and then plummeting over the side of the ship to the roiling sea below.

"*No!*" I shout into the wind, throwing myself against the railing to look into the waves. The faintest hint of Delphine's dress bobs in the white caps, but my long hair whips across my face, blocking my sight. As I push the wet strands away from my eyes I frantically search the sea, finding the water crashing violently against her and the ship. Somehow Lennox is at my side within moments, a panicked Lyra with him.

"What happened?" Lyra wails, eyes wide with panic. "Did she jump?"

"I think she fell," I reply, still desperately scanning the water.

Lennox bumps me with an arm, and I snap my eyes to him, realizing he holds a long length of rope in his hands. He wraps it around his waist, knotting it securely under his arms.

"You can't!" I gasp, grabbing his arm with white knuckles as I realize what he plans to do. Terror runs through me at the prospect of him in the rough sea, even if I can't bear to think of Delphine crushed below the churning surface. The storm shows no signs of letting up, the ship tosses in the rough waves like a child's toy.

"I have to try. We can't just let her die," he replies in a grim tone, but his face shows the same fear I do. "Here, Pike. Hold fast."

Spinning and wiping rain from my face I come face to face with Pike, Daniel, and several other crew members who hold the length of rope securely behind us, bracing their feet against the gale.

"See what you two can do to help," Lennox shouts in my ear, then kisses me. Before I can protest, or say anything at all, he leaps from the deck.

"No!" I choke on my fear, gripping the railing again and following the rope down to the water, trying to spot him in the depths.

While I usually find resolve in Lennox's confidence, his

belief that I can control the wind and waves of a storm is daunting. This is nothing like flipping the pages of a book on a breeze or transferring liquid from a glass, even with the extra strength Salome's power gave me. Fear courses through me, as I fight tears at the thought of Lennox and Delphine pummeled beneath the waves, but imagining them injured steadies me enough to focus my emotions to try.

Lyra sobs once before I grip her arms, forcing her to face me. "Lyra! Look at me!"

She stutters, wiping her nose on her sleeve and staring at me through the dark curls plastered to her cheeks. Forcing myself to be calm, I take as deep a breath as possible in the heavy rain, then explain, "Remember your lessons. Remember what I've taught you. The weather is just the elements on a grander scale. You focus on the wind. I'll focus on the water. It's up to us as much as it is to the ones holding the rope. Do you understand?"

Blinking through the storm, Lyra takes a deep inhale and nods in understanding. Clutching one another's hands as tightly as the crew holds the rope behind us, we step to the rail and begin to concentrate, our *glow* illuminating the space around us as we stare over the sea into the storm. The wind whips around us, relentless in its ferocity until slowly, so slowly I barely even realize it's happening through my terror for Lennox and Delphine, it begins to cease in a bubble around our ship. Without the wind, the rain eases its violence, even though it continues to fall. The waves begin to steady, to still, until the sea gently laps the edge of the ship. Through the patter of the rain I hear muffled voices and the sound of feet on the wet deck, but I stay focused on the water below, willing it to remain calm as Lyra trembles and holds the storm winds at bay. My eyes dart over the ocean's surface, running down the thick length of rope that tethers Lennox to us. My heart slams in my chest and my throat tightens with panic as the rope remains below the surface of the sea. Minutes feel like an eternity as I search for any sign of the two of them.

Suddenly, a gasping Lennox breaches the surface, and somehow, in his arms clings Delphine.

"Heave!" Pike's deep voice thunders and the rope creaks at my side as the crew begins to pull them toward the boat. I squeeze Lyra's hand in mine but don't break eye contact with the two figures in the water, concentrating on keeping the waves still. Just outside the edge of the forced calmness, the storm still rages, lightning flashing angrily as if our power insults its fury.

Faster than I could anticipate, Lennox's wet head is close enough to the railing for Pike to reach a thick arm over and grip him by the back of the shirt to haul him and Delphine onto the ship. Lennox releases his hold on her and rests against the side of the hull, tipping his head back as his chest rises and falls in great gasps. Pike unties the knot around his chest, causing Lennox to grimace as it pulls free before he rests his elbows on his knees, head dropped between while he catches his breath.

Delphine is on her hands and knees, pale hair dripping as she sputters and coughs water onto the deck.

Emotions overcome me, and I drop my control of the water, the waves crashing against us once again. Lyra must do the same because the winds whip around us when she drops to her knees next to Delphine. She pushes Del's hair away from her cheeks, studying her pale face as she holds her close. Before anyone speaks a word, she pulls Delphine's face to hers and kisses her fiercely.

Breaking away almost violently, she shouts at Del, "Don't you ever be that fucking stupid again, Delphine! And don't you dare say no one cares about you!" Lyra sobs as she pulls Del into her chest, gripping tightly. With a shocked expression, Delphine holds her tight in return, fingers tangled in the wet fabric of Lyra's dress.

"Are you all right?" I ask, kneeling at their side.

"I… Yes. Yes, I am," Delphine croaks. She begins to tremble as she holds tight to Lyra, shivering both from emotions and the cold. "Thank you," she says, looking at Lennox who grabs the side of the ship to pull himself up to his feet.

Lennox looks down at the young woman with a stern expression and nods. "Of course. We never leave anyone behind," he answers. "Although your debts to me seem to be racking up. This is twice now I've saved you."

I jerk my attention to him and find there is no jest to his words, his expression still serious as he looks down at Delphine. She dips her head to him without another word, keeping her eyes focused on the planks under our knees.

"And thank *you*," Del says to me, looking up through her sodden hair. Her eyes shine with tears as they fall in earnest, mixing with the rain falling around us once more while Delphine trembles, holding back her sobs.

I nod once, beginning to stand as well, but Del releases her hold on Lyra and grabs my sleeve.

"I apologize. For how I have acted toward you, Nerissa," she says earnestly. She pulls away from Lyra fully to turn to me, raising to one knee so she kneels as she holds my sleeve. "You have my promise, I'll try harder. I won't disappoint you," she pauses looking between me and Lennox before continuing, a sob breaking her voice, "either of you. Again."

My expression softens at her words, her contrition is obvious as she diverts her eyes.

"This is far from the end of your story, Delphine. We all deal with our grief differently, but you're never alone," I reply, placing my palm on her shoulder. "We're here for you, even when it's difficult."

Delphine just nods in response, pulling Lyra against her again and burying her face into her shoulder as she cries.

The wind whips around us once more, seeming angrier now after the lull. "Let's get inside the cabin. I don't think the storm is near over and I don't have the energy to hold it at bay again." The wet wool of my skirt squelches and sticks to me as I drag myself to the cabin door, followed by Lyra and Delphine. I look over my shoulder once, finding Lennox's outline in the rain where he remains on deck with the crew as the storm continues to rage. I want to run to him and pull him into the cabin with us as if he'd be any safer there, but I force myself to step through into the warm space and shut the storm out.

"Here, change into this." I dole out two clean, dry shifts to Lyra and Delphine, turning my back and stripping my soaked gown from my body as Lyra starts to help Delphine out of hers. When I turn back to them, Delphine stands trembling with glassy eyes while Lyra has pulled a spare blanket from the bed I share with Lennox to wrap around her.

Lyra chafes her hands over the wool blanket, trying to warm Delphine even though she must be just as cold as Del and I are. My fingertips are wrinkled and goosebumps still cover me even though I've shed my wet clothes. I wring my hair out and knot it back before pulling a small iron stove from the corner. We rarely use it — a fire can mean sure devastation on a ship — but I'm confident in my ability to control the flames, so it's a risk I'm willing to take despite the rocking of the ship. Anything to get the chill out of the air and warm Del and Lyra. Closing my eyes and drawing on the comforting memory of the bonfires of Delosia, I hold my hand out to guide my intention to the small stack of kindling in the stove, igniting it immediately. It heats quickly, radiating warmth through the cabin.

"Bring her over here, Lyra," I instruct, piling extra blankets on the rug next to the stove. "You could both stand to get warm."

Lyra leads Delphine to the warmth, guiding her onto the floor while she crouches at her side by the flickering stove. I cross my arms over my chest, rubbing my palms over them to slake the chill, watching as Lyra gently pushes Del's lank curls from her face. Exhaustion starts to weigh on me. The adrenaline surge from seeing Delphine fall has fully dissipated, and the use of my power to control the water was more than I expected. Even though I was able to easily light the small fire, I feel weak and tired.

"Lyra, how are you feeling? Would you like anything?" I ask, retrieving the brandy decanter from Lennox's desk.

"Brandy. For both of us," Lyra says, still kneeling beside Del and holding one of her hands.

I bring glasses of brandy, placing one in Lyra's hand and a second next to Delphine, then retrieve my own, before huddling under a blanket beside the warming stove.

"Delphine," I say softly once I've taken several sips of the fine brandy, swirling the rich amber liquid in the glass.

She holds her glass but barely sips it as she stares into the fire. After a moment Del finally looks up, stormy eyes clearing as the warmth of the flames sinks in. "Yes?"

"Are you all right? Do you need Lyra to heal you?"

Del's eyes are uncharacteristically soft. Even when we shared intimate moments in New Aphros, I never saw her gaze as vulnerable or gentle as it turns when she gazes at Lyra, who now sits warming her hands by the stove. "She already has. By not giving up on me." Del reaches over and takes one of Lyra's hands in hers.

As we rest, the winds seem to calm, the rock of the ship lessening with each passing moment until dim sunlight peeks through the roiling storm clouds outlined in the back windows. Soon, the skies are as blue as if we had imagined the squall, but when I step onto the deck I shudder at the darkness we sailed through still looming behind us.

The crew is soaked, battered, and exhausted as I look over them from where I stand in my shift, wrapped with a blanket. A headache throbs at my temples and my body aches with exhaustion from the use of my power, but relief floods me when I locate Lennox.

My bare feet carry me over the wet planks automatically, until I hold his wet form against me, pulling his mouth to mine with hands on each side of his face. He wraps his arms around me and holds me tight, soaking through my blanket and shift. We've all made it safely through yet another potentially fatal event, and my mind reels wondering when our luck, or the Goddess' favor, might run out.

CHAPTER 11

"How are you feeling? Are you certain you don't have any broken ribs? Do you need me to get Lyra to help heal the bruising?" I ask Lennox the same questions for the third time as I inspect the angry reddish-purple line around his chest where the thick rope dug in as he saved Delphine and was hauled back onto the ship. I already treated it with an arnica and lavender ointment and tried my hand at healing him myself using my power, even if it isn't one of my stronger skills, but it made no visible difference. I've only just begun to toy with the healing powers Salome mentioned in passing once she realized Lyra would likely master them. Since her initiation ceremony, Lyra's healing skills have improved dramatically, far exceeding mine, and she could likely have the mark completely gone from Lennox's chest in a few minutes.

"I'm fine. If you remember, I healed up after a blade to the ribs, Nerissa. A rope burn won't kill me," Lennox jests, standing from the chair he sat in. His smile fades when he looks down where I still kneel in the crouch I assumed to inspect his injury and sees my expression. He nearly died on our first voyage from the blade to the ribs he so casually brushes off, and I'm certain the memory of those days is written on my face. "Don't fret, my love. Let Lyra rest. *You* should rest."

"I will," I assure him, pressing my palm to his stubbled cheek. He rests his larger hand on mine, stroking his thumb over my wrist. "I'm going to go check on her now that things have settled, then I'll come back."

After the storm cleared, the inspection of the damages began. One of the sails on the *Vengeance* was damaged, but the *Kraken's Maw* and *Selkie's Tears* were left unscathed aside from overturned barrels and shaken sailors. The *Island Queen* was farther behind, and we can only hope she fares well. We all rendezvoused close enough to shout to one another, making sure no one was lost and no ship was beyond repair before continuing on our course. From the distance, it was hard to tell for certain, but Siobhan looked horrified after the storm. My stomach sank at the sight of her so shaken, knowing her hope of *Seeing* a storm in time to warn us all is dashed. But Erik wrapped a huge arm around her as he shouted to Lennox, offering comfort that will hopefully be enough to keep her steady as we approach our homeland.

Lyra and Delphine had retreated from the great cabin shortly after the storm ended, hands tightly gripped between them as they lugged their damp clothing down into the hold. My heart felt light at the sight of them together, hoping they would each begin to find happiness again, but a shudder of sadness danced along my spine at the memory of Lyra's loss of Charlie and the dangers that potentially await us, especially knowing what I'm going to present to the captains at the meeting on Nemi. The memory of Charlie's death gives me pause, making me close my eyes against the worry of how many more deaths I will witness in the coming months.

Back out on the wet deck, I make my way past the few crewmembers on shift. The sun set hours ago in a grand show of red, orange, and pink, and now the sky is inky and peaceful alongside the gentle lap of the waves, belying the violence of the storm we passed. The air has a biting chill to it tonight, due to our increasingly northern latitude, but I'm comfortable in the breeches, tunic, and coat I changed into after being soaked in the storm.

I carry a sachet of herbs for tea to leave for Delphine, hoping it will help soothe her in the absence of her favored rum or wine. While Lyra is capable of healing any of Del's physical injuries, she hasn't fully mastered herblore yet. Since Delphine has never mentioned any interest in healing, I take it upon myself to offer the tisane, just in case.

Making my way down the stairs and into the hold, I pause outside Lyra's cabin — the same one she and I once shared. I listen at the door for a moment, not wishing to intrude, but when only silence greets me, I quietly crack it open, refraining from knocking in case they're asleep. Dim light spills through the slim opening as I push the door open, the small space lit by a low-burning candle on the table. On the floor in the center of the room, both mattresses have been turned into a large sleeping pallet. Delphine lays on her side in the middle, her pale curls now dry and wild across the pillow, eyes shut and face youthful in slumber. Behind her Daniel snores, laying over the blankets with an arm protectively resting across her waist. Facing Delphine, their foreheads almost touching, rests Lyra, her slim tan fingers crossing Daniel's arm to wrap Delphine. The little black cat that was enamored with Lyra on our first voyage has even joined them, curling herself into a tight ball behind Lyra's legs.

Both Daniel and Lyra breathe deeply, and I smile at the sight of the trio cuddled together like a litter of puppies keeping one another warm. All of them have endured so many hardships in their young lives and they deserve whatever comfort they can find. Even if Daniel and Delphine haven't fully disclosed their past to me, their bond is evident, and the knot of worry I hold in my chest releases a little knowing they all have one another.

Placing the packet of herbs on the plain chair sitting near the door, I retreat from the space before my presence is sensed or I disturb any of the sleeping inhabitants. With my heart full, I climb the stairs, nodding to the crewman I pass on the way back to the great cabin.

"WELL, THAT WAS A HEARTWARMING SIGHT," I ANNOUNCE AS I walk through the door of the cabin.

Lennox sits at the table sipping a glass of brandy. His chest is still bare, but the stove burns nearby, keeping the chill at bay. His brows raise in question as I remove my coat. "What was?"

"Delphine, Daniel, and Lyra seem to have all become *very* comfortable. They were all sleeping when I went into the cabin. Together."

"That's news." He rakes his fingers through his hair as he sits back to study me. "I was always under the impression Daniel was only a friend to Delphine, especially after catching him with Tom on the beach."

"I'm not saying he's anything more than that; they were just sleeping, after all. She mentioned before that he came with her from Selennia and kept her safe, but how did they know one another before that?" I ask taking the chair next to him.

"I don't know all the details, but they grew up together in Murias. They escaped when the temple outside the village was ransacked and caught passage to New Aphros on a fleeing fishing boat, then a merchant ship. Daniel has been like a brother to her throughout the years after her mother died, from my understanding."

I nod, glancing at the map still sprawled on the table. Murias is the location of one of the eastern temples, sitting just north of the mountains that split Selennia. It's a smaller site than the temple in Athene where I lived and trained, but the town had a small port, explaining how they were able to escape.

"But she was an initiate at the temple?" I ask, remembering Salome explaining that Del hadn't completed her initiation before fleeing Selennia. That's why Salome had performed it herself, then trained Delphine once she took her in and saved her from the priests' pyre.

"Yes, but she was young. I'm not sure she lived in the temple very long before Blackwell invaded. She never talked about it much around me." Lennox finishes his drink, tipping the glass up before clapping it on the table-top. Standing, he drags a hand aimlessly across my shoulders, caressing my hair as he does. I lean into his touch, following his movements, and turning my head to watch him as he prowls toward the bed. "Let's go to bed, my pretty priestess. I'm not sure about you, but I'm exhausted."

I continue to watch him, the muscles in his scarred back flexing as he pulls the coverlet back and unbuttons his breeches. My cheeks heat, pulling my lips into a smile when he pushes them down to reveal the paler skin they cover.

"I might stay up a bit longer. I wanted to try to get through a bit more of Salome's journals. But I can lay with you for a bit," I say, approaching where he sits on the edge of the bed. I step between his thighs, cupping his face in my hands, and pull his gaze to mine.

"Rest, Nerissa. I know you didn't sleep well last night. I know when you toss and turn, even if you won't tell me what's bothering you. The journals will keep," he murmurs, smiling into my palm before placing the softest kiss against my skin. Looking back up at me, he asks, "Do you want to tell me what you've been dreaming? What's bothering you?"

"Besides the obvious?" I retort, sliding my palms down to his broad shoulders. I step back, removing myself from between his legs to sit on the feather bed next to him. He merely cants his head to the side so he looks at me with a raised brow and sideways smile, as if to say he knows I'm avoiding answering. Sighing, I kick off my boots and stand again, unable to sit still. Pacing the floor, my bare feet pad on the exotic rug that lays across the wooden planks, as if the movement will order my thoughts. "I worry we aren't ready. I worry that I'm leading everyone to their deaths. I worry that the other captains will refuse to help or that they'll betray us. I worry that some flaw in the plan will cause the bricks to crumble and crush us all beneath the weight. And…" I pause, the words catching in my throat.

"And?" he urges, his emerald eyes tracking my incessant movements.

"And I've been having dreams… nightmares… visions." I haven't quite figured out how to describe the images that haunt my nights. "Memories?"

"Since when?"

"I've always had dreams about the past; they would come and go. I told you when we sailed from Selennia that the rites kept coming back to me in my sleep. Sometimes it would be pleasant memories, like that night, or time spent with Adelaide. Others weren't so pleasant. But now… since New Aphros… they've become more frequent and *different*."

"Like Siobhan's visions?" Lennox questions. His eyelids droop and I know exhaustion threatens to drag him to sleep, but if I don't answer he'll continue to force himself to stay awake.

"No. I don't need to use divination devices for them. They're just *there*. I've been having dreams of my mother… and Blackwell."

Lennox's eyes grow wide and his shoulders tense, the weariness transforming into energy that has him sitting forward. "Siobhan used to sometimes get visions out of nowhere. I remember Erik saying she could look too long in a cup of tea that had been stirred, or at a fire, and have them come to her. But, Blackwell? Have you met him before?"

I shake my head. "That's the thing. No. None of it's from a time I was present. It's like… it's like the closer we get to Selennia the stronger they're becoming. Like I'm seeing things that happened. I've been wanting to speak with Delphine about it, but she either wasn't sober or wasn't willing to speak with me. I can only hope she can shed some light on it. Maybe she can—" I start, the sudden pause making Lennox quirk a brow. "Maybe she can channel Adelaide? I know next to nothing about how that works for her, what it would entail, but I have to know if these are just figments created by my worried mind or if they're true occurrences that are being gifted to me in my sleep." I look at him with hopeful eyes as he scrubs a hand over his tired eyes and stubbled jawline.

"I don't know how her power works either. She's never mentioned how she channels or if she's done it frequently. All I've ever seen her do is her work with the shadows. At least until she transferred Salome's power to you."

His words are like a punch to the stomach. Even though we've all made our peace as much as possible with Salome's passing, guilt presses against my chest and brings tears to my eyes when I remember her laying in a pool of blood in the square of New Aphros. The knowledge that she, Siobhan, and Delphine all knew what might occur that night, yet never told me, is something I haven't fully come to terms with. I felt betrayed initially, then guilty that Salome sacrificed herself to siphon her full strength to me, even if it was Salome's decision and not my own. The pressure on me to succeed grows heavier each day, knowing that after the meeting on Nemi, we approach Selennia and the cruel man who killed my mother and stole her throne.

The fear that I will fail, that Salome's death will have been for nothing, is almost paralyzing.

"Maybe it's something manifesting from Salome? She was talented with divination," he reminds me — as if I could forget. "Speak with Del tomorrow. I have a feeling after today she might be more amenable. If you need me to, we can have Siobhan rowed over for a day or so, too. We aren't many days out from Nemi; she can be apart from Erik for a bit." Lennox stands, striding naked through the cabin to catch me mid-step as I still pace. He pulls me against his warm body. "But tonight, rest."

With a gentle press of his lips to my forehead, he pulls away and tugs my hand until I follow him to our shared bed. I strip from my clothes before curling under the blankets against him where we both fall into an exhausted, uninterrupted sleep.

CHAPTER 12

The morning sun glints off Siobhan's copper hair as she's rowed across from the *Vengeance*. We spent yesterday recovering from the storm, the crew resetting crates and supplies that were tossed around and making any repairs needed on the ships while Lyra, Delphine, and I rested and made sure everyone was all right after the harrowing experience. Even though most of the crew had been through severe weather at sea before, it doesn't seem like something one ever fully gets used to. Lennox rang the loud bell on deck, signaling to Erik that Siobhan would be required to work with us the following day, to which she agreed.

She nimbly climbs the rope ladder in her breeches and tunic, swinging her leg over the railing like any of the other sailors aboard, then greets Lennox and me with a warm smile before wrapping me, and then Lyra, into a hug.

"Did you all fare well?" Siobhan asks, raking her eyes over each of us.

"In the end, yes." I cut my eyes to where Delphine waits

at the top of the stairs to the hold. "Let's go down to the surgery and see what we can achieve today, shall we?"

Lyra leads the way, taking Del's hand in hers so they walk down the steps together, while Siobhan and I walk behind. Siobhan looks over at me with a curious gleam in her eyes, then gestures with a nod toward the two younger women, brows raised in question at Delphine's change in attitude. I answer with a smile and a small nod, then mouth, "I'll tell you later." Siobhan chuckles softly in response, following me into the hold.

The surgery space is small, but we all find places to settle around the room. A pot of tea waits along with mismatched mugs for our refreshment and we each hold one to warm our chilled hands. While it may be nearing springtime, the temperature grows cooler near Nemi, making the cozy closeness of the surgery a welcome change compared to the cool dampness of the decks above.

Cutting right to the chase, I turn to the women. "Siobhan, I have questions about divination for you. And Delphine, some for you, too."

Siobhan pauses, her drink halfway to her mouth as she asks, "What is it you wish to know?"

"Have you ever heard of someone having visions without seeking them? I ask, sipping the relaxing chamomile tea while I study her expression. "In dreams perhaps?"

"It's possible. For those with strong gifts, yes. I've had visions arrive when I've been unfocused or looking too deeply at something. Fire, for instance." Her brow creases as she looks between all of us. "Why? Which of you has been *Seeing* things?"

"Me." All three women tense at my admission, a long pause lingering as they consider this new information.

"I assumed Delphine," Siobhan responds, looking over at Del who remains silent while we talk. "But Nerissa, I thought you never trained in divination?"

"I didn't. That's why I'm asking. I've always had memories surface in my sleep, but these are not *my* memories." My mind goes back over the last dream I had, remembering my mother's final moments I'd watched play out. "These are like visions of the past. Of Adelaide and Blackwell, of things I was never privy to. They're short, but they're unnerving and confusing."

"They're being sent to you." Delphine finally breaks her silence, meeting my eyes.

"What?" I narrow my eyes. "Sent? By whom?"

"The Goddess. It used to happen to Salome in her sleep. It's how she knew Queen Adelaide had passed before word ever spread to New Aphros. She woke one morning *knowing*," Delphine explains, her voice trembling when she speaks of Salome. "Salome wondered if this might happen once she shared her power with you, that you might begin to tap into what she could do without having to train for it."

"What have you *Seen*?" Lyra asks me, resting a soft hand on my forearm.

"I *Saw*—" I start, taking a deep breath before recounting the parts of the dream I remember. "I *Saw* my mother slash a man's cheek with a blade, then watched as her body was dragged from her chambers. Blackwell stood in the doorway, ordering his men. I've never seen him in person, but she called him by his name."

Remembering the scene makes me tremble; my mother didn't struggle or scream, simply clutched something in her hand and went still. Night after night I've watched her die before I wake up covered in sweat. Swallowing the emotions the vision brings, I turn to Delphine. "That's where you come in, Del. I was hoping you could tell me more about your ability to channel. Is it true you can speak to those who reside in the Afterlife?"

Lyra turns quickly to Delphine, studying her as though she expects her to leave the room, but Delphine briefly closes her eyes. "Yes, although I've only done it a few times." Her voice drops to a whisper, grey eyes meeting mine. "It isn't a pleasant experience. I didn't understand what happened the first time I did it. I was recovering from my burns at the Den when Daniel came to visit me. He brought me a blanket that belonged to my mother, one I'd managed to bring with us on the passage from Selennia and had stored away in my room. He thought it might bring me comfort, so he dug it out and tucked it next to me.

"When I pulled it closer it was like my mother was there. She spoke to me, whispered in my ear that I would be all right, that it wasn't time for me to join her in the After-life. When I opened my eyes I saw Daniel, but I also saw her sitting on the bed next to me. Only…" Del swallows again, her eyes pained. "Only, she looked the way she had when she died — hollow and wasted from the fever that took her, and so many others, in a season. I started screaming as she spoke. I had no idea what was happening, and neither did Daniel. When I flung the blankets off me the connection broke and Daniel held me until I could rest again. It was only after telling Salome that I came to learn it was part of my gifts."

"Delphine, I'm sorry. That's a terrible way to discover such a skill," I soothe, worried that her story means she's unwilling to try to tap into that power again.

"It was, but Salome helped me learn. Once she did my initiation I was able to control it better — the channeling, the shadows, all of it. I still need an object that belonged to the person, but I can tap into it at will once I have that; it doesn't just take over anymore."

"Would you be willing to try to seek Adelaide for me?"

"Yes. I can try," Delphine agrees. "But, do you have anything that belonged to her?"

Sighing, I scan through the inventory of my belongings in my mind: articles of clothing and things I've accumulated in the years since I fled the temple. "Unfortunately, at the moment, no. I never had the chance to take anything of hers before Blackwell came. I can only hope something might be left behind once we arrive in Selennia."

"What *is* the plan for when we arrive, Sister?" Siobhan asks, drawing my attention away from thoughts of Adelaide. "Erik told me we should be at the island of Nemi within a day or two to meet with the other captains, but what will we do after that?"

"Lennox and I have yet to finalize everything, but hopefully we'll bring the other ships to our side and sail to Selennia. His idea is to attack at different ports and move inland, drawing the soldiers from the castle so they're easier to take on in smaller groups. But it all depends on how the meeting goes."

We won't be able to fully determine a course of action

until we know how many support us. Even with the pirates' help, it will ultimately be up to me to face Blackwell — to remove the head from the griffin, crumbling his regime so we can take our island back from the grip of him and the priests who support him.

"Don't worry, Siobhan. We won't leave any of you in the dark," I soothe my friend. I wish I could reassure her that this will be a peaceful endeavor with few lives lost, but I can't tell that lie. It isn't even one I can convince myself of.

"Now, what should we work on today?" A smile teases my lips as the words leave them, reminding me so much of Salome during my training in New Aphros as though I have truly stepped into my role as their leader and High Priestess.

———

"YOUR HEALING HAS GOTTEN IMPECCABLE, LYRA!" SIOBHAN gushes as Lyra heals a cut on one of the crewmen's arms an hour later. He arrived at the surgery shortly after we began working with a deep slash bleeding all over the floor, expecting to be bandaged up. Instead, Lyra stitched the wound together with her power. Now, only a thin white scar remains on the man's weathered arm.

"Thank you, Miss Lyra, " he says, awe filling his gaze as he inspects the smooth skin. "What a wonder!"

"You're welcome." Lyra beams back, her tawny cheeks pink with happiness. "Thank you for letting me practice on you."

When he leaves, she turns to me and says, "Aunt

Nerissa… I mean—" She halts her words, eyes wide at the title she addressed me by. "I'm sorry, I mean Nerissa."

"Why are you being shy? You may call me aunt if you wish," I reply. My heart swells with affection for Lyra like it always does, but now it's almost painful. Lennox and I have still not made our handfasting common knowledge, so Lyra must have taken it upon herself to think of me as family, which pleases me deeply.

She smiles, then says, "Very well. I was only going to say, have you noticed you feel stronger the closer we get to Selennia? I can't tell if it's because I've been practicing more or if it's the distance, but it seems like I'm able to do more with less energy expended."

"I've noticed the same," Delphine adds. She snaps her fingers and darkness coalesces immediately throughout the small room, only allowing the lantern light to shine from where it sits on the desk.

"And you, Siobhan?" I ask as the shadows turn to wisps and disappear at another flick of Del's fingers.

"The images in my visions are clearer, but unfortunately they're no easier to understand. It isn't uncommon since the future is fluid, but I'd hoped they would show me something solid," Siobhan sighs. "But the elemental powers work much faster. I've been practicing a bit in our cabin each day and can do more than I was able to in New Aphros."

"I think we're all getting stronger, then. Never would I have imagined that Lyra and I would be capable of calming that storm enough to get Lennox and Del out safely, but we did. I wonder what that means for when we actually step onto Selennian soil?" I muse aloud, hoping this will be the advantage we need, not only to convince the captains at Nemi but to defeat Blackwell, too. We all look at one another curiously before moving on to our next task.

"I suppose we'll find out soon enough," Siobhan murmurs, meeting my eyes over her mug. A look of worry that mimics the feeling that curls around my heart dims their brilliant cerulean depths.

CHAPTER 13

The following evening I stand on the deck, staring up at the moon shining in a cloudless star-filled sky, while the crisp air cuts through the wool of my dress. The waxing gibbous moon gives off white light and reflects on the rippling ocean below.

"Nerissa." Lennox's voice is soft at my side as I gaze at the horizon. The waters are no longer crystal clear like those around Delosia, and the darkness reminds me of the emotions that wrap around me, threatening to drag me into the deep. "Come inside, it's getting cold and you don't have your cloak."

He places his hand on my lower back to gently guide me toward our shared cabin. I allow him to steer me, knowing his concern has grown since I admitted to having unexplained visions in my dreams. I haven't confided that I'm growing more concerned myself. Hearing from Del and Siobhan that this may be a result of Salome's shared power doesn't make the things I see less upsetting, even if knowing Blackwell never had a chance to physically harm my mother is a relief. I've seen her lifeless form so many times, dead before he ever laid a hand on her.

The darkness from the years I was lost clutches me, pulling me under the closer we get to Selennia. Memories of freezing nights in mountainside caves, of the sharp tang of fear that flooded me each time a patrol walked by while I hid beneath my cloak in the streets of Athene, rise to the forefront of my mind. But I don't want to make Lennox worry more than he already does.

I can do this, I can be strong.

I *will* survive.

I've done it before.

Having people to survive *for* will keep me focused, even if the plan we've concocted disquiets me, causing me to turn the pieces over and over in my mind.

I haven't told Lennox that I don't think all the parts will work, or that my idea he refuses to consider is the most likely way to get to Blackwell. I won't bring it up again tonight, not when we both need to rest to be confident in our roles tomorrow.

"Are you well?" Lennox asks as he hands me a glass of brandy once we return to the cabin. The oil lamps are lit and one of the cabin boys has brought us our simple dinner to enjoy in peace this evening. Though it often does me good to be with the crew, I've needed more time for reflection as of late — to formulate our plans, to steel myself for facing the man who took my life from me, and to make sure I'm just as unflinching in the face of soldiers wearing his colors as I am the pirates we meet with tomorrow.

"As well as I can be. Do you really think they'll agree to it?" I ask, for the hundredth time.

"I do. I know the captains and many of their crews. Even if they do have some true villains in their ranks, most of them are made up of people who hate Blackwell as much as we do."

"The enemy of my enemy—"

"Is my friend," he finishes the statement, lifting his glass in a mimed toast.

Lennox is confident that, between him and Jackson, their influence will be enough to encourage Trevino and di Micios to join our cause. Erik's family is loyal to him and is sympathetic to our cause. Lennox's assurance that we will have their backing, and the fact that Captain Morel and the Delosian militia have shown no signs of faltering, bolsters not only our numbers but my confidence, as well. I have reservations about revealing my identity and our plans to some of these lawless men, but we have no real choice. As I told Marie in her sunny dining room months ago: I have no forces of my own beyond Lennox's crew. I'm just a single woman with a birthright. No matter how much it pains me, I *must* ask for help.

After we finish our meal, I curl under the blankets on the bed while Lennox scratches away in his ledger and studies the map spread across his desk. My eyes memorize the planes of his face, running over the scar on his right eyebrow as his golden brows draw down in concentration. I have no idea whether he's calculating for tomorrow, or if he's simply writing a log for the day. Whatever it is, it consumes him as he works. I continue to watch him for a few minutes before his eyes meet mine. He smiles slowly at having caught me admiring him. When I return his grin he closes the ledger and lays his quill on the desk, takes the last sip from his glass, then stands slowly and stretches his long body — arms reaching overhead to grip the low beam across the ceiling.

"Is there something I can do for you, my pretty priestess?" he asks, before prowling toward me.

"I can't sleep," I pout, desire for his lean frame winning out over the worries swirling in my mind. "I could *hear* your brain plotting."

A chuckle escapes his full lips at my teasing as he nears my side. "Do you need my assistance?"

"Well, I'm nervous about the meeting with the other captains. Perhaps you could *distract me*?" I sit up, allowing the shoulder of my shift to drop down, revealing the top of my breast as I recline on the pillows.

Another masculine chuckle rumbles in his chest, surely at the memory I hoped I would invoke — when he *distracted* me in the Port of Athene, the first time we shared this bed. He walks to the side of the mattress and leans down, meeting my lips with his own as he cups my now fully exposed breast, running his thumb across my hardened nipple. I sigh at the sensation and he deepens the kiss, pushing me down into the mattress as he holds himself above me.

"How should I distract you tonight?" he asks when we break apart momentarily, lazily running his hand over my shift, then caressing my bare thigh. "With my hands?" I take the question as rhetorical because he reaches my slick core and slides his long fingers over me, capturing my moan in another deep kiss. He makes a low sound in the back of his throat as he slips a finger into me, pressing the heel of his hand against the apex of my thighs. "Or perhaps my mouth?"

Lennox slides farther down on the bed, alternating kisses with nips through the thin fabric of my shift until his mouth replaces his palm between my legs. As he continues to work his fingers in time with his tongue, I grip his hair and rock against him, the stubble of his growing beard pleasantly tickling my smooth skin. Soon, my release coils and I buck under him, grinding myself against him as I pant with my pleasure.

Lennox hums against my skin, a satisfied sound in the back of his throat before nuzzling and kissing the sensitive skin of my inner thighs while I run my fingers through his hair.

"I want you, Billy," I moan as his kisses drift back up to my breasts. *"Please."*

He smiles against my chest, glancing up at me as he runs his tongue across my bared nipple, pulling it between his lips and grazing it with his teeth.

"I didn't think queens were supposed to beg, my pretty priestess," he murmurs against my flushed skin, palming my breast as he presses the evidence of his own need against my thigh.

Gripping him by his shirt, I pull him up so he faces me and demand, "Fuck me now, *Captain.* Is that better?"

He gives a wicked grin, then pulls his shirt over his head while I quickly unfasten the buttons on his breeches. Slowly, he pushes the light shift, which by now, barely covers me, up my legs. Tapping me on the hip so I raise them, he pulls it up and over my head. With our clothing shed, his mouth finds mine once again — passionate, yet unhurried. His fingers run through my loose hair as we kiss. Always the more impatient one, I reach down to grip him, guiding him to my entrance. He pulls away from our kisses and presses his forehead against mine as he slowly slides into me.

I gasp at the sensation of him filling me, any words I might utter turning to a moan as he begins to move. When his pace picks up I wrap my legs around his hips, pulling him deeper as I meet his thrusts, wanting him closer. My fingernails trail down his scarred back as I kiss his chest and throat.

"Oh, Goddess," I breathe against his heated skin and feel a moan rumbling low in his throat. My pleasure tenses in my belly once more as he thrusts deeper into me, causing me to clutch him closer. "Please don't stop."

He grips the sheets tightly and his decadent movements push me over the edge. Shuddering, I cling to him as the waves of my release grip me, stifling my cries against his shoulder. A few more thrusts are all it takes before Lennox finds his own pleasure and rests his forehead against mine again, breathing hard along with me. He presses a soft kiss against my brow, where my sigil rests, uncloaked until the meeting, and runs his fingers through my hair before cupping my cheek.

"Distracted enough?" he whispers, a cocky smile tiling the edge of his lips.

"It will do," I smirk. Emotion overcomes me as I run my thumb over his full lower lip. "I love you."

"I love you, too," he says, then rolls to lay beside me, pulling me against his chest. A few moments later he murmurs, "I know you're apprehensive about the meeting.

Don't be. I don't think you understand how badly change is needed for Selennia, how much the people will love you. And remember, I'll always be with you. I won't let anyone harm you again." He squeezes me in our embrace for emphasis. "I know you're more than capable of taking care of yourself, but I'm always with you, Nerissa."

"I know," I murmur, pressing my face against his chest so he can't see the worry written on my face.

CHAPTER 14

The morning of the captains' assembly dawns crisp and still. Since the single storm, we've been lucky to avoid any additional interruptions on our voyage, and today the sails hang slack from the masts as we prepare to descend in row boats. A small cluster of islands lay ahead of us covered in craggy cliffs and evergreen forests. The largest is Nemi, which is utilized for the annual meeting of the captains, ensuring neutral ground to discuss politics as they pertain to those who hunt these seas, or in this case, to Selennia.

The *Bartered Soul* is anchored near *Andromeda's Vengeance*, the *Kraken's Maw*, and the *Selkie's Tears*. The *Island Queen* approached from another direction, stopping in an alternate bay farther out from shore, as planned. A ship I'm not familiar with floats near the *Vengeance*. I don't see its name, but the figurehead is a fierce black dragon with a plume of golden fire exploding from its jaws. Other ships dot the waters farther out with small boats at the ready tied to their sides.

"What ship is that?" I ask Lennox as we prepare to climb into the rowboat, pointing toward the dragon.

"Ah, the *Hadriel*. Erik's cousin's," he replies, holding out his hand to steady me as I take my seat. I've foregone all semblance of femininity for this showing, tucking my hair up neatly and hiding it and most of my face under a dipped tricornered hat. I don a leather coat similar to Lennox's, except his has the repair from where he was injured attacking the *Archangel*, while mine is unblemished. At first glance, I look like one of the crewmembers — exactly as I wished. Even though the captains met me at Marie's last fall, I wish to listen in unobtrusively at this meeting before I make my presence known.

Tom rows us together with Erik toward the island, his dark curls tumbling over his eyes as he works the oars to cut through the calm waves. Jackson and several of his crewmen row in alongside us, our alliance unmistakable to anyone who may be waiting for us ashore.

On the beach ahead, a few other boats litter the wet pebbles of the rocky beach, but no one stands near them. As we come to a stop on the shore I leap out of the boat like the men, not wanting to be seen in Lennox's arms by anyone who might be observing. The cold, salty water seeps into my leather boots and I curl my lip at the unpleasant sloshing and chill that permeates my lower body but keep my head dipped as we wade onto the beach. Erik, Tom, and Jackson join Lennox and me, none of them flinching at the chilly water as we plod through the slick, shifting pebbles toward a clearing hidden behind the large rocks that line the edge of the shore. Beyond the natural stone bulwark is a large canvas tent our crew erected the night before. The front flap stands open and a large man with long sandy hair and laughing blue eyes stands just outside the entrance, a sword across his back, tattooed arms crossed over his massive chest.

"Ulf!" Erik calls out, a broad smile gracing his face. It's so rare to see Erik openly smile away from Siobhan that my heart lightens at the sight despite the seriousness of our endeavor.

"Cousin!" Ulf replies, his stern countenance brightening at the greeting as they slap one another on the back in welcome. "Lennox, Jackson," Ulf greets the other men, his smile waning, but not disappearing, at the sight of allies, not family. His eyes shift to Tom and me lingering behind the captains, a brow raising in question. "And who are your companions?"

"Tom, quartermaster under Erik, and one of my crewmen from the *Bartered Soul* come to serve refreshments," Lennox quickly interjects, avoiding an outright introduction for me. Ulf gives a wry smile, looking between me, Lennox, and Erik, but doesn't press the issue.

"Who's inside already?" Erik asks his cousin while we step out of earshot of the flap.

"So far, the captain and representatives of the *Hadriel* and Morel with men from the *Island Queen*. I thought I saw di Micios land on the beach shortly after us, but he hasn't turned up yet. The *Calypso* is in the other bay, so I expect Trevino will be washing ashore soon," Ulf advises.

"Well, let's get on with it. If di Micios and Trevino don't arrive in the next half hour we'll start without them," Lennox remarks, indicating with a jerk of his chin that we should follow him into the tent.

Erik and Ulf step through the flap first, inspecting the interior for any possible subterfuge, followed by Jackson, then Lennox, Tom, and myself. In the center of the massive space is a large table and chairs, which disassembles for ease of transport. On one side sits Morel, flanked on the right by a younger, lighter-skinned man with dark brown braids in a similar style to those Marie wears. In the seat to Morel's left is another young man who looks almost identical to the captain of the *Island Queen*, except his hair isn't shaved; he wears it in tightly cropped, coarse curls.

Facing Morel and his companions is a slight, cloaked figure. With their back to me, I can't make out the features of the person, but a small axe is laid across the table in front of them and a dagger glints from their boot as it rests casually across their knee. The choice of weaponry makes me assume this is another of Erik's relatives. Erik claps the figure on the shoulder and they turn quickly to greet him, face still hidden by the hood of the cloak. I retreat to the corner of the tent as we planned, hoping to not draw attention to myself as I take up a pitcher and act as though I'm only there at my captain's bidding.

"Morel, we didn't see the *Island Queen* after the storm. Any losses?" Lennox asks as he takes the seat at the head of the table. Erik sits next to him, Ulf between him and the cloaked figure. Jackson walks behind Lennox to sit at the chair to his left, next to the youngest of Morel's crew. The older man blows out a final puff of herbal smoke, the scent so like that of the hand-rolled cigarettes Salome smoked that I find comfort in the aroma as he stubs out the end on the ground.

"No losses, thankfully, Lennox," Morel answers.

"Though I hope the storms are finished for the season and we can get home before the late summer ones arrive."

I exhale a small sigh in relief that they didn't sustain any damages, grateful once more that these men will stand with us, even though our fight takes them far from their sunny shores and calm waters.

"That would be ideal," Lennox agrees, his mouth grim. "You're lucky you were far enough behind us to miss the worst part of the one we rode out. We can only hope everything moves quickly after today."

We have a plan in mind, outlined bit by bit each evening in our cabin, but it all depends on the cooperation of men who are known for being uncooperative, and the actions of a king whose only predictability is brutality. I keep my head down as they make small talk, still waiting on di Micios and Trevino to arrive.

The men in the tent so far have reasons for standing against Blackwell — alliances based on love, kinship, or revenge for direct damage suffered at Blackwell's command. Those we await are not bound by such things, and my heart clenches as I let my worries circle in my mind standing near the canvas wall.

Minutes tick by as we wait, interrupted only by the motion of Jackson checking the time on a pocket watch he pulls from his multi-hued waistcoat. Finally, footsteps sound outside the door and an elegant, pale-skinned, blond man sweeps through the flap. He's tall and broad with icy eyes and a stern expression as he takes in the group waiting for him. Two men follow closely behind him — crewmembers I assume — taking up places near the wall of the tent like Tom and I, waiting for instructions from their captain.

"Trevino. Nice of you to show up," Jackson sneers at the man, standing from his seat.

"I got caught up with the Tomcat, rambling nonsense as usual. Apologies for the delay, gentlemen. What have I missed?" Trevino glances over at me briefly, scanning each of us standing along the wall, but takes the seat next to the cloaked figure, his back to me. His no-nonsense attitude is refreshing, especially if he already shows signs of irritation with di Micios — the one I fear will make this meeting a challenge.

Just as I think of the man, he appears in the doorway with a crewman trailing behind. Although he still glistens with gold rings and preens like a peacock, his clothing is muted compared to the last time I saw him, pawing all over me at Marie's masquerade. Lennox's jaw twitches, likely remembering our last altercation with the man, as well. As he enters the room, di Micios makes no excuses for his tardiness, and simply takes the seat next to Morel's man at the end of the table, smoothing his black hair back from his tan forehead and steepling his fingers on the tabletop. No one sits with their back to the flap, ensuring there will be no surprises at their backs.

"Bit of a delay this morning, di Micios?" Lennox questions sarcastically, eyes hard and narrowed as they observe the man's calm demeanor.

"I'm here now, Lennox. I'm flattered you still welcome me after our last party together. Is there something pressing causing you to be so eager to get underway?" Di Micios' tone bristles with animosity, causing my nerves to kick up a notch higher while I watch the men cast their eyes about at one another. The tension between di Micios and Lennox may be an issue today if things continue in this vein.

"Hold your tongue, di Micios," Trevino snaps unexpectedly. "If you didn't want to attend, you shouldn't have set foot on the shore. Lennox, what *is* so important that we needed to meet immediately upon arrival?" His tone brooks no argument from the Tomcat, who glowers at the others like a scolded child.

"Thank you, Ivan. We have much to discuss…"

CHAPTER 15
LENNOX

If di Micios runs his mouth one more time, I swear I will fucking kill him, I think to myself as I prepare to explain our gambit.

There's always been enmity between the two of us, but it's only worsened since Nerissa was brought into the equation. Mario "the Tomcat" Di Micios isn't a bad man, just cocky and used to flattering his way into everything he wants, whether it be riches or women. After last fall and how he treated Nerissa, I can hardly look at the man without grinding my teeth.

Trevino's chastisement seems to have silenced him for now, his anticipated ally proving to be as fickle as I'd hoped. Confident, I clear my throat to begin, only allowing myself to offer the ghost of a glance to where Nerissa stands in the corner of the tent. Jackson has a clear view of her at all times, which eases the tension coiled in my chest, even though I'm certain she can more than take care of herself.

"I have a proposition for you all," I begin without preamble. "Some of you know firsthand that Dargan Blackwell's reach has overstepped the shores of Selennia. He pressed against the northern islands soon after taking power in Selennia, disrupting trade and attempting to send priests to infiltrate their shores." Ulf and his companion both nod, confirming the statement. "Now he's crossed the sea to attack Delosia and New Aphros. If he were successful in those attempts, it would thwart our business at our most lucrative ports and safe harbors. His harbormasters already take substantial portions of our haul in bribes to avoid the gallows, it's time we take a stand to stop his power grab before he can take hold elsewhere and spread the pestilence of his reign."

Before I can continue, di Micios opens his smug mouth again. "Seems to me it's your whore's fault for him turning his sights across the sea. Rumor has it that Blackwell is looking for the priestess who's been warming your bed. Wouldn't it be better to just give her to him and continue on our way? Or can you not bear to part with your treasure, William?" His smile earns every bit of his nickname — he sits looking like a cat that got the cream. I'm surprised the Tomcat doesn't lick his fucking paw.

Although my hands tremble with rage, I bite back my fury. As much as I hate to admit it, the asshole isn't wrong. He just hasn't laid out the reason Blackwell wants her, though these men aren't fools and have surely suspected it since Marie's dinner.

"Are you finished?" I ask blandly, choking down my irritation while I force myself to relax my fists and steeple my fingers. The other men watch me warily, except for Trevino who smirks at my hands as if he knows the restraint it requires for me to keep them from balling into fists. His distaste for di Micios is well-known, and I'm positive he would love for me to backhand him.

"Mario, this isn't a pissing match. If you aren't here to at least lend your consideration then leave now, before we all lose our temper," Jackson chides, like he's speaking to a child who needs his ears boxed. Jackson cuts his eyes to me and gestures for me to speak, lighting another cigarette. "Get to the point, William."

"The point is, though he claims he's looking for one woman, it's only his excuse while he tries to expand his empire. Blackwell *must* be stopped. This isn't just about my homeland anymore. He's destroyed Selennia, and you'd be a fool to think that he won't come to yours next. He's a threat to *all* of us, as it stands. There is no love or loyalty for the King in this room. Isn't it time we do something other than just harry his ships for prizes? Together, we can take Selennia back."

"And who will rule in his stead?" Trevino questions, his eyes locked on me. I knew he would be one who needed convincing. Beyond our trade contact on Delosia, and occasionally in New Aphros, he has no meaningful tie to any of us, and, while always civil, we aren't what I would consider friends. His light brows furrow above piercing eyes as he assesses me and my allies. "Unless what I deduced on Delosia is correct? That your woman is, in fact, Adelaide's heir."

Jackson's crystal blue eyes flicker to where Nerissa stands in the dim light. She's still hidden enough with the other crewmen to not stand out despite her slim figure, but I don't want to reveal her until she's ready.

"Regardless of who will rule, my men and I would like

to hear the plan. The ruler of Selennia has no bearing on Delosia, except when they are invading our island. If we are guaranteed peaceful trade in the aftermath, we will fight on your side," Morel interjects, his voice as warm as the island he hails from, belying the penchant for violence I know he possesses. His companions nod their heads in agreement.

I'm pleased with his choice of words. The others needn't know Morel and the *Island Queen* were already aligned with us from the start.

"The Northmen feel the same. What is it you are proposing? Once we hear the plan we will make our decision," Ulf offers, his lilting accent so like Erik's. The big man receives a small dip in response from his cloaked companion. Why they're keeping this air of secrecy I don't know, but I won't question it at the moment.

I proceed to outline the plan that Nerissa and I have discussed. The men gathered around the table sit forward as I unroll a map of Selennia and place stones in strategic places while I speak, indicating where temples once stood in defensive locations and where Blackwell's navy keeps its fleet distributed. I've made assumptions in my mind as to which crews will agree, which will balk at different parts, and who will want to leave outright. So, it's a shock to me when Trevino sits back, without discussing with his men, and states without any questions, "The *Calypso* will fight with you."

Di Micios seems more surprised than me at the outright pledge, his mouth dropping open so that his gold tooth glints in the lanterns. Ivan Trevino is known to be brave, but cautious, so a firm agreement wasn't guaranteed.

"Close your mouth, Mario," Trevino snaps, leaning back

in his chair. "Despite your words on the beach, you know how I feel about Blackwell. My family was forced from their home by Blackwell's grandfather on the continent a generation ago. Then, once they were settled and prosperous in Selennia, this shit with a chip on his shoulder comes through and put us through it all over again. I'm ready to pay him back. I'll offer assistance to rid us of him. I know my crew will agree with my decision."

"Well, I don't see how this benefits me or my crew, especially without telling me who will be taking charge of Selennia or any guarantees to our immunity afterward. It exposes us to more loss than the *Hellcat* will wish to risk for little to no gain," di Micios states and pushes away from the table, visibly unhappy that he's the only one who challenges me today.

As I start to speak, the sound of a throat clearing and the snick of a blade from its sheath comes from where Nerissa stands. All eyes turn to find her dark blue stare fixed on di Micios.

Nerissa no longer wears her hat and has allowed her sigil to shine on her brow, this time accented by the scrolling knotwork that spreads across her forehead and disappears into her temples like a permanent crown. It glows in the dim tent and di Micios takes a step back when he recognizes her.

"*I* will rule, Captain di Micios." Her voice is as chilly as the waves we stepped in to reach the island earlier as she prowls forward.

My she-wolf, indeed.

"If that doesn't suit you, I welcome you to leave. But first—" She nonchalantly runs her blade through the flame of the brazier that helps to heat the tent, watching as it glows red with heat. "I'll need to ensure you don't spread word of our intentions."

Di Micios looks between me and Nerissa rapidly, his black eyes showing fear and confusion. "Mistress, what do you mean?"

"Your tongue, of course. I'll need to remove it so you can't tell anyone what you've heard or seen today. Don't worry, the blade will seal the bleeding. It will be over soon." Her words send a shiver over me as I meet di Micios' eyes, full of disbelief. But I know mine have gone feral listening to her threats, my lips lifting into a savage smile.

"What is this, Lennox? An ambush?" he gapes, looking between me and Nerissa, bristling like a wildcat. When I remain silent, he turns his attention to the others around the table. "Are you all going to just let her walk in here and take charge? A stranger with no proof or guarantees?"

Jackson blows another puff of smoke from his lips as he sits back in his chair. Trevino appears amused, one corner of his lip lifted slightly at di Micios' distress. Erik and Ulf are mirror images with their arms crossed over their chest on either side of their cloaked brethren, while Morel and his men cast their eyes between one another.

Not one of them offers a challenge to Nerissa as she holds her blade. Not even the man di Micios brought with him from his crew steps forward at the sight of her fury.

"Are you finished?" Nerissa asks, taking a step forward without hesitation, brandishing the blade.

"No. I mean, yes. I—" di Micios grinds his teeth together then takes a knee before her. Defeated, even though his eyes are alight with hatred when they glance at me. "Forgive me. My crew and I will do your bidding, Mistress. Whatever you ask."

"I'm not sure I should allow a coward to join us," Nerissa muses, inspecting her blade. "But today, I'll offer you mercy. Know this though: should you betray me, or any of the men in this room, I won't need a knife to end you." She places the tip of the still-warm blade under di Micios' chin, forcing him to look up at her with a wince.

"Yes, Mistress."

"It's *Your Majesty*," she corrects, stepping back and gliding to my side.

The cloaked figure at Ulf's side finally moves, tattooed hands rising from their lap to begin a slow applause. After a moment a feminine chuckle escapes from the hood before their slim fingers push it off to reveal the woman within. Her strawberry blond hair is a shade darker, and several shades redder, than Ulf's, but they share the same blue eyes and quick smile.

"Well done, Your Majesty," Revna Gunnarsdottir chuckles. "You have the full support of the *Hadriel*. You would have anyway, knowing Lennox as we do, but after that show, I would not wish to align myself with anyone else."

"It's about time you show your face, Captain." I smile at Erik's other cousin, Ulf's twin — Captain of the *Hadriel*.

CHAPTER 16

Tom quickly moves the empty chair from the end of the table so I sit next to Lennox. Under the table, Lennox's hand steadily soothes me, tracing small circles on my thigh through my wool breeches. The sensation is almost as distracting as the wicked smile he gives me, heating my core and making me clench my thighs together while trying to focus on the captains waiting for one of us to speak.

Di Micios sits quietly, not meeting my eyes again after the spectacle of my threat. I tell myself that I wouldn't have really cut out his tongue, but then, perhaps I would have.

Little does he know, I wouldn't need a knife if I wanted him silenced. I wouldn't even need to touch him.

I've known men like di Micios before, all bluster and bravado to demonstrate their manhood, but when it comes down to it they're more cowardly than any woman I've met. Whatever animosity he bears toward Lennox is likely only because Lennox commands respect without trying, whereas di Micios has to claw for it.

The smoke from Jackson's cigarette curls around our end of the table, the sweet scent of the burning herbs reminding me of Salome and restoring my calm confidence as the meeting progresses. Lennox designates locations for raids to each crew, and the captains nod and agree to the plan as it unfolds.

"The *Hadriel* will land at the Northern Point, drawing allies from the Northern Isles to retake the temple at Airmedan. Once secured, Revna and Ulf will return for the attack on Aphros. Trevino, you and di Micios, will circle to the northeastern coastline, north of the Cybelene woods near Murias. Hopefully, that will keep Blackwell's forces in the east delayed," Lennox revisits each point. "Morel and the militia will land and take Cybele itself, then move through the woods toward Aphros to offer support on land. Jackson will take the coastline at Athene and will return with the *Hadriel* once the western coast has been secured. Erik and Pike will wait hidden off the cliffs of Aphros until I give the signal. We can keep the *Kraken's Maw* with them in case we need it."

Lennox speaks confidently, each piece of the plan clear and precise. But I haven't shared the true lynchpin yet. The part that I know must happen, but that I'm most fearful of. Blowing out a deep breath I explain, "The most important part of the plan is for me to make my appearance in Selennia. For the people to know I still exist, that Adelaide's heir has returned. No matter how many victories you may secure, I need the loyalty of the common folk to back me. And I need to see and hear firsthand what's been happening under Blackwell's rule. To do that without fail, without hiding, I must get close to Blackwell." I pause, a tremor passing over me as nausea turns my stomach at the idea. Lennox cuts his eyes to me, his hand freezing on my leg as I speak.

"So, you will attack the castle directly? With Lennox's crew?" Morel questions, his eyes darting between Lennox and me.

"No. I must convince him that I wish to make an alliance. *Not* that I'm there to overthrow him. He cannot know that any of you are working on my side. I need him to recognize my legitimacy… to make me his consort. To name me his queen, on my terms, publicly." The words are bitter as I speak them, causing me to swallow nervously while Lennox's hand squeezes my thigh and the muscles of his jaw twitch. I can almost hear his teeth grinding.

Even though I've suggested this before in private, Lennox has insisted that there is another option than offering myself on a platter to Blackwell, yet we haven't figured out what that might be. He hasn't agreed to this portion, but I know he won't question me in front of everyone now. Doing so would shake the solid foundation we've constructed, undermine the confident front we present, and could potentially make the others question their choice of alliance. Even though I hate this plan, it will be easier to tempt Blackwell into trusting me and welcoming me back to the castle in Aphros than to plot a full-scale siege and take over. The loss of life should be fewer, and the risk to those helping me lessened.

"Isn't that exceedingly dangerous?" Morel asks, his eyes wide as he cants his head to the side and considers my words. The entire group looks shocked that I would place myself in harm's way, especially knowing Blackwell was more than happy to murder the last queen to steal the throne.

"It is. But not if he believes it. I'm confident I can handle him if necessary. It's of the utmost importance that he believes I'm not in league with you. He needs to trust me." I don't offer any additional information; they don't need to know the full extent of the power that Salome and the Goddess have bestowed on me and my sister priestesses. Not yet. Their only tasks are to follow Lennox's commands and do as we ask: distract and draw the King's forces around the coastline, take strategic locations, incite rebellion in the villages they breach, and stand beside us when we need them.

"We're only a week out from Aphros," Lennox begins, improvising a plan on the spot. "We can send a messenger with a letter to the King to offer her proposal to meet. Once he responds we'll know how to proceed. In the meantime, you'll each have your orders to complete. We need the country to be in chaos. Blackwell's soldiers must be spread thin and be far away from the castle. Erik and I can handle things in the city if the rest of you do your jobs."

"What exactly is in it for us in the end?" Captain Trevino asks. Unlike di Micios, Trevino has not been hostile, but his cool mannerisms show he's still weighing the options even though he already agreed to help us.

"Once this is over we can discuss that — depending on how well you play your role, Captain," I reply coolly. "Our first goal is to dispose of Blackwell. But, in the end, wouldn't it be easier for you all to sail under a legitimate letter of marque from the crown, rather than risk being hanged as pirates by neighboring kingdoms? Assuming we can come to an agreement like you have in Delosia and New Aphros, I'm willing to discuss options once we've regained our footing at home. You could have a safe haven for trade on the east side of the sea like you've established in the west."

Trevino doesn't ask any other questions, but he appraises Lennox and me then sits back again in contemplation.

"I think that's enough for today. After the full moon, we can depart to enact our plans. I hope you'll stand with us as promised," Lennox says, standing, the nicety thinly veiling the threat of what he'll do if they do not uphold their portion of the bargain. The men, and Revna, approach and shake his hand, then bow to me. Revna gives me a little grin when she stands back up, before gathering with her brother and Erik.

When the others file out we join the trio and Jackson. "Ulf, Revna, will you join us on the *Bartered Soul* this evening for dinner?" Lennox asks, clapping Ulf on the back.

"Only if my captain allows it." The big man laughs, deferring to his sister. "I'd like you to meet my wife, cousin," he tells Erik, then turns to Lennox and me to add, "She's from your homeland."

"Of course! I hear Erik's lover is with him this time. I must meet the woman, and get to know you as well, Your Majesty," Revna replies pleasantly, turning to me.

STEPPING BACK ONTO THE DECK OF THE *BARTERED SOUL* I CAN feel the frustration radiating off of Lennox at my side. He hasn't spoken to me since we said our farewells on the beach, his silence louder than any shouts I might have expected. I swallow nervously, wondering if I should have told him my plan to announce my proposal before the meeting, but I wasn't ready for him to offer alternatives or other solutions. I needed the captains to know I'm as willing to go to battle for my throne as I expect them and their crews to be.

My pulse thrums nervously as I lead us back to our cabin where Lennox holds the door open, jaw tight, before following me in.

As the door clicks shut, his voice turns icy. "What the hell was that?"

"What?" I ask, turning to face him. His eyes shimmer with checked anger — the kind of anger I've seen him level at others, but never at me.

"Why would you say that? Why would you tell them you would offer yourself in marriage to Blackwell? I told you we have other options."

"Because I will. And *what* options? If this is how I can get close enough to take the throne back, I'll act the part. We know he's looking for *me*," I explain, frustration leaking into my voice. "We know that even with all these ships in agreement we don't have the forces to defeat an entire army. If I have to act as bait to fool him then I will. I can't imagine any other options."

"We're supposed to do this *together*, Nerissa. Why would you hide this from me? Surprise me like that?"

"Oh, as though you yourself haven't *surprised* me several times in the past?" My own anger begins to simmer in my chest to match his, to smother out my self-doubt and fear. "Do you fear that I *want* to be with the man? That this is something I *desire* to do?"

"*No*, of course not. I simply want you to trust me and discuss these things as we move forward. I know you are our queen, but I won't have this go the way it did in New Aphros. Salome thought she knew best and look at what happened. Do not dismiss me the way she did!" His voice cracks and my anger falters.

The guilt I carry over Salome's death, that Delphine carries, also weighs on Lennox. He hasn't spoken of it before now, but his words betray his silence. He warned Salome that meeting the priests in the open on Winter Solstice was folly, but she hadn't listened. Now I understand it's because she knew what the outcome would be, knew that she had to die to pass on her power to me, but even so, Lennox apparently harbors guilt over not pushing harder against it.

"Billy," I start, reaching out to trace my fingers over the cuff of his coat. "I should have discussed it with you, but I knew what you'd say. There's still time to determine our final path, but we needed their agreement. Who's even to say Blackwell will agree to it?"

"He will." Bitterness coats the two simple words as he stares at my hand on his sleeve. "He's sent soldiers halfway across the world to find you. He won't turn you away when you're a willing sacrifice."

Stepping closer, I force him to look into my eyes, sliding my palm against the stubble along his jaw and cupping his cheek. "His greed will blind him, and then we will take back what is ours." Although I mean for the words to offer comfort a chill skates down my spine at the sorrow in

Lennox's eyes before he presses his forehead to mine in resignation.

———

As the sun sinks into the ocean, Lennox and I stand on the quarterdeck waiting for Erik's cousins to row over from their ship. Our argument from earlier may be concealed behind our pleasant demeanors, but I'm certain the discussion hasn't been laid to rest.

The island of Nemi isn't far, its rocky beach and outcroppings dark in the fading light. A few fires shine from the shore, other ships having disembarked to camp on the beach for the next few days until our plans are all settled. Occasionally the sounds of merriment drift over to us from the people there. Four figures sit in the approaching boat — Ulf, Revna, Ulf's wife, and a crewman who rows the vessel. Erik and Siobhan wait near the rail of the main deck to greet our guests, and Siobhan's happy laughter floats on the breeze as they speak quietly to one another.

"Is it common for the Northmen to bring their wives on their voyages?" I ask Lennox. Although Erik and Lennox each have their partners by their sides now, it isn't something I ever considered when I thought of pirates in the past.

"It depends on the wife, but it isn't unheard of. Many of those who choose this life have partners and families back on land, wherever that might be. Oftentimes you make a better living doing this than you would on a legitimate vessel, even if there's a risk of being put to death if you're captured." He wraps his arms around me, pulling me close for a moment before we must descend to meet our guests. "I don't know how I could ever leave you behind again," he whispers into my hair before pressing a kiss to the top of my head and releasing me.

Even though the weather is mild, the coolness of the impending night surrounds me at the loss of his warmth and I shudder because I feel the same way. I don't think I can bear to be apart for a long period of time again, but I have to bury the worry that niggles at the back of my mind thinking about the upcoming months when we may have to do just that to defeat Blackwell.

The small boat reaches us and a rope ladder is dropped for the guests. As they climb, Lennox and I descend the stairs to the main deck. Revna crosses over the railing first, followed by a woman with dark brown hair braided tightly back from her face. This must be Ulf's wife. As she reaches for the railing, she lifts her head to look over the deck and my heart stops in my chest, causing my feet to still as I pause gripping the rail of the stairs I still descend.

The woman has fair skin and clear green eyes. Her forehead has markings similar to those Erik has tattooed on his scalp, but in the center just above her brows is an upturned crescent. Outlined with the ink that was used for her others, the sigil is dull and scarred like mine was before I accessed the Goddess again with my sisters. It's been nearly nine years since I've seen her — since the night we both fled the temple. But I'd recognize her anywhere. As she climbs over the railing her gaze meets mine and a wide smile breaks across her face.

Confusion knots his brow as Lennox glances behind him to find me still frozen on the stairs while the woman smiles.

"Sister," she says softly while Revna and Lennox look between us.

"Aisling," I reply barely above a whisper, finally remembering my breath and propelling myself toward the woman to wrap her in a tight embrace.

CHAPTER 17

"Aisling," I say again, as I hold her away to study her face, then pull her close once more, clutching her to me as if she's a phantom that might slip away. "How? How are you here?"

"Nerissa," Aisling replies, stepping back to look at me. She's slightly shorter than I am, but, aside from the tattoos on her face, she still looks so similar to me it's eerie. "I escaped that night, but I thought I was the only one. I was so relieved to know that my visions were true when Ulf told me about you being at the meeting. It's only because of my visions that I insisted on coming on this voyage." She runs a hand over her abdomen and I realize that her belly swells slightly under her loose dress, showing early signs of being with child.

"But... how?" I study her face again, so shocked to see my old friend that I forget the others surrounding us for a moment.

Lennox clears his throat, gently placing his hand on my shoulder as I stare at the newcomer. "Welcome," he says to

Aisling and then to Revna and Ulf. "It seems that your wife and m— Nerissa know one another, Ulf." He stumbles, almost revealing our handfasting to the guests, but catches himself. Ulf and Revna share a look, one that enforces their bond as twins with an unspoken understanding, and the big man nods once.

"My love insisted she come on this voyage. Even though she is already showing with our child, I cannot deny her anything she desires," the large man replies, casting a warm smile down to Aisling. "She sailed with us before we married. Her gift is useful in determining where we choose to travel."

"You are a *Seer* like my Siobhan?" Erik asks, arm wrapped proudly around Siobhan's shoulders.

"She is," I reply, still holding Aisling's hands tight in mine. "She trained alongside me in Athene. We escaped the same night." Aisling was specifically chosen for how closely we resembled one another. Since I'd never seen or heard from her again, I'd assumed she was captured or killed the night we all fled from the temple. Her bold personality was always the opposite to my reticence, and I remember her challenging our High Priestess when she told us to flee that night.

"Let's all go to our cabin. We can share a meal and get to know one another better," Lennox says as he places his palm on my lower back, bringing me back to the present as I release Aisling's hands.

"Yes, please. This way," I echo, gesturing for the group to follow Lennox toward the great cabin.

Once we take our seats around the table in our cabin, adding an extra chair from Lennox's desk to accommodate our number, Lennox pours wine while we wait for the cook to bring us the meal he's prepared.

"So, Aisling, how did you and Ulf meet?" Lennox opens the conversation, looking between the large Northman and his Selennian wife.

"Sheer luck," Aisling answers, glancing over at her husband with a smirk.

"Her Goddess delivered her to me. She is just less effusive about it than I am," Ulf refutes with a smile. "I found her on the docks when we were leaving Athene. We never meant to be in Selennia during Blackwell's overthrow, but it was a surprise that his men were already there at the time we were. When we saw the forests set fire we hurried to depart. As we prepared to weigh anchor I saw her running down the docks as if she were a water spirit ready to cast herself back into the sea, so I grabbed her and carried her on board the *Hadriel* before she could refuse."

"You kidnapped me and nearly scared me to death," Aisling murmurs with a teasing air, smiling at her husband and running a hand over her belly.

"Ha! You nearly scratched the side of my face off for my troubles. I think we were equally surprised, my love," Ulf chuckles in response.

"This is true." She sips her watered wine and smiles at me. Her smile falters as she adds, "I ran out the front escape way into the burning woods. I only thought of making it to a ship and stowing away. I didn't even know how I would do that, just ran blindly through the ashes that rained on me. The next thing I knew I was on the docks and then some brute snatched me up, tossed me over his shoulder, and carried me onto his ship. I was relieved and terrified at the same time when I found it was a Northman, but to be honest, I didn't think I would be better off with Blackwell's troops."

"You wouldn't have." The soft words are past my lips before I can stop them. Aisling, Revna, and Siobhan's expressions all change from gentle to grim at my answer.

Aisling swallows, looking down at her hand in her lap before speaking again. "In the end, Ulf was exactly who I needed to find me. He took me to Revna and they carried me to the Northern Isles with them once they left Athene. There they valued my visions and welcomed me into their village as a holy woman of sorts since their goddess legends aren't terribly different from ours. And, well… one thing led to another and I ended up with this one," she smiles jutting her thumb toward Ulf, "and our babies." Ulf and Aisling share a look full of love and friendship and my heart both aches and soars for them.

"Babies? This isn't your first?" Siobhan asks.

"No, this will be our third. The older two are safe with our village while we assist you."

I'm happy Aisling was saved that night. I would never wish for the horrible things that happened to me and my sisters to happen to anyone else. But I also regret not having found the comfort and safety she did so soon. Fear hounds me thinking of what I'm asking of Ulf and the crew of the *Hadriel*, knowing the dangers they may face at my behest and what he and Aisling both risk leaving behind.

"I *Saw* you, Nerissa. For the past few years, your face has come to me. I could never tell where you were, or when the visions were from, but I always knew it was you and that you were alive. I saw you on a ship, marked by a wolf." Aisling's eyes flicker over to Lennox who silently drinks his wine. "When Ulf told me he was coming to Nemi for the annual meeting I had to come. To see if you were really with them."

"What of Layla?" I ask, remembering our other companion priestess who trained with us and fled through the passages that night as well.

Aisling looks down at her wine, shaking her head. "No. Never."

I knew it was too much to hope that all of us had survived, but I still have to squeeze my eyes tight to keep the tears at bay. Siobhan, seated next to me, reaches over under the table to grip my hand, squeezing it gently as I breathe deeply.

The silence lingers until a tap at the door announces Davey and a few of the crew who carry our meal. They lay out the dishes, then exit the cabin before anyone speaks. As we pass the food around — flakey white fish in a savory broth with cabbage, potatoes, and carrots — quiet conversations begin. Ulf, Revna, and Erik discuss news of the Northern Isles, and Siobhan and Aisling confer over methods of divination, but Lennox and I remain silent, looking over the group gathered before us.

"So," Revna begins, looking between Lennox and me. "What is your plan for Selennia once you have taken it back?"

"As we said in the meeting, I plan to rule," I reply, glancing at Lennox with confusion.

"Yes, but what of those who have supported Blackwell? The prisoners and soldiers who aren't killed in battle? Should we aim to kill as many as possible in the takeover?

Or do you wish to hold a public execution?" Revna's questions are asked as simply as if she's discussing what type of cake to serve with my coronation tea, not the fate of men's lives.

"I…" I stumble for words. Up until now I'd been so focused on gathering allies that I haven't considered what to do with any survivors that might oppose me. I'm not a fool; I know we should expect some resistance. But, even though I'm not a tyrant like Blackwell, anger grips me when I think of men blindly following his orders to torment the inhabitants of Selennia at his behest without question. "I wish for them to suffer, this is true, but I confess I hadn't thought past defeating them as a whole." I'm not certain whether this admission is too candid, but Lennox and Erik are so at ease with the twins that I don't check myself in my response.

"Surely you won't kill them all just because they're trapped under Blackwell's thumb?" Siobhan's gentle voice cuts through.

"Siobhan, you were held captive by them and forced to treat their wounded. Then, your home and business were destroyed by the soldiers Erik killed on Delosia. Why would this be any different?" I can't fathom why Siobhan would possibly defend any of the soldiers we might face and I'm more confused by the look shared between Erik and Lennox.

"I was, but the army physician I worked with was Selennian. He was just unlucky enough to be captured and held by the army, the same as I was. He did his best to keep me safe despite our situation, just like I'm sure others have had to choose to do. Not everyone can be as brave as all of you," she replies, her cheeks pink from speaking up. "Some of them may be more than happy to join our cause if given the chance."

Revna and Ulf make similar sounds of disgust in their throats. "Cowards who would turn their coat to save their skin are not ones we should want on our side."

"I do not think it is as easy as that," Erik adds, surprising me. "I will take any man's life who threatens me, Siobhan, or my friends and family, without hesitation. But, then, I also know I would be willing to make sacrifices I never thought I would to protect them as well."

"Siobhan, I know we've had this conversation before," Lennox adds. "I understand your viewpoint, but I will defend what is mine. If anyone threatens one of you I won't hesitate regardless of their motivation. However, I'm willing to listen to what you want to do, Nerissa." His gaze, along with the others, weighs on me. Another decision I must make that I don't feel prepared for, one that I won't have an answer to by the end of this meal.

"I'll let all of you know before we part ways in the next few days. My instinct is to capture any prisoners who don't fight back but don't hesitate to defend yourselves or any who might harm the innocents of Selennia. Whether they bear Blackwell's colors or not." I drink deeply from my wine and pick at the rest of my meal, sinking into my thoughts as the others nod in acceptance. Siobhan's eyes catch my gaze, but she smiles and turns to speak softly to Erik without pressing the issue.

After dinner, we sip brandy together, comfortable in the company of friends both old and new, as if battles don't wait for us in the days ahead.

"Tell us how you two ended up together," Aisling nudges Siobhan. "It seems fated for two *Seers* to find two Northmen, especially cousins!"

"Aye," Siobhan agrees, smiling. "It took a bit longer than for you and Ulf, but I believe the Goddess brought us together as well. Erik and William found me in Athene, hiding from soldiers in an alley."

I haven't heard the tale of Erik and Siobhan's meeting. I didn't know it happened in Athene.

"It was a song that sealed it. That, and Lennox's matchmaking," Erik adds, looking at Lennox and rolling his eyes as he shakes his head in jest.

"Matchmaking, hmm? You really are a romantic at heart aren't you?" I smile as Lennox grins over his cup.

"I don't believe either of you has thanked me for it either. You would both still be giving each other sidelong looks and blushing if it weren't for me," Lennox teases.

"Tell me the song!" Revna interjects gleefully, clapping her hands in excitement. "What song was it?"

"A lullaby from home," Erik replies.

"Sing it for us?" I ask quietly, my heart still heavy from our earlier conversation.

Siobhan and Erik share a nervous glance, then look at all of us as if asking for permission. Lennox and I raise our brows and nod in encouragement, and Ulf and Aisling cheer them on. It's only moments before Siobhan's brogue lifts into a lullaby, soon harmonized by Erik's deeper voice. Ulf and Revna smile and join in on the second verse, singing along until the end of the song.

"It *is* a lullaby! Auntie used to sing us all to sleep with that song. But, how do you know a lullaby from the Northern Isles, Siobhan?" Revna asks when the song ends.

"My mother was from the north," Siobhan answers. "Erik promised he would take me to her homeland once this is all over."

"Aye! We will welcome you in our village," Aisling enthusiastically agrees, lifting her cup.

While I try to remain positive, I can only hope that between Aisling and Siobhan's gifts, they speak from divined knowledge that we will all, in fact, make it to the other side intact, my own dreams still showing me nothing beyond the fate my mother met.

CHAPTER 18

The night of the full moon comes and goes off the coast of Nemi. Bright moonlight shines stark white against the grey rock and black outlines of the trees that stand as sentinels on the island. Siobhan, Delphine, Lyra, Aisling, and I hold a small ceremony on the pebbled beach accompanied by our closest crew, but each of us returns to our respective ships in preparation for the battles to come, the chill of the rocky isle not as enticing for lingering as the soft white sands we left behind. The celebration is a quiet affair compared to the one we shared on the beach of Delosia, most of us turning inward toward thoughts of the coming weeks ahead. We have one additional night before all eight ships plan to depart, heading east and then breaking off to the north and south. Each captain has instructions on which ports to target, which temples to take back, and which towns to sweep, hopeful that we can lure contingents of Blackwell's troops to battle across the island and not congregate at the castle gates.

The morning we're slated to set sail dawns crisp with a

dense mist surrounding the rocky coastline. A light frost coats the decks and railings when Lennox and I step out of our cabin, pulled from the warmth by shouts from the crew. The sky is pale blue and the sun shines brightly overhead, reflecting off the dark ocean and white waves crashing on the shore.

Pike approaches at a faster clip than is usually warranted so early, drawing my attention. "Captain!"

He holds the spyglass out to Lennox with a severe expression. We all knew the likelihood of making it the entire way between Nemi and Selennia without encountering any of Blackwell's naval vessels was slim, but the cry of *"Sails!"* that now drifts through the misty air so close to remote Nemi is an unwelcome surprise.

We anticipated having time to send a messenger under a white flag to Aphros within the week, but now, just days after our meeting, a vessel flying the griffin of Blackwell's fleet shows in Lennox's glass.

"Seems this may be our first test, my she-wolf," he says grimly, handing the glass back to Pike. His lips are set in a hard line as his eyes meet mine, but I feel a surge of energy tingling under my skin.

"Do we have a ship we can risk?" I ask, scanning the vessels in the water surrounding us as an idea takes hold. "If we truly wish to test our abilities, to show the others what we can do, this might be our chance."

Clenching his jaw, he studies my face, then joins me in scanning the ships. "The *Kraken*. It's recognizable as one of theirs from a distance, so they might be fooled. The crew can easily be split amongst other ships should it be lost. What are you thinking?"

I quickly explain the plan that takes shape in my mind, unsure if it's even feasible. Lennox's eyes narrow and his jaw clenches tighter with each word, but he holds his tongue until I explain in full.

"I will not risk you," he hisses when I finish.

"I won't be at risk. I'll have you and Delphine at my side. The others will be close enough. You know we can do this. I need to see what we're truly capable of when it matters." I grip his hand in mine, hoping the confidence I feel isn't foolishness. "How much time do we have?"

"Not long. We must move now, before they see us."

I run down the steps to retrieve Delphine, explaining as we dash back up the steps what she's to do. Lennox shouts orders across to the *Kraken's Maw* and it pulls alongside us, dropping a boarding bridge for Delphine, Lennox, and me to cross. Orders ring out between ships, all of the others opening their sails and departing on our signal until only the *Kraken's Maw* sits alone in the water. The crew is tucked against the hull, sitting on the deck so they're hidden beneath the railing wearing ill-fitting uniform coats, while Lennox, Delphine, and I wait on the deck under one of Blackwell's leftover flags.

A DENSE, DARK FOG RISES FROM THE OCEAN SURROUNDING Nemi as the crown's ship nears. It blocks the sight of any waiting ships, except for the one we stand on. Lennox hails the King's vessel, wearing the most serviceable of the officer's coats that were saved when Erik took the lives of the men on the beach of Delosia. As the other ship comes alongside, their captain observes us, looking around nervously at the ominous shadows that wrap around his ship.

"Hello!" he shouts across the gap between vessels. "How did you come to be here? Where is your crew?"

"Hello!" Lennox returns amicably, if a little nervously. "My crew and I were caught in a storm on the way back from Delosia. Many were lost to the squall, and those who weren't took refuge here to rest. But those that left the ship are lost in this neverending fog. This island is treacherous, friend. I have too few of my crew remaining, not enough to make it back home on our own. I retrieved the woman I was sent to find by King Dargan. Might I bring her aboard and we can return her to Selennia together? I'm sure we could split the glory." He grips my arm, roughly pulling me forward as if to show me off to the other captain.

"I get a bad feeling from this place. I've heard too many tall tales of it. I'll lower the bridge and we can be away," the other captain returns, his eyes frantically scanning the darkness that continues to roil around his ship. He speaks a quiet oath under his breath, as though it will protect him from what lurks in the shadows.

"Let me gather the men still on board, then I'll be over with her," Lennox says. A few of the crew stand, ready to follow us.

I take a calming breath as Lennox tightens his grip, dragging me behind him as he steps onto the boarding bridge that traverses the gap between ships. The water below is dark from both the fog and the depth, and for a moment my nerves ratchet my heart into a faster rhythm as

I stare at the waves. Blinking the fear back down, I focus on my footsteps and those of the crew following behind.

"Welcome, aboard, Captain," the King's captain greets us as we climb on deck, his eyes raking over me. "So this is the whore Blackwell seeks? Is she worth all the trouble that it's been to find her?"

"I can't say, Captain," Lennox replies, releasing his grip as he pushes me forward so that I appear to stumble away from him. I keep my head down, eyes averted in false fear as the sailors take me in.

The other captain approaches me, his boots slapping on the deck as he forces my chin up so my eyes meet his. He's middle-aged, his face lined from years on a ship, and his formerly worried look seems to dissipate as he drags his attention from the mysterious fog to take me in. "She's pretty enough. Have you taken a taste?" he asks over his shoulder, continuing to leer at me while ignoring the additional crew members who make their way over the bridge to his ship.

"I haven't had the pleasure," Lennox replies, barely hiding the contempt in his tone. "Yet."

"I might just have to keep her in my cabin for a bit, once we get out of this God-forsaken fog. I thought it was a priestess Blackwell was seeking, though. This one bears no mark, Captain… What *is* your name, sir?" The man turns as he addresses Lennox, brow knitting as he looks at the crew that now stands aboard, beginning to realize his error at not clarifying before he eagerly welcomed us aboard.

"It's Lennox," Lennox's voice rumbles across the deck before he exhales a dark laugh, nodding toward me with a devilish smile as he adds, "and she is."

The enemy captain jerks his head back to me, only to be blinded by my shining sigil as my lips curl bearing my teeth into a vicious smile. He steps back rapidly, finding Lennox at his back as he tries to retreat.

"Now, Del," I calmly order. Delphine pulls the shadowy fog away from the water, stepping from the group of crewmembers with a smirk as she reveals the seven pirate vessels surrounding the King's ship.

CHAPTER 19
LENNOX

The idiotic captain's reaction to Nerissa's sigil is almost comical as he stutters and retreats from her as though a viper coils on his deck. He makes it all too easy for me to wrap my arm around his throat and hold him against my chest with my cutlass threatening him.

"Listen up, men!" I shout over the waves to the King's sailors. "Drop your weapons! You've been taken."

The clatter of swords and daggers rings out as the sailors do as they're told. Some grit their teeth in anger, looking at Nerissa and Delphine as though their Devil stands amongst them, while others stare with wide eyes, mouths agape at the power in their midst. Pride swells in my chest as I watch Nerissa, but I can't allow myself to be distracted. "On your knees!"

Sailors kneel as my crew walks past picking up their discarded swords, dirks, and other weaponry. A few have the gleam of violence in their gaze and have to be forced to put their knees to the wood, but most are so distracted by the two women with unexpected power standing before them that they don't struggle long.

"Delphine, I think it's time we see what we can do. What do you think?" Nerissa's low voice drifts on the breeze, drawing a smile from Del's lips.

"Whatever you command, my Queen," Delphine replies, her expression serene as if she's finally in her element — causing chaos.

"*Queen*? What is this treason?" the captain sputters in front of me. "This whore is no queen!"

"Bold of you to speak so confidently, you bastard," Delphine spits, her hard stare causing the man to flinch. Her sigil shines alongside Nerissa's and the bright illumination hollows her cheeks as her eyes bore into him.

"*Witch*," he returns.

"*Enough.*" I tighten my grip across the man's throat until he begins to struggle, gripping my forearm with white-knuckled fingers as he tries to pry me away.

"Captain Lennox, release him," Nerissa says from across the deck, pulling my eyes to her in confusion. Her only response is a small nod.

I loosen my grasp, letting the man fall to his knees coughing and sputtering on the deck.

"Heathen witch. You will burn for your sins," a man's voice cuts through the air met by Nerissa's laugh as she turns to face the speaker. Looking over the crew kneeling on the deck I locate the speaker, a middle-aged, black-clad priest in their ranks, fuming in Nerissa and Delphine's direction. "You and your Goddess will never rule again in Selennia, God is on King Dargan's side. The rightful king. The true God."

"Your brothers thought the same in New Aphros, Father," Nerissa says, her voice emotionless and low as she steps toward the man. As though her acknowledgment emboldens him, the priest stands and takes a step toward her. "They were wrong. And so are you."

He takes another step, reaching into his robe despite one of the sailors grabbing at his leg in an attempt to halt his movements. I move forward as well, instinctively wanting to protect Nerissa. In the moment it takes him to pull a blade from under his garment, Nerissa's hand swipes through the air, sending blinding light streaking across the space. The priest's forearm falls to the deck, still clutching the knife as he begins to scream. A cold smile spreads across Nerissa's face once more, mirrored in the grin Delphine wears.

"What is this sorcery?" the priest screams, holding his bleeding arm as he collapses to the deck in a dark puddle.

"What should have met you and Blackwell when you first landed years ago," I say proudly, striding across the deck to fist my fingers into his hair, yanking his head back to force his eyes to meet Nerissa's. She is a vengeful goddess before us, the way she was when she punished Crewes for his transgressions against her, terrifying and beautiful in the *glow* that shines from her. "What's coming for you now."

"Finish him," Nerissa orders, calmly turning to the captain who still kneels before her. I take heed of her command, drawing my dagger across the priest's throat and leaving him to bleed out among the sailors. Some hiss and curse under their breaths, praying to their new God, while others openly follow Nerissa's movements with glassy eyes as though they are witnessing a miracle they never expected to see.

"Shall we end them all?" Delphine asks, deferring to Nerissa for guidance.

Nerissa remains expressionless as she assesses the men kneeling on the deck, considering. Her eyes drift back to the captain who sneers up at her, not daring to move after what she did to the priest. A shout from the *Kraken* draws all of our attention to Lyra climbing over the railing and nimbly crossing the bridge to meet us.

"Aunt Nerissa!" Lyra calls, stepping onto the deck. I gesture to my crew to hold the King's sailors at bay so I can approach the three women. Lyra's words are soft as she addresses Nerissa, "Heed Siobhan's advice, don't slaughter them all just because you can. You'll be no better than Blackwell."

"Do you think any of these men give two shits about our lives? That they wouldn't follow orders to rape and murder us, Lyra? Can you be *that* naive?" Delphine hisses, but Lyra merely stares her down, unflinching at the harsh words.

"I think some of them would side with us if given the chance. Uncle Billy, weren't you yourself held prisoner in the King's Navy? Would you not have sided with us if the opportunity was presented?" Lyra pleads, looking at me, then turns to Delphine emboldened. "Or Daniel, trapped in the cathedral? Those who joined us from New Aphros have proven to be loyal."

As much as I hate to admit it, Lyra is right.

I can almost hear Nerissa thinking as she looks out

across the deck at the men there, analyzing the hatred in some faces, the fear in others, the awe in many. She closes her eyes, the sea breeze whipping her dark hair around her as she clenches her jaw.

CHAPTER 20

Lyra's words ring true, and a part of me regrets sharing Siobhan's thoughts with the girl in our recent lesson now that she's reminding me of them. But, as much as I wish I could ignore them and let my anger toward Blackwell guide my actions, there is a real possibility that some of the men on this ship are trapped like Lennox was at one point. Men at the mercy of the King's command to save their own lives, not willing to be a martyr for their beliefs, or simply trying to survive until tomorrow for themselves or their families.

Although I recognize it as truth, I also believe Delphine — some who are trapped in servitude wouldn't hesitate to mete out our deaths should their captain order it, regardless of their conscience.

I open my eyes slowly, allowing the sound of the wind and waves to come back to me as the sun momentarily blinds me. Casting my eyes across the decks I search the faces there, attempting to root out the emotions that play across the men's hardened expressions. The priest lies bleeding amongst the sailors, his color fading to a pallid grey in death. His death doesn't trouble me — he believed his ugly words and curses and would have gladly buried his knife in my chest — but some of the men near him try to distance themselves as they plead with their eyes.

"Tell me, Captain." I turn to approach the officer still kneeling on the deck with one of Pike's blades to his throat. "Why do you serve Dargan Blackwell?"

The man merely sneers at my question before answering, "Fuck you, witch."

"You wish," Pike scoffs, letting his knife nick the man's bobbing throat.

"No response, then?" I calmly ask the man, offering one final opportunity to determine his loyalties. "Is it because you follow blindly with no reason, or because you think you'll survive this by not answering?"

His only response is to grit his teeth, the lines on his face deepening as he watches me.

"Very well. Step back," I order. Pike does as asked, moving to the side quickly as I approach the captain. "Your refusal shows your loyalty to Blackwell. My enemy, and someone who wouldn't hesitate to strike down any of those who stand with me. Therefore, today you die."

Before he can respond, I slice my hand across the space separating us, sending a bright slash of light through the man's throat. He falls forward, so I'm not forced to see his eyes as he bleeds out at my feet, the dark liquid pooling under the toes of my boots. Shuddering gasps spread through the crew of the King's vessel at the sight, as though they had imagined the priest's injury and are only now realizing the extent of my powers.

"Now, who's next?" I ask, turning to face the rest of the men, holding my hands out in front of me so they see I bear no weapons.

One by one, the men of the King's ship are dragged forward, far from their companions, to tell their tales. Some cry and plead for their lives, expressing loyalty to the Goddess and sharing lash scars and stories that mirror Lennox's experiences to prove they're prisoners on the ship.

Others, however, vehemently support their King, cursing me and the rest of the crew to their Devil before being executed by my *glow* or Lennox's blade.

In the end, twenty men join us to be split amongst the other ships to join our cause after swearing fealty to me as their queen. More than double that have been left behind to color the decks, and the hem of my skirt, crimson.

Back on the deck of the *Kraken's Maw*, I decide to test the strength of my power. As I stare at the vacant ship littered with bodies left for whatever seabirds wish to make a meal of them, I slice my hand through the air, sending light to sever the ropes so the sails hang limply. Then, I close my eyes and concentrate on the gentle ocean breeze, forcefully sending it toward the mast, curious if my intention will work. My thoughts are answered by the loud *crack* of wood splitting as it echoes across the expanse of sea. I snap my eyes open in time to watch the main mast break in half, crashing to the deck and busting the side railing.

With another deep breath I push my power outward once more, the fury I managed to keep tamped down now freed as I reflect on the men's hatred and their ugly words as they cursed me — cursed all of us — as though *we* are the villains. Flames begin to lick over the surface of the enemy ship, traveling swiftly over the bodies, then down into the hold to the few barrels of powder that were left aboard by our men. While explosions ring out across the sea, I look around at the pirates' ships in our fleet. Captains and crews stand at the railings or perch in the rigging to watch as the King's ship is torn to pieces by my elements.

As the wreckage sinks, cheers from our crew float on the breeze over the crash of waves. The other pirates join in, ringing their ships' bells with glee over the carnage. Slowly each ship, including ours, raises a new flag — one with a grey field bearing a black wolf's head with a white crescent sigil above its brow, the new symbol of my reign. The flags were passed out after the agreement, but aren't to be flown until my takeover is secured. Their impromptu show of solidarity now is a relief, an action that I take to mean I have fully proven my abilities and secured the loyalty of even those who might have doubted me before.

My chest grows lighter than anticipated at the sight of the flags, even after the bloodshed and brutality of the day. But as I move away from the railing, turning to face Lennox, my vision blurs and the world seems to tilt under my feet. I catch myself swaying with black spots on the edge of my periphery, gripping the wood again as he rushes to my side. The short-lived relief fades rapidly as panic takes root. Perhaps I'm not quite as strong as I thought.

"Nerissa!" Lennox grips my arm to keep me standing. "Are you all right?"

I try to breathe deeply to steady myself, but my head still swims as Lennox scoops me into his arms and retreats toward our cabin.

"Do you need my help?" Lyra asks, watching as we pass.

"No. I'll be fine. I just overdid it," I reply, my voice much softer than I expected, as Lennox sweeps past everyone, kicking the door closed behind us.

His boots echo in the cabin as he approaches our bed, laying me on the coverlet and crouching at my side. "Why did you push so hard?"

"I had to see what I could do. I needed to show them what we have on our side," I reply, laying down and curling so I face him. "You said it yourself that they wanted to see my full power, see what they're fighting for. Who they're fighting with."

"You don't need to prove anything more than what you already have. You certainly don't need to push so hard you nearly pass out on deck," he scolds, moving to brush my hair away from my cheek before checking himself. His hands are crusted in dried blood from the takeover, and he pulls back quickly before he touches me.

"I do, though, don't you see? If they're willing to do this for me, I should prove I'm willing to do the same. I won't just stand back and order them all to their deaths," I explain while he steps away to rinse his hands in our basin. Although I'm not pleased at how weak I feel, I'm relieved that I didn't pass out completely this time like in the square in New Aphros when I first acquired my full power.

"You're our queen, Nerissa. You aren't meant to be in harm's way..." He trails off, as though considering whether we should have this conversation now. Then, he changes the subject as my eyes begin to feel heavy. "Can I bring you something to eat, some broth? Should I send Lyra in?"

"No. I think I just need to rest for a bit. It's all an experiment at this point," I answer, blinking my heavy eyelids a time or two before exhaustion drags me under. Before I slip completely into unconsciousness I feel the mattress sink beneath Lennox as he sits by my side, running a heavy hand over my hair. By the time he whispers something, I'm too far gone to comprehend his words.

BLINKING AWAKE, I SEARCH THE CABIN, BUT MY ONLY COMPANY is a lantern glowing dimly in the twilight. I must have slept for hours, and frustration overpowers any concern for my condition as I rub my eyes and peer around the room. Although it didn't cause any complications today, I hate the risk we face if I were to expend too much power too quickly in a battle. It would endanger not only myself but those with me if they're depending on me in Selennia. Gritting my teeth, I slip from the bed. I'm still wearing the stained gown from earlier, but rather than change, I wrap a blanket around my shoulders to ward off the cool night air and open the cabin door.

On deck, all is quiet under the illumination of the waning moon and a splash of stars. The crew who remain above board monitor their tasks, barely taking note of me, aside from a few dips of chins here and there. I search the shadowy figures for Lennox's broad shoulders and tall frame, to no avail.

"Mistress! You're up and about! Shall I fetch the Captain for you?" a feminine voice calls across the deck. Hadley, one of the long-time female crewmembers, smiles as she approaches me, dipping her head in respect before meeting my eyes again. Even though her tone is light and her smile is pleasant, something lingers behind her eyes as she studies me. I can't tell if it's concern for my well-being, or to do with the small massacre earlier in the day.

"Do you know where he is? I feel fine, I can go to him," I respond, eager to breathe in the briny air instead of retreating to the cabin already.

"I believe he's down in Miss Lyra and Del's cabin," Hadley answers, cutting her eyes toward the stairs leading down into the hold. I nod my understanding, holding the blanket tighter and scrubbing my hands over my arms against the chill breeze as I make my way across the deck and down the stairs.

The hold, while always dim, is shadowy without the lantern I left behind in our cabin, but I remember the way between the stairs and the cabin easily enough after spending so much time traversing between the two on the way from Selennia to Delosia. Lennox's voice rumbles through the door as I approach, the warm sound soothing me and bringing a small smile to my lips. Lyra's higher voice mingles with Delphine's as I get closer.

As I reach my hand up to knock, I overhear, "I don't want her to think she has to do this alone. I won't allow her to risk herself again."

Sucking in a breath at Lennox's words, I let my fist fall against the wood as irritation swells in my breast once again. This time it isn't at my perceived failure, but at his presumption to have this discussion without me present. The door swings wide almost immediately, Lennox standing in the doorway while Lyra and Delphine sit at the small table where a pot of tea rests with three cups.

"Nerissa," Lennox breathes, relief coloring his words as he reaches out to pull me into an embrace. "You're awake! Are you all right?"

Lyra stands and approaches as if to inspect me, but I shrug out of Lennox's arms and step back to avoid both of them. "I'm fine." I look between each of them in turn, finding Delphine smug, while Lyra looks guilty. Lennox studies me, his lips tightening the longer I remain quiet. "Discussing anything important, Captain?" I ask, bringing my eyes back to his.

"Only his concern—" Lyra starts, but Lennox stops her with a raised palm.

"Let's go to our cabin, Nerissa. We can talk there," he says, his voice flat.

"This isn't going to go well," Delphine murmurs, taking a sip of tea while Lyra snaps her head in the other woman's direction. Delphine simply shrugs as she bounces her eyes between Lennox and me where we stand staring at one another.

Finally, he pulls the door open, holding it for me to exit before following behind. We walk in silence up the stairs and back to our cabin where I wait for him to open the door for me to enter. Once inside, Lennox takes a seat in one of the dining chairs, sighing deeply as he runs his palms over his face and through his hair. When he looks up at me the rumpled effect almost makes me go to him, to pull him against me for comfort, to ignore what I briefly overheard. Instead, I toss the blanket on the bed, then cross my arms and sit in the chair next to him.

"Well, are you going to share your concerns with me, or just your niece?" I ask, the hurt bleeding into my words without me meaning to allow it.

"Nerissa, my love," Lennox begins. "We all saw what happened, both today and in New Aphros. We have all seen what you are capable of. But at what cost? You cannot face Blackwell and his men alone."

"I already explained in the meeting with the captains, I won't be facing them alone," I reply, my frustration turning to anger as my skin heats with irritation. I knew this conversation would come. Lennox has already expressed his reluctance to proceed as planned, but I didn't want to discuss it with tensions running this high. "I do not intend on entering the country to immediately wage war. I expect that I can get him by himself. One man is nothing against what I can do, Billy. I will convince him that I wish to ally with him and then can take care of him when the opportune time presents itself. There's still so much I don't know about the state of the country that I need to find out before we just take it back. It isn't like I plan to take down his army single-handedly."

"And you expect me to stand by while you walk into the lion's den *alone*? With that beast?"

"I already told you why when we first discussed this option, Billy." I can no longer control my emotions and my words come out far more agitated than I intend. "We couldn't convince random people in a strange city that we weren't in love. How do you think we'll fare under the scrutiny of that tyrant? He can't find out about us; I can't bear the idea of him using you against me!"

"Nerissa, you're my *wife*! Do you think *I* can bear the

idea of him near you? Of allowing you to walk into his grasp without being there to protect you?" Lennox's voice rises along with mine.

"I'm your *Queen*, Captain. You do not *allow* me to do anything." My voice is hard and cold, like the steel of his favored cutlass as it cuts through the tension in the air.

He sucks in a sharp breath at my statement as I move to stand, the urge to pace, to storm out, getting the better of me. As I rise, his rough palm circles my wrist, the same one I wear his bangle on, tightening and pulling me toward him. When I'm close enough he spins me, gripping my chin and forcing my eyes to look into his face.

"Damn it, Nerissa. Don't do this," he hisses through clenched teeth. "Don't push me and everyone else away because you're trying to prove something. Don't twist my words. You know fucking well what I meant. I know you're my queen. I know you could cut us all down if you wish. That you can protect yourself. But what kind of husband would I be — what kind of man — if I won't risk my life for yours? How can I watch while the woman I searched for nearly a decade — my Queen, my wife, my whole heart — strolls into that castle without me guarding her back?" his voice cracks, shattering my heart with it.

"I can't risk you, Billy. I can't risk our relationship being known once this farce begins. It's bad enough if I take Del or Lyra with me, to place them in harm's way, but if someone on the docks recognizes you we're finished then and there. Even if I *can* take down Blackwell and some of his men, there's no guarantee I can protect the rest of you or defeat them all. It would be *my* fault if any of you were harmed, and I can't live with that." I tremble where I stand, the idea of being met with a show of force as soon as we step onto land sending fear prickling over me.

"I can't live without *you*, Nerissa. If we face him together and lose, so be it," he murmurs, standing and pulling me against him. I tuck my face against his chest, trying to force my eyes to remain dry. "I would rather die with you by my side than live without you again. But, look at me," he says, drawing my eyes to meet his once more. "I will not fail you. He will not know me, or who I am to you. I will not be careless again like I was in New Aphros. I can do this. *We* can do this."

I tremble in his arms, swallowing my fear as he holds me. Finally, I ask, "What's next? How do we get word to the bastard?" I step away, wiping the few angry tears that have slipped free from my cheeks. Although I'm not fully convinced, I'm not willing to argue about it anymore tonight. I'm still weak from earlier and need food and more rest before I feel up to revisiting things.

"Let me handle that part. I think some of the men we took on from the ship earlier can help. For tonight, rest. We'll strategize tomorrow. We only have about a week before we're within sight of home."

I shudder at his words, both fear and excitement weaving a cocktail of emotions through my system as I melt against him again. If we only have another week like this, I'll take advantage of his warmth until I can't any longer.

CHAPTER 21
BLACKWELL

"What is it now?" I grit through clenched teeth as Charleston listens to a newly arrived messenger.

"Very well, you're dismissed," the Commander tells the man, ignoring me and stoking my irritation. Closer to me than my own brothers, Charleston knows exactly how fine a line he walks with his boldness — something that endeared him to me when we were just boys, and which has kept him by my side ever since while making my name away from home.

"You're not going to be pleased." He steps to my side with a scrap of paper extended between his blunt fingers. Instead of the casual lunch I expected, today has gone the same as the rest of the week, filled with continual interruptions and messages from the different ports around the country.

"Another one?" I snap, snatching the paper from him, allowing my knife to clatter on the plate and eliciting a cringe from the serving girl waiting in the corner to clear the table when I finish.

"Yes, it seems that a crew from Delosia sank several ships near the harbor at Cybele and slaughtered the crews. They've taken the city. Perhaps this explains why we haven't heard from the ships that we sent south before winter."

"First the Northmen rising up, now these barbarians from the south? What the fuck is happening? Any news from the eastern shores?" I drain my wine, holding the glass out for the girl to refill, forcing her to part from the wall she clings to and retrieve the pitcher on the table to do so. She never meets my eyes as she fills the glass and darts back away. At least I maintain fear *somewhere*.

"Is there word about the local Selennians in Cybele?" I read the scribbled words quickly, not finding anything more detailed than Charleston relayed. "Did some of them join these invaders like they did in the north?"

"That's to be seen. I would assume that if there are hidden pockets of rebels hiding in the outskirts of Cybele that they would have."

"Perhaps it's time we send more men to deal with Delosia. I won't stand for them thinking they can send criminals to destroy our shores, nor can we allow it to rekindle talks of rebellion amongst the natives." I watch as Charleston's brow furrows and his lips thin.

"Perhaps you should allow me to refocus my men *here* instead of casting them about for this priestess you've become obsessed with," he mutters, adding, "Your Majesty," as I glare at him.

"Are you saying this is *my* fault, Charleston?" While I value his opinion, especially in military matters, I'm not willing to deal with his ranting about this again. He's been bitching about the ships we sent to Delosia and beyond for months now.

"I'm saying that first, you sent the contingent to pose as priests in New Aphros, then the ships to Delosia. None of those men returned and we are suddenly under attack with no word from anyone we've sent out. Use your brain instead of your cock, Dargan. This obsession with a *true heir* is getting dangerous and you're beginning to sound as bad as the peasants you claim are just superstitious fools. We won. You beat Adelaide. If you want to keep your throne I'd think you'd be happy with ruling here instead of trying to overextend your reach seeking out a woman who might be a figment of a frightened thief's imagination. We do *not* have a surplus of soldiers to keep throwing at your fantasies, and I cannot recruit or hire more from back home quickly enough."

"Check yourself, Russell," I growl in frustration, cutting off any further argument. "You'll send your men *where* I tell you, *when* I tell you. It seems like the warming weather is stirring all the beasts that prowl the seas. Send soldiers to the different port towns; they're already partially fortified and can be held if they have enough men in them. Then, we can decide whether we need to send ships to deal with Delosia."

Charleston throws his hands up in irritation but holds his tongue. "As you say, Your Majesty."

As Charleston turns to leave, a timid knock sounds from the door. He looks over his shoulder with raised brows before yanking the iron ring to reveal the page that waits outside. "Commander, sir. Your Majesty," the boy stammers, dipping his head and extending a rolled parchment toward Charleston. "This just arrived, for the King."

Charleston sighs, taking the roll and returning to me to deliver it. The wax sealing the parchment is a dark navy with the faintest shimmer of silver, but no symbol marks it to reveal the sender's identity. Glancing up at Charleston I crack the wax and open the letter, finding elegant, feminine script:

BLACKWELL,

Rumors swirl that you have sought me out, even going so far as to cross the sea for me. But perhaps that's just the romantic desire of a woman who misses her home.

You seek the rightful heir to the moonstone throne to further your line. I seek my rightful title and position. I believe we can both find what we seek should we join together as King and Queen.

If you are amenable to an agreement — an alliance if you will — I will willingly return to Selennia to stand at your side where I belong.

Send word with the messenger who delivered this within two days and I will meet you on the docks of Aphros on the first day of the new moon cycle. If you refuse or seek to meet me with treachery, I won't be so easily found again.

Sincerely,

The rightful heir of Selennia,

Nerissa Faelan

. . .

"THIS AUDACIOUS BITCH," I WHISPER, READING THE WORDS again, but a smile tugs at my lips wondering what kind of woman would be so bold as to hold herself out in such a manner. The challenge in the words, even when she should be begging, seems to match the thief's description of the whore, and intrigue captures me as much as my desire to secure my reign over this island.

"Excuse me?" Charleston rumbles from the seat he's taken while he waits, sampling some of the food still laid out on the table.

"This woman. Whoever wrote this," I reply, waving the letter in the air. "She claims she's Adelaide's heir and wants to join with me to reclaim her rightful title."

Charleston holds his hand out for the paper, reading the text slowly as I finish my wine. "Do you believe the heir actually wrote this? Or is it some farce the rebels have concocted?" Always the more cautious of the two of us, Charleston's skepticism is plain in his words.

"Regardless, if we can fool the people into thinking whoever wrote it *is* the heir — and that she's willing to side with me — it will crush their hopes. We can dispose of her however we see fit once it's complete. Girl!" I snap at the servant still standing in the corner. "Bring me ink and a quill, and my sealing wax."

"You're responding immediately?"

"Yes, and you will follow to see who takes the letter from the messenger, and to where it goes."

"I'm not your errand boy, Dargan."

"No, but I don't trust any of them like I trust you, Russell. Find out what you can and report back. We will be prepared to slaughter them if there's treachery. Otherwise, we will finally clinch my rule over this island."

Sighing at the placation, Charleston inclines his auburn head, his permanently scarred grimace widening in acquiescence.

CHAPTER 22

"I still think he must be desperate if he responded that quickly," Siobhan says, sitting in the surgery toying with the flames of the lantern on the desk. She flicks her fingers to make it dance with her powers, staring into the center with unfocused eyes. "The rebellion in Selennia must be more threatening than Captain Jackson led us to believe. This is good news."

"Or he's stupid. Or planning a trap," Delphine adds, watching from where she leans against the door frame. She's taken to wearing the clothing of a sailor and I can't help but think how it suits her insouciance. While her attitude has improved and her drinking has lessened, I still see the sadness in her eyes when we gather to train. I assume the memories of Salome still aggrieve her, as they do me, even more so since she had so many more years with her.

"Have you *Seen* anything, Siobhan? Did Aisling mention anything before she left on the *Hadriel*?" I ask yet again. We haven't heard anything from the Northmen's ship since it departed Nemi over a week ago, and I can only hope they were successful in their early attacks on the King's outpost at Airmedan and the surrounding northern coastline.

I rub my hands over my face, pressing on my eyes as though I can dispel the ache I feel behind them. Despite my growing confidence in our plan, my nerves have kept me awake at night. Between the visions and nightmares that creep into my sleep and the anxiety that prevents me from dozing, exhaustion tugs at my senses, keeping me distracted and unfocused.

"No. Unfortunately, nothing new has come to me. I try to scry, but it's more of the same," Siobhan sighs. "Are you certain you won't accept a sleeping draught, Sister? You look like you're barely able to keep your eyes open."

"No, thank you. And pardon me for the candor, but you aren't one to talk with those circles under *your* eyes." Siobhan's cheeks pink, throwing the dark circles in even more of a contrast. "Let's review our plan for when we arrive. Lyra, you and Delphine will come ashore with me. Are you both certain you're comfortable with that?"

"Of course," Lyra answers, glancing at Del who merely nods in agreement.

"And Delphine, you're capable of minding your tongue?" I ask with a wry smile.

"I know my duty." She rolls her eyes, but a matching smirk tilts her lips. "Daniel and I will be there to help pass messages and gather information. I can be a pretty hand-maid for everyone else."

"Good. Siobhan, you will remain with Erik. If anything comes to you, you'll send word through Tom. He has connections at the port that are trustworthy. They'll know to expect him, or his messages, at the hidden caves. The caves aren't far from the castle; I remember sneaking out to them occasionally when I was younger." I run through the plans out loud again, more to soothe myself and confirm everything than because the women in my close circle require the reminder.

A quick tap comes at the door before it swings open revealing Lennox standing in the doorway. "Good evening, ladies. Siobahn, Lyra, may I borrow you?"

"Of course!" Lyra hops to her feet to join him near the door. Siobhan moves more slowly but drags her focus from the lantern to do the same.

I narrow my eyes, noting this suspicious request. "What are you up to?"

"You'll see. You can come join us in a bit if you wish, just give us a little while first." He smiles but reveals nothing more as he steps aside to let the women pass through the door before trailing them down the hall. Delphine and I share a curious look as the door swings shut, but neither of us knows what's happening.

"The amount of secrets that float around on this ship is ridiculous," Delphine mutters, taking the chair Lyra vacated.

"Oh, like you're one to talk. But, you have no idea," I agree, thinking about all of the things that have been revealed to me both on this ship and in the company of its inhabitants. "Would you like some tea?" I offer, standing to pull some dried herbs from their storage.

"I'd prefer coffee, but I know that's unlikely away from

New Aphros," she sighs wistfully, twirling a curl around her finger.

"Oh, Del — as you said, secrets abound." I grin as I pull a small pouch of roasted beans from a hidden drawer. "I don't have any milk, but I did manage to stash some of these for my personal use when we left. For medicinal purposes of course." I wink, grabbing a mortar and pestle to grind the coffee.

"Smart woman. I knew you were more than just a pretty face." Delphine allows a rare, real smile to spread across her face as she watches me, taking a deep inhale of the aromatic beans. "I guess I was right in the end."

"Let's hope so." With a sigh, I pour hot water from a kettle over the ground coffee and let it sit. We wait in near silence as the coffee steeps, then I pour her a cup and take one for myself, returning to my seat at the table across from her.

"Delphine," I say as she sips and closes her eyes as though savoring the flavor. "How are you doing?"

"Shouldn't we be discussing how *you're* doing?" she deflects, taking another sip while inspecting me over the edge of the cup with narrowed eyes. The motion is so similar to how she behaved while drinking tea in Salome's office that my heart aches at the memory of our times with our mentor. I merely tighten my lips and tilt my head, encouraging her to speak instead of answering with another question.

"I'm fine, Nerissa." Her efforts to be nicer haven't gone unnoticed since the storm, and she's started opening up more. Placing her cup down, she looks me in the eyes.

"Salome isn't the first person I've lost. It just seems to hurt worse than the others."

I nod, sipping my coffee before addressing something that's needled me since her outburst on Delosia. "When we were at Lyra's birthday, what you said, about our night together in New Aphros… if that night hurt you, I'm sorry."

"Don't be." She shakes her head. "I only said that because I knew it would wound you. I wanted you — everyone really — to hurt like I did. Your intentions were clear from the beginning that night — it was all in good fun. What I said was unfair to you."

Relieved that Delphine holds no lingering resentment, I quietly sip on the bitter coffee and relax into my chair. "I understand what it's like to hurt, Del, and how hard it can be to let go of the defenses that have protected you for so long."

Del nods, and after a beat admits, "I confess, I wish Lyra wasn't involved in this endeavor. But I trust you and Lennox. I trust in my own abilities. All I can do is look forward to the other side of this, or at least until I get to see Blackwell bleed." Her eyes darken, the storm of emotions I sense whirling in her showing only momentarily as she smirks and I can't help but note how similar we are — I also look forward to seeing Blackwell bleed.

"I wish she weren't involved either, Del." Settling into my seat, I ask, "I take it the two of you are getting along better than on Delosia?"

Del's returning glance is intended to be withering as if annoyed with my prodding, but she ends up smiling before answering, "She's too good for me, and I'm certain she will recognize that as soon as the stress of all of this is over, but damn it if I'm not falling in love with her."

"She's easy to love." The days I spent with Lyra on our voyage from Selennia endeared her to me, and it's obvious from the honesty in Del's smile that she's more than endeared herself to Delphine.

"Could we not convince her to stay with Siobhan when we return to land? To keep her safe?"

"Del, we might need her healing abilities should things turn against us, and you know she won't stay behind. We'll keep her safe. Lennox and I won't allow anything to happen to her. I know you won't either."

"No. No one will hurt her as long as I can stop them." Delphine's voice suddenly has the edge I'm used to, and I know with utmost certainty that should Lennox and I fall, Delphine will keep Lyra safe.

When our cups are drained and all that remains of the small pot of coffee are the dregs, I stand, smoothing my wool skirt as the energizing liquid fizzes through my veins. "Let's go find out what they're up to, shall we?"

Delphine stands, gesturing with an extended arm for me to lead the way.

I don't knock before entering the Captain's cabin; it's my space, too, and Lennox *did* tell us to come find them in a bit. Since none of the party was present on the main deck, I assumed they would be assembled here, but I'm surprised to hear soft chanting through the door. Erik and Siobhan's voices harmonize once again like they did singing the lullaby they recounted at our dinner. As I push the door open quietly, I'm not prepared for the sight we find.

Lennox sits in one of the chairs, gripping Lyra's slim hand in his. His niece sits crossed-legged on the floor at his side while he breathes calmly with his eyes closed. His golden hair has been shaved on the sides, revealing his scalp in the same style Erik wears. The middle portion is braided tightly down the center to keep it off the bare skin. Erik and Siobhan stand on either side of him, both holding sharp shards of bone in one hand and small cups in the other, their fingertips stained dark blue to match the ink visible on the sides of Lennox's head.

"I was wondering when your curiosity would get the best of you, my pretty priestess," Lennox says, smiling as he opens his eyes.

"What are you doing?" I ask, stepping through the entry ahead of Delphine. She pulls the door closed while I cross the carpets to inspect the sigils and markings that now decorate his scalp. Some are already inked permanently, while others are just outlined, waiting to be completed. I expect them to be red and angry, but the finished marks appear healed and aged, almost as much as those that adorn Erik's skin.

"You wanted to make sure no one recognized me in Selennia. They expect Lennox to be dark-haired and clean-cut, not a blond Northman," Lennox offers with a wink.

"And I'm practicing," Lyra adds, explaining the healed tattoos. "I'm healing them as they complete them, making sure they look older so it's not obvious he just had them done."

"Is it painful?" I ask, tenderly touching one of the healed marks with my fingertips.

"I can think of far more pleasant sensations," Lennox

murmurs with a huff of a laugh. "But, I've felt much worse. It isn't much more painful than my other tattoos."

"We're blessing them as we mark him," Siobhan adds. She and Erik both patiently wait to finish their work until I cease my inspection. "I learned the methods when I was a child watching my grandfather and uncles."

"I figure any blessings would be welcome," Lennox says as I step back to let Erik and Siobhan resume their work.

"I agree," I answer, sitting on the worn rug next to Lyra. Delphine joins us, silently drifting up and taking the spot on Lyra's other side. "Perhaps we could all use the extra help."

HOURS LATER, THE EXCESS BLUE INK WASHED FROM OUR SKIN, each of us bears new marks blessed by the north, just as we bear our cloaked sigils from the Goddess. Having never seen Siobhan undressed, I never knew she had the blue-black ink on her back and shoulders, gifted to her by her family before she left home to join the temple, and added to when she and Erik parted the first time.

Lyra and Delphine now have healed tattoos inside their upper arms, hidden from plain view by regular clothing. Mine runs down my breastbone, the same way my ceremonial chain falls, easily hidden by modest clothing choices. We aren't able to cloak the tattoos like we can our sigils, but should my garments be removed against my will, the offender won't leave in a state where they can expose my secrets to anyone anyway.

Standing in our cabin that evening wearing only his

breeches, Lennox looks fierce. Black ink covers his arms and chest as always, but the severe cut of his hair and the new tattoos covering his scalp highlight the wildness in his emerald eyes as he readies for bed. A set of leathers, similar to those Erik has for battle, are laid out across our trunk — a gift from Ulf for our arrival in Selennia.

We only have a couple of days before our arrival on the docks of Aphros. At best, the ruse will work and my guard and handmaidens will be invited to the castle without incident. There I will glean whatever I can about any rebellion and how to best take the country back with as little bloodshed and loss of life as possible. At worst, we will be met with violence immediately and I must prepare to defend myself, and those I love, with everything I have.

"Nerissa?" Lennox's voice comes softly from near the bed, pulling me from my musings where I sit at the table.

"Hmm?"

"Come here." The dark command in his tone sends a shiver over my skin and heat to my core as I tilt my head to the side with a sideways smile.

"Is that an order, Captain?" I tease, pulling my lower lip between my teeth, but remain seated.

"Yes. You'll be ordering me about frequently in the next few weeks; it's my turn tonight. I want to take my time with you while I still can," he rumbles. I clench my thighs together at his words, my heart speeding in my chest, but I remain in my chair with a wry smile spreading across my face.

"Come and take what you want then." His eyes glitter in the flickering lantern light, muscles rippling as he prowls through the cabin toward me. "Isn't that what Northmen are rumored to do? Take what they want? You might need the practice."

"I want *you*, my pretty priestess," he whispers against the shell of my ear, leaning over me so I'm trapped in my chair. "My she-wolf," he murmurs, nuzzling my cheek with his nose. "My Queen." With that, he picks me up and carries me to the waiting bed.

CHAPTER 23
SIOBHAN

"Siobhan, my love." Erik pulls my attention away from the flames of the brazier in our cabin. "You must come to bed. You *must* rest before tomorrow."

I know a day starting before dawn awaits us, but the flames have been teasing me more each day, as have the waves, the mugs of tea, and my dreams. Even if the meanings are just out of reach.

"I know. I just don't know what I might *See*. You know rest hasn't come easily lately," I reply, forcing my feet to move toward him and away from the heat of the fire. As I curl into the bed next to his large frame I'm shocked to find that he feels cool to the touch for once, evidence of how long I'd been standing without moving next to the brazier.

"Do you wish to tell me about it? Would it be easier for me to take you to Nerissa now to speak with her before tomorrow begins?"

I lean into his embrace, feeling grateful for the man at my side. Erik is always thoughtful, always thinking of what would make things easier for me, but he doesn't realize that sharing the truth of the future isn't so simple. Oftentimes I have no idea what the portents might mean, whether they're true or mere possibilities for the future, or whether they will soothe or shatter the ones who appear. Too often in my youth, before I fully understood my gifts, I offered my insight only to find the recipient of my help more distressed than before, and often without need, which was part of the reason I hadn't shared my vision of Salome's fate with Nerissa in New Aphros. I'd hoped there was a chance it would turn out to be false.

"I only see blood, Erik," I whisper against his chest. "Saltwater and blood. Steel and blood. Wolves and blood. So much blood. I have no idea whether it's ours or the enemy's, whether it means victory or death. I don't want to share that with her, not when so much depends on tomorrow. It will wait, I have faith in her and the Goddess."

Easy silence ticks by as he rubs a soothing hand over my skin. "Have you any *Sight* with regards to the *Hadriel*?" His tone is nonchalant, but his concern for his cousins is clear.

"No, nothing. At least… nothing I discern with clarity," I answer, sighing deeply with frustration as I sit up.

I rub my hands over my face, then untie the ribbon at the end of my braid, letting my hair fall loosely around my shoulders. Erik runs his fingers through the heavy strands, studying me as though trying to root out any hurt to soothe. Since we met, his gentleness has always been a surprise, something I missed dearly when he was away from Delosia. Now, even though we spend each night together, he still treats me like I'm a treasure that might wash out to sea, something he has to handle delicately to avoid losing. Curling against him, a soft brush of his lips on my forehead, my cheek, my throat, then more firmly on my mouth dims the worry in my brain.

Though I've practiced keeping things to myself — knowing what may come without concerning others and shouldering the burden without breaking — it's harder around Erik. He knows me well enough to look closely, but I smile at him and hope it's enough to cover up any sign of wariness. Unease for all of us buries itself in my heart as I settle against his warm body, even if the steady beat of his heart thrumming under the muscle lulls me to restless sleep.

In the darkest part of the night, Tom rows Erik and me across the waves to where the *Bartered Soul* waits. Our crew on the *Vengeance* has opened its sails and weighed anchor to be certain they're farther out to sea, beyond any possible sight of the port or patrols. We want no possibility of suspicion this morning. Tom secures the rowboat against the hull and surprises me by climbing up after us. When we stand on the deck I understand why as he strides confidently across the boards and pulls young Daniel into a tight embrace, cupping his face and kissing him deeply. We all have goodbyes to say this morning.

"Erik, Siobhan. You both look striking this morning," Lennox greets us with a sarcastic half-smile, eyes traveling over the two of us. I know he hides his nerves with his swagger, and this morning is no different. I can only hope he can keep his temper and scorn under tight control for the next few weeks. He's right though — seeing Erik in a frock coat and tricorne this morning was a shock. With his braid tucked down the back of his coat, he almost passes for a Selennian gentleman, or at least a gentlemanly rogue like Lennox. Wearing the breeches and tunic I've come to favor on the voyage, I don't look much different than the other sailors. Erik braided my hair tight to my scalp and tucked it under a knit cap to keep me warm on the short row over. I feel more secure in disguise than I would in a gown.

"You look fierce, William. I almost don't recognize you," I reply, observing the leather and furs he wears as Erik claps his closest friend on the back. Pike approaches, looking like a kindly, yet ill-at-ease grandfather. His presence sends a ripple of dread over me, but the reason is just out of reach. The confusing visions have come so frequently lately that I've started to have trouble keeping them straight.

"Where's Nerissa?" I question, chafing my hands on my arms in the cold breeze. Selennia is cooler this time of year, but even though the weather isn't unusual, it's more biting than I expected on the open water. It almost feels like the chill wind is trying to claw through my flesh and into my soul.

"She, Lyra, and Del are finishing up in the great cabin. You're welcome to go join them, Siobhan. Go get warm and have some tea," Lennox advises with a smile and nod toward the cabin door. With a squeeze of Erik's hand, I gratefully retreat to the cabin while the men circle up to finalize the morning's plan.

Casting my gaze to the shore in the distance, I can't help but look at what was once my home. Being on the ship away from the soil of my homeland, or that of Delosia where I could sink my hands into the garden and remind myself that I was safely one with the earth, has left me feeling as adrift as one of the little boats we ferry back and forth in. I'm not sure if it's the reason I can't get a grasp on the visions, or if it's why they are flooding me like the tides, but it's been increasingly hard to focus since we left Nemi. Once we win this, and Nerissa has retaken the throne, I plan to discuss a permanent home with Erik. Hopefully, he'll agree to somewhere for us, even if I feel guilty asking him to stay on shore with me.

My knock on the door is answered quickly, Lyra holding it open with a broad grin when she sees me, one I can't help but return, even if it feels forced because of my frustration at my visions. My Sisters' presence is always soothing, and a part of me wishes I was heading to shore with them, if only so I could feel grounded once again. "Good morning, Sisters."

"Good morning, Siobhan. I wish I could say it's good to see you, but I know that means it's almost time and I hate to admit... I'm fucking nervous," Delphine says, cupping a mug between her hands. The circles under her eyes are so dark they look bruised, and I wonder if she's been having an equally difficult time resting as I have. "Please tell me you've *Seen* something to make me calm down?"

Nerissa turns from where she was finishing her hair using a small mirror propped on the dining table, dark ocean eyes studying me as I consider Delphine's question. If she's worried I can't tell, her expression remains unreadable. Nerissa's ability to hide her feelings has always been unnerving, but today it fills me with relief. If I, her friend, can't tell what she's thinking, surely the men on shore will be unable to as well.

"What is it, Siobhan?" she asks, tilting her head to the side like a crow, sending a wave of inky black hair cascading over her shoulder.

"Nothing that I can tell for sure... just... a lot of blood. Have you had any more dreams?"

Nerissa merely shakes her head in answer and gives a tight smile, one that does nothing to soothe me. Is she being as cagey as I am?

"Wonderful. *Blood*." Delphine huffs a breath and downs the rest of her mug. When I stare at her curiously she adds, "Don't worry. It's coffee, not alcohol. Probably the last I'll have in a very long time." Lyra joins her, taking her hand once she sets her mug down, looking between Nerissa and me with those sparkling hazel eyes. She's so young — she hasn't been broken and reforged into steel like Nerissa or Delphine, at least not in the same way.

"Lyra, are you certain you don't want to stay behind on the *Vengeance* with me?" I ask for the final time. I already know her answer, but I also know that Lennox, Nerissa, and Delphine would be relieved to have her outside Blackwell's grip, so I make the offer anyway.

"No. I'm going with them. Remember, we're all doing this together, whether we win or lose," Lyra answers, showing that there *is* some steel in her already. I simply nod in response.

"Very well, what can I help with? Do you need anything, Nerissa?"

She stands, tall and proud as always, the bearing of a queen evident even when I first met her in the apothecary. The front portion of her hair is in the coronet braid of a priestess, the rest hanging loose to her waist in a dark

218

curtain, but every other mark that might give her away is cloaked, hidden away with all her emotions so she's like a regal statue before us. "Only if you can tell me you've *Seen* that this isn't going to end very badly," she scoffs, letting a smile tug her lips up to hide the anxiety I can feel radiating off of her. "Otherwise, I think we should say a prayer to the Goddess. Hopefully, She'll know when we arrive and will guide us." With that, she takes a black cloak from the bed and wraps it around her, securing the clasp.

"Is that a Northern Isles cloak?" I ask, noting the grey wolf fur lining and the knotwork on the heavy silver clasp.

"It is. Aisling gave it to me before they sailed off," Nerissa answers. "I hope you rendezvous with the *Hadriel* soon, and that they've been successful at inciting troops to be sent north. I'd feel better if you had another priestess with you in case you run into trouble." As she speaks, she runs her fingers through the fur as though it brings her comfort. The symbolism of her family's name isn't lost on me at the sight of that pelt, and I know it won't be lost on Blackwell either. A tiny jab to begin the battle.

I can only hope the wolves in my visions are the ones drawing the blood and that this isn't already a bad sign. Choking down my worry, I approach her and wrap her in an embrace as the crack of the sails sounds through the cabin door and the *Bartered Soul* sails the final leg home.

PART TWO
HOME

CHAPTER 24
BLACKWELL

A shadow slips over the sun, high in the sky, as my destrier snorts and paws at the cobblestones leading to the dock. Evidently, he's as impatient as I am awaiting Nerissa's arrival. With every passing moment, the sky darkens during the eclipse. The townsfolk around me titter superstitious nonsense, grating on my nerves, but none more so than the priest who breaks from his brethren to approach me.

"Your Majesty!" the priest pleads, black robes billowing around him in the wind coming off the sea. "This is a sign of evil, you *must* stop whatever plans you have!"

"I thought you were a man of God, Father," Charleston chides. "Surely, you aren't afraid of peasant nonsense."

I can't help but smirk at his words, agreeing whole-heartedly.

"Of course not, but this is a dire omen!"

"Silence," I order. "The skies do not rule things here. *I* do."

My words end any debate the cleric might have had

planned. The priest ducks his head in subservience before moving to rejoin the others before I turn my gaze back to the sea. Just as the sun peeks back out from behind the moon, I see the rowboat finally moving toward the docks.

Taking the spyglass from Charleston's outstretched hand where he sits on his matching destrier at my side, I raise it to examine the pirate's ship sitting in the harbor. My teeth grind as I look at the ship — the *Bartered Soul*. Lennox's ship. We've been allowing this *Captain Lennox* to skirt our guards for years despite the rumors that he and his crew seek out royal ships as targets. The vessels never return, and the dead can't point fingers, so I've never had any proof of his piracy that outweighs how handsomely Lennox pays off my harbormasters.

Seafarers and soldiers alike tell tall tales of the man who mutinied on the *Griffin's Destiny*, killing the captain and quartermaster before sinking the ship a little over a year after I wrested Selennia from Adelaide. But the physical description of the infamous pirate has continuously changed, and his bribes are always in gold, so concessions have been allowed when he's docked at the more distant ports. This is the first time Lennox has sailed into Aphros itself, and the cargo he carries is far more valuable than hanging a pirate.

I'll see what condition the woman he brings me is in, and, if she pleases me, I'll let him think he's slipping through my grasp again when he departs the port.

For now.

After hearing about Lennox's behavior with the whore from the thief who saw them together in Athene, I've wondered if their arrangement was one of business or emotion. The former I can understand, while the latter… Well, if the bitch cares about him, then I can have him captured and held as collateral to ensure her cooperation.

I raise the glass again to view the huge, dark-haired captain standing on the deck almost improperly close to a fresh-faced, red-headed cabin boy. If *that* is the company he keeps, perhaps I shouldn't be concerned about him having used the whore, or that there are more tender feelings at play, after all. He's dressed in a frock coat as if that masks his true nature, but heathen tattoos adorn his scalp, peeking from under the tricorne he wears, marking him for the criminal he is. Perhaps this brutal styling is what's boosted his reputation these past years.

Typical.

Focusing on the small boat bouncing on the waves, I inspect the three figures cloaked in wool with hoods hiding their features. One blond Northman pulls the oars. His hair is worn in the fashion of the raiders who still harry the northern coastline, shaved on the sides with the long center knotted in the back. As he rows he speaks to the others, his eyes flashing up once to where the Commander and I wait, hatred burning even at this distance. Surprisingly, a young priest in black robes also rides in the craft, piquing my curiosity.

"Shall we go down and see what they've brought us, Commander?" I ask, handing the glass back to Charleston. He and I both wear matching plain helms, an attempt to confuse our enemies in case anything goes amiss today.

"As you command, Your Majesty," he responds.

We turn our horses to make the short walk down the main road to the dock. The street closest to the quay is lined with soldiers from my infantry, a show of force in case the pirate has a grand plan today. Through the glass, it wasn't clear who is cloaked in the boat, and I won't risk a surprise attack on the capital city. Our horses' hooves clatter on the cobblestones as the boat reaches the docks, drawing the eyes of the townsfolk as we pass them standing along the street, eager to see what brings a royal procession to town. The Northman expertly ties it off and the priest is the first on land. He's younger than I thought and looks weary, but a sigh of relief passes his lips when his feet touch the firm ground.

The young priest turns to offer a hand to the first cloaked figure, a young woman with pale blonde curls and an achingly pretty face. Her eyes look haunted and wary as they run over the crowd lining the street, but it almost makes her more desirable. Next, another young woman reaches her hand out to the priest for assistance. This one has light brown skin and glittering hazel eyes that flit around the city as if she's never been to one before. I glance at the Commander with pleasure, and I can just see his brows lift in appreciation through the slit in his helm. I expected one woman, and here are two additional beauties for my court.

Finally, the last cloaked figure stands, reaching out to the tall Northman who attends to her. All I can see at first is the pale skin of her hand, one thick gold ring adorning her middle finger while the fur-lined hood of her black cloak hides her face fully. The Northman steadies her as she steps onto the dock, then, pulling her hand back, she reaches up and folds back the hood.

It feels as though the air has been forced from my lungs.

The audible gasp that registers through Charleston's helm matches my own, while the surprised chatter of the townsfolk mingles with the sound of the gulls crying overhead.

There is no mistaking who this woman is.

Staring at the black-haired beauty who stands on the docks is like looking at a ghost of Adelaide.

Any doubts I had about her identity disappears. Dark blue eyes travel over the soldiers lining the street and the townsfolk gathered behind them. Then, those cold eyes land on the Commander and me, still mounted on our matching warhorses. Her full lips flatten slightly, but she makes no move toward us, nor does she turn back to the boat. Adelaide's heir merely stands with her chin lifted proudly, waiting for us to approach.

As I study her, I'm shocked at how closely she resembles the version of Adelaide I first attempted to court, but I can see this is no lighthearted songbird like her aunt. Her gaze is piercing like a raven's, intelligent and waiting to pluck your eyes from your skull should you fall.

My heart rate increases as I observe her elegant movements and ruthless expression, my chest and stomach tightening with greed and desire. I want to possess her more than I ever wanted her aunt.

Her hair is styled in the manner of the priestesses, long and loose down her back with the front portion braided into a crown, but she doesn't bear the cursed mark of their ridiculous Goddess on her brow. Curious, since I know she was living in the temples when I took power.

"Go get her for me, Commander," I mutter to Charleston. He dismounts, handing his reins to a stable boy who waits nearby and approaches the small group. The

Northman has stepped in front of them, his hand resting on the hilt of a sword at his hip.

"Lady Nerissa?" Charleston's voice carries over the lap of the waves on the chilly breeze.

"Who might you be?" Her voice is low, deeper than her aunt's, and suspicion clouds her words as she steps to the side of the warrior in front of her, studying Charleston.

"I'm Commander Russell Charleston, leader of the King's army," he replies, removing his helm to show his scarred face. Many flinch at the first sight of the scar that draws up Charleston's mouth and cheek, but no one in the party reacts, as though scars and violence are to be expected.

"Is your King too frightened to meet me on his own?" she mocks, raising a dark brow, her eyes shifting to me.

No. She is *nothing* like her trusting, lighthearted aunt.

"I've even brought one of your priests along to show I'm open to discussing compromise." She waves her hand dismissively toward the young priest who waits with the two other women on the dock behind the protection of the Northman.

Charleston's lips lift into a smirk, turning his head to glance over his shoulder at me in challenge. The bastard. I will *not* be mocked in front of the entire crowd. I dismount and remove my own helm as I stalk toward the group, eyes locked on the woman as if she's my prey. The haughty bitch never flinches. Never blinks.

"I fear no one, Lady Nerissa," I state as I stop before her. She rakes her eyes from the top of my hair to my boots before returning them to my face. A cold smile graces her full lips, finally.

"Bow to your King, harlot!" shouts one of the graying priests who trailed the army, and now stands observing on the edge of the crowd.

I grind my teeth at his impudence; I did not ask these fanatics to be here for this. They have been a means to an end, and I give them free rein to do as they wish to keep me in power by controlling the inhabitants of the country, but I will not have them ruining this.

Before I can reprimand him, Nerissa laughs. A deep, throaty sound that makes my cock twitch at her boldness.

"*Bow*, Priest?" she sneers. "Perhaps you should visit that ship in the harbor. Ask the crew what happened the last time they saw me kneel before a man in public." Her words are disquieting, but she continues, marking the priest in the audience with her cold gaze. "Since *I* am the rightful heir to the throne he sits upon" — her gaze swings back to me and I almost have to stop myself from taking a step back at the flicker of rage in her stare. It's only there for a moment, then her expression is unreadable once again. "Perhaps *you,* and *he*, should bow to *me*."

The priest begins to sputter, ranting about a woman's proper place, but I give him a look that brooks no argument. "Stand down, Father. Allow me to greet my bride properly."

Shocked whispers rise behind me as the townspeople react to my announcement. I hadn't planned on accepting her proposal publicly, but the priest has forced my hand. Plus, her spirit has won me over, even as I want to break it and have her groveling on her knees.

"Oh, I'm your bride already?" she questions, but her lips twitch into the hint of a smile. The Northman at her side flinches slightly but remains silent with his palm still casually resting on his weapon.

"I *tentatively* accept the proposal from your missive. We should return to the castle to discuss it further. In private." My words are neutral, but if the rumor of her past years in a brothel is correct, she knows what I expect. I turn to the man at her side. "You are dismissed, sailor. Return to your captain."

"Oh, no. *I* command him. He's my personal guard and will remain with me at all times," she firmly states, and it doesn't escape my notice that she has refused to address me with my proper honorifics. She never even looks away from me, making me wish to avert my eyes from her bold stare. Disgust at my weakness makes me grit my teeth, while Charleston's insolent smirk rankles my ire.

I will *not* be walked over by a woman, especially not by one coming to me as a beggar seeking a throne.

"You have no need of a guard, now that you're safely back in Selennia, Lady Nerissa. Especially not a violent Northman," I soothe, assuming a softer hand might lower her guard. "My soldiers will protect you."

Her eyes darken at my words, nostrils flaring as she sucks in a breath. "I know firsthand how your soldiers *protect* women," she snarls the words through her teeth. "*He* is trustworthy. I will not have him taken from my side until I'm assured of my title. My handmaidens will also accompany me, as will the young priest who is tutoring me in the way of the true God." She looks to the other members of her retinue in turn before returning her eyes to me in a challenge, no hint of fear anywhere in her expression.

The pirate's vessel still waits in the harbor. Unless my

men attack and forcibly restrain them, they could easily hop back into the rowboat and out to sea at her discretion.

The townspeople have all heard her words and whispered gossip of the Queen's heir is likely already spreading through them as we stand here. I cannot risk them rioting if their foolish hope of a returning heir escapes back into the ocean. This woman is more clever than I anticipated. Clenching my jaw to hold myself in check I finally state, "Of course, my dear. As you wish. But first…"

I signal to one of the soldiers to bring in my surprise. Let's test the bitch's mettle before allowing her to proceed so confidently. Keeping my eyes trained on her, and the guard at her side, I watch for any reaction as the soldier brings forth our captive.

"I believe you know this man," I remark, studying her stern face.

The soldier roughly pushes the dark-haired pirate forward so he stumbles and stands in front of him, arms chained behind his back.

"I've met him before, yes," Nerissa says with no emotion in her voice, her face betraying nothing. "Captain di Micios, I believe?"

"Aye, we've met," di Micios replies with a sneer.

CHAPTER 25

I had taken the eclipse as a sign of good luck standing on the deck of the *Bartered Soul,* allowing the sight to boost my confidence as I prepared for the days ahead. But now I worry I was mistaken as I try to avoid swallowing or showing any other sign of nervousness while Mario di Micios stands bound before us. If they've captured him on the east coast, what is the fate of Morel or Trevino?

Has our plan already failed?

We could easily be walking into a trap if they've all been captured. Especially if he, or any of the others, made a deal or told Blackwell our plans. The sneer on di Micios' lips causes my stomach to flip and my heart to race as I watch him.

"Now tell me, *Captain* di Micios. Is this woman the one you met before? The one who accompanied Captain Lennox?" Blackwell questions, a smile twitching on his face as though he knows he has me pinned. Lennox stands firm at my side, completely impassive. He never moves or reaches for his weapons aside from the hand that has casually rested on his sword hilt since Charleston approached us. He merely observes as though there is nothing unusual about the exchange.

"Aye, she is." Di Micios nods, running his eyes over me with a smile. I focus on the gleam of his gold tooth as I struggle to breathe evenly, hoping my fear doesn't show in my pleading gaze.

"And the man she stands with, her *guard*. Have you seen him before?" Blackwell asks, raking his dark eyes over Lennox, suspicion lingering there.

Di Micios drags his eyes from me almost casually as he studies Lennox in silence. I'm certain my heartbeat is audible to anyone standing near me. Although I keep my hands at my side and don't flinch, I prepare myself for what I must do if we are exposed.

"No."

I almost sob with relief. For whatever reason, di Micios has remained loyal; he hasn't betrayed our plans when he easily could have. It's difficult to keep from sagging in place, but I maintain my posture while I watch Blackwell.

"Very well. Thank you, di Micios," Blackwell answers, looking satisfied with the answers, albeit disappointed that he hasn't caught me in a lie. Di Micios seems to relax, although it's unclear what agreement he has cooperated with. Blackwell turns to the soldier who brought di Micios forward. "Take him, brand him, and hang him," Blackwell orders the guard, who reaches out a large hand to grab di Micios by the arm. "And sink his ship."

Panic surges anew in my chest, forcing me to fight against it to keep my expression neutral at the command.

"*What?*" di Micios shouts and pulls away from the

guard, chains clanking together from the sudden move-ment. "I agreed to your terms. My *men* agreed to your terms. I honored my word. I know nothing other than that this is the heir to the Selennian throne. I told you what you asked for!"

"And yet, you're a pirate. Your men will be released into the sea to survive as best they can, but they will *not* return to your command. *You* will not threaten these waters again."

Di Micios opens his mouth and my heart stutters. Although he's acted untoward and disrespectful in the past, I don't wish for him to hang. But, if I defend him or show my hand, all our plans will be dashed before they have even begun. I don't know if my power can take down enough of these men to save us. My eyes meet the Tomcat's and for a moment his lips part, as though he will confess the truth. But he only lifts his chin, a muscle twitching along his jawline, then bows his head and takes a knee. "I wish you well, my lady."

The soldier who brought him forward yanks di Micios from his knees and drags him back the way they came. As he passes Blackwell, di Micios turns his head, shocking everyone when he spits at the King.

"*Fuck you*, Blackwell. You are no king. You've shown your honor today." His voice grows louder, carrying over the crowd as he shouts, "The people will remember!"

The soldier lands a blow to di Micios' cheek as he turns to follow him, knocking him back a step and causing him to spit blood on the cobbles underfoot. Then, di Micios laughs and calmly follows to meet his death.

"Well, now that we've established that. This way, my

dear." Blackwell sweeps a hand toward the town at his back.

As I pass through the lines of soldiers, I can barely control the tremors that threaten to take over. So far, I've managed to maintain the ruthless air I'm striving for, even as sorrow for di Micios clouds my mind. But, as their eyes rake over me and the dim sunlight highlights their uniforms, I'm reminded of the terror I've felt each time I was in the presence of Blackwell's red and black.

Blackwell and his commander both seem to assume the dark-haired pirate watching from the *Bartered Soul* is Lennox, just like we'd hoped. Di Micios conveniently confirmed their suspicions to his own detriment. They don't know the blond Northman who guards my side is the captain they seek. He remains in disguise as much as I do, another wolf in sheep's clothing joining them.

The castle awaits down the main road and outside the town, surrounded by orchards and a protective wall on the city side. Another side faces the cliffs and the crashing sea beyond, the others lead to the forest where the Central Temple stands, overlooking the coastline and sacred grove. Or, at least, the temple stood there before. From this distance, I can't tell if Blackwell has had it destroyed like the others. The tallest turrets of the castle are all I can make out over the stone buildings that crowd the dock, but I know from memory that it should only be a half-hour ride from where we stand. As we traverse the dock toward the town, a black carriage waits, its door open and inviting.

"Hiding me away already?" I question, looking between the coach and the King as he remounts his stallion, his chainmail rattling as he settles in his saddle.

"It's appointed for your comfort and the comfort of your ladies. It's a long walk on foot to the castle," he replies. He's polished. His answers are smooth, but I'm pleased that I seem to make him uneasy as he cuts his eyes to his commander. He didn't expect someone with an opinion, someone who wouldn't be caged in immediately because she has no other options. Someone who doesn't flinch at the ease with which he orders men's deaths.

"I can ride. Someone bring horses for my guard and me. My handmaidens can ride in the carriage with Father Daniel." I gesture to the coach urging Lyra, Delphine, and Daniel to all step toward it. Pleasure ripples through me at the muscle twitching in the King's jaw. I know I'm pressing him too quickly, but I won't show weakness yet. A small huff sounds from within the helm Charleston has resumed wearing, and I wonder if it's one of annoyance or amusement.

It's all I can do to maintain control over myself in their presence. I have to concentrate to battle the urge to strike the King down. The desire surges through me each time he runs his gaze over me, but I remind myself that I wish to learn about his reign, about Charleston's loyalty, and to see how the citizens of Selennia react to me. I must be patient to allow our men to carry out their portion of the plan first before I take my revenge.

I study the King's profile as he waves to two of his men to dismount and bring Lennox and me their horses. He isn't overly handsome, but he isn't unattractive either. Despite being at least twenty-five years my senior, he's still lean and muscular, although shorter than his commander or Lennox. Close-cropped dark hair peppered with grey tops his tan face, and his dark eyes dance with barely veiled malice when he looks at me, but he offsets it with a pleasant, almost indulgent, smile. If I were a less experienced woman I could ignore the greedy lust that seeps from him, mistaking it for kindness or sheer desire. But I know better, and each lingering glance feels like insects dancing on my flesh, making me glad I have Lennox at my side and Salome's training for support.

A soldier guides a grey mare to me. She shuffles her feet nervously as she nears the King and his larger mount, snorting and rolling her eyes as she sidesteps the stallion pawing at the ground. I take her reins and run a hand lightly over her neck, whispering soft words of comfort to her.

"Are you certain you wish to ride, my lady?" the young soldier asks, looking between me and the nervous horse. Lennox already holds the reins of the bay he was given, a stout beast with gentle eyes, and watches me with concern.

"Yes, I'll be fine. Thank you," I answer, stroking my hand over the mare's neck once again. When the soldier walks away she calms slightly, snorting as she stares at me. Her dark eyes shine with intelligence, and I speak softly to her again while the other men mount up. "You'll be all right, girl. Let's just get through this together."

"My lady?" Lennox's voice rumbles behind me, drawing my gaze from the mare. "May I help you?" He bends to offer a step up to the stirrup, which I accept, tossing my leg over the mare and adjusting my skirts. A squeeze to my ankle, so brief I barely believe it happened, is the only contact he makes with me before quickly mounting his horse and reining up beside me.

Although a few murmurs of disapproval run through the crowd, mainly from the priests who watch me with contempt as I proudly ride astride through the street, many of the townspeople wave or bow their heads to me. Some go as far as to cross their arm over their chest with a closed fist on their heart as they drop their head in respect. The same way they honored my mother. Emotions catch in my throat and tighten my chest, choking me as I scan the people and buildings we pass, so familiar, yet so changed in the years since I last saw them.

I remember visiting Aphros when I was younger. It was always a highlight of my month when I exchanged the white walls of the palace for the cozy interior of a carriage accompanied by a guard to get a peek of the town. Whoever was tasked with my safety would make the driver park the unobtrusive carriage outside the busy center, and would then follow me through the streets, allowing me a taste of freedom while making sure no one knew who the girl in the hooded cloak was.

I remember bustling rows full of open shop doors, smiling merchants, and pleasant snippets of conversation from shoppers enjoying the harbor town. Now, everything — the inhabitants and the town itself — looks sullen and dim. The shops are still open, and the port is still active, but the overall life has been tamped down by years of Blackwell's rule. It's a shock to see the difference his immediate presence has had on Aphros compared to Artemisia and Athene farther north, where his soldiers patrol but the King never visits.

Blackwell rides ahead of us with his commander at his side. Both wear dark helms that match their red and black chainmail and hide their faces. People bow and avert their eyes, but it's unclear whether it's out of true respect for their ruler or only fear. Watchful eyes scour me from the sidewalks, the doors, and the upper windows of the buildings, making me uneasy at how open and on display I am, but I refuse to dip my head, meeting gazes head-on and observing everything I can. Lennox rides silently at my side, the only sound between us is the hoofbeats on the cobbles and the wheels of the carriage following slowly behind.

Outside the city wall stands what used to be the vast southern orchards. I nearly gasp in surprise when my eyes light on the withered fruit trees, still bare from the winter. This time of year the trees should be welcoming new leaves and budding flowers to produce the apples popular for cooking and cider-making later in the year. Instead, they're still skeletal, only the smallest leaf buds peeking on a few branches.

"What happened?" I whisper, pain lacing through me at the sad sight.

"My lady, the orchards have done poorly for years now. It seems to worsen each spring," a young guard riding at our flank murmurs, looking at me from the corner of his eye before his gaze flickers to the Commander ahead. He can't be much older than Delphine, but his face is drawn and serious as he slows his horse to keep pace with my mare. I look over at Lennox who shares a worried expression.

"Has anyone sung to them?" I ask, cutting my eyes toward the young man to observe his reaction to my query. Tradition held that in the late winter, groups were to sing to the apple trees to encourage their growth. It's doubtful anyone would dare do so since Blackwell's rule, and it seems the orchards, and in turn, the farmers and cider makers, suffer for it.

"No, my lady." The young man's lips thin as his expression hardens. "Not since the King took power."

"What's your name, soldier?"

"Ciaran McAllister, my lady." He dips his dark head in respect, nervously inspecting Lennox by my side with subtle glances.

"Have you served the King long, Ciaran?" I question, curious about the men who surround us and do Blackwell's bidding. None of the others have offered more than a glance, but the young soldier's cheeks pink at my attention, so I take advantage.

"I've been in the guard for four years now. Most of my family has passed on and I had no other opportunities since…" His voice trails off as he flicks his attention toward Blackwell and Charleston, then the other soldier riding near, as if worried they might hear him. Lowering his voice, he continues, "Since my family's orchard was burned, my lady. We used to grow apples as well. Not that I'd have had a choice anyway — Blackwell ordered all men over the age of sixteen into the army for mandatory service — but I'm a farmer at heart. That's why I heeded your question. My sister and I fled afterward to the city. She's since married for the second time. Her first husband didn't make it after the invasion."

"McAllister! Back in line!" an older soldier barks ahead of us.

"Pardon, my lady. I must return," Ciaran dips his head,

then nudges his horse into a trot to rejoin the men who line our party.

Before I have time to further consider the death of the orchards, the bridge and wall of the Grand Castle loom ahead. The light grey stone is dark with lichen and moss growing up the sides and the huge oak gates are closed tight, waiting for the King and his retinue to return. Archers wait on the top of the wall, crossbows casually held as we approach. The sight of the soldiers with their crossbows freezes my heart, so similar to the ambush that waited for us in the square of New Aphros. My fingers tighten on the reins, and my mare gives a sideways shuffle as she tosses her head, feeling my fear through my grip.

"Forgive me, girl," I soothe, loosening my hold. I can't fool the horse like I can the humans; she can feel my distress even if I pretend I'm not fazed by the return to my former home. Pausing for the gates to open, I study the stone of the protective wall. Dark stains drip below spikes inserted along the top and into the sides of the stones. Bile rises in my throat, burning as I swallow it back down when I spot ragged remains of clothing still clinging to some of them. What has Blackwell done to my home? I grit my teeth at the defilement and cut my eyes to Lennox, who, to his credit, has maintained a mask of silent indifference the entire ride.

Unease sits in my gut as the gates finally widen enough to allow us to ride through, followed by the carriage and the remainder of the King's retinue. The gates slam shut behind the final horse, locking us in. The yard beyond is mostly unchanged — the main entrance of the castle beckoning straight ahead, while the stables sit to the left. The sounds and smells of the animals within are soothingly familiar.

The only difference is any decorative greenery or plants have been cleared from the entrance, and only packed earth waits for us to dismount. I slide down from the mare's back easily without assistance and wait holding her reins. Stable boys rush forward to take the horses, keeping their eyes focused on their feet as they approach. After handing the mare over, I turn in place to fully view the yard. When I rotate to look at the closed gate at our backs my heart stops.

Above the gate, a stone has been pried from the wall and a gleaming white skull is inserted in its place.

My eyes study the grisly adornment, dread gripping my chest and making it hard to breathe. I can't pull my gaze from it, even as Lennox's eyes drift over my shoulder and he steps forward protectively.

"So she can watch over how a kingdom *should* be ruled," Blackwell's dark voice gloats over my shoulder.

"Excuse me?" I whisper, gripping my cloak so tightly that my fingers ache while struggling to maintain control over my raging emotions. I turn to see him removing his helm, dark eyes glittering in his weathered face.

"Adelaide, of course. I wouldn't want her to miss out on how I've improved her beloved Selennia, would I?"

CHAPTER 26

Disgust churns in my gut as my vision swims.

Logic warns me that Blackwell is baiting me — this could be anyone's skull and he's trying to gauge my reaction. But another part of me, the one so connected to the soil of the land I stand upon, knows that he has desecrated my mother's remains just to stroke his ego.

Blackwell's pride is so fragile that he must view the destruction he's wrought, down to the bones of my mother, to make himself feel better about his tenuous grip on Selennia. I remind myself that Adelaide is in the Afterlife now; she has no need of the bones she left behind. He can't own her in death any more than he could in life.

This is a moment I could lash out and end him immediately, but as I take ragged breaths my eyes flicker over the parapets. The archers wait, arrows nocked, all pointed at me. Delphine steps from the carriage and watches me with wariness while Lyra peeks from the doorway, observing me with a hint of fear in her wide eyes. If I strike now, I might end Blackwell, but I can't guarantee his soldiers won't kill my friends before I can stop them, even with surprise on my side.

Breathing deeply, I look into Lennox's eyes once, steadying myself and forcing calmness to win out over the anger pulsing in my breast, then turn to Blackwell. "What of the rest of her remains?"

"Tossed to the beasts of the forest. Isn't that the way of your Goddess? Worship like an animal, return to the animals?" Blackwell drawls, a smile twitching at the corners of his mouth as he watches me for signs of discomfort.

Rage darkens my vision and I struggle to steady my hands. My nails dig into my palms to keep me from dragging them across his face as I study him with what I hope is no expression on my face. Forcing myself to hold it together, I look him in the eye and answer, willing my voice to remain steady, "Seems a morbid choice of decor. I hope you haven't used the same techniques to decorate my chambers."

Charleston removes his helm, the sun glinting off his dark auburn hair as he steps next to Blackwell. The Commander studies me intently, a hand resting on the hilt of his sword in a mirror image of Lennox, his stare calculating and cold. I force my hands to relax under the Commander's scrutiny; even if Blackwell is more focused on tormenting me, his second is dangerously observant.

Blackwell's brow furrows, something akin to disappointment in his eyes. Momentarily flexing his jaw, he answers, "I have left them relatively untouched. I assumed you would be comfortable in the former Queen's chambers until you take your place in mine." Lust fills his eyes as he drags them over me. I allow him to inspect me openly — he's no different than any other man I fooled in the *House of Starlight* — while I study the courtyard more thoroughly.

Sadness washes over me, and I know my already worn indifference slips when my inspection finds the shell of the former hothouse. I'd assumed the contents would be decimated or removed based on the appearance of the orchards and courtyard, but nothing prepared me for the destruction of the place that housed my fondest memories of my mother.

The glass is smashed or missing, the roof trusses hang into the center of the building, and the back wall appears to have collapsed completely. While the rest of the space is tidy, the hothouse is like a tattered skeleton left to taunt me, just like the rags on the spikes lining the walls and the skull smiling down from the gate. The happy memories of sweet-smelling flowers and learning and laughter that I shared with Adelaide are all that remain of the spaces my mother loved.

"My maids and I are tired," I state, feeling my resolve falter as I offer only a sideways glance to Blackwell. "Can someone from your household lead us to my chambers? I assume they will take the ones adjacent. We can discuss the rest of our arrangement tomorrow."

"Your maids may attend you, but your guard will remain with my soldiers in the barracks," he says, directing his words to both me, Lennox, and the Commander who stands to the side. Charleston's amber eyes continue to monitor me, the scarred grimace across his face masking whether his lips twitch into a smile at the King's growing frustration or whether it's merely a muscle spasm.

"*My guard* will remain where *I* tell him. He's more than capable of staying outside my door or in an adjacent chamber. You may have taken this castle, Blackwell, but don't think I will be so easily captured." My words cut, and some of Blackwell's soldiers eye one another nervously. "Father Daniel is happy to share chambers with him and to ensure my virtue is protected if that's what you fear."

Blackwell takes a step closer to me, his breath hot as he leans forward. My instincts scream for me to step back, but I refuse to heed them, locking my muscles instead. "I fear *nothing*, you mouthy bitch," he whispers through his teeth, quiet enough to hide the insult from his men, dark eyes boring into mine as he looks down at me. "And I have no doubt you possess very little virtue at this point."

Glaring back at him I realize how thin the line I toe has become. It's only the first few hours since my arrival and I'm already about to lose the control I cling to on my power. Taking a shaky breath, I swallow, then cast my eyes downward and huff, "That may be, but he remains with me." I can feel the anger radiating off Lennox at Blackwell's proximity, but he remains motionless."Now allow me to retire."

Satisfied by my slight submission, Blackwell steps back, his false smile returning as Delphine, Lyra, and Daniel join me. "Molly! Take Lady Nerissa and her companions to her chambers. The maids will take the chamber adjacent and the priest and her guard will take the one across the hall," Blackwell commands, addressing a short, middle-aged woman who waits in the doorway leading into the castle.

"Yes, Your Majesty! Right away," she says, ducking her head as she approaches me and my companions. "Welcome, my lady. Are your belongings on the carriage?"

"Hello, Molly. Yes, all our belongings are in the trunks. Please have them brought."

"Right away, my lady. Follow me, please." She dips her head again and scurries ahead of me. Delphine walks behind her, Lyra at my right side, while Lennox and Daniel take places behind me. As we approach the doors, once so familiar and comforting to me, a sense of dread sinks in, wrapping itself around my heart and tightening my stomach. So much destruction has already been viewed; what awaits inside the place I called home? Taking a deep inhale, I step through the opening and into the palace.

We wind through the grey and white marble halls behind Molly's quick steps. While the exterior of the castle has been brutalized by Blackwell and his takeover, the interior seems mostly unchanged, much to my surprise and relief. The main difference is that any symbol of the Goddess or the previous queens has been covered by red and black tapestries or Blackwell's griffin emblem. The halls are pristine, the floors free of any dirt or disorder, and the large windows allow the sunlight to shine through, illuminating our way through the castle to the wing I will forever associate with Adelaide.

With each step closer to her chambers, my heart beats a little faster, unsure whether I can believe Blackwell's statement that he's left the Queen's quarters as they always were, or whether a macabre prison awaits me. Ever so quickly a brush of fingers grazes my lower back, raising goosebumps on my arms while warming my heart at the same time.

Lennox is with me.

My Sisters are with me.

The Goddess is with me.

We cannot be so easily defeated, whatever waits beyond the door.

"Here we are, my lady," Molly says, standing to the side of the door with her head bowed.

The surface is different, the carvings that once adorned the wood of Adelaide's quarters missing. Destroyed during the takeover. Tracing my fingers over the smooth wood, memories of one of my nightmares flash through my mind — visions of the door being busted down. Had I truly *Seen* her fate, then?

"Your maids can reach their chambers through the adjacent door within, or through this one to the side, whichever you prefer. Men, your room is there," she adds, more brusquely, pointing down and across the hallway in turn to each of the doors.

"The King doesn't reside in this wing?" I ask the older woman.

"No, my lady. He refurbished the wing near the throne room for his purposes. He rarely comes to this portion."

Good, I think, grateful to avoid him for now.

"Your trunks will be up shortly. Should you need anything at all please ring the bell," she concludes. Then, more quietly adds, "We are so pleased to have you back, my lady."

I ponder her words as she quickly dips her chin and retreats back the way we came.

"Was she here when you lived here before?" Lennox asks, watching the woman's form disappear back down the staircase.

"Not that I remember," I answer, racking my brain for

any memory of the woman. "I haven't seen anyone I recognize. I can't imagine he allowed anyone to live who served Adelaide." Sighing, I turn my sights back to the closed door. "Let's see what awaits."

Lennox steps forward to turn the iron knob, keeping me behind him in case someone or something looms in the empty space beyond. The hinges creak loudly, the silence reminding me to breathe as my heart pounds. A gentle breeze greets us through the open window across the room and, as I step through the doorway, I'm shocked to find that Blackwell hasn't lied.

The room is almost exactly the way I remember it from when I lived here. The large feather bed sits in an alcove to the right, while a desk rests in front of the open window facing the door. A seating area around a cold fireplace is directly to our left, the latter filled with a stack of logs waiting for a fire. Completing the room is a small table and set of chairs, the place where I dined with my mother for tea while discussing plants or other trivial things.

I float through the space, my eyes running over each piece and finding it all as pristine as the halls we passed through. Surprisingly, no dust or cobwebs adorn anything, it's been cleaned and freshened in anticipation of my arrival. As I try to fathom what game Blackwell is playing, a sudden, sharp gasp behind me jerks my attention back to the center of the room.

Delphine kneels on the rug that I just walked over, the only thing in the room I'm not familiar with now that I look at it more closely. One palm presses into the woven surface, the other arm wrapped around her waist as if warding off sudden pain. I can only see her wild blonde curls shudder as she sucks in ragged breaths with her face turned toward the floor.

"Del? *Delphine!*" Lyra kneels beside Del, reaching out to comfort her, but before she makes contact Del's face snaps up to meet mine.

Delphine's voice quivers through her shallow panting. "I found the connection you needed."

"What?" I quickly return to her side, kneeling next to her as well.

"Pull up the rug. I know how to channel your mother."

CHAPTER 27

"**W**hat?" Lennox hisses, looking back toward the closed door once before crouching next to Delphine's other side.

"I haven't been pulled into a vision of the dead in a very long time, but something is here to do it. Something of hers." Del blinks slowly, swallowing as though she might be sick. "Pull back the rug."

Delphine crawls to the edge of the carpet, leaning against Lyra as she takes deep breaths. Lennox and I exchange a concerned glance before he and Daniel begin to roll the rug off the stone floor, but I already have an idea of what we will find.

If the dream I had of Adelaide and Blackwell is true, this is where my mother made her last stand. Where she gave blood in offering to the Goddess with her final prayers.

As we near the spot Delphine collapsed, a faint brown stain appears on the pale floor. It's obvious it's been scrubbed, the stain barely visible except in the cracks between the stone, but it's there.

"It's her blood," I whisper, touching the stones with my fingertips.

"Is this… is this where he killed her?" Lyra asks softly, her eyes studying me as though I might come undone. But I already suspected that what my dreams had shown me was true, and I know Blackwell can't claim her death directly.

"He didn't kill her," Delphine says, eyes unfocused. "She did it herself."

"*What?*" Lennox looks between Delphine and me in disbelief.

"She's right. I *Saw* it in a dream. Adelaide drank poison Salome left her. She maimed Charleston, then prayed here, before the poison took her. Blackwell just took the credit rather than admit that she beat him, even at the end."

Unexplained pride burns in my chest knowing that my mother did what she could in the end to prevent Blackwell from having her, even if I now offer myself to him. Even if it's an act, a constant doubt chimes in my mind — *what if I'm not able to outsmart him? What if I've somehow given him what he needs to take my home completely and her sacrifice was for nothing?*

"I can use it to channel her, Nerissa," Delphine whispers, looking at the spot with a nervous glance. "It started involuntarily when I stepped onto the spot, even through the rug. I can control it and reach her for you if you still want me to."

"What do you need?" I ask. I sense this will be difficult for her — and I know in my heart it will be equally as difficult for me — but I need to know anything Adelaide can tell me before we get too far into this situation.

"Just time to do it where we won't be interrupted. And time to rest afterward," she replies.

"Tomorrow night. Our belongings will be settled by then, and hopefully, after dinner, no one will bother us." I scoot over to take Del's hand in mine. "I won't ask this of you more than once if I can help it. We can get what we need tomorrow and be done with it."

She nods her head in agreement as Lennox replaces the rug.

THE REST OF THE AFTERNOON AND INTO THE EVENING IS FILLED with servants bringing our trunks, offering refreshments, and seemingly making up excuses to get a glimpse at me. So far, I recognize no one from when I lived at the castle before, but it's been nearly fourteen years. I expect that most of Adelaide's attendants were either killed or escaped during the takeover, but it would be comforting to find at least *one* person I remember from my time here as a girl.

Earlier this evening, a large meal was sent for all of us, one we hesitantly nibbled on. It seems unlikely that Blackwell would poison us — he hasn't had enough time to try to make me fear him or bend to his desire yet, so we gave in to our hunger and finished the food.

"I want to walk the castle and grounds before it's too late. I want to see what he's done," I tell Lennox, tossing the linen napkin on the tray and standing.

Lyra and Delphine have already slipped through the adjoining door into the room they'll share while we're here, the one my mother's lady's maid used when I was small.

Daniel went with them to help unpack before he retires to the room he and Lennox were assigned across the hall.

"Whatever you wish," Lennox answers, standing and retrieving the sword he's taken to wearing in place of his favored cutlass. As he sheaths it and turns to face me, I take the chance to cup his face and pull it to mine, kissing him deeply — the first time we've truly touched since docking. His warm hands grip my waist, holding me close even as our lips break apart and I press my cheek against the leather of the Northman's armor he still wears.

"We've made it through the first day," I whisper, looking up into his face. Even with his beard longer and hair knotted behind him, his eyes gleam the same as they always have, burning with his devotion.

"We'll make it through all the days, my love," he murmurs back, kissing me once more before releasing me. "Now, let's go explore."

Wrapped in my cloak to ward off the chill of the night air seeping through the stone walls, I lead the way down the hall to the curving stairwell that descends to the lower levels. There, the kitchens and servants' exits wait. This wing seems to have been deserted since the takeover. Many rooms hold nothing at all instead of the furniture and decorations that once adorned the different spaces of the former royal wing. Between the desolation of this wing and the destruction of the hothouses when we arrived, I can only begin to wonder at what has become of the music room, library, and gardens so beloved by my mother and myself.

Sweat threatens to bead on my brow as we descend toward the kitchen door — the kitchen has multiple entrances for servants to easily run to the different wings.

Lennox and I stand in the one that leads to the Queen's wing, watching a few people milling about in the heat of the fires. It takes several moments before anyone notices us, but when an elderly woman carrying an empty copper pot catches sight of me she gasps and drops it in a great clatter to the stones underfoot before struggling to bow.

"Great Godde— I mean…" the woman stumbles over her words as she trembles, a hand over her heart. "My lady, we didn't know you would be coming down. I'm sorry for the inattentiveness!"

"Think nothing of it, we interrupted your work," I reply, gesturing for Lennox to go retrieve the pot and help the woman to her feet. A young girl, likely the scullery maid, and a teenage boy all keep their eyes averted as he briskly strides past to assist the woman.

"Did your dinner displease you, my lady?" the woman asks when she's standing again. The fear in her eyes makes my heart ache, wondering what kind of treatment she's experienced to result in such a reaction.

"Not at all, dinner was excellent. Thank you," I reply, cocking my head to the side. Something strikes me as familiar about her lined face, but I can't place it. "What's your name?"

"Bridget."

"Have you worked here long, Bridget?"

"My lady, I've worked in the castle for nigh on twenty years now. I… I remember you well, even if I never spoke to you," she answers, dipping her head.

"How is it you still serve the King?" Lennox asks, his deep voice and false Northern accent causing Bridget to step away from him as though he struck her. "How did you survive the takeover?"

A look of shame crosses her face as she flicks her eyes between the two of us. "I swore fealty to the man to save me and my grandchildren." She lifts her chin toward the youths in the kitchen with her. Now that she's pointed it out the resemblance is obvious. "Their father was one of the soldiers Blackwell's men hung on the walls. I couldn't let the same happen to them."

I clench my jaw, grinding my teeth together at the brutality that follows Blackwell, and that has physically and emotionally stained the castle. "You have nothing to be ashamed of, Bridget. I had hoped to find an old friend in these walls and it seems I may have tonight." As I let the words sink in, I watch the elderly woman stand straighter. She looks me in the eyes and I see the resolve in them that rescued her and her grandchildren.

"Aye, my lady. You do. Within and without," she whispers, then crosses her right arm over her chest to rest a fist over her heart. Her grandchildren kneel and make the same gesture.

"Rise, quickly. Before someone else enters," I tell them. "I welcome your kindness, and I'm pleased to be home, even if it is to meet with my future husband." The lie tastes oily on my tongue, but I don't know these people. I can't risk them thinking I'm here for anything other than the potential union with Blackwell, even if they claim to support me. "We'll leave you to your work, now." Turning to Lennox, I nod toward the exterior door next to the hearth, "Let's go."

"Be well, my lady," Bridget murmurs as I pass her.

Stepping through the door to the outside, a chill breeze greets us. A part of me misses the warm humidity of Delosia and New Aphros, but the crisp air refreshes me and clears my mind as I stare up at the dark sky where stars glitter across the expanse. Torches line the wall surrounding the castle, but only a few guards walk along the top. We'll need to monitor their activity to see how they keep watch in case we need to send word to the caves or leave the castle grounds in secret.

"This way," I whisper, trying to keep our presence hidden from the watchmen. While I can claim I'm simply taking the air after my evening meal, I nevertheless dread running into one of the soldiers this evening. Lennox walks at my side, quietly scanning everything as we stroll toward the space that was once the garden.

Passing through the archway and into the walled garden, I'm surprised to find that not all is destroyed. While the beds are overrun with dead grass and weeds, the great oak in the center still stands, one of the few that still defiantly clings to its leaves. In the dimness of the late evening, with no moonlight to guide me, I can't tell if the other shrubs or perennial plants thrive, but I'm relieved, if only slightly, to find that Blackwell hasn't fully decimated the entirety of the home I missed. We walk the pathways between beds with only the crunching of old leaves and dead foliage under our feet until I'm finally chilled enough to want to return to my chambers. Turning at the back edge of the garden, my eyes snag on a latch hidden under a riot of dying vines.

"What is it?" Lennox asks, stepping closer as I run my fingers over it and press my hand to the center of the stone door. His warmth seeps through the furs he wears and warms me through my cloak. I ache to press against his side but don't dare in the open in case the guards on the parapets noticed us and decided to follow.

"A gate I'd dismissed before. It requires a key of course, but it leads out of the castle and into the forest. There's a sacred grove a ways away on foot. It used to be where the townsfolk worshiped… if it still stands." The door is made in such a way that the stones blend with the wall, and the overgrowth of wilted vines covers the hinges, so only one who knew it was there would know to seek it out. I can only hope that Blackwell wasn't able to identify the grove. One wouldn't know it for what it is without knowledge of the Goddess in this area, but until I'm able to venture out and explore the nearby villages I won't have a clear image of what he's done outside of the castle walls.

"It would be good to have the key, then. Just in case," he whispers against my hair, sending an ache of longing through me.

I swallow, resisting the urge to lean into him. "I'll have to see what we can find in my chambers. Perhaps there was an extra? Or perhaps we can figure out a way to pick the lock. It would be useful if we need to let our reinforcements in through these walls." Running my fingers over the vines, I hope they lay naturally enough to re-cover the door, then I turn to Lennox. "Let's head back, I'm cold and a fire sounds nice."

As we stride out the gate and back into the main courtyard, I can't help but detour toward the broken hothouse that looms nearby. Sadness again tugs at me over the unnecessary destruction, but I'm shocked back to reality when Commander Charleston steps from the shadows into my path. Lennox's fingers wrap around my arm protectively, halting my steps as he pulls me close to block me from the other man. He drops his grip immediately when he sees who stands before us, murmuring, "Apologies, my lady," as though he shouldn't have taken such liberties.

One of the sooty torches lining the wall illuminates Charleston, the flames casting shadows across his scarred face as he lifts the unmarred side of his mouth into a chilling smile. "Well well, already out and about with your *guard*, Lady Nerissa? Didn't want to take even the first night to settle into your new home?"

The way his eyes drift over me and Lennox sends panic surging through my veins, and I hope he can't see my pulse thrumming under my skin at the insinuation. If the Commander already senses our lie then Blackwell will know soon enough, and I'll have to make my stand with few reinforcements. It was a risk bringing Lennox with me, but a risk I had to take. I won't be without him ever again.

Standing straighter, I study Charleston in the torchlight. Although I saw what happened to his face in my nightmares, I almost pity the man for the damage done and wonder if it causes pain all these years later. But as my inquisitive gaze reaches his eyes, all sense of pity dies at the predatory gleam staring back at me. I force myself to stay in one place, not allowing my feet to step back or shift my weight. "This castle was my home once, there's no need to *settle in* somewhere you grew up." I tilt my head, studying him. "Is there a reason you're following me, Commander? Worried about a lonely woman reminiscing about her losses?"

He chuckles, the sound menacing, making me evaluate if *he* is the true threat here, not the King. "Simple coincidence, my lady. I was merely curious where you and your heathen bodyguard were off to in the darkness when I saw you slip out the kitchen door. I was just on my way to the barracks to receive my nightly report from my men."

Lennox exhales loudly at my side, his lips tight as he glares at the man in his black and red uniform. I pull my cloak closer, feigning a deeper chill than I feel now that my anxiety has spiked. "Well, nothing to worry about on my account. I'm returning to my room now to retire. Goodnight, Commander."

As I pass, Charleston starts to reach his hand toward me, but Lennox tightly grips the other man's forearm as he moves for the dagger at his belt. "Watch your familiarity," he snarls through gritted teeth, his false accent faltering momentarily.

Charleston merely smiles and narrows his eyes, raking them over Lennox's hand and up to his face. "Interesting. A Northman with a Western Selennian accent. Calm down, dog. I was merely going to remove that from the lady's cloak."

I twist to look and find a dried leaf clinging to the wool. Brushing it off, I gesture for Lennox to follow me, but my blood runs cold when another of Charleston's chuckles follows us through the darkness.

"Do you think he truly suspects anything?" I whisper once we reach my room without another incident. I hang my cloak and turn for Lennox to unbutton my gown. I know he can't remain in my chambers overnight, but that reality doesn't negate the fact that I wish I could pull him down with me into the cold bed that waits.

"No. I think he's playing a game to see if he can frighten you or make us reveal something. Keep up the nonchalance and I'll try to keep my damn mouth shut," he answers roughly, frustration coloring his tone, as he finishes his task. His hands are warm through my shift as he runs them down my sides under the wool of my dress, and I lean back against him for a moment before using my power to light the fire in the fireplace across the room.

"I don't want you to be provoked by that man. He's already looking for any reason to take you from me. Then I'll have no choice but to take matters into my own hands earlier than planned."

"I know, but I won't allow one of them to touch you without permission. It wouldn't be allowed by *any* decent guard." Lennox spins me in his arms and presses a kiss against my forehead. "Rest, my she-wolf. I'll be across the hall with Daniel. Keep your door barred until I return in the morning."

"Goodnight, I love you." I raise up on my toes to kiss his lips quickly before he pulls away and heads to the door.

"I love you, too," he whispers, slipping out the door before I bar it and curl under the coverlet of the big empty bed.

CHAPTER 28

Delphine and Lyra wait in my chambers the next morning before the kitchen maid brings our meal. Lennox's firm knock at the door alerts us to her arrival and Delphine dutifully opens the door as though I can't be bothered to do such menial tasks on my own. This dynamic feels unnatural now but I was taught the ways of royalty early and know it would be viewed with suspicion if I did these simple actions for myself. The maid dips her head and silently leaves the tray covered with dishes before scurrying back into the hallway, avoiding eye contact with Lennox as though he might gobble her up.

Dread skips down my spine when I find a note beside the pot of tea and dish of eggs on my breakfast tray. A glob of black wax holds the edges together and my appetite disappears when I open it to find a note from Blackwell himself.

. . .

IT'S TIME WE DISCUSSED YOUR PROPOSAL AND OUR FUTURE. Dine with me tonight in my private dining room. Someone will retrieve you at half past seven. -Dargan

I SIGH IN IRRITATION, TOSSING THE PAPER ACROSS THE TABLE where Lennox picks it up. His lip curls as he reads, making a sound of disgust in the back of his throat.

"Tell me again why we can't just kill the bastard?" Delphine muses, looking between the two of us as she raises a forkful of eggs to her lips.

"If only it were that easy. It's been so long since I was here. I need a better idea of how things are being run right now, of what will happen after I seize my rightful throne once more," I explain yet again, even as I roll my eyes and suspect her question was rhetorical. "And I don't want to put all of us at risk should I tap out of power. We need it to be a coordinated effort."

"Or, you could just seduce him and murder him in his sleep and be done with it," Del pushes, smiling wickedly around her breakfast. Lyra and Lennox both shoot matching glares at Del, and the similarity of their expression is almost enough to make me laugh. Almost.

I wish Delphine's suggestion was that simple. If it were, I might be able to stomach one last seduction to rid us of Blackwell, but I have a suspicion that I would regret that course of action.

"I want Daniel to come with me tonight. If I'm to discuss this sham of a marriage with him I want 'my priest' to attend with me. To ensure I understand the expectations of the King's religion, of course." Lennox gives a wry smile in response, but it does nothing to ease the nervousness twisting my gut.

"We'll have to try channeling Adelaide after the dinner, Del. Do you have everything you need?" I ask, turning my attention to Delphine and the other source of my tingling nerves.

"I don't need anything but the blood," she replies, taking a deep sip of her tea before giving me a tight smile. Lyra runs a hand over Del's arm in an attempt to soothe her, but I'm fairly certain Delphine is just as tense as I am. "Are you sure it will be such a short meal? What if he requires you for more than dinner?"

"*That* will not be happening," Lennox snarls from where he stands by the door.

"That's why Daniel is attending. To remind Blackwell of all of his religion's rules." My voice shakes despite myself because I know that even if the religion that supports him insists that celibacy is the only choice before a man and woman wed, the reality is Blackwell may very well assume he can take whatever he wishes. Just like he took this castle.

Clearing my throat, I change the subject, not wanting to think about what would happen if Blackwell attempts to take me as well. "Lyra, I want you to come with me today. I'm going to walk the grounds to see what else has changed. That way you can get your bearings as well. Del, I trust you can slip in the shadows to explore on your own? Out of trouble?" I toy with my meal as I speak, raising my brows at Delphine.

"My pleasure," Delphine retorts while Lyra nods in agreement.

"I'm going to go across to eat with Daniel. I'll come back

with him when we finish and we can do as you wish," Lennox says, stepping forward to kiss the top of my head before leaving the three of us.

Within an hour all six of us gather in my chambers. When he returned with Daniel trailing behind, dressed in his black robes, Lennox advised that Blackwell's men now stand at either end of the hallway and at the top of the stairs we descended last night. "It seems Charleston has told his men to keep an eye on us after our run-in last night. Each of us must be careful," he says, almost as though he's reminding himself as much as the rest of us.

"We all know what to do, William. Calm down," Delphine chides, pulling a dark cloak around herself. "I'll see all of you later." She kisses Lyra's tan cheek, running her thumb across her cheekbone before slipping back into their room and presumably out the alternate exit while we prepare to depart the main door.

In the morning light the hallway is bright and airy, the way I remember it as a child. I run my hand over the pale walls as we stroll toward the stairs, ignoring the red and black-clad soldiers in the hall. As we approach the top of the stairs, a broad-shouldered guard, the older of the two stationed there, steps in our path barring the doorway.

"Where is it you think you're going, heathen?" he challenges Lennox who has stepped in front of me in response to the guard's movement.

"I wasn't aware I was a prisoner in this wing," I remark, looking up at the soldier with irritation. Lennox's jaw flutters, but he remains still and calm. "We're taking the morning air. Let us pass."

"The Commander told us to keep you under watch."

"Did he also tell you to speak disrespectfully to your queen?" I sneer, marking the lack of proper courtesy in his tone and manner of addressing me.

"You aren't queen yet," the man starts, but thinks better of himself when he looks into my face, finishing with, "my lady."

"Not officially, but I will be. What is your name?"

"They said you were an impudent little thing," he snipes, then chuckles. "It's Hopper."

"Very well, Hopper. Watch your tone with me, or when I sit on my throne beside Blackwell I'll make sure you have no tongue with which to address me at all. Now move. If your commander has anything to say about it, tell him to find me himself." Breathing deeply, I step past Lennox and push past the man. The other guard who still stands by the doorframe dips his head to me respectfully as my retinue and I pass through.

I can faintly make out the men's voices behind us over our light footsteps as we walk down the grey stone stairs, the irritation of being so closely watched chafing me. I knew I wouldn't be able to roam as freely as I'd hoped, but their presence grates on me. I'm going to have to work harder to keep my temper in check, to keep my reality cloaked from the soldiers I will face daily now. The only consolation is that instead of the fear that usually grips me at the sight of a red and black uniform, I only find frustration at the challenge.

"Father," I address Daniel, catching his attention and causing him to stride past Lyra and Lennox to walk beside me.

"Yes, my lady?" Daniel answers, matching my pace. I

glance over at him in his black, so different from the rough-spun I've seen him wear these past weeks on the ship. He's still lanky, but although he's younger than me by several years, he looks older with his hair trimmed close like the other priests.

"I'd like to visit the temple. Have you heard anything from the others about whether it still stands?" I ask, knowing Daniel has already visited with the resident priests.

"From what I've gathered, it does. Blackwell has ordered changes to it to better suit the true religion, but for some reason didn't have the Central Temple destroyed like he did the others," Daniel whispers. "The priests here haven't been forthcoming on their own, but they answer my questions. They are very interested in *you*, my lady."

"I'm sure they are," Lennox murmurs from behind us, his disdain clear.

"What have they asked?" I wonder aloud as we stroll through the gleaming hallway. Sunlight streams through the large windows and reflects off the shimmering white stone, highlighting the gilded sconces and soaking into the black and red banners that cover the engraved sigils, friezes, and reliefs that decorate the walls of the palace. Our footsteps are muffled on the long black carpet runner underfoot. At least it isn't red. I know well enough that blood ran through these halls without a visible reminder of the fact.

"They want to know if you were truly a priestess and, if so, why you aren't marked as one."

"And what have you told them?" I murmur.

"I told them that you sought salvation, and that when I

blessed you and cleansed you of your sins the mark vanished. A *miracle*," he replies seriously. When I turn my face toward him a youthful gleam lights his eyes and his lips twitch from trying to hide the laughter simmering underneath.

A slow smile spreads across my own face at his cunning storytelling. "A miracle indeed."

"The better question is did they believe you?" Lennox softly rumbles behind us.

No one stands guard in this hallway and no steps follow behind, but we still keep our voices low in case the tapestries and banners have ears. We can't be seen pulling them back to check, so we continue to murmur our conversation as we near the back entrance of the castle, the one that leads to the rear courtyard and then the path to the Central Temple beyond.

"They seemed to. Most of them are younger here, except for their higher-ranking elders. They all acted as though they were in awe of my skills after I told the tale."

"Is the old sod who yelled out on the docks their leader?" Lennox asks.

Daniel nods. "I believe so. I wasn't able to meet him last night; he had already retired to his prayers after speaking with the King."

"I wonder if he'll be at the temple today," I muse. I'd prefer to visit alone, without the hateful eyes of the priests scanning in search of my secrets in such a sacred place. But, now that Blackwell has men monitoring us and my meeting with him looms, I don't want to miss the opportunity to visit the temple. This might be the only chance I have before things get underway and I'm unable to walk even as freely as I can now.

"I don't know, but I caution you, several expressed their displeasure at how bold you were yesterday and how sharp your words were. As you know, God requires women to be subservient and obedient. You may have to work on that if you're to be convincing as a convert."

Squinting against the brightness as we step from the castle, I breathe in the crisp air of a Selennian spring morning. It helps cool the irritation Daniel's words elicit, even if he's only relaying information that helps achieve my goals. "I'll take it under advisement, Father. Thank you," I reply with narrowed eyes and a sideways smile. Daniel returns the look, sensing my annoyance.

Closing my eyes for a moment, I take one more deep breath. I've missed the sights and smells of home, even if all has changed since I was here last. Continuing on, we walk briskly across the cobbled yard, ignoring the stares of stable boys and soldiers who ready horses and the blacksmith with his ringing anvil.

The main pathway to the temple is clear, the gate stands open, and the trail is apparently trodden frequently enough that the dirt is packed and free of overgrowth. We follow it into the silent forest that surprisingly still stands near the castle. After the destruction of the groves in Athene and the surrounding countryside, I assumed we would find the forest around the castle demolished as well, but relief floods me as the wind whispers through the naked branches and caresses my cheeks. Although I still wonder why the trees are this bare so late in the year, I exhale a sigh of contentment as our group strolls through to the clearing before the Central Temple.

The relief I felt in the whispering forest disappears when the temple comes into view. The path from the castle leads to the side of the temple, wrapping around to a private entrance for those who approach from the palace. Another wider, sloping, main pathway leads down to Aphros at the bottom of the hill. Trees would usually surround the gleaming structure from all sides, but the ones that should continue around the building and onward to the sacred grove are gone, cut nearly to the bare soil.

"That fucking bastard," I whisper through my teeth. I knew what to expect, knew there would be changes — there have already been worse ones — but seeing the forest decimated tears at the grip I hold on my emotions.

"Rein it in, Nerissa," Lennox warns softly, his eyes flickering from the barren earth to my face and back.

"I'm fine," I mutter, stepping from the woods into the clearing. "Let's see what else they've done."

When we reach the private entrance Lennox tries the door. The wood creaks as he tugs at the iron handle, but doesn't budge. The wind whips around me, swirling my dark cloak around my ankles as my frustration rises, but I swallow it down. Daniel leads the way to the front of the temple where we're greeted by two priests, one on either side of the door. The older man hisses through his teeth at the sight of Lennox's tattoos, leathers, and furs. He appears every bit the part of a vicious Northman as he intends, in no way a friend to these priests or their God. Then, the priest turns his calculating gaze to me.

"What is *she* doing here?" the man asks.

"She's here to worship. The same as everyone else who visits," Daniel gently replies as if the priest's words don't ooze with condemnation.

"Did King Dargan allow her to do so?" the younger priest asks, his eyes traveling over me as though he suspects I'm indecent under my cloak.

"King Dargan did not stop me. I've sought education and conversion from your brethren. Now I wish to see where you worship since the temple has fallen. Do you not welcome all who believe in your God?" I ask, feigning confusion and shock, laced with barely hidden irritation.

"And *do you* believe in our God?" the older priest questions, looking between me and Lennox. Lyra remains silent at my side, eyes downcast as though she knows her place among the men.

"Father Daniel has said as much, both to your brothers and to the King. Now allow me entry, or else I will tell my future husband that you were disrespectful and deserve to be replaced." Lifting my chin slightly I take another step forward, my eyes level with the younger priest on the top step. "Surely if my words prove false, or my presence is deemed a sin, your God is strong enough to strike me down upon entry. My handmaiden and priest will attend me, my guard can stand at the entrance if his presence offends you."

Lennox tenses at my side, a small motion no one would notice if they weren't as aware of his movements as I am, but I don't fear these men. I have my dagger in my pocket and power in my veins. Stepping past the priests who finally relent and move aside, that power surges momentarily as I cross the threshold into the temple, catching my first glimpse of the open space. Heat spreads over me and I struggle for a moment trying to calm it. Now is not the time to allow the *glow* to shine and reveal the truth.

I'd noticed that my power seemed different the closer we got to Selennia, but now I'm certain. It curls and surges under my skin now that I'm back in my rightful home as if it draws strength from the land itself. As if it's as offended as I am by the changes wrought by the King and his priests. I glance over to Lyra who takes measured breaths at my side, as if her power is acting similarly unruly.

Turning my head slightly to Daniel, I whisper, "Tell them I wish to have privacy, that I only want *you* to attend me in this place for now." He simply nods and turns to speak in soft tones with the men. The older man's grumbles travel up the aisle behind me, but I step farther into the space and ignore him. Soon, the doors close and I'm left with only Lyra and Daniel.

"You have your wish," Daniel advises.

"You're certain no one watches?" I ask, scanning the room warily.

"Yes. The remainder live in barracks similar to the soldiers near the palace. Only a few man the doors through the day and night."

At his confirmation, I sink to my knees and allow angry tears to roll down my cheeks. The loss of the forest and grove cleaved my heart, but the damage to the temple completes the rending.

The floors have been covered with wood, relatively recently hewn — likely from the trees that were cut just outside. The protective sigils and marks of the Goddess are now all hidden beneath the planks. Glass covers the once-open windows surrounding the top of the walls. The windows had allowed air from the forest to surround worshipers, while fires around the edges of the room would keep the chill at bay on cold days and nights. But now the room is sealed like a tomb. Even the clear glass opening in the ceiling has been altered, the view of the sky blotted out with black. It's unclear staring up at it whether it was painted or if the glass was changed altogether, but any glimpse of the sky from the interior of the temple is blocked to those within.

The other windows that line the walls have heavy wooden shutters covering them, only torches along the walls light the space, leaving sooty streaks snaking up the pale stone walls from their fires. I assume in warmer weather they might still open these windows, but I have no way of knowing.

"Nerissa? Are you all right?" Lyra crouches beside me, rubbing a small hand across my shoulders as I kneel with my head bowed. Her power tingles against my own as if she can't help but send a wave of comfort to wash over me.

Breathing deeply, trying to steady my voice, I wipe at my eyes before looking at her. "I will be. We all will be."

"Is it so very different?" Lyra asks, looking around the dimmed space.

"The temples, all of them, used to be so open. Air flowed freely, fire flickered in braziers, the gentle lull of water ran in healing fonts, and the moon shone down through the glass in the ceiling. Even on the darkest nights, when the moon was missing, the stars were always there to keep us company. This..." I hold in a sob, looking around once more. "This is so stifling, so controlling. It doesn't allow us to be one with the rest of the world, only closes us off from nature. How does it not suffocate them?"

As I speak it feels as if the walls press in on me, stealing my breath as my pulse begins to race, and memories of the night the temple in Athene was attacked start to claw to the forefront of my mind. I can't allow this to happen now, not with the eyes of the priests so close and the dinner with Blackwell looming.

"Let's leave this place." I grind my teeth, pressing my palms against my eyes to stop the tears that threaten to return, then stand abruptly. The room tilts slightly, forcing me to grip the edge of one of the benches but a few more breaths steady me enough to stride confidently back to the door and into the warm embrace of the sunlight and cool kiss of the breeze. Lennox stands straight, pushing off the wall where he was leaning, the panic in my chest easing at the sight of him waiting.

"Thank you, Father, for allowing me time alone for my prayers," I direct to the older priest. His eyes widen slightly, as if surprised at my gentle words, but says nothing as I breeze past him and down the pathway back toward the forest followed by my attendants.

"What did you find?" Lennox asks as his long strides eat up the path to walk at my side.

"That they've covered everything with misery inside just as they have the rest of the country. I hope this dinner is swift and we're successful with Delphine later. I want this to end sooner rather than later."

He huffs in response, quietly keeping pace the entire rest of the way back through the woods.

CHAPTER 29
BLACKWELL

"Yes, but what were they *doing*?" I demand. My frustration with Charleston is like a living thing between us as I stare at my second. My patience wears thin.

Why had he not come to me immediately after he saw Nerissa and that Northman last night in the courtyard? How could he only just tell me about this *now*, shortly before I'm slated to dine with her?

"There was nothing to tell," he answers nonchalantly, studying me with amber eyes and a twisted smirk. "They weren't *doing* anything that I could tell off hand. It looked like they took a walk in the old garden and then returned to her chambers."

"But you said he *touched* her."

I assume the woman has been touched by numerous men over the years if she spent time as one of the whores they called priestesses, and then in the Houses of Artemisia. But the fact that she would dare flaunt it in *my* castle inflames my senses, making me lose the focus I'd been honing in preparation for our discussion tonight. I will not have her stolen away from me by her guard like Adelaide was.

"You misunderstand. As much as I would happily rid us of the Northman, he did nothing different than I myself would have in his position. I saw nothing intimate in his gesture. I'll monitor them and keep my men in her wing. But, unless you want to create more animosity than already simmers in her, we need to bide our time."

His words are truthful, his thinking measured, as always, but they still cause me to clench my jaw and pace the room. My manservant stands in the corner, eyes downcast, waiting to finish dressing me since he was interrupted by Charleston's arrival.

"That is of course..." Charleston pauses, his smile widening as his eyes glint with malice.

"Yes?"

"If you don't plan on just taking her by force anyway, I mean."

I chuckle in response. "No. I need her to cooperate, at least at first. Let her think I welcome her and want her. It won't do me any good to break her before the people see her as queen. You saw them at the docks: the whispers, the gasps. The fucking *awe*. If we can tame all of them, and convert them like she seems to have been, it will clinch everything. An heir will finalize it. My brothers will seethe knowing I've subdued an entire country while they merely lord over their measly fiefdoms across the sea."

I know I need to gain control over my emotions but a feeling akin to glee fills me unbidden when I imagine my family hearing about my successes. While *they* maintain the tidy estates they never thought I could manage, *I* rule an entire country. Their disapproval will mean nothing when I have the official heir at my side to soothe any remaining unrest that hasn't already been rooted out. Once we produce a child to ensure my name lives on, it will prove my family's doubts about my abilities wrong. They'll fear *me* when I can crush my hateful, snickering brothers with my power.

I pour a glass of whiskey, drinking it in one burning swallow to temper my feelings. If I expect to have a conversation with the woman without her balking, I'll need to convince her that I actually plan to let her hold some power at my side. I saw her on the docks. I sensed the hatred in her. But, even if I refuse to admit it to Charleston despite his prodding, I can't help but want her.

To call her mine and keep her here to do with as I wish.

To finally claim her, like I attempted to do with Adelaide years ago.

It's a fitting revenge that Adelaide's heir has come back to me now, willingly. All that effort to keep me out and here she is, offering herself freely. I could cut down every tree on this island, destroy every hothouse flower and thing of beauty Adelaide held dear, and none of it would compare to how sweet it is to know her heir will crawl before me and give me full control over this land in the eyes of its people.

"Finish dressing me, it's nearly time." I snap at my manservant, ignoring Charleston's pointed gaze and the lust now clouding my mind.

"Are you sure you're going to be able to control your temper?" he prods, needling me as no one else is allowed. As if *he's* my brother instead of one of the assholes across the channel I share a bloodline with.

"Fuck off, Russell. I've gotten us this far, I'll tame the bitch and have an heir in her by Midsummer."

"I believe *I* aided in getting us this far," he scoffs, then adds, "I look forward to watching the show tonight. I'm curious which of you will be the better thespian." He unfolds his lean frame from the chair he lounged in and bows slightly before opening the heavy door to exit my chamber.

<hr>

I ARRIVE IN THE PRIVATE DINING ROOM TEN MINUTES EARLY TO find it lined with guards as expected. Charleston stands behind my seat, acting as a personal guard like I expect Nerissa's Northman will do for her. One of the serving girls steps forward, pouring wine into my goblet as usual. She waits for a moment, but tonight I don't pull her onto my lap or fondle her as I normally would. Tonight, I need to present a civil front to my future bride. The thought nearly makes me snicker.

The woman is a fool to think one man guarding her is enough to keep her safe should I wish to take her and dispose of him. The men in this room could easily dispatch the brute, but I'll bide my time. See what she has to say tonight, and what proposal she offers.

After fifteen minutes, steps sound in the hallway beyond the door of the private dining room. The torches lining the walls and the candles in the hanging candelabra all flicker, the flames dimming slightly and casting thick shadows in the edges of the room, before the steps halt outside the door. A few of the younger soldiers shuffle their feet as a knock sounds but stand straight after a stern look from Charleston.

A younger guard pulls the door open, revealing the servant tasked with escorting Nerissa to the dining room who steps aside to allow her entry. She's flanked by the young priest from the docks and her damned shadow of a guard. Much to my disgust, my soldier bows to the woman standing framed in the opening — she has no title, just a claim. A claim I had originally thought to dispute. But as she stands in the flickering light it's undeniable. She looks just like Adelaide and my head clouds once more with desire.

Tonight, her slim curves are covered from throat to wrist and all the way to the floor in midnight blue wool with black embroidery trimming the high neckline, wrists, and the short train trailing behind her. The tracery of inky lines forms the intricate knotwork designs so popular on this island, irritating me at her show of loyalty to her homeland. How she could afford such garments astounds me — was she so good at whoring that she became rich? Was the pirate who took her so generous with his treasure?

Before stepping through the door she observes the men lining the walls, the table laden with food, then her eyes land on me. They show no emotion, her lips don't tip up or down, and for a moment I'm almost impressed by her apparent calmness.

The tall Northman is still dressed in the stinking leathers he's worn since their arrival. The brute's coarse attire and uncivilized visage disgust me. Anger surges to the forefront of my mind at the thought of him spending time with what is mine, but I shake it away as Nerissa finally takes a step forward into the dining room.

"Good evening. Welcome," I greet amicably, gesturing for her to sit down. She silently approaches the table, standing beside the assigned chair waiting for someone to pull the seat away from the table. I toss my fingers toward the seat and one of the guards steps forward to pull it out for her. He dashes forward, but before he can push the chair back in, the Northman steps in the way and does it for him, shooting a glare at the young soldier whose eyes lingered for far too long on her face. I'm surprised the younger man doesn't cower like a chided puppy, but to his credit, he merely steps back to his place along the wall.

"So many guards for a simple dinner, Dargan?" Nerissa's voice is low, and while she teases she doesn't smile. The disrespect in her address is noted but I'll ignore the slight. For now. "Where shall my priest sit? I want him present for our negotiations."

"Bring another place for the priest!" I call to the serving girl, never taking my eyes from hers. The deep indigo is depthless and the anger behind them simmers like a pot left to boil over, even as she breathes slowly and maintains a calm facade.

Good.

I look forward to stoking that fire.

CHAPTER 30

The young woman who was hidden in the corner of the room dashes forward with another plate and goblet for Daniel, placing it next to mine and scurrying off to bring utensils and a napkin. Her eyes drift up to mine once before she dips her head with the slightest smile and retreats again to the corner.

"So," Blackwell begins, fondling his goblet as I sit straight in my chair staring at him. I maintain my silence, allowing the tension to stretch out between us, and note that his fingers grip the goblet more forcefully the longer I hold my tongue. Enjoying the challenge, I merely raise my brow at him and wait for him to speak.

Finally, he takes a deep drink and insists, "If you wish to discuss our arrangement you must, in fact, speak."

"Indeed. However, I already made my proposal in writing. I agreed to wed you in exchange for my rightful title as Queen. What do you offer *me* in exchange for my presence to calm the rumored unrest in this country?"

"*Rumored* being the key word. Nothing you need to

concern yourself with. You'll have the comfort of the castle, of your title, what more do you need? Or do you wish to be turned back out to fend for yourself?" His words are harsh, his tone derisive, as though he knows exactly how I have fended for myself these years.

"We both know this isn't a love match, but this marriage can be mutually beneficial. My sources say you still struggle to win over the common folk. You're still seen as a foreign usurper. I can help endear you to the common people in exchange for me being able to live my life without the fear that's trailed me these past years. But I require the ability to help the people of Selennia. I will not sit back with the comfort of a title or as a figurehead for you to rule behind. You must allow me to visit the common people, to help them however I can, whether it be with charity or healing. I saw the ragged people on the docks, I saw the way the orchards struggle to bloom. Allow me to assuage the suffering that's followed in the wake of your arrival." I keep my hands in my lap to keep them from shaking, to hide the fact that I would much rather pull my dagger from its place at my thigh and thrust it through one of his dark eyes that rove unchecked over my body.

"You make many demands for someone who comes to me as a beggar. But, very well. Under the supervision of the priests, you may do as you say, for both our benefit. Charity is a Godly virtue, after all. It's the very virtue that convinced me to heed your plea when the messenger brought your missive." Blackwell's voice is laced with sarcasm and Charleston seems to be fighting with himself to keep from smiling. I bite the inside of my cheek so hard I almost bleed to force myself to hold my tongue as he continues, "But *you* must submit to my authority. The people must see that it is *I* who rule this country. *Not you.* You will convince them to convert to the new religion and abandon the wild ways and the Goddess some commoners cling to. Just as you have."

Breathing deeply, I finally reach to pick up my wine glass. Lennox steps forward, taking it from my hand before smelling it. He takes a sip, waits a few moments, then places it back in my grasp. Glancing up at him, I find his expression serious despite the dark wine staining the golden beard around his lips. "It is safe, my Queen," he mutters in a false accent strikingly similar to Erik's.

"Do you think I would poison my future bride at my own dining table, you cur?" Blackwell snarls.

"You stole this castle and placed Adelaide's skull in the front gates. How could I *not* be wary of your intent, Dargan?" I reply, taking a small sip of the wine. It's of fine quality, and I take a second drink before placing it down and sitting back in the hard, carved chair. Each time I address him by his name instead of an honorific I note Blackwell's jaw tightening further, sending a little thrill through me.

"War and conquest have no rules, Lady Nerissa. I assure you, I will not poison my future queen." Blackwell's voice softens, an attempt to put me at ease, something that will never happen in his dark presence.

"I agree with you on that, Dargan. Now, shall we discuss our marriage and my coronation? When will your priests be ready for the ceremony?"

"I thought it best we hold it on an auspicious day, one that would bring the most townspeople to view the union.

Perhaps one that aligns with one of the old holidays of the people so it can be celebrated for a proper reason instead of an uncivilized one. Don't you agree?"

The upcoming days silently tick through my mind. We've passed the Equinox by a couple of weeks and are only another couple of weeks away from… my breath hitches as I realize the day he means. "Beltane?"

My birthday.

"Don't the people here believe it's a day to usher in fertility? What better time to have our wedding? Then they will believe that our union — that *we* — are the reason for the health of Selennia. Not some fictitious Goddess or ridiculous ritual in the forest. And what better night to make an heir together? Unless, of course, I can tempt you to start on that task sooner?" His eyes rake down my body yet again, desire clouding his vision as he finishes his second, possibly third, goblet of wine.

"Your Majesty, that would be against the teachings of your church," Daniel speaks softly from his place at my side, saving me from snapping at the foul creature leering at me. I drink deeply yet again as Blackwell's attention shifts to the young priest.

"What was that, Priest?" he asks, as though startled the young man would dare interrupt.

"I only remind you, Your Majesty, that my mistress has repented of her past life. She has been cleansed of all sins, and it would be against the church's law to lie with the lady before you are wedded in the eyes of God."

A snort of laughter escapes Charleston before he can turn his head to cough, hiding the mirth that shimmers in his eyes. Blackwell's expression hardens, his fingers clenching the goblet and his jaw tightening as he grits his teeth so hard I fear they might splinter in his jaw.

"Something funny?" Lennox asks from behind me, his tone gravelly with irritation.

"Only a cough. There must be dust in my throat, heathen," Charleston retorts, pursing his lips into a sarcastic sneer.

"You will be silent," I chastise Lennox over my shoulder.

While our guards stare at one another with thinly veiled animosity, Blackwell's eyes meet mine, hatred and lust warring behind them, but I simply gaze up through my lashes, glancing away as I suck my lower lip between my teeth. When Blackwell speaks it seems I've won, at least for tonight. "You speak true, Priest. One wouldn't want to cause the lady's virtue, or the paternity of our heir, to come into question before our wedding night, would they? Now, let's eat."

The remainder of dinner is a quiet affair as I pick at the roasted meat and now cold vegetables that lay on my plate. Charleston continues to stare over my head, presumably at Lennox standing at my back, while Daniel eagerly shovels food into his mouth as though he can't be clear of the tension soon enough. Blackwell picks at his food, watching me as he continues to drink goblet after goblet of wine. When the servant girl steps forward to pour another glass he grips her backside firmly, drawing her close to his body.

The clatter of my fork on my plate breaks the silence and he immediately releases the girl, eyes flashing at me. "A problem, Lady Nerissa?"

"You will not grope the girl at the table, or against her will again, Dargan."

"You dare speak to me as though you rule this hall?"

"I dare speak to you about what is proper, regardless of who rules. If you wish to earn the respect of the people of Selennia — if you wish to earn respect from *me* — you will cease to act like a rutting beast and start acting like the *king* you claim to be."

"I will not have a whore speak to me about rutting beasts! God knows how many men you've allowed between your legs!" Blackwell pushes back from the table, staggering slightly from the wine as he shouts across at me, spittle escaping with his vitriol.

"And there he is. The *King* of Selennia." I curl my lip in distaste, unable to stem the sarcasm dripping from my lips as he gawks gripping the edge of his seat. "Make no mistake, Blackwell. I know what kind of man you are. I will be your queen. I'll help you rein in the people. I'll even agree to bear an heir to the throne when the time comes. But don't you *dare* presume to shout at me like I'm some timid servant girl. You will regret it, you drunken fool." Turning my attention to Charleston, I sneer, "And *you*, control your *king* before he embarrasses himself beyond repair."

Standing, I gesture to Daniel to follow. "Goodnight."

"You bitch!" Blackwell sputters and shouts at my back as I walk toward the doors. "You dare speak to me as if you are my equal?"

"*Calm yourself!* Don't allow her to provoke you further," Charleston hisses, causing me to wear a secret, satisfied smile as I walk through the doors and into the hallway beyond, giving the smallest glance over my shoulder to catch his amber eyes appraising me while he holds Blackwell from either stumbling after us or into the food on the table.

Our steps echo on the stone floor as we walk swiftly back to my wing of the castle. I hope the servant girl was clever enough to get out of the dining room before Blackwell took advantage of her. I can only do so much without tipping my hand this time, but his disrespect could not be ignored.

"I will hasten to say prayers with the other priests, my lady," Daniel says softly, taking his leave down one set of stairs as Lennox and I turn toward those that head up to my wing.

"You push him too hard," Lennox whispers as we climb the stairs. "If you don't pretend to be at least somewhat docile he'll figure you out."

Torches light our ascent, casting shadows over the stone walls shimmering with inclusions of crystals in their polished surface, and I focus on the glittering flecks as his words sink in.

"I can't bite my tongue at all times, but I know I push too hard," I admit, silently admonishing myself for failing to ask any pertinent questions of Blackwell tonight. Instead, I riled the man and am no richer in knowledge for my troubles. "I have to let out some of the anger or else I fear I'll completely lose control over my power too early." As we walk, I run my hand along the smooth stone, caressing it as though it can soothe the fire in my veins. A rough, warm palm covers mine, fingers finding the grooves between my own and pulling my hand away from the wall. "He's repulsive."

"I know, my love. I know. It's all I can do to not stab him through the heart and drive my sword into Charleston's sneering face, but we must hold. We must allow our ships to finish their work and gather. Then we strike like you wished." Lennox's voice is soft, his breath warm against my cheek, my neck, as he leans over me to brush a kiss against my skin. "Only a few more weeks until they should be close by."

"Billy," I breathe, pulling him closer, my fingers gripping the leather of his jerkin.

"Nerissa," he replies, our breath mingling in the dim stairwell, chests pressing together.

I tip my face up to look into his eyes, then pull his mouth to mine. The scrape of his beard is still novel against the soft skin of my cheeks, and I smile against his lips as it brushes against me. Melting against his chest, I push him against the wall, deepening our embrace as he cups my face, moaning against my lips.

A throat clearing stops my heart and I jump back, nearly stumbling down the stairs.

"Are you two going to stop groping one another in the darkness so we can get on with this channeling business, or may I climb into my warm bed?" Delphine's voice finds me as she steps from the shadows above us.

"Delphine!" I gasp, hand pressed to my chest as I try to catch my breath.

"*Nerissa*. Your mark," Lennox murmurs, his face lit by the silvery glow of my sigil shining on my brow.

"I thought you had learned to cloak that better."

Delphine rolls her eyes, stepping down the stairs until she stands just above us. "You two will be the end of us all if you can't keep your hands off one another." She crosses her arms in dismay, but there's no malice behind her taunts.

Taking a deep breath, I close my eyes and the glow fades from my sigil, only the torches lighting our way once again.

"Are you ready for this?" I ask, looking toward where Delphine waits.

"I'll be fine. The question is, will *you*?" she returns.

"I guess we'll find out," I sigh, squeezing Lennox's hand tightly once before pulling mine free and following Delphine up the remaining stairs.

CHAPTER 31

Delphine and Lennox wait in the hallway, bidding me good evening for the benefit of the guards at the end of the hall before I enter my room for the night. We decided the best way to conceal Lennox being in my room would be to make it appear that Delphine sneaks him into hers often.

Lyra waits perched on one of the plain wooden chairs when I step into my chambers. She and Delphine must have eaten their evening meal here since a half-empty tray and decanter sit on the polished table. The rug has already been rolled up and moved aside, and candles are placed around the stain on the floor in a circle large enough for Delphine and me to sit within. A few moments later, Delphine and Lennox enter through the adjoining door from the room Lyra and Del share.

"I hope they didn't expect too much of a show. You didn't seem nearly as eager to get into my room as you were with Nerissa in the stairwell," Delphine teases, earning an eye roll from Lennox. Hastening to my side, she waves her hand toward the candles and their flames flicker to life, illuminating the space.

Lennox stands with his back to the door after barring it with the lock and an additional board in case anyone were to think of intruding. It wouldn't do for the King's men to find us tonight. Lyra brings him what's left of their dinner, which he readily accepts with a smile.

Del reaches her hand out to me, taking my palm against hers and lifting her skirts to prevent them from touching the candle flames. Her touch once raised a spark of desire, but now it raises goosebumps from the nervousness of attempting to channel my mother. I have no idea what to expect, or if it will even work. Exhaling forcefully as if my breath will take my anxiety with it, I lift my skirts and step over the candles into the center of the circle at Delphine's side. She drops my hand as we sink to our knees across from one another, our skirts fanning out to cover the stones, leaving only the bloodstained portion in the center.

"Do you need anything, Del?" Lyra asks from outside the flames.

"Just a moment," Del whispers, blinking rapidly and breathing deeply, as though trying to calm her nerves as well. "I'm fine. Are you ready?"

Dipping my head in the affirmative, I take a deep breath as Delphine reaches her palms toward the bloodstain on the floor, pressing them flat against the stones and closing her eyes. The candles flicker violently as if a breeze blows through the window but all openings are sealed to the night air and apprehension tickles my senses.

For a few moments, a skin-prickling silence fills the

space. Delphine's breathing evens out as she looks up from the floor to meet my gaze. Her eyes are unfocused and soft compared to their usual challenging storm.

"Del?" I whisper, cocking my head to the side as I study this sudden change. "Are you all right?"

"My darling. Oh, my darling, Nerissa," Del's voice is soft and sad, so much gentler than she has ever spoken before. So similar to Adelaide's that I choke on a sob.

"Mother?"

"Yes. I don't have long, I can't risk using up your friend. But, Nerissa, I'm so sorry for what you've endured, for how I left things for you. I thought I was doing what was right, what would protect you, but I failed you terribly. One day perhaps you'll be able to forgive me for my choices." Del reaches out and clasps my hand urgently. *"We descend from the Goddess Herself, Nerissa. But when your father was killed I lost myself. I didn't know how to take my revenge as She did. I'm sorry for not telling you. I was a fool for thinking I could hide our love. Perhaps if I'd been less concerned about appearances I could have held the country with Gareth and Salome at my sides. I'm sorry for raging against the Goddess in my heart for his loss. I should have used that rage instead of burying it. I think... in the end... She heard me though."*

The vision-dream is fuzzy in my head now, only bits and pieces standing out, but I remember as Adelaide died I heard a howl. Was it the Goddess?

"I'm here. I'm alive. I will avenge you and my father, and all of our people, Mother," I answer. "I have enough rage for all of us."

"You do, my darling. You have enough love, too. I left you

what you might need. It's hidden in our spot, just in case. I thought you would have Seen it in your dreams. I sent them hoping you would See the truth. It's all there." Delphine's eyes cut to the wall near the desk before her hand raises to my cheek, caressing it, then brushing my hair back as she studies my face. Her expression hardens, resembling Delphine's normal state more than any look I ever saw Adelaide make. *"Take it back, my girl. Take it all back."*

"I will. I promise." I clutch at her hand, as though I can truly touch Adelaide once more. "I love you, Mother. I forgive you."

Delphine's brow creases as beads of sweat build and her breathing hitches wildly. A small drop of blood appears at her nostril, slowly trailing down to her lip.

"I love you, too, Nerissa. I've never loved anything more than you. I'm always with you. The Goddess will guide you, She's always protected you and will keep you safe. Now, I must go for the girl's sake."

"Mother!" I plead, having failed to ask any questions, so consumed by the surprise of speaking with her directly. I grip Delphine's hand as if I can hold Adelaide here, but Del gasps, shuddering, then falls against my shoulder breathing rapidly as her eyes flutter. The candles flicker and die, leaving only the torches on the wall and the small fireplace to light the room.

"Delphine? Del?" I shake Delphine's limp shoulders, pulling her against me as I sit back, wiping tears from my cheeks. "Are you all right?"

Slowly, Delphine's eyes open, returning to their usual focused and sharp gaze, glancing up at me and then over to

Lyra and Lennox who silently crouch outside the circle of now unlit candles.

"I'm… I'm fine. It hasn't happened like that before though," Delphine mumbles with a furrowed brow, wiping her nose with the back of her hand and smearing blood across her cheek. "I usually just see them, can speak *to* them. I've never spoken *for* the dead before."

She swallows, looking worried at the development, even as she pushes away from me and rises to her knees to try to stand. In her weakened state she stumbles slightly, relenting to Lennox who easily picks her up and carries her to the chamber she shares with Lyra.

When he returns he crosses his arms, leaning against the mantle over the fireplace, and watches me where I still sit on the floor with my palm resting on the stain on the stones. "Do you know what she meant? 'Your spot'?"

Standing from the stones, I lift my embroidered skirts and step over the cooling candles, then walk toward the window and the desk that still sits in the same spot it has for years. Striding behind it, I press my fingers against the stones of the wall, feeling foolish that I hadn't done so earlier. As I explore the cracks in the wall, my fingers find the spot I seek — a loose place between stones — and grip the single scrap of aged parchment hidden within.

My breath hitches as I pull out the intricately folded piece, shaped the same way notes from Adelaide had always been when I lived here. I *Saw* it in the dream of Adelaide dying, but for some reason, I only focused on her ending, not the note she tucked away. I cradle it against my chest, closing my eyes tight against the memories of

Adelaide. The times she hid notes for me. The times I didn't know I should cherish.

"Nerissa?" Lennox whispers from behind me, a large hand resting on my shoulder as I fold inward, trying to calm my thoughts and breaths.

"I'm all right," I reply. "It's all just… this is all so much. This has all happened so quickly. So much depends on me now." I sigh, but can't seem to pull in enough air in the closed-off room. Stepping away I open the window over-looking the courtyard and stare out across the castle walls toward the woods beyond.

"We're all with you, Nerissa." Lennox turns me so I face his broad chest, then tips my chin up so I look into his eyes. Through the window, the rustling of the wind in the distant trees carries the mournful call of the wolves who must still live deep in the remaining forest. The sound is so similar to the battle cry of the crews we left on our ships that my heart fills and my breathing settles.

Lennox is right, he's not the only one who stands with me now.

I'm not alone.

"I know." I give a tight smile as I place my palm against his cheek. "Let's see what it says."

Lyra slips back into the room through the adjoining door as I unfold the letter while Lennox paces in front of me.

"Is Delphine all right?" I ask, looking up at her before reading the letter.

"She said she will be. She's already asleep," Lyra answers. She crosses the room and sits on the edge of my mattress as I start to read.

. . .

My darling,

If you've found this it means I've fallen, but you've returned and remembered. I can only hope your homecoming is at your behest and not under duress. You'll find new histories beyond the wall, where I've kept my notes for you alongside the freedom you might seek. Keep your eyes down and ears open.

The Goddess will be at your side when the time comes. She has been waiting for you and I trust in Her to watch over you, even now, when She can't stand beside me. I've done my best to gather what you need to truly take the throne and save our home. It's up to you now.

I'm sorry I couldn't explain in person, but your father and I will see you in the Afterlife.

With all my love,
Mother

CONFUSION MUDDLES MY THOUGHTS AS I READ THE WORDS over and over. Adelaide wrote vaguely, not addressing me or giving any real information for understandable reasons, but I'm no closer to the knowledge I might need than I've been these past weeks at sea scrutinizing Salome's journals. With a grimace and growl of frustration I stand from the desk still clutching the letter, wrenching open my trunk and pulling out a bottle of whiskey I'd stashed before departing the *Bartered Soul.*

"What is it?" Lennox asks cautiously. He's stopped pacing and sits next to Lyra, watching me as I uncork the bottle and take a drink directly from it.

"More riddles to decipher," I answer with annoyance, handing him the parchment as I take another drink. Between the dinner with Blackwell, Delphine's channeling, and now the letter, I want to drown my thoughts more than I care to admit. The sudden urge to do as Delphine suggested, to walk into Blackwell's chamber and kill him outright, tempts me, but I take another drink and sit on the other side of Lyra as Lennox reads. Rash decisions within the walls of the enemy's court won't solve our problems.

"Is there a passageway?" Lyra asks, having taken the letter from Lennox's hands when he placed it in his lap.

"What?" I ask.

"A passageway? The letter says 'behind the wall'. Does she mean outside the castle wall? Or does she mean literally *behind the wall*?" Lyra's hazel eyes flick from the letter to the stone wall where I pulled the note free.

Looking across his niece, Lennox leans forward to meet my stare. "It's possible there would be an escape way for the Queen. What do you think?"

"It's worth checking. She never showed me anything more than the little notch, but maybe…"

I return to the wall quickly, the whiskey warming me as I study the stones and press my fingers against them. Gripping the stones around the notch I push and pull, tugging each one with no result. Lennox joins me, mimicking my motions until both our fingers are sore. With a frustrated sigh, I throw up my hands and lean back against the surface rubbing my hands together to soothe the rawness.

Suddenly, with my full weight pressed against them, the stones shift slightly, causing me to stumble back with a start as the wall begins to move. Lennox steps to my side and pushes against the wall with his shoulder, forcing it to move more until the space widens enough to allow a person to squeeze through.

"I knew it!" Lyra claps her hands together as she bounds from the bed to look into the darkness with both of us.

"Well, grab a candle. Let's see what she's left me."

CHAPTER 32

"You really didn't have any idea this was down here?" Lyra asks in awe, turning in place in the center of the open space we found waiting at the bottom of the worn stairs. Her feet rest on the full moon carved in the center of the floor, the rest of the phases spanning across the length of the room.

"No. None," I answer, just as mesmerized. Somehow we're only one flight down, yet I can't imagine where we're tucked in relation to the architecture beneath my chambers.

A light coating of dust covers the surface of shelves of books, ancient weapons, and detailed carvings that adorn the walls. Several tables are laid out in the space with more stacks of books and long empty inkwells accompanied by disintegrating quills. A painting of the Goddess, Her consort, and the wolf She supposedly morphed into — similar to the drawing Salome showed me in her office in New Aphros — graces one of the short walls that aren't lined with bookshelves. The other short wall has a heavy tapestry of the night sky covering it from floor to ceiling.

From where I stand at the base of the steps, it looks like the moon is the center point with constellations embroidered in the weave using silver threads that dance in the candlelight against the dark blue field.

I run my fingers over the dust, tracing lines through it as I walk around the edges of the chamber. A table sits in the center with a heavy wooden chair topped by a ragged cushion on the seat. A newer book waits in the center filled with Adelaide's looping handwriting — another journal. The sight brings forth a heavy sigh, both of nostalgia and frustration. Once again, the pain of her absence mingles with the irritation of her secrets as I flip through the pages.

Lyra sneezes, snapping my eyes from the turning pages to find her inspecting the tapestry on the wall. Lennox remains near the stairs, as though he worries we might be discovered.

"Looks like more reading is in my future," I mutter sarcastically, earning a small smile from him.

"Oh!" Lyra gasps, interrupting my thoughts once more, pointing at the tapestry. "Look! These aren't just stars."

Lennox and I both join her, eyes searching the tapestry. Close up the words are in fact names, but not names of the stars themselves. They're names of the daughters of the moon, the Goddess Herself.

The firstborn daughter of each generation is listed, some marked as high priestesses, but all queens. They spiral around the tapestry, creating constellations in the false sky until Adelaide, then me. The proof of Salome's tales in plain text on an ancient cloth. I didn't need to see it in writing, but the sight brings forth my emotions nonetheless and sends a wave of love over me at the acknowledgment.

Looking at the different names, two stand out. I can tell Lennox sees it at the same time I do because he reaches a hand up to gently touch the fabric.

Genevieve and Cordelia.

The names from Salome's journal.

The ones that were listed to discuss with Adelaide. Counting the generations back, my suspicion is confirmed: the sisters are five generations in the past, matching the timing of the waning powers of the Queen of Selennia and corresponding with the transition to her leaning on the High Priestess of the Central Temple for guidance.

"What happened to you?" I whisper, staring at the names. The way they're sewn into the fabric makes me wonder, *Why would both be listed when it should just be the firstborn?*

"It seems we have more questions than answers, yet again. But at least it's a start," Lennox sighs at my side.

"I should go check on Del," Lyra whispers after completing a circle of the room. "Do you need me for anything else? I can come back down right away, if so."

"No, thank you for your help. I'm not sure I would have found this so quickly without your idea," I reply, gently cupping the girl's cheek. The small show of affection lights her face, and she dips her head once before trotting back up the stairs.

Once she disappears, I start to circle the room, eyes scanning the tomes along the walls. Ancient pieces of my ancestry scattered around in a shroud of dust.

"Nerissa," Lennox calls, still standing at the tapestry, this time holding it away from the stone wall. "Come look at this."

"Freedom." The word Adelaide used in her letter suddenly makes sense when I reach his side. "This is what she meant by 'the freedom you might seek'." Behind the ancient tapestry, a narrow doorway is just visible in the stone of the exterior wall. A keyhole stares at me from the shimmering white bricks, but it's an escape nonetheless.

"Do you think this key matches the one you need for the garden wall?" Lennox asks.

"We could only be so lucky. But we still need to find it."

Hours later, eyes heavy with exhaustion and watering from the dust, Lennox and I climb the stairs back to my chambers. We haven't found anything resembling a key, nor have any of the books I pulled from the shelves at random told me anything enlightening. Lennox walks ahead of me and stands in the doorway watching as I hold my skirts up to avoid tripping on the worn stones.

Clank. I pause three steps from the top, my foot held aloft at the noise and shifting rock underfoot. Pressing my foot gingerly on the third step again, the sound echoes down the stairwell. *Clank.*

Eyes down and ears open.

"Everything all right?" Lennox asks from the backlit door.

"That's to be seen." I glance up momentarily as I crouch on the stairs, running my hands along the step to find out what caused the sound.

One of the stones wiggles under the pressure from my fingertips, not easily removed, but not secure either. Pulling my dagger from my pocket, I wedge it in the crack and pry it upwards, hopeful that I won't break off the tip of the steel. When enough of the edge is raised, I cast the dagger aside and pull with my fingers again until the stone comes away fully, revealing a compartment under the step.

"Hand me a candle, Billy," I murmur, holding my hand up. But, instead of placing the holder in my waiting hand, he sits on the top stair illuminating the space so I have both hands free. After clearing the stray cobwebs in the corners of the small opening, I reach in and pull out two slim books. Setting them to the side, another sweep of my hand brushes against cool metal, sending my heart galloping into a rapid rhythm to match my excitement. When I pull the metal from the compartment, I grip a key.

"Seems like luck may be on our side after all," Lennox whispers, a smile spreading across his face in the flickering candle flame. "Let's test it."

We replace the stone, then turn back down the stairwell to the chamber below. Lennox holds the tapestry from the wall while I fit the heavy key into the carved lock. Taking a deep breath, I look up into Lennox's eyes, then turn the key.

The door doesn't open smoothly, nor is it easy to slip through the small space when it does, especially for someone of Lennox's size, but it does indeed open. Lennox pokes his head through to find an empty courtyard outside the castle wall, close enough to escape into the walled garden with the other secret stone door with little likelihood of being seen.

"If this key works in the garden wall as well, we have the perfect way for Daniel or Del to take messages to the cave to send word to Erik and the others. We'll have to test it the next time we're able to explore the garden," I explain to Lennox.

"We can send Daniel and Del tomorrow evening to try

it. We need to get word to Tom in the caves to let Erik know that we need to be ready for battle on Beltane if that's to be your *wedding day*." Lennox crosses his arms with a smug expression. "It's the best time to show your might to the most people at one time. Don't you agree?"

"Yes. That gives Del time to rest so she can hide them, if need be. We can tell them in the morning. Should we write a note or just tell Daniel what to pass along?"

"I'll tell him what to repeat. We can't risk him being caught with anything written." I nod in agreement as Lennox runs a hand down my back, then turns to push the stone door back in place.

We may have no need of the doors tonight but my breathing comes easier and my heart settles into its regular rhythm again. I'm comforted now that I've found the key, knowing my friends can escape the castle should a sudden need arise.

Thank you, Mother. Thank you, Goddess, I think to myself, glancing once at the tapestry of my lineage as it falls over the door before we repeat the climb up to my chambers, my heart lighter and pocket heavier for our efforts.

CHAPTER 33

I shouldn't be affected by Blackwell's colors decorating the halls leading to the throne room after the sight of the changes in the Central Temple yesterday, but they still irk me. I remind myself over and over as Lennox walks just behind me that the banners and carpets are only textiles; their colors mean nothing. They'll all burn when I retake the throne. Even so, each scarlet- and coal-colored step makes my anger ebb higher in my chest like a rising tide crashing against the shore.

I haven't seen Blackwell or Charleston this morning — a relief, even if their men still stand guard at the end of my hallway. As we near the great doors of the throne room their voices are easy to discern. Another voice mingles with the first two, male from the deep tenor seeping from the small gap in the slightly open doors. If the voices weren't enough, the guards standing outside the door are all the confirmation I need to know the men are within, but they don't halt my steps as I near.

"It's unacceptable, Your Majesty! She marched up the

steps demanding to be left alone to worship, and with that demon of a Northman trailing her! I question whether that young priest she travels with has truly taught her properly with how boldly she acts," the third voice rants.

"Calm yourself, Father," Charleston answers. "Mind your tongue when you address your King."

"What is it you would see me do?" Blackwell adds, his tone surprisingly mellow and unimpressed. "She claims to have converted and her priest guided her appropriately enough at dinner last night."

"Remind her of her place, the place of *all* women. It won't do for her to be inciting rebellion when so many of the people refuse to properly obey as it is. It could be a threat—"

"A threat to whom, Father?" I ask, stepping through the doorway on silent feet to surprise the old priest where he stands before Blackwell and Charleston. "Good morning, Dargan. Charleston." I dip my chin in greeting, even if the action irritates me at its small submission. Lennox stands in the doorway behind me, arms crossed over his broad chest when I chance a glance toward him.

"Ah, my lovely bride-to-be!" Blackwell stands with a sarcastic smile. "We were just speaking of you, Lady Nerissa. Weren't we, Father?"

"We, uh… yes, we were."

Charleston's eyes glitter with suppressed amusement as the old man looks between the King and me with uncertainty.

"It seems I have displeased you in some way, Father? I had no idea my desire to pray alone in your church would cause such trouble. I merely sought comfort upon my return home. Something I thought your house of worship was designed for."

The old priest seems cowed as I stand before him in my modest gown, hands innocently clasped before me. I tilt my head to the side, my eyes boring into his.

"Well… Yes, it is… But you don't know your place! You cannot just—"

"And what *is* my place, Father? Beneath you? On my knees, perhaps? I'm to be queen, am I not? Does a queen hold less power than a priest, Dargan? Does a *king*? Are *these men* who truly rule here, then?" I feign confusion, looking between the priest and Blackwell.

The priest's eyes widen at my words, but he's too focused on Blackwell's reaction to offer a rebuttal. When Blackwell's jaw tightens and his eyes harden, I know I've said the right thing. His distaste for the priests he's used to gain control was evident on the docks, and then again when I used their rules to block his attempts at forcing me into his bed, but now the suggestion that *they*, not *him*, are more powerful has done what I needed.

"Father, you are dismissed. I will handle reprimanding Lady Nerissa," Blackwell states, waving away the man who scurries past me, ducking away from Lennox to escape through the doors. "Charleston, you and the lady's guard wait outside."

Charleston promptly steps from the dais, strolling past me toward the door. I turn to watch him as he ignores Lennox and walks into the hallway.

"My lady?" Lennox bristles, looking at me for instructions. Although I have no desire to be alone with Blackwell,

I have my dagger and, should I need it, my power. I dip my chin at him in dismissal as well.

The oak doors shut with a clank as the metal pulls strike the surface. When I turn back to Blackwell, he's risen from the moonstone throne and stepped closer to me. Not close enough to touch, but closer than I desire him to be.

"What brings you to my throne room this morning, Nerissa?" Blackwell asks, eyes lingering on my face as he inspects me.

"I had hoped to view more of the castle today. It's been so long since I've seen it," I reply honestly. The grey and white stone I remember fondly still shimmers in the sunlight streaming through the large windows, but the black and red banners soak up the light instead of allowing it to reflect around the space, dulling the awe I once felt here.

"I see. And what do you make of the changes?" he steps closer, still out of reach, but pitches his voice lower.

I swallow, looking into his dark eyes, hoping to push down the hatred and distaste. Deep lines cut into his skin, etchings from years of frowning at those beneath him, covered with a light silver and black stubble. The lines deepen as I take a moment to consider his question.

"It's all very different. I haven't had time to decide what I think."

"Hmmm… and what do you think of the priest's request that I reprimand you?" he steps closer to me, but I refuse to give up my footing in the center of the room.

"I think that perhaps you let the priests believe you follow their orders far more closely than you do if the desires you expressed at dinner last night are any indications," I reply coldly.

"Ha!" He surprises me with a loud chuckle. "You wield your words sharply, my lady. Both last night and today. What is it you really want coming here?"

"As I said — I wanted to see what you'd done to the throne room and to speak with you. I would like to take a horse into town to visit the people and see Aphros. May I?" I nearly choke on the request, but after last night I hope to soothe his bruised ego.

"Ah, a request. Interesting," he answers, as he circles me, forcing me to turn to keep my eyes on him. "What is it you seek in town?"

"Just to see how you rule, how the people fare. I've not been able to move freely amongst them in some time. Perhaps you could tell me news as well? The state of the coffers? How are the crops? These are things that interested me when I was younger and they still interest me now. I could be of assistance to you."

"Straight to the point then." He retreats back toward his throne, leaving me standing in the center of the room in the stray beams of sunlight streaking through the space. I hadn't noticed before that the sun forces one standing here to squint to see the ruler on the throne at this time of day, making it impossible to see their expression clearly at this distance. I tighten my fingers in the fabric of my skirt as I wait for him to answer. It would be easier if he'd just give me permission so I don't have to sneak a horse out at night to visit the town.

"You did say I could help the people, Dargan," I remind him when the silence stretches on uncomfortably.

"The crops fail because of the laziness of the crofters. But never fear, *our* coffers remain comfortable, regardless of how the common folk live. All thanks to men like the one who brought you to me," he answers, a cruel smile creeping across his face. "Criminals. Brigands. Pirates. They all serve a purpose for a time, and then when they don't, I dispose of them."

"So that's why you never stopped Lennox, or any of his fellow pirates, before? The payoffs? Not because his prowess at sea won out over your ships?" I press, looking up through my lashes, repressing the shudder at his admission — that anyone who ceases to be of use is killed.

Leaning forward to look down on me, his smile turns into a sneer. "Don't worry, piracy won't be an issue much longer. I've sent men to deal with the ones rising up and leading these raids on the coasts. Just like we'll deal with any who try to use your return to their advantage on land. You needn't worry about anything aside from calming the people, and looking pretty for me once we are wed."

"I see." My hands tremble with anger, gripping the fabric of my skirt tighter. "I hadn't realized there was such a threat from the sea. Are you worried for your men? You must be close with them."

"Very curious today, Lady Nerissa," Blackwell mocks, but to my surprise, he continues to speak, as though he can't help himself. "No. Charleston manages the soldiers. He's always been better at dealing with them, so I leave him to it — to recruit, conscript, or hire as he sees fit. I don't care what they do as long as they enforce my wishes."

"Oh, I see. When I saw you in your helm on the docks, I only assumed you were close with the men. Not like other rulers who allow them to win their battles for them, but then again, I don't know much about soldiers or warfare. As far as any fomenting rebellion — it's best if the people have affection for us *both*, of course. I'll do my best to win them over. Do you find that they enjoy it when you visit Aphros?"

"Oh, I don't visit the town. I have no need to see what the common folk are up to; that's what my soldiers and patrols are for."

"But, isn't it best for you to have the love and respect of the people? Not just their fear?"

Once again, Blackwell barks a laugh, as though I'm some kind of novelty for his amusement, a jester telling a joke. "I don't give a fuck about their love. Love didn't hold this land for Adelaide, but fear keeps them in line for me. Whether they fear my wrath, or that of God, it's all I need." He pauses, running his thumb over his bottom lip as he considers me and my request. "You may visit the town, the crofts, wherever you wish, Nerissa. Just be wary. I wouldn't want any harm to come to you now that you've returned."

"Of course. Thank you," I answer through my teeth at his condescension, my power aching to shine through as my irritation grows. "Good day, Dargan."

I spin on my heel and yank the door open, eager to escape his gaze but he stops me, his voice echoing from my back in the vast room. "Be prepared for court tomorrow evening, Lady Nerissa. You'll want to present your best self now that you've returned, won't you?"

Swallowing once, I turn to look over my shoulder and give a small nod before escaping into the hallway with Lennox on my heels.

CHAPTER 34

"What are *you* doing here?" I try to keep my posture relaxed and the anger from my voice as Commander Charleston strolls through the open doors of the stable while the groom finishes saddling the grey mare I rode a few days ago, but irritation is plain in my tone and I curse myself for it.

Lennox tenses, rising from the stool he reclined on to join me facing Charleston.

"Saddle up Leonidas," Charleston orders, spurring one of the other young grooms into action so that he pulls the large destrier from the stall at the end of the row. "Good morning, Lady Nerissa. I'm joining you and your party in the city today."

"I see. Have you a particular interest in the ills of the townspeople, Commander? Or merely coming along to spy on me like a good pet?" I stroke my hand down my mare's neck, calming myself as much as I soothe her.

"You should be careful, my lady," Charleston murmurs, his voice resonating in the quiet of the stables. "Your smart

319

mouth may rile the King, but it just might endear you to me yet." His grimace twitches, the red scar tissue tugging at the corner of his mouth as he smiles at me with a flirtatious glimmer in his eyes. The look sends a shiver over me despite the warmth of the cloak wrapped around my shoulders.

"Perhaps it's *you* who should be more careful. Especially with regards to how you speak to me, Commander," I reply casually. "One might think you're trying to woo me away from your king. Dargan doesn't seem like the type to share nicely."

The Commander's grin widens as he laughs. "Oh, Lady Nerissa, you might be in for a surprise if you think that. You can't believe you're the only one who allows their guard a taste now and then," he responds, then turns to inspect the groom's work as Lennox's eyes bore into his back. I swallow and meet Lennox's stare, worry written on my expression as we ready to mount.

Our party is small as we ride out of the front gates of the castle and down the bridge toward Aphros. Lennox and Charleston flank me, while Daniel rides in the back, bouncing roughly as though he's more suited to a wagon's bench than on horseback. Hopper, the grizzled guard who confronted me in my hallway the morning after I arrived, takes the lead, silent as we ride toward town. I would feel more comfortable with Delphine or Lyra at my side or with the young guard Ciaran at my flank since he was willing to share information on our first day, but this is a quick journey and no one expects us in town. I don't want to attract a crowd with my presence or garner too much attention with a large entourage, especially not with Charleston nearby in case anyone refers to the Goddess or my mother.

Since Blackwell agreed to allow me to meet with the townspeople, I'm determined to seek some out today. Then, I'll go through the nearby countryside in the coming week. The people in town live close to one another, residing over shops, in public houses, or in narrow rowhouses along the cobbled streets that make up the port city. Those outside of town live in manor houses or cottages depending on their station and occupation. These rural estates once dotted the fertile land between the castle and town, separated by orchards and crops. Breathing in the fresh morning air, I close my eyes briefly, letting the cool breeze and sharp clap of the horses' hooves on the pathway settle my nerves as I prepare to face my countrymen.

When I reopen them though, my heart sinks, any calmness replaced with unease when I scan the open countryside more closely. Without a contingent of guards lining the road or the nerves of our recent arrival riding me, I notice several of the crofters' cottages are damaged, their fields stand fallow, and no animals graze or call out for feed or milking. They would have suffered greatly from Blackwell's takeover since their homes were in the direct path of the soldiers who approached from the forests or the town. But after this long, why hasn't anyone rebuilt? Did they all end up like Ciaran — like all of us — torn from all they knew and now surviving however they had to?

"Charleston!" I snap.

"Yes, my lady?" he replies with a note of confusion, almost as if he's shocked I address him at all.

"Where are the crofters? The lords of these farms? Why does this land lay barren?"

"Collateral damage of a usurpation," Lennox mutters on my other side, barely audible over the hoofbeats.

"Their supplies were seized during the siege. Many didn't agree with that arrangement, or with Blackwell's rule, so they were taken care of," Charleston responds, ignoring Lennox if he heard him at all.

"And yet, after over eight years, they still lay in ruins? How does Blackwell expect the country to prosper if there are no crops? If the people starve? How is he making up for this? Who fills the granaries and stores?"

"No one will farm these lands, Lady Nerissa. It isn't for want of trying on the King's part. Maybe you should speak with the countryfolk you seem so fond of. Their silly superstitions hold that these lands are haunted. They say ghostly wolves and restless spirits prowl the land seeking vengeance for the death of the Queen. No one will set foot here to farm it. Not even the threat of punishment has encouraged their cooperation," Charleston replies. For once, no mockery laces his tone, even as he rolls his eyes at the thought of haunted lands.

"I see."

I swallow my other questions, and we ride the remainder of the way into town in silence. My eyes scan every bit of land that I can see from the road, goosebumps creeping along my skin at Charleston's words as the pit in my stomach grows with each empty field we pass.

When we reach the town, the older guard leads us to the back of a public house where the stable groom takes our mounts and leaves us on foot.

"Remain here, Hopper," Charleston orders the guard. Hopper nods once, sitting on the bench outside the stable to wait, ankles crossed casually as he settles against the wall. Then Charleston turns to me, crossing his arms. "Where to first?"

I walk just ahead of Lennox and Charleston, Daniel still trailing behind stiffly as though he's saddle sore from the short ride. We turn onto the main thoroughfare, the same one that was lined with townsfolk when we made our way up from the docks upon our arrival. Now that the sidewalks are bare and Blackwell's red celebratory banners are missing, the dingy shops stand in full view. Far from being the vibrant and sophisticated port city I remember, full of bustling shops and a busy market that I longed to escape to as a child, Aphros is dull with forlorn inhabitants trudging through the damp streets. Bits of rubbish snag in the cobblestones, some of the buildings themselves are in disrepair, and the scent of nightsoil tinges the air as we pass a darkened alleyway. All the crisp cleanliness I remember is wilted in the watery mid-morning light. Even the cries of the gulls at the docks sound like mourning songs instead of a greeting as I inspect the signage we pass.

"My lady, have mercy," an older woman pleads from a bench as we pass. She reaches out as if to touch my cloak, but Charleston grips her forearm roughly, wrenching her from her seat and causing her to cry out.

"Commander! Release her," I order, drawing stares from the few people on the street who dare look the man's way. I yank his grip from her as the woman kneels on the sidewalk, holding her arm against her hollow chest.

"No one is to touch you, my lady," he snarls, jerking his arm from my fingers.

"She's an old woman! How dare you treat her with such cruelty?" I chastise him, kneeling at her side. Lennox steps next to me, glaring at Charleston while I inspect the woman's arm. "What is it you need?" I repeat.

The elderly woman studies my face with rheumy eyes, her matted silver hair pulled back tightly from her haggard face. "Your Majesty, is it you? Have you come back?" Her voice is shaky and her expression is confused as she reaches up to touch my cheek with bony fingers. "Queen Adelaide? Are you a ghost?"

"No. I'm not Adelaide. I'm Lady Nerissa," I whisper, gently taking the woman's hand in mine. The touch of her cold fingers on my face is unnerving. They're much easier to tolerate held this way instead of probing my cheeks. "What is it you need?"

"Your Majesty, you've returned," the woman repeats, tears forming in her eyes. "The Goddess has heard our prayer. You've returned. You've returned." She begins to weep fully now, sobs shaking her frail shoulders as her cries grow louder. A middle-aged woman rushes from the door of the neighboring townhome holding a small child in her arms and looking both ways in a frenzy.

"Mother! Mother, there you are! Where did you — Oh! Oh, my lady! I'm so sorry," the woman says, pausing briefly as shock passes her face when she realizes who I am. "Mother, you must come back inside. Leave the lady alone. I'm so sorry, please forgive her. She's not right in her mind any longer. She hasn't been since..." The woman's voice dies as her eyes flicker toward Charleston who looms large, leaning against the side of a nearby shop. Lowering her voice she steps closer and says, "She hasn't been right since they invaded, my lady. Please forgive her."

"There's nothing to forgive," I reply. Standing, I reach out a hand to help the elderly woman to her feet. At my side, Lennox offers his as well. As her daughter wraps her free arm around the old woman I grip her bony hand once more, pulling her close and whispering so she and her daughter can hear, "And you're right, I *am* back. I'll do my best to make sure things are different going forward." I squeeze the old lady's hand before meeting her daughter's surprised expression. Then, I gently cup the toddler's cheek and smile before stepping away so they can return to their home.

———

THE NEXT HOUR PASSES MUCH MORE QUIETLY. MOST PEOPLE stay inside the homes and shops as we peruse the streets of Aphros, none as eager to speak to me as the elderly woman on her bench. I sense curious eyes on me as we pass by open windows, but don't attempt to draw the citizens out. They're understandably wary of me, especially with Charleston by my side. The time will come when I can announce my plans, but I can't show my hand yet, even if I wish there was a way to alleviate their doubts and reassure them now.

I haven't seen the city since I left for the temple, but I assume most of the more dramatic changes have occurred since Blackwell's takeover. They're similar to those I witnessed in Artemisia when I ventured out from the *House of Starlight.* But at least there, far from the watchful eye of the castle and king, trade and commerce still seemed to thrive, even if it was fueled by pleasure houses, secret payoffs, and contraband.

Aphros used to boast a busy market square where the local farmers sold their produce and goods, and fishermen carted their catch each morning to fill people's cook pots that evening. Several bakeries, butcher shops, and eateries completed the space, but now only a few remain and no one sells in the abandoned stalls of the square itself. The central fountain still spills water, but no one casts wishes under the carved crescent moon centerpiece, likely scared off by the only people who stand around the fountain now — a couple of black-robed priests handing out parchments and prayers.

"Are they from the Central Temple?" I ask, nonchalantly.

"The Central *Cathedral,*" Charleston corrects. "And yes, they come to prevent the leftover heathens from praying at the fountain. So they can direct them to salvation by the true God." His words are rehearsed and hold no conviction.

Does he believe in his King's God? Does Blackwell? I wonder, but keep my questions to myself as we pass the square and move down another street.

The seamstress shop, haberdashery, and cobbler remain in place, but several other stores on their street have shuttered, or are being used as living spaces. The windows are covered in old linens to block the view of the interior instead of being open and inviting.

"Why have so many businesses closed?" I wonder.

"Those moving from the countryside have piled into

the city, but they don't have coin for purchases, so the shops closed in favor of renting them out. Several families can fit in one shop, so it suits everyone," Charleston replies.

"Hmpf... I bet it does," Lennox drawls sarcastically.

"Don't your people live in one big hut, Northman?" Charleston goads, amber eyes glittering with contempt as he tries to rile Lennox, but Lennox merely flares his nostrils and continues to keep watch as we pass through the streets. When he receives no response Charleston continues, "Fewer ships arrive at this port to trade than they once did. Many prefer to anchor farther north."

I wonder why, I think, noting the patrols wandering the docks, more priests walking down from the hill, and the people surreptitiously scurrying away from them like rats fleeing a barnyard cat.

"I'd like to make one final stop, then we can go through the countryside and back to the castle," I announce, turning onto a street a block over from where our horses await.

The little bell tinkles overhead as we step into the apothecary shop. Charleston purses his lips in disapproval as we enter but keeps any protests to himself. I'm curious as to whether he will report every step of our visit to Blackwell and want to see how he reacts to me purchasing healing herbs.

"Hello, welcome—" the shopkeeper greets as the men step in before me, but snaps his mouth shut when he sees me. "Oh, uh, my lady. You aren't supposed to be here. King's orders." His eyes dart between me and Charleston.

"Hello." I smile. "I believe some of the rules can be bent just a bit, don't you? I had hoped you carried some new soaps. I prefer to select my own scents, you see, and I need a few simple herbs for tea. For my nerves."

"Ah, I do have some fine soaps and oils that ladies are permitted to buy. But as to the medicinals, that's something your priest should assist you with, my lady. I'm not at liberty to offer such items to you. Only God can truly offer the peace you seek," he answers, stumbling over his words as he stares at Charleston.

"Commander Charleston," I sigh, giving Charleston a pointed look. "Surely you can ask this man to make an exception for his future queen. I merely seek tea, not salvation."

"Give her whatever she asks for," he commands, waving his hand from me to the counter as if encouraging me to approach the shopkeep.

"Yes, sir," the man replies, dipping his head with fear in his eyes as I step closer.

After smelling a few of the soaps, I make my selection, then tell him which herbs I seek. His eyes widen as I place my order. It's obvious he knows I request things other than those for nerves, but he passes my test, nodding and packaging all the items quickly into a tidy bundle for me.

"No charge for you, my lady. Seek me out at any time you need," he whispers when he hands me the parcel. He glances again at Charleston, who stares out the window in annoyance, before crossing his arm across his body and placing his fist over his heart.

"Thank you, sir. I will." I grin then turn to head out the door.

Hopper meets us with a scowl in front of the tavern. "The people are getting rowdy, Commander. We'd best be off," he says softly, keeping pace as we stride by, heading toward the stable. As we pass, two men stumble out the front door. The sun hasn't even made it to the midpoint of the sky, it's far too early for people to be this drunk.

"Fucking barbarian," one of the men taunts, grabbing a stone from the street and throwing it at Lennox. Without a word, Lennox's sword is in his hand, a dagger in the other. The drunk seems dazed and backs off slightly at the sight of the big man now holding cold steel but his friend moves closer, staring at me.

"You traitorous bitch," he snarls at me, taking me off guard. It's one thing for them to challenge someone they think is a Northman — the prejudices toward them still permeate some parts of the country, especially with the rumors of their recent raids traveling down the coastline, even if they're at *my* command to rid us of Blackwell. It's another thing entirely to address me in such a manner. "Queen Adelaide would be sick knowing you were fucking that bastard in the castle."

"Step back," Charleston snarls, his sword in hand as he steps in front of me to stand next to Lennox.

"Go get on your horse," Lennox orders. Both men glance back at me to check whether I've obeyed, then refocus on the drunks.

"How dare you desert the Goddess, whore? How dare you side with Blackwell? Convert to his God?" the man shouts, his words cutting deeply, even though they aren't true. I can't deny his accusations out loud though or I risk revealing myself in front of the Commander.

Before I can think further, the man charges forward, pulling a blade from his belt in a drunken fury. I gasp and take a small step back, bumping into Hopper in my haste as my hand instinctively moves to my pocket and the dagger hidden within. Before the drunk can get any closer he chokes, gurgling on blood, as Lennox drives his sword through his chest.

"Get on your horse, *now*," Charleston repeats Lennox's earlier words, staring as Lennox pulls his sword free and wipes the blood on the man's shirt before sheathing his weapons. "Welcome home, Lady Nerissa."

Mounting quickly, we ride directly to the castle. I knew it would be impossible to achieve universal adoration from the people of Selennia — some may have truly converted to the new religion, some may feel like I abandoned them in the first place, and yes, some might believe that I side with Blackwell now — but it's sobering to face it in the streets, to see blood spilled for such things.

Leaving Charleston and Hopper in the stables, I make haste to my chambers with Lennox on my heels. He carries the package from the apothecary, any excuse for him to need to enter my chambers for a moment. As soon as we're safely behind the door of my room, Lennox grabs my hand and pulls me close, dropping the parcel and whispering, "Nerissa, are you all right?" He presses his lips to my forehead, then tucks me under his chin and holds me close against him.

"I'm fine. Are you?" I ask, pulling away to study him for a moment before laying my cheek against the leather of his jerkin once more.

"If it's a choice between your safety or the life of another, you will always win. I'm fine," he answers, speaking into my hair. "Is the town as you expected?"

"No, it's much worse. Even if the people don't trust me, they need the alliances we can bring. Selennia can't continue in the state he's driven it to." I pull away, looking up at him as I continue, "I didn't see any signs of latent rebellion, but I didn't expect the people to be forthcoming once I knew Charleston would be in town with us. Nevertheless, I don't think we can wait as long as we thought. I wish I didn't have this idiotic court event tonight so we could return to the study, but there's no way around it. Perhaps I can at least scout who may be potential allies or find out something useful to help rid ourselves of Blackwell."

"I agree," he replies softly, then runs his thumb over my cheek and kisses me quickly before resuming his post outside my door.

CHAPTER 35
BLACKWELL

"What did she think of her beloved Aphros?" I ask when Charleston storms into my study without so much as a knock. A smile creeps across my face knowing my commander's presence was likely a thorn in her side rather than a reassurance, perhaps it will have rattled her enough to keep her in line this evening. "Was she pleased to have you accompany her? Any surprises to encourage her to behave?"

"Why didn't you tell me you planned to have Hopper pay drunks to attack her?" Charleston snaps, hands pressed to the top of my desk as he stares at me. "I should have been privy to that. To be prepared."

"I knew you could handle it. I didn't want it to seem like you knew. I wanted her to know not everyone is happy to have her back. Reassure her she's safe with *my* men."

Each time I've come across the woman she's entirely too self-assured in her belonging here. She needs to learn her place. To show proper respect. Perhaps scaring it into her and showing her she needs protection from real soldiers will accomplish the task.

"Except *your men* aren't the ones who kept her safe. *Her* man killed the drunk, Dargan." Charleston throws his hands up in irritation as he details the altercation. "The Northman never even flinched, just ran the man through as though he was a bag of sand, wiped the blood away, and waited for more."

"Why didn't you take care of it?" I snarl. Anger burns through me as I listen to Charleston, and I feel my cheeks heating despite myself. Why didn't he step in and handle the situation?

"I didn't know if you'd want me running citizens through on the street," he challenges, his anger rising to match mine. "We already worry about rebellion; how do you think it would look should your second in command kill a drunk local? Plus, I assumed exercising temperance would make you and your soldiers more trustworthy to her. You cannot make these decisions without telling me, Dargan."

"We need to be rid of the Northman." Standing from my desk, I begin to pace as Charleston crosses his arms.

"How the fuck do you propose we do that? He guards her constantly. She's made it clear she won't stay without him."

"Who cares what she wants? We can hold her here and dispose of him."

"I have a feeling she might be tougher than you give her credit for. I wouldn't discount her fury yet, my friend." His words make me pause, as does the sudden smirk that tugs at the edges of his mouth.

"What are you talking about?" I halt my pacing to study my second. I can usually read him without trouble, we've been as thick as thieves since we met thirty years ago. Through the years we've grown to be friends, even if his challenges irk me. We know one another better than most, but something seems almost gentle about him when he speaks now.

"She barely flinched when the men came out of the tavern yelling. Even when the one spat at her and called her a 'traitorous whore' she stood her ground. For a moment I thought she might actually draw a blade herself the way her fingers twitched. It was quite a sight."

"Are you sure you didn't miss the opportunity to kill the man because you were busy admiring my betrothed, Russell? Are you developing a soft spot for the bitch?" Jealousy burns in my chest, but is it jealousy that my second desires the woman? Is it that he might somehow shift his loyalties to her? Or, is it because he speaks of her almost with pride in her actions?

"Oh, trust me, Dargan, *soft* is not how I feel when I think of your *lady*," he chides, giving a wink.

I choose to ignore his double entendre. "How did she react to their taunts? Did she refute the statements?"

"No. They berated her for coming to your side, but she didn't deny it or speak out against you at all."

"Hmph…" I had hoped she would stand up against the men and deny her alliance with me, but it seems she didn't take the bait if her true intention was to take over. The missive laying on my desk draws my eye and my ire once again, the information contained within what I was processing before Charleston intruded.

"There's something you need to read," I advise, handing him the letter.

"When did this come?" he asks after scanning the letter. "When did this happen?"

"The rider arrived shortly after you left. I sent him to the barracks if you need more details, but we need to send men to the eastern coast."

"If enemies from Delosia have already taken the fortress at Cybele there's no use. They can easily hold it and kill our men while they do so. This can't be a coincidence, Dargan. Her arrival on a pirate ship, these attacks… Use logic and end this engagement. Even if she didn't speak against you today, how do you know she isn't here just to incite the rebels? Cancel tonight's event and hang her for a pirate, mount her head on a spike like you did Adelaide for all I care." Charleston crumbles the note and tosses it on my desk, his words clearing any lingering jealousy over his loyalties. "She's beautiful, I'll give you that. I wouldn't deny her a place in my bed. But I caution you again, don't let your bruised ego from Adelaide allow her to steal the throne back."

"You know this island will only truly fall in line if I can bring her to heel. After seeing the glimmer of hope in them at the docks, I'm almost certain of it. Murdering her as an example would only cause *more* problems. She has a sharp tongue, but I can cow her. I'm certain that the small rebellions, the apathy of those conscripted, and the spiteful refusal to work will end if she cooperates and provides an heir. It will crush the final spark in her and in any who oppose me. It will prove that no one is coming to save them."

I return to my desk, pouring goblets of wine for myself and Charleston while he stands before me unconvinced. "Send a contingent east, and form another to send west in case of repeat attacks at Athene. Keep some on hand here of course, but I'm depending on you to protect the coastlines now. The castle can withstand an attack. Perhaps we need to move the wedding date up, after all."

Charleston doesn't move to take the goblet I push forward. Instead, he narrows his eyes as his jaw works, the muscles popping as he holds back his words. He's always been far too attached to his soldiers, it's why many are loyal to him and readily do as he asks — but what use are they if they aren't disposable?

"Fine. I'll write to hire some men I know from the continent to bolster our forces, but I can't guarantee they'll answer, or how quickly they can arrive. In the meantime, don't tell her anything. Don't let her know when to expect the wedding. If she's playing a game, even a long one, shake up the board as much as you can."

"Agreed. Now, send my man in to prepare me for this evening."

CHAPTER 36

Outfitted in an emerald green gown accented with shimmering gold floral and knotwork embroidery at the wrists, neckline, and hem that matches the gold jewelry that kisses my throat and fingers, I allow Lyra to place the finishing touches on my hair. She's woven gold threads through the thick plaits and curled the dark strands, pinning all of it back to accent the high collar of my gown.

Tonight, I dress like a queen — regal, reserved, elegant — hopeful that I can ingratiate myself with the courtiers in attendance and fool them into believing I've truly crossed to Blackwell's side, or that I'm a trustworthy ally if they themselves aren't in total agreement with the King.

"Are you ready for this evening?" Lyra asks as she inspects her work, then steps back to allow me to see my reflection in the mirror.

"Yes. Although I was never presented at court myself, I spied on Adelaide at parties and other functions enough to know what to expect. As long as the courtiers behave the way they always have, at least."

"Good luck." She smiles brightly even though it doesn't reach her eyes, then she gives me a quick peck on the cheek. Returning her smile, I smooth my skirts, more out of habit than need, reminding myself that my dagger is close at hand in a deep pocket, then turn to exit my chamber.

Lennox waits outside, still dressed in the leathers of a Northman instead of formal attire like the rest of the party will be wearing. The hilts of his sword and dagger catch the light of the wall sconces. The glimmer draws my eyes for a moment and highlights the dangerous aura wrapped around him. I offer a soft smile when he rakes his gaze over me, pleased at the hungry look in his eyes, despite the knowledge that he can't admire me like this openly beyond my doorframe.

"Good evening, my Queen," he murmurs under his breath with a half smile and a wink.

"Good evening. You look perfectly barbarous for court," I reply with a smirk.

"Good. Perhaps it will remind any who seek to get too close to you to think twice."

Sighing, I square my shoulders and turn to the end of the hallway, making my way to where the guards wait, the sound of Lennox's boots following close behind a small comfort.

"This way, my lady," a middle-aged guard greets me in monotone at the top of the stairs.

Before I can answer, he turns his back and leads the way down the stone steps and into the wide hallway below. I follow silently, unsure as to whether Blackwell holds court in the throne room or whether he will attend to his guests in the formal ballroom this evening. Passing the throne room doors we trail down the hall to the former library to find Blackwell waiting outside the door with Charleston in a fresh red and black tunic by his side.

As we approach, Charleston chuckles at something Blackwell whispers, then they turn their attention to us.

"I heard of your exploits in town today," Blackwell remarks once we are closer. "Did you even manage to wash the blood off yourself, Northman? Do you own other clothes?"

"You should be thanking him for protecting me. If not for him, I might not have been able to be at your side this evening," I reply coolly, looking between him and Charleston while Lennox remains silent. The muscle in the Commander's jaw flexes for a moment, but he maintains the sarcastic smile that I'm growing accustomed to.

"I suppose you're right. Thank you for keeping my bride safe. You will remain quiet and hidden away tonight, do you understand? I will not have my court thinking I support your kind after their attacks on the coast recently. And you—" Blackwell turns his attention to me, stepping forward so I can smell the clean scent of his soap.

This close, his dark eyes are like the roasted coffee beans I brought from New Aphros, just slightly darker than his wide pupils, and I swallow softly to keep myself from pulling away as he looms over me. "You, my dear, will mind your manners this evening. You will keep that sharp tongue silent and act the way a reformed harlot seeking refuge ought to unless you wish for any of the privileges you've bargained for to be rescinded. Do you understand?"

When I clench my jaw in response he grips my chin and forces me to meet his stare. "Well?"

"If you tighten your grip any further you'll have to explain to your court why my face is bruised," I snarl, pulling free. I'll concede to behaving tonight, if only because it serves my purposes. "But, yes. I understand."

"Good. You do look lovely tonight, I wouldn't want to be blamed for the ruin of such a pleasing sight, would I?" Blackwell chuckles, stepping back. "Now, walk with me so we can present ourselves to our court."

With that, he extends his arm for me to take. As I do, I sense the tension radiating off of Lennox, but he steps out of the way, obediently taking his place next to Charleston to follow us back down the hallway toward the throne room.

We once again pass by the oak doors, following the tapestry-covered hallway until we reach the ballroom. I don't pay close attention to the imagery woven on the cloth, focused on the heat of Blackwell's arm touching mine even through layers of cloth. I have to fight to keep from pulling away, reminding myself over and over to stay calm and in control of my emotions.

"How many people are you expecting?" I ask as we wait to be announced.

"Not too many; perhaps thirty. Mainly the remaining merchants and courtiers who live outside the palace in the countryside. The kitchen staff has laid out buffets and tables, much more casual than you might expect. I simply wish to show you off before our nuptials. Allow those of importance to get to know you."

Wish to prove I exist and have rumors of me being on your side passed through the country, you mean, I think to myself but nod my understanding and keep quiet. I'll act the part of a penitent, reformed sinner, come to beg for my place for him and his court tonight, if only to serve my own needs.

The din of people chatting and dishes clinking reaches us in the hallway, but after Charleston's sharp rap on the wood, silence descends as we're announced: "King Dargan Blackwell and Lady Nerissa Faelan have arrived!"

Two guards swing the doors wide to allow us to enter, the courtiers waiting within standing along the sides of the carpet runner to observe as we approach the dais at the head of the room. A quick glance over my shoulder allows me a glimpse of Lennox stepping to the side where he walks along the perimeter of the room near the long tables laden with food and drinks instead of behind us where Charleston follows. Despite the indifferent air I hope to present, my heart hammers in my chest knowing that some in this room might have been responsible for aiding in my mother's death, while others might readily support my return.

Blackwell indicates I should take a seat in the chair next to his, a false smile plastered on his face as I obey him to look out onto the fine silks and wools worn by the men and women of the court. Then, he sits next to me, waving over goblets of wine for us while the courtiers line up to greet their sovereign, congratulate him on his upcoming marriage, and admire his future wife. They bow and scrape before Blackwell, then turn to me, allowing me to study each one, hopeful that I recognize someone from before.

As their faces begin to blur, an older man bows before me. "My lady, it's wonderful that you have returned to wed our King," he says, rising with a smile. Something about him chills my blood, his cordiality seeming to hide something ugly beneath it.

"Thank you, sir. But, do I know you?" I ask, tilting my head as I parse through my memories. "You seem familiar."

"Oh! Well, I visited the castle often… before–"

"Before Adelaide was murdered?" I cut him off coldly, recognition sinking in. "You were on her council, weren't you? What's your name?"

"I…well, I…yes. I was. I'm Archibald Tiernan." He looks nervously between me and Blackwell, but the King has turned his attention to the next courtier and pays us no mind.

"And you remember me from that time?"

"You were but a slip of a girl. I didn't realize who you were when I saw you flitting through the halls. She didn't speak about her sister's child often." His fingers twitch on the stem of his goblet and he looks once more at Blackwell, licking his lips and rolling his eyes like a nervous horse.

Had he betrayed Adelaide? Had this man been responsible for confirming my existence once she was gone?

"But, you knew she had an heir? You confirmed that information so I could be sought out?" I press, leaning forward and capturing his gaze with mine in challenge.

"Well, my lady, I knew you were at the castle for a time and then that you'd departed. I didn't think–"

"What's all this, Tiernan?" Blackwell turns, finally noting the apprehension growing in the older man.

"Lord Tiernan is simply telling me of how he recognized me from when I was a girl, weren't you, sir?" I answer for the man.

"Yes, yes, I was. I remembered her from when the Queen ruled."

"Ah, well, isn't that nice." Blackwell's voice has turned icy as he looks between the two of us. "You're excused, Tiernan."

"Yes, Your Majesty. Lovely to see you again, my lady." Tiernan almost falls over his feet turning away so quickly to escape my stare.

"Fond memories?" Blackwell questions as I watch the man retreat.

"I barely remember him. Though, I confess I'm surprised you would allow someone so close to my aunt to live in your court."

"Ah, he aided in my conquests and has proved valuable since then with his connections to the common people. You never dispose of something so valuable until you're certain you've used it to its full advantage." He chuckles, suddenly gripping my hand in what appears to be a good-natured squeeze, but is bone-grinding.

"Indeed," I answer, taking a long drink of my wine and slipping my hand from his grasp.

Another hour passes sitting at Blackwell's side while people introduce themselves and fawn over us. The novelty of my presence dissipates quickly though, and many of them simply greet me and then continue in their conversation with one another as though I'm not there aside from a few sideways glances. Looking out over the sea of well-dressed guests nibbling on delicacies and drinking fine wine I sigh deeply — how did my mother do this for years?

The press of humanity around me is exhausting, more so even than being trapped on a pirate vessel with a rowdy crew. The false flattery and undeserved power within the room are infuriating, and I have to focus to keep from standing and walking through them and out the doors.

I once hid in alcoves dreaming of being exactly where I am now, dressed in shimmering silks and cloaked in frivolity. Now, I can't wait to escape to my room with the man I love and the people I trust most. Is that what Adelaide had found with Gareth? What she mourned so deeply after he died?

A few courtiers linger at Blackwell's side so I sit back, nibbling on little biscuits and tarts while quietly listening to their requests and reports, trying to soak up anything useful as they speak to both Blackwell and Charleston.

"The crofters north of here have tilled and planted. Time will tell if they reap anything from their efforts…"

"We may have to ask for taxes to be raised again, but I don't know if any of them will pay…"

"We may have to cut more of the trees to sell off to the mills on the continent…"

"A few rebels were found south of Athene, but rumors say the townspeople hid them before the soldiers could root them out…"

"The Northmen sailed away from Airmedan, but many have crossed the channel between the islands and the coastline and hold it still alongside the rebels there…"

"There's talk of wolves from the Cybelene woods. The peasants are becoming more restless on the edge of our manor than they have in ages…"

"My lady?" A deep voice surprises me, grabbing my attention from where it focused on the whispers around me.

When I turn to find the speaker, a man around my own age bows before me.

"Yes?"

"I wished to greet you and welcome you home. I'm Lord Gavin Delaney. My wife and I were pleased to hear our king has made such a fine match for himself," he replies, straightening to his full height with a gentle smile. His frock coat is simple, yet well-made, and his chestnut hair is combed back from his lightly lined brow. He waves at a blonde woman who stands nearby, inviting her to his side. She dips into a low curtsey before me, her deep plum skirts fanning around her. "May I present my wife, Lady Tieve Delaney? Some might call us superstitious, but we hope your return brings prosperity and luck to the throne and Selennia."

"Thank you, sir. I'm pleased to be back home and to bring the needs of the people to our king. Perhaps knowing you both will aid me in that endeavor." Gavin inclines his head in agreement but looks curiously at his wife. "You seem far too young to have been at court when Adelaide ruled, yet your accent tells me you're from this area."

"Ah, my father knew her well, Lady Nerissa. However," Tieve answers glancing toward Blackwell and Charleston before continuing in a softer tone, "he did not survive the siege. My husband took his place as Lord Delaney once everything was settled. Should you need a lady at court or anything else, feel free to call on our household," she adds with a gentle smile, even as her eyes bore into mine. "I heard tales of your struggles. I hope your time aboard that pirate's vessel was kind to you. We've all heard the rumors about Captain Lennox."

My eyes cut to Blackwell, but he's deep in conversation with another courtier. Charleston stands nearby, and I sense that he's listening much more closely. "It was much gentler than one would expect. Despite his reputation, the Captain treated my ladies and me with respect. I'm thankful to him for his service in returning me home."

"That's shocking indeed, but I admit it's a relief to hear," Tieve replies. She opens her mouth to say something further, but quickly dips into a curtsey as Blackwell turns in his seat toward us. "Your Majesty."

"I bid you good evening, my lady," Gavin says, bowing once more to me and moving over to speak with Blackwell. "Your Majesty, congratulations on a beautiful bride. My wife and I look forward to your wedding."

"Yes, she is a beauty, isn't she? I'm very lucky," Blackwell replies, running his eyes over me yet again. I smile briefly, then down the remainder of my wine, handing it to a passing servant, before standing.

"Thank you both. I'll keep you in mind should I need any additions to my household. Now, I fear I'm growing weary and must excuse myself." I dip a small curtsey to Blackwell, ignoring Charleston's piercing gaze and inquisitive expression, then nod to Gavin and Tieve before catching Lennox's eye where he's stayed tucked away behind a curtain all evening. Swiftly striding through the center of the room, I smile at the courtiers who dip their heads or bow to me, then meet Lennox at the door and slip from the ballroom without looking back.

Whispering as we pass back down the hallway, far from the guards at the door and those waiting at the stairs to my wing, I fill Lennox in as best as I can in the short time we have alone. "It sounds like small pockets of rebellion may still be present like Jackson told us; some hold Airmedan with the Northmen. The economy is shaky at best, but Blackwell seems to be keeping them in line. I need to speak with more of the people to see if I can find out what's happening. We need to ride out to the countryside. *Without* Charleston."

"I agree. In the meantime, let's keep reading and see what your mother might have found out."

I nod as we begin the ascent to my wing and then slip into my chambers for the evening, leaving Lennox standing guard in the hallway.

CHAPTER 37
LENNOX

The dust lays thick over the books we haven't browsed yet, covering the surfaces that were neglected in the secret study for almost nine years. My eyes itch from it each time I pull down a new book to hand to Nerissa or to thumb through myself, but I rub them and recline in the hard chair, flipping through texts alongside her each day without complaint.

She hasn't requested to venture into Aphros again, not since I killed the drunk that morning. Each time she claims she's all right I sense the falsehood. Even without her admitting it, I know her well enough to see the man's death bothers her, even if she would have killed him herself had he gotten close enough to be a threat. After our many conversations at sea, I'm well aware that she's afraid of becoming a tyrant like Blackwell, murdering people just because they don't agree with her, but I couldn't bear the thought of any harm coming to her.

She becomes more restless and withdrawn each day we sit in this dim room searching for the names of the two women on the tapestry with no luck, especially after the evening spent at court reminded her how much has changed and how suffocating life as a royal can be. Each day I bite my tongue and remain silent in the presence of Blackwell, Charleston, and the stream of taunts by the guards who stand watch at the end of the hallway. Nerissa and I both long to make a move, to strike Blackwell down now, and retake her throne. But we're both adept at waiting, and we must continue to do so until the time is right and our crews are close enough to aid us.

The approaching full moon likely has something to do with her moods as well. Even *I* feel its power tugging at me to leave the castle, my body begging to roam in the open forest beyond the walls in the night. I can't imagine how it feels for her and the other two priestesses kept within these walls. How she felt during those years in the *House of Starlight*. At least through all my pain I had the open skies and sea air to comfort me.

Sitting in the private space below her room, Nerissa allows her sigil to *glow* openly, trying to release bits of her power while hidden. She's struggled to keep it controlled recently since she's unable to freely use her gifts like Delphine does sneaking around in her shadows, or Lyra can by effortlessly ebbing and flowing with the emotions of those around her.

"What do you want to do for the full moon?" I ask, closing the book I've finished skimming.

"What do you mean?" In the silver *glow,* her indigo eyes study me, dark brows drawn down as if my question is a surprise.

"Do you wish to celebrate? To leave the castle for a ceremony? We have the key, the ability to do so." I nod toward the tapestry where the door to the courtyard hides, unable to hide the eagerness in my voice.

Selfishly, I long to escape the confines of the castle to hold her without worrying about being seen by one of the numerous soldiers prowling the halls at all hours. Even our brief caresses in the stairwell, and stolen moments when we take breaks in this study, feel like a single drop of water to a man parched in a desert. I wish for nothing more than for her to be happy, to take her in the moonlight under a blanket of stars, where I know her spirit will be lighter and her heart freer than it can ever be here in secret.

"Yes," she whispers. "I think we'd have to travel fairly far on foot to reach a sacred place without the soldiers seeing us, but I fear I must risk it. It's becoming harder for me to control my power and cloak my sigils. Every time I feel my temper flare it threatens to shine forth. Del and Lyra seem to be managing their power fine, but mine is aching to be used now that it's grown stronger. Even though they'll want to come, they'll have to stay behind. It's not worth the risk to *all* sneak out, especially if Blackwell suspects anything."

"We'll leave them behind with Daniel. Claim you're all praying with him, perhaps?"

She worries her lip as she thinks, still flipping through the pages of the journal she's opened on the desk. Glancing down as she flips the pages she pauses all movement, frozen in place by something on the page.

"It's them," she whispers as if speaking the words too loudly will erase the ink from the parchment. "It's the story we've been looking for."

Standing to look over her shoulder I scan the pages, locating the names she points to — the ones woven in silver on the tapestry hiding the doorway to the outside.

"They were twins," Nerissa reads, absentmindedly placing her hand over mine where it rests on her shoulder. "Genevieve was the eldest, the High Priestess-Queen. Her sister, Cordelia, was born a few minutes later and was next in line to the throne. But Cordelia was never strong; even from birth she was a sickly child." Nerissa's words fade to a rapid whisper as she reads, her eyes roving the pages for several quiet minutes. "Oh. I think I understand now."

"Understand what?" I ask, stepping back around the desk to pull my chair close as she continues to read.

"Cordelia was already weak, but at some point, she became gravely ill. Queen Genevieve tried to heal her. When she wasn't able to do it alone, she sought help from the other priestesses and even had her second, a high priestess who could channel like Delphine, try to channel Genevieve's strength into Cordelia. It drained Genevieve, but she wouldn't allow them to stop when they begged her to. She gave everything to save Cordelia and never recovered from it." She pauses, and when she looks up her eyes are sorrowful. "It killed her."

"Is that possible? To drain all your power like that?" I sympathize, understanding how someone could give up all of themselves to save someone they loved — I would have done it for my mother. I would still do it for Celeste, Lyra, and Nerissa. But even if I understand making that choice, knowing that pushing too far with her powers, like she's almost done several times now, could strip her of the power Salome died to give back to her, strikes fear into me.

354

"It must be. Salome did. It explains why following their generation the queens didn't wield power any longer. Cordelia was still weak, even after the channeling. She never had the power her sister did to begin with, but after Genevieve died, Cordelia refused to use what she'd taken. See, here—" She points and I crane my neck to read the words under her finger. "This says she cursed the Goddess for not protecting them and ended up deferring to the High Priestess for any source of power thenceforth. After Genevieve's death, Cordelia mourned for years. When she finally had a daughter, Cordelia refused to allow her to train in the temple, as was tradition for the queens before her. She never wanted her daughter to be forced to face the same kind of sacrifice and ended up cutting the next generations off from their birthright."

Nerissa's eyes flicker swiftly over the pages, soaking up the information with a knit brow. "That's also when the fear of shadow work gained traction. Cordelia banned Genevieve's friend, the High Priestess who helped channel the power that saved her, from the court in her anguish. Without an explanation from the Queen for her banishment, the commoners assumed the High Priestess did something nefarious. Rumor spread that instead of passing the power to the younger sister, she stole the Queen's power for herself," Nerissa continues reading, looking up at me from time to time. "This is horrible — that one person's fear and hurt can cause so much damage. How it can seep through generation after generation. Look at us now, all still suffering over the grief from a single death."

"And no one thought to question the reason until Salome and Adelaide." I sigh, wondering if Adelaide might have had the latent power needed to fight back against Blackwell if she'd only been trained like Nerissa was. It does no good to speculate, but if Adelaide and Salome had found this earlier, perhaps together they could have made a convincing stand when he invaded.

"Sometimes it's easier to just follow along instead of pushing against the current. Look at all the effort Salome put into this, and she still ended up essentially banished across the sea for her troubles."

She's right, but then, Salome did more good being across the sea than if she'd ended up slaughtered in Blackwell's takeover. At least she managed to save some of the women I helped escape and trained Del and Nerissa. Salome accomplished what she'd hoped, even if it meant sacrificing herself. Perhaps Salome had known all along, another secret vision she kept to herself.

"We need to tell Delphine and Lyra about this. I'll have Daniel touch base with Tom to share with Siobhan and Aisling. None of you can risk stripping yourself of power, not when you may need it more than ever. Promise me, Nerissa, no matter what, you won't drain yourself."

Her eyes are sad as they meet mine, and she takes a deep breath before whispering, "I can't promise that, Billy. If I could save one of you, how can I not?"

"You aren't the only priestess now, and Del can channel power; none of you need to make that sacrifice." My muscles ache from the tension running through me. I knew she'd never make this promise — it isn't one she can keep — but I can only hope my words will sink in and that she remembers them if the time comes for her to need them.

"I know," she answers softly, glancing back over the text again.

"Nerissa," I whisper, stepping around the desk and sinking to my knees at her side, drawing her gaze to me. "Don't sacrifice yourself for me. No matter what happens."

Tears line her eyes when she looks at me, turning in her chair so we face one another. "How can I make that promise when I know you won't make the same one to me? Remember what you said before? If we lose this, we lose together. I won't be separated from you." Before I can speak, a tear falls on her cheek and she pulls my mouth to hers.

"I know, my love. I know. We only have a few more weeks until this is done." I caress her cheek and press my forehead against hers, trying to change the subject. "Do you still want to visit the crofts in the next few days? I'll arrange for all of us to have horses if so, or we can take a wagon or carriage."

At her small nod, my mind turns to Ciaran. The young guard who spoke with her on the ride from the docks is always quick to bow in respect to Nerissa and her maids. Although he rotated through standing guard in her wing early on, I haven't seen him in these halls in a while but I can seek him out. "Ciaran said he had connections with the remaining crofters. If we can bring him to our side, he may be able to bring more of Blackwell's men to it as well."

"Yes, let's make sure we get through tomorrow night and then we can see who still lives in the countryside."

"I'll see it done."

"Ciaran, a word."

The young man's head whips in my direction when I find him standing guard in the main hallway of the castle the next morning. "Aye, sir… what is it you need?"

With a lift of my chin I draw him from his place, just a few paces down the hall into an alcove. It's far enough from his companion, an older man who never says anything when we pass, but not so secretive to arouse suspicion. "Lady Nerissa would like to visit the crofts surrounding the castle in a few days time. You mentioned when we met you that you grew up outside the city, so we thought you might be able to guide her during her visit."

"Oh! Well, I would have to check with my superiors, but I would be honored to assist the lady." Ciaran's face lights up with my request, a look I recognize from other young men who wish to be of importance to their leader. From this look alone, I can tell he's more inclined to side with his rightful queen than with the usurper responsible for the destruction of his life.

"Of course, you'd do well to say the lady asked for herself; they won't be eager to grant the wishes of a Northman."

"Yes, sir."

I give a curt dip of my chin and turn to go, but am drawn back by Ciaran's halting voice, "Sir? What am I to call you?"

"Excuse me?"

"Well, everyone has just been calling you 'the Northman' or 'the lady's guard', but what's your name?" Ciaran almost looks like he's afraid to ask, but no one else here has — they've all avoided me or looked at me with scorn.

"Ulf." Erik's cousin's name is a fairly common one and amusingly means *wolf* of all things in their mother tongue, so it seems fitting for me to borrow it for now.

"You honor me with your request, Ulf. I'm happy to assist my lady however she needs." The young man's eyes stare into mine, his expression harder than I've seen on his otherwise youthful face. A promise and an offering from him to Nerissa.

"Thank you. I know she will appreciate your words, Ciaran."

CHAPTER 38
SIOBHAN

Not knowing how things fare on land is driving me to distraction. We've only had reports from Tom gleaned from rumors and whispers in the taverns in Aphros, but nothing has come directly from our friends since Daniel's first report explaining the secret exit from the castle and the library Nerissa never knew existed. I worry for my Sister, especially after Tom told me about the man Lennox killed for threatening her.

My attention aboard *Andromeda's Vengeance* is pulled in so many directions that any attempt at scrying is dashed for lack of concentration and worry. When the visions do come, they bear down swiftly, yet are painfully unclear. I *want* to know how Aisling and Erik's family are in the north; how Nerissa, Lyra, and Delphine are surviving court life under the scrutiny of Blackwell; and how the other crews are succeeding in their missions around Selennia. Instead, I receive images of flowing blood, hear howling wolves, and am blinded by the flash what I can only assume is the sun glinting off steel. With the full moon set to rise tomorrow my power itches under my skin, as irritating as poorly spun wool. Despite this, I hope I might be granted a clear view of what awaits us under its light.

The last time I had a truly clear vision was in New Aphros alongside Salome. Now I plead with the Goddess that She will bestow something to soothe my nerves about my friends' fates.

"Siobhan, Tom returns," Erik announces, stepping into the cabin and pulling my attention from my musings. Smiling up at him, I stand and peek out the back windows to see a small boat bobbing along while the dark-haired quartermaster rows back to the ship.

"Perhaps he'll have had word from them today," I say hopefully. "How long should we expect it to take before we receive word from the *Hadriel*?"

"Not long now. Revna and Ulf should have had enough time to hit the important points along the northern coast and to recruit villagers from both sides of the channel between the Northern Point and the isles to hold the temple. Morel will have reached Cybele by now, too."

"I worry for Aisling. A ship would be a terrible place to give birth," I add, trying to dim my concerns for everyone else by focusing on Aisling's welfare.

Erik hums in agreement, smiling down at me even though I know I don't fool him. I've been uneasy for days now waiting for *some* news, either from Tom or the Goddess. The sight of di Micios being hanged at the port is still burned in my memory. We were forced to stand impassively on the deck of our ship as they branded him and strung him up like an animal. I continually worry for the fate of Lennox and my Sisters. Shuddering at the memory and those of other deaths I've witnessed at the hands of Blackwell's followers, I grab my cloak and tuck into it to join Erik on deck.

"Tom! Any news?" Erik calls across the deck when Tom's curly hair pops over the railing.

"Yes, Captain," he replies. "News from the Queen. Daniel said she and Lennox have found information that's imperative to be passed along to Mistress Siobhan."

My eyes widen at his words, wondering what could be directed to me specifically.

"Go on, Tom," I encourage.

"Daniel said that she found a journal explaining the loss of power in the queen's line. One of her ancestors drained her power trying to save her twin sister. The Queen died because she expended too much power and couldn't recover. Queen Nerissa insists you heed this warning — do not overextend your power or else you might lose it, or your life," Tom relates, dark eyes examining me for my reaction.

Erik wraps a large arm around my shoulders and pulls me closer while I absorb Tom's words.

"I see. Thank you, Tom. That *is* valuable information. I wasn't aware our power was finite, or that using it could cause death. I should hope it won't come to that."

"It will not. You will not expend all of your power, my love," Erik states, the command in his voice clear. "Is the wedding still set for Beltane? Any news on that front?"

"No changes that I know of. I've seen troops sent out from the castle, and the number of men on the walls dwindles by the day. They're staying on watch for longer hours, so I think the plan is working. Blackwell is spreading his men too thin, just like Lennox hoped."

"Excellent news. We will wait for Revna and Jackson to return and plan to sail the evening before Beltane. You are dismissed to return to your regular duties, Tom," Erik says. He won't be slated to return to the port for two days. In the meantime, if anything needs to be passed to us one of his contacts in Aphros is responsible for rowing out to us.

Just a little longer, I think.

Just a little longer until Beltane and the false marriage ceremony Nerissa is counting on as a distraction for us to strike.

I step to the railing and stare toward Selennia. We've managed to anchor hidden amongst some of the rocky outcroppings that dot the sea north of the port of Aphros without notice. It's a place that most ships don't dare seek out for fear of damage, and no cottages overlook the sea due to the inhospitable cliffsides, but the *Vengeance* is smaller and we hide successfully from any patrols that might seek out unfriendly ships. Erik explained to me when we anchored that Blackwell's navy has never been his strongest force. He depends on infantry and cavalry to police the island. Nevertheless, I catch myself scanning the sea for unfriendly vessels. Satisfied that we remain safe in our cove and pleased to hear our friends are still safe, I take a deep breath of relief. I'll be certain to give an extra offering in thanks under the moon tomorrow.

CHAPTER 39

A tingle of power surges under my skin as I pace like a restless beast in my chambers. It claws at me almost painfully, worsening each day I hold it in, and I fear my control over it will fail like it did in Salome's study if I don't let it free soon; exposing me too early and risking all of us.

I've kept it to myself, but each time my anger surges at one of Blackwell's slights, I struggle to hold my power in, to keep from cutting him and all his men down without regard for the repercussions. Now that I know what's at risk if I overextend my or my Sisters' power, it reinforces the need to wait until we have the full might of our crews before making our move to take over completely. I can't bear the thought that one of them might perish because of my failure and I'm not naive enough to think I can take over the country with my power alone.

Between the revelation of the journals and the bright white light of the full moon that taunts me through the open window, I can't calm my thoughts or soothe my spirit any longer. Tonight is my best opportunity to release some of my *glow* and call on the Goddess for aid.

The remnants of the roasted chicken and vegetable dinner I shared with Lyra and Delphine still sit on the table. Silence lingers in the room after we discussed that they can't join me outside tonight — we can't risk sneaking such a large group beyond the walls. As much as I want them to join me in ceremony, I suspect that Blackwell and Charleston may have instructed the guards to watch all of us more closely tonight.

Now, as I make another turn to walk past the table, both hazel and grey eyes follow me wearing down the carpet. Lyra accepted my decision without argument even though her disappointment is evident in the pout that turns her lips downward. Delphine remained shockingly silent when I explained why they couldn't come, but she's never hidden her annoyance well, sitting with her arms crossed and frowning at me when I meet her stare. Lennox stands guard outside my door and confirmed that soldiers remain at the exits of the halls on this floor, just as they have since the first full day since we arrived.

"Are you going to leave soon, or not?" Delphine finally presses, unable to bite her tongue any longer as she toys with the leg bone of the chicken resting on her plate, tapping it against the dish. "You're driving us both mad with your pacing."

Exhaling deeply, I look between her and Lyra before coming to a stop at the window where I stare up at the full white moon high in the sky to determine whether the time is right. Sighing once more, I stride to the door and open it.

"Guard, please send the priest in. I wish to pray; you may join us if you wish."

"Yes, my Queen," Lennox murmurs.

I close the door behind me, pulling my cloak from its peg and wrapping it around my shoulders in time for Daniel and Lennox to tap at the door and enter. Lennox quietly locks the door before looking at me expectantly.

"All of you stay in my chambers until we return. Try not to draw any attention. Should anyone seek to interrupt, please answer and tell them I'm at prayer and wish to be left alone for the rest of the night. If they attempt to enter, bar the door and retreat to the caves through the hidden exits. I'll leave them unlocked for you."

They all nod their understanding. Worry over leaving them behind gnaws at me, even if I know Lyra and Delphine both carry hidden knives and Daniel keeps a pair of daggers beneath his priest's garb. Although they've all been training since New Aphros, their best chance is to run rather than challenge any of the soldiers should my absence be discovered.

With Lennox on my heels, I snag a wineskin from the table, then he presses the secret spot to open the passage-way. Our steps are silent as we descend the narrow stairs to the small library chamber, then to the outer door where I peek out into the illuminated courtyard for any signs of activity before creeping into the moonlight.

Fewer guards walk the walls or prowl the castle grounds since Blackwell has sent men to the coasts, making our getaway tonight easier. Crossing the empty courtyard, we hurry through the deserted garden. My heart pounds in my chest so loudly I wonder if Lennox can hear it but he remains silent as I look around once more before inserting the key into the hidden door that opens into the forest behind the castle. I take one final deep breath, saying a silent prayer that no one waits for us, before turning the key and cracking the door. With a final glance behind us, I fully separate the vines dangling over the garden wall and step free of the castle proper, Lennox close on my heels. The forest is cast in a silver glow from the moon, strikingly similar to my sigil's light.

"Let's move swiftly. We can complete the ceremony and be back before anyone suspects us missing," Lennox says under his breath, placing his hand on my lower back. Warmth surges through my core at his touch, eager to complete the ceremony and steal a bit of time with him in the grove while we can.

The trees near the castle walls have finally begun to sprout their foliage, but it's mainly bare branches that whisper in the cool breeze as we rush through the remaining forest. Panting, we move as swiftly as we're able, veering away from the cut trees near the Central Temple, and not slowing until we're far beyond the sight of the castle.

By the time we reach the grove, the moon is high overhead, shining directly over the center circle that stands clear between the thick tree trunks. My heart lightens in the open air, relief flooding me at the discovery that the sacred place is untouched by Blackwell's blades, even as I gasp for breath after our flight. Freedom from the watchful eyes of the castle and the ability to hold Lennox close for the first time in weeks lifts the heavy weight of worry I've been crushed beneath.

We catch our breath as I remove my cloak and drape it over a stone at the edge of the trees then kick off my boots. I decided to forego my robe tonight, choosing a simple long-sleeved dress instead — if we'd been caught while I was fully dressed as a priestess, no excuse for my being in the forest would be believed. Not that I'm foolish enough to think I would be spared should I be caught anyway. Lennox stands aside, keeping watch, his eyes sharp in the bright moonlight as I stack a few larger twigs in the center of the clearing, close my eyes, and project my power to light the fire.

Since arriving on the coastline the power of the Goddess seems to pulse just under my flesh, and now I can barely contain it as the flames dance in the gentle breeze. Closing my eyes, it flows through me, the *glow* shining along my entire body as I offer a prayer. Standing amongst the forest I can feel the connection between myself and the trees that protect us, the soil beneath my bare feet, and the wind whispering all around us.

"Goddess, we've returned home. Even though you've traveled with us in our hearts, I know we're closer to you now, here on the soil of your forest, than we've been for a long while. On this night I make my offering to you, to ask that you return to us and aid us in our endeavor to reclaim this land as yours. As *ours*. I beseech you in reviving your island with us. In kindling the spark reignited long ago by Salome and my mother. Help me — help *us* — when the time comes."

After I speak, I pour half the wine into the fire where it sizzles and steams, then raise my voice in the song of the

Full Moon. Lennox sings softly along with me, his support warming my heart as it always does.

After our song ends, I look toward Lennox with a sultry smile. "Do we have time?"

"I'm at your command, my Queen. We have time for whatever you wish." His voice is thick as he approaches me, his eyes traveling over my face, then lower as he pulls me close to him, pressing me against the hard planes of his body that I've craved. My breath becomes ragged at the heat in his gaze. It's been weeks since we've lain together, always worried we'd be found out, even in the secret room beneath my chambers.

"I hate to say we need to make it quick. I'd love nothing more than to take my time with you, but I can't go another moment without touching you, Nerissa," Lennox whispers, tangling his fingers in my hair before his mouth slants across mine.

I'm breathless when we break apart, but he pulls away before I can kiss him again. Grabbing my cloak from the stone, he spreads it across the soft, forest floor before returning to me and taking my hand, leading me to the makeshift blanket.

Our mouths clash together as we sink to our knees on the cloak. Although I haven't worn my robe, my dress is simple and pulls over my head easily before I tug at the buttons of Lennox's breeches between kisses. Something feels different tonight between us, not just the urgency of our need, but the tingle of power still dancing under my skin almost in time with the rustling of the breeze in the branches and the pounding of our heartbeats. The moon illuminates the small clearing and makes the dark ink decorating his chest, arms, and scalp seem like shifting shadows on his tan skin as his muscles flex beneath them.

Pushing Lennox onto his back, I shift so I sit astride him, heat pooling in my belly at the sight of him ready for me. Desire sears through me, vanquishing any lingering worry about being tracked or caught by Blackwell's men. Mimicking our position on the beach in Delosia and the night of the rites, I slide myself onto his length gasping at the sensation. For a moment, the memory of the masked boy and girl flashes through my mind, but the breeze is cooler and the trees are bare — nothing like the lush warmth of midsummer's eve like our first night together. Gooseflesh rises on my moonlit skin, but the warmth of Lennox's hands on my hips overshadows the bite of the breeze as we begin to move our hips.

"Oh, Goddess," I moan, leaning down to press against his chest as we share slow, lingering kisses. Lennox runs his rough hands up my back, then tangles them in my hair as he cradles my head and kisses me deeply. Digging my fingers into the dirt beneath us, I can almost feel the spirit of the forest surrounding us like it did during the rites years ago when I committed to the Goddess. And Lennox, unbeknownst to us, committed to me.

As our movements grow more urgent, I sit up, pulling him up with me so we look into one another's eyes. The feeling that this is different than the other times we've made love deepens as we move, almost as if the emotions that flow between us are tangible this evening, buoyed by the blessing of our homeland, and my heart swells with the love that resides there. My release nears and Lennox wraps his arms around me, holding me close as I tumble over the edge, dragging my fingernails down his back. Hissing at the sting, he increases the tempo of his thrusts until he sighs my name with his climax. Our breath mingles as we pant, brows pressed together for a moment. Lennox runs his hands over my bare skin before kissing my forehead, my cheek, and then lower.

"This is new," he murmurs with a smile against my illuminated breast, glancing up at me with awe in his emerald eyes.

Blinking, I realize it isn't just my sigil or the full moon that shines — it's my entire body. My chest rises and falls as I catch my breath, but I'm confounded as to why I would be *glowing* when not in ceremony or battle. "Perhaps because we're home? Maybe it's a sign the Goddess heard our prayer? Did it feel *different* to you this time?" I still sit astride him, looking into his eyes, when I hear the twig snap behind me.

Lennox tenses and gently lifts me, leaving my questions unanswered as he pushes me to his side and reaches for the sword resting near his discarded clothing. I draw the edge of my cloak over me, scanning the forest beyond as I grip my dagger. Fear floods me momentarily as I curse myself for being so distracted. At least the illumination that surrounded me has faded and only the pale moonlight reflects off my bare skin now.

"Nerissa..." Lennox's voice is barely loud enough for me to hear him over my heartbeat, but when I peer into the forest my heart stutters and I suck in a breath as my eyes land on what has him staring motionless.

Just inside the treeline waits a massive black wolf, eyes shining silver as they reflect the moonlight. Panic surges in my breast as the beast steps into the clearing, its bright eyes staring into mine as it stalks forward.

The memory of the drawing Salome showed me during a lesson in New Aphros flashes in my mind — the Goddess and her consort alongside the wolf she supposedly transformed into — and all my fear subsides.

If my instinct is correct, this is no ordinary wolf. If I'm wrong, then I'll find out soon enough.

Rising to my feet, I allow the cloak and dagger to drop from my hands while releasing the control over my sigil and mark.

"*Nerissa!*" Lennox hisses through his teeth, grabbing at my hand as I step forward. At his sudden movement, the wolf's muzzle quivers, baring its fangs.

"Wait. Trust me," I whisper, squeezing his hand before prying my fingers loose and stepping forward again. Moving slowly, I approach the animal, keeping my eyes focused on it as I pad over the forest floor. When I'm only a few paces away, I reach a hand forward, palm up.

"Goddess? Is it you?" I whisper as the wolf studies me. Its forehead has a faint mark in silver fur, and in the *glow* of my sigil, the crescent shape is clear, matching mine.

For a trembling heartbeat, I worry that I've made an error, that I'll be attacked as I stand naked in the forest with my hand held out to a wild animal like a hopeful fool. But upon my second breath, the wolf whines and tucks its warm head against my hand then presses against my bare leg as I bury my fingers in its thick coat. A sob leaves my parted lips as I sink to my knees and wrap my arms around the wolf's neck, burying my head against the warm fur and holding tight to the comfort that floods through me.

"It *is* you. You didn't forget me. You heard our prayers."

———

THE FOREST AROUND ME FADES, REPLACED WITH THE HEAT from the she-wolf as I cling to her. Lennox calling my name vaguely registers as if he's far away from me instead of a few paces, but I can't stop the tears flowing onto the thick black fur, the years of heartache pouring forth from me as my chest fills with warmth.

The she-wolf emits a whine as she nuzzles against me, and suddenly images and emotions begin to flood my mind and take over my body.

As I watch, misery overwhelms my senses when a handsome man in a crowned helm is run through by a sword. Familiar blood-boiling rage consumes me before my body shifts to all fours, then leaps toward the man's attacker. Hot blood fills my mouth as the enemy falls beneath my bite, barely struggling as he dies. But sorrow overrides satisfaction as I howl in anguish for my lost lover.

Confusion clouds my mind when the taste vanishes, replaced by a tight hug from a young woman with tears in her eyes as she pleads, "Great-granny. *Mórai*. Must you leave me? Can't you stay?"

My voice answers, but it's not *my* voice. It's Hers, the Goddess, the she-wolf. "The time has come for me to depart, my dear. You have the power you need to rule. I've taught you and the others well, just like I taught your mother. Just call on me if you need me and I'll do what I can to help."

Then, the image of two girls with matching faces and

hair as pale as the moon's light playing in the forest flashes in the wolf's mind. Before my eyes, they transform into grown women, one supporting the other on a much slower walk along the path. The trees were so much smaller than those that surround us now, but the sacredness is the same. In a blink, one of the women is clinging to the other's limp frame, screaming her name while a wolf howls with grief in the distance.

Genevieve and Cordelia.

Soon after, the vision swirls and the wolf and I watch as a different cloaked woman rides from the castle, kicking her horse into a gallop as shadows wrap protectively around her. Tears cover her face as she pushes the horse into a lather, fleeing for her life. A bright sigil glows on her brow when she looks back over her shoulder — this must be the High Priestess who channeled Genevieve's power.

The memories change rapidly like I'm inside the wolf's mind, filled with centuries of memories and emotions as my power dims and I watch queen after queen pass through the castle without calling on her latent power or training in the temples. Selennia's protection, once provided by the priestesses, falls by the wayside and, even though they hold ceremonies and exercise some minor control over the elements, divination, and healing, the she-wolf — the Goddess — silently laments the memory of the strength they should be honing.

The strength she once gifted them.

With a sharp pain in my heart, another vision appears: my mother stands in the grove smiling brighter than I've ever seen. Her hair is shiny and black in the moonlight as she runs into the arms of a tall, lean man with dark brown hair and beard.

My father. Gareth.

The wolf's emotions flow through me, pride and love filling my chest as my tears flow harder, dripping onto her dark fur. I can just barely hear her voice as my mother says, "I'm with child." Gareth's eyes soften as he begins to cry despite his smile.

Again, the images change and the forest is choked with smoke, sending fear through my veins. Blackwell is here. The she-wolf's power has nearly weakened to its limit from sending so much of it to the land She loves. But She runs with a pack toward the castle, braving the ashes and heat on their paws. The coppery scent of blood reaches us. It coats the walls and seeps into the soil of the courtyard. The guards of the castle have perished; She and Her pack are too late. But then, the distinct scent of another's blood reaches Her.

Adelaide.

The prayer in Adelaide's mind reaches the Goddess. A prayer to watch over her daughter, the last heir. *Nerissa.*

In another blink, I'm transported to a different burning forest, watching through the wolf's eyes as a black-haired girl in a torn robe and covered in blood flees through an army camp into the burning woods. She struggles in hiding, but each night the wolf creeps to her side to keep her warm. To keep her alive. In the caves and crevasses of the mountains, she's watched over and comforted in secret.

"You saved me," I whisper, receiving a gentle whine in response.

Then, I see through the eyes of an old woman as I carry

the girl with more strength than I should possess into the hut on the edge of the mountains to revive her and strengthen her for the battles to come.

With a gasp, I sit back on my heels, feeling the chill of the night wrap around me in the absence of the warm fur. Lennox strides forward slowly, his footsteps barely audible at my back on the forest floor. Then, the warm wool and fur of my cloak wrap around me.

Throughout the visions the she-wolf's strength seemed to ebb and flow, as though the faith of the queens, priestesses, and people of Selennia sustain Her — regardless of where they reside. But She has remained here in hiding all this time. She's shown me through our connection that *She* is how I survived my journey to Artemisia, though She was weakened further in her human form. Now, I hope that the faith I've held close can return the favor.

"Nerissa? Are you all right?" Lennox whispers, kneeling at my side with a warm palm on my shoulder.

I nod, looking between my love and the she-wolf seated before me. "I think we all will be now."

CHAPTER 40
SIOBHAN

"Erik! We must sail!" I shake Erik's muscular shoulder harder than necessary, rousing him from deep sleep even though we've only been abed a few hours. The full moon illuminates our cabin despite the hour and I only have to use a drop of power to light the candle on the table.

My moonlit prayers have been answered in the form of a distressing vision in my dreams, clearer than any I've had in some time, waking or asleep. I can only hope the events I *Saw* haven't occurred yet, but the ice in my veins tells me we may be too late.

Erik's voice is thick with sleep as he turns toward me. "What is it, my love?"

"I've *Seen* something. We must sail north immediately," I answer, tugging a shirt over my head and pulling on breeches and boots while Erik does the same. "It's Jackson."

On deck, Erik shouts to those who are already awake, ringing the bell for the sleeping crew to rise and help with weighing anchor. Departing with haste, we sail from the rocks leaving the *Bartered Soul* and *Kraken's Maw* anchored under Pike's command as our canvas catches the wind. Hoping to speed our journey, I push some of my power forward, urging the wind to fill the sails and carry us to our allies' aid.

"Tell me again what you *Saw*," Erik demands as we sail north. The chill pre-dawn wind bites my cheeks so they feel as cold as the blood in my veins as worry continues to weigh heavy on my mind.

"Blackwell's ship was firing on the *Selkie's Tears* and the *Hadriel*. They were heading south to meet us but were taken by surprise. Jackson was lost, and Revna was severely wounded. We must reach them." I recount the vision, hands trembling from my panic as I use my power to will more wind to push us faster.

"Where was the sun?"

"What?"

"In your vision, where was the sun?" Erik repeats.

I take a moment to think back, closing my eyes to picture it again. "It was just fully over the horizon."

Erik nods. "We are not too late, then. We will save them."

His confidence shows in the hard set of his jaw and, for a moment, I think he might be right. The dawn is at least an hour off. For it to be as bright as it was in my dream we have a few hours. But what if it isn't even the right day? Worries flash through my mind, each more distressing than the next — what if we just left Lennox and Nerissa without allies? What if I've asked Erik to sail us to our own deaths?

But it's too late for those worries now. Our course is set and must continue until we find Jackson and the *Hadriel*.

MY EYES ARE GLUED TO THE HORIZON AS THE SUN BREAKS OVER it, casting a bloody light over the sea. The farther we sail north, the more I begin to think I was wrong. No ships come into view, even as we move quicker over the crashing waves. For a moment, I breathe easily — perhaps the vision was incorrect and this has all been for naught. Maybe we'll be there in time to sail with them and be on guard for Blackwell's ship.

Just as the thought slips through my mind I see the first charred board cresting over a wave. Then another.

Pieces of wood, then torn canvas float on the surface of the water as we continue north and bile rises in my throat.

When the first body floats by wearing the mismatched attire of a pirate, torso torn by cannon fire, my tears begin to flow in earnest. I search the bodies, trying to identify anyone through the burns and brutal wounds.

"Siobhan, you should go inside," Erik murmurs at my side, rubbing his hand over my back to soothe me as the waters carry more victims and debris toward us. I grip the railing, my fingernails aching with the pressure as I look for anyone we can pull from the sea amongst the wreckage. But not a soul cries for help, no one reaches for a rope to be thrown to aid them. I've failed them all.

"Captain!" Tom shouts, drawing us to his side of the ship where he points to the depths. A patchwork coat floats on the waves, partially ripped from the battle. Jackson and his crew are lost.

"I was too late." I turn from the sight, sniffling and trying to stop my tears.

"This is *not* your fault," Erik insists, but even if I believe him, I still feel the weight of shame for being unable to stop this loss.

"But where is Revna? Where is Blackwell's ship?" I wonder, dashing my tears with the back of my hand and looking over the bow to desperately search the open water. "There!" I shout, spying the smallest speck in the distance.

"Bring me the glass!" Erik roars over the sound of the sea. Tom comes forward with it, lips pulled down in a tight frown.

"It's the *Hadriel*," Erik announces, handing it to me to see.

Relief and panic war in me, hoping we aren't too late. "Go! Perhaps we can stop whatever comes next!" I plead. "I can move us quickly!"

Not waiting even a moment longer, Erik orders the crew into action. Pushing my power outward as I focus on the wind, the sails catch and we travel over the sea at a rapid pace. If I wasn't so panicked I would relish the sharp kiss of the cold ocean air on my cheeks drying my hot tears and the power thrumming through my veins. We near the *Hadriel* as a swift ship flying black and red sails appears from the coastline.

"*No.*" I force more power forward, determined that we will reach Erik's family before the enemy. My head begins to ache as something in my chest burns from the exertion, but I push past it, thinking only of the wind.

Breathing heavily, my power ebbing with use, we drift closer to the *Hadriel*. I spy Aisling's small figure on the deck next to Ulf and Revna waving at us. Blackwell's ship looms, turning so its broadside faces us, cannons at the ready, as though their superiority is undoubted and the two smaller vessels have no chance against their might.

When we come alongside the *Hadriel* Aisling shouts over the wind, "Siobhan!" to draw my attention. With one hand on her rounded belly, she holds the other out toward me and, whether it's because of our shared gift of *Sight* or just that we are Sisters under the Goddess, I'm certain of her intention. A long-buried instinct guides me, telling me what we must do. What the priestesses of long ago did to protect Selennia against its foes.

I don't allow myself to think about my past arguments with Lennox and Nerissa when I insisted that some of the men aboard the enemy's ship might be innocent. Now, I simply clear my mind and steel myself to push more strength into controlling the elements, even as my body protests after using so much of my power to get us here.

Together, even through my exhaustion, Aisling and I turn toward the oncoming ship and send our might toward it.

Several cannons fire from the enemy ship as we work together, grapeshot ripping through the railing to my right, while more lands in the water just shy of the *Hadriel*. Fear laces through me as more flies but between our wind and the distance they don't make it to our decks. Revna's muffled shouts carry on the wind and the *Hadriel* returns fire. Shortly after, the *Vengeance* does the same, the *boom* of the cannons reverberating under my feet, but I breathe deeply and ignore the noise and the threat of the dangerous iron that's sent toward us, focusing on the damage *I* can cause.

Screams from the men aboard Blackwell's ship travel

over the ocean as their masts crack from the force of the wind Aisling and I control. Remembering Nerissa's show of power off the coast of Nemi, I turn my concentration to fire, hoping I haven't overextended myself as I force heat and flames toward our foes. Aisling must do the same because the men's screams soon become more frantic. Some throw themselves overboard as an orange glow licks over the decks from both bow and stern, traveling up the broken masts, and catching the canvas of the sails before slithering down to the powder hold.

The ship's explosion is barely a distraction from the sudden, sharp pain that surges through my head as I continue to focus. My chest heats, burning as intensely as the fire across the water, causing me to stumble against the hull to keep myself standing. Something drips from my chin, but all I can think about is defending those around me and taking justice for those left dying in the sea from the *Selkie's Tears*.

Erik's voice calls over the wind whipping around me, "Siobhan! Siobhan, stop!"

His fingers circle my bicep as he tries to pull me from where I stand but I don't have time to respond before my knees buckle. Steady as always, Erik catches me as I collapse to the deck underfoot.

WHEN I AWAKEN, A COOL CLOTH GENTLY SCRUBS AT MY NOSE and chin. It takes a few moments for my vision to clear, blinking in the bright light from a lantern on the bedside table. Finally focusing my blurred vision, Aisling's tattooed face greets me with a soft smile.

"Welcome back, Sister. You had us very worried," she whispers, tilting her head toward the chair where Erik sleeps. He opens his eyes at the sound of her speaking and is at my other side in moments.

"My love, you must not do such things again." He grips my hand firmly, holding it against his chest as he studies my face. "You heard the warning from Nerissa — if you use too much power you could die."

"I'm fine," I soothe, but then I note the cloth Aisling holds. Blood stains the tan linen, just as it tints the water in the basin next to her as well as several other bloody rags at her feet. "Oh."

"Oh, indeed," Aisling says quietly. "You've been unconscious for several hours, Siobhan. Rest, my Sister. I think you'll recover, but you must be more cautious." Her eyes linger on me as she says, "Erik, I know you wish to comfort her, but Siobhan and I need some time to speak. About our powers, as *Seers*. As priestesses."

"I understand," Erik replies. He leans forward and brushes a soft kiss against my brow before rising from the mattress. "We are already on the way to rejoin Pike. Aisling will sail with us until we reach our anchorage. Take as much time as you need."

He strides toward the door, looking back once with a strained smile before exiting.

"Now, Siobhan. If you're feeling up to it, let's discuss what we've both *Seen*. Perhaps we can figure out how we can help win this and get all of us home safely."

CHAPTER 41

My body protests the bright sunlight that wakes me the morning after the full moon. My muscles ache after the long trek through the moonlit woods, but it's a satisfying kind of soreness as I stretch and sit on the edge of the featherbed. We snuck back to the castle a few hours before dawn, creeping through the empty garden and into the secret study before climbing the stairs and retreating to our rooms. There was a risk that Lennox would be spotted by the guards at the end of the hall but, when Lyra poked her head into the hallway, one was asleep and the other was wrapped around one of the serving girls, so he slipped out their door while Delphine pretended to bid him a blushing farewell. So far their ruse hasn't been questioned — it wouldn't be the first time a guard and a lady's maid held secret trysts.

The memories of the Goddess replayed in my mind as I tossed and turned before sleep finally took me, both comforting and distressing me in turn. I hope that my return will strengthen Her, that She and the pack She brought forth into the grove can come when I call.

With the she-wolf on my mind, mysteries about my heritage and Selennia's past swirl with my hope for the future as I nibble on the edge of my toast and sip scalding tea, straining to view the trees we worshiped under in the distance.

A brisk knock at my door has me spinning on my heel before Lennox steps into the room. "Are you ready for a ride, my pretty priestess?" he asks, his tone lighter than I've heard in weeks.

"Do you think we can slip away without unwanted guests this time?" I ask, tidying my hair and pulling on my boots under my wool skirts.

"Ciaran said he and another guard would accompany us. He seemed adamant about having this one as his companion, so I think we'll be unmolested by Charleston this time," he answers, drawing me close for a quick kiss and running his hands over my sides and hips.

I take a few more sips of my tea, stuff the remainder of my toast into my mouth, and grab my cloak from its peg before following him into the hallway. Ciaran waits for us at the top of the stairs, dipping his head low as we approach, then he leads us down, out into the courtyard, and to the stables where our horses are all saddled. Another guard, similar in age to Ciaran, is already mounted and waiting for us. He bows his head deeply, then waits in silence while we mount.

"What's your name?" I ask the young man pleasantly, but he only looks at me curiously, tilting his head in confusion before glancing at Ciaran.

"His name is Sebastian, my lady. I should have explained further when I insisted he come along. He cannot speak."

"Since birth? Or from injury?" I wonder, smiling at the young man. His eyes are gentle as he once again looks at Ciaran.

"Injury, my lady." Ciaran guides his horse closer to mine as we head toward the gate before whispering, "He was punished for speaking against the priests. They removed his tongue when he refused to repent."

"*What?*" I don't know why I'm surprised. I know the kind of cruelty the priests are willing to dole out, but seeing this man wearing the red and black of Blackwell gives me pause. "Why would he choose to serve Blackwell then?"

"With the conscription, there isn't much choice. He was already punished terribly for merely speaking out; can you imagine what they'd have done if he flat-out refused to serve?" Ciaran replies. "We've been close since I arrived though, I trust him. I think you can, too."

Sebastian meets my gaze when I look in his direction, then his eyes dart around as if searching for anyone who might be observing us. Satisfied no one is watching, he dips his head and crosses his arm over his chest before resettling his hands on the reins. Revulsion at the torture he endured churns my belly, making me glad of my light breakfast, but I'm pleased that the men in the barracks may not all be the villains I expected, reminding me of Siobhan and Lyra's counsel to offer leniency to those who might wish to return to my side.

Our horses carry us out the back gate of the castle and over the worn pathway through the forest toward the

Central Temple. We pass behind the temple and through the clear-cut stumps before reaching the edge of a field belonging to one of the closest crofts. Even from the road, I can see the thatched roof has collapsed inward and what used to be a barn is only charred beams. We ride in silence past it to the next, but I say a quick prayer under my breath for those who once lived here and for the land that surrounds it.

The next croft has rows of fruit trees out front, but they stand barren without leaves. A small flock of hens scratch in the kitchen garden next to the house when we ride up and a little girl runs from where she collects eggs in the coop to the cottage, her bare feet dark with dirt. Lennox dismounts and reaches a hand up to help me when a woman not much older than myself steps from the front door. An infant clings to her in a cloth wrap while the little girl with the eggs peeks from behind her skirts.

"Caitriona!" Ciaran greets brightly, tying his horse to the fence post and stepping inside the gate. The woman's grim expression transforms into a smile at the sight of the young soldier, and the tension in her shoulders visibly fades.

"Ciaran, you had me worried in your uniforms. Oh!" Her eyes widen when she sees me and Lennox step up behind Ciaran. She tries to bow, but between the infant and little girl, it's clumsy at best. "Oh, my lady! Welcome!"

"Mistress." I dip my head in respect. "Thank you for allowing us to interrupt your morning. I apologize if the timing is inopportune."

"No, never! You're welcome here, my lady. It's a surprise is all. How may I help you?"

"Ciaran is taking me on a bit of a tour. It's been a long

time since I was here last. I had hoped to visit some of the crofts and homes outside of Aphros to see how the people are faring. Yours is the first one we've come to that's inhabited."

"Ah, yes. I came into this one by accident, but it's served us well."

"May I look around?" I ask, examining the state of the home, which is in surprisingly good repair compared to the destruction I've seen elsewhere. The hens are fat and a goat bleats from the back of the yard. "I don't wish to disturb your usual routine more than necessary."

"Of course, let me show you." She frees her skirts from the little girl's hands, crouching down next to her to whisper, "Now go see Ciaran. He'll play with you for a bit while I show the lady around. You have nothing to fear, my darling."

Ciaran smiles at the girl and holds his arms open as he crouches down; she giggles and grins before running to him and wrapping her little arms around his neck. "Let me introduce you to my friend Sebastian. He's very quiet but very kind."

Standing, Ciaran carries the little girl with him over to the horses to meet Sebastian. The gentleness of these men reminds me of the guards I grew up with in the castle.

"My little brother is the reason we are here safe. My husband is abroad at the moment, but I hope he'll return within a few weeks," Caitriona explains, patting the baby's back, seeming to comfort the babe and herself in equal measure.

"Ciaran is your brother?" I ask, looking between them and noting the same dark hair and hazel eyes.

"Oh, yes! Did he not tell you? I'm not surprised. He doesn't want many people to know, just in case."

"In case of what?"

"In case of any retaliation if he were to anger the King, one of the other soldiers, or the priests. He doesn't want people to know he has family near to use against him. That's the way they like to keep people in line, you see," Caitriona says bitterly.

I hum noncommittally. Have I risked his secret by coming here today?

"But enough of that, *you* have to share walls with the beast," she says before clapping a hand over her mouth as her eyes widen. "I'm sorry, my lady. I meant no offense to the King, I—"

I hold my hand up to stop her from fretting. "You have nothing to fear from me; your words will stay here. It's a relief to speak plainly. It's been years since I was in this part of the country and to see it so changed is… painful. How have you managed? They say no one is willing to farm, but it can't be superstition keeping people from working."

"I fear the Goddess has been chased away, my lady. She cannot bless a land where people are afraid to call on Her. But not everything is lost." She leads me to the wattle fence that surrounds her kitchen garden and what I find is a world apart from the dead fields we passed on our way here. "I keep it hidden as much as possible to avoid questions, but you see, some of us do not fear to call on the Goddess still. This is proof."

The garden boasts vegetables and herbs, some newly sprouting through the rich dark soil while others wintered the cold season well and continue to thrive. Medicinal herbs are kept in one corner while rows of food fill most of the space.

"I share with the few neighbors I have and make teas and remedies from the herbs to trade in town when Ciaran can take them for me. I can't travel far these days with the little one, plus I fear being caught with them. But it does help, and it keeps us fed and able to help others when they need it."

"I'm pleased to hear that and to see that I may have friends both inside and outside the castle. As I said, it's been so long since I've been here and not everyone seems pleased to see me back."

"Oh, to be sure, my lady. I heard rumors of what happened in town when you visited. But I haven't met any neighbors who speak ill of your return. We're pleased you're here and can only hope you can help convince Blackwell to change the way things have been," she confides. "There's just so much fear of Blackwell and his men that most people wouldn't dare confront him now. A few challenged him after he first arrived, but not for a while now. Everyone's too tired and broken, but we haven't all given up."

After another half-hour, we take our leave. Ciaran passes a small parcel to his sister before hugging her and kissing the two little ones goodbye.

"Mistress," I call before mounting my mare. "If you should hear of anyone who needs help, please let Ciaran know. He'll be certain I'm told and if there's anything I can do, I will."

"Thank you, my lady. Thank you for visiting us. I wish you good luck and health." She squeezes my hand in hers, then backs away to stand behind the fence as we ride to the next few crofts.

The people in the next locations are less open, showing more fear than Ciaran's sister. Despite her reassurance that her neighbors are pleased about my return, they only offer guarded answers and silent stares.

Evidence that Blackwell's soldiers and priests have been ruthless with the people is visible in almost every home. Some are maimed, like Sebastian, while others have been broken in spirit by loss and hopelessness from attempts to stamp out embers of rebellion or dissent.

Sadness fills my heart as we depart the final croft, my hot tears barely held in check as I mount up to return to the castle. Riding through the orchards and fields I say more silent prayers to the Goddess for rebirth, the way I would have in the temple as a young woman with my Sisters.

Beltane nears, then the Summer Solstice, both dates of renewal and fertility, and I pray that those things will come to pass for the land and its people now that we've come back to restore it.

Returning to the castle, I watch the sun sink low in the sky, setting the clouds ablaze with its departure. For a moment, I force the fear of Blackwell to fall away and survey the land and forests kissed by the fiery light.

This is home.

My home.

Our home.

The power of the full moon ceremony last night, the return of the Goddess in Her wolf form, and this visit through the countryside have given me the boost I need to stay focused on the fight ahead.

CHAPTER 42

S houts of soldiers carry on the warming breeze that sneaks through the cracks in the shutters, provoking my concern and dragging me from the warmth of my bed the next morning. When I push the shutters open, the sun is higher in the sky than I expected but what catches my eye are the men moving briskly through the dusty space, milling around like insects toward the gates to look outside the walls.

Draping a light cloak over myself, I open the door to find Lennox and Daniel both in the hallway chatting in low voices.

"What's happening?" I hiss, looking between them.

"Come here," Lennox replies, motioning for me to follow him to the large glass windows. When I reach them I gasp, stepping back at the sight. From this vantage, I can see beyond the castle walls, all the way to the Central Temple, the forest, and the crofts we visited yesterday. The trees, bare of all but the smallest leaves yesterday, have foliage unfurling on their limbs in the early morning light.

A sea of varying shades of green spreads as far as I can see. Rushing to the other side of the hall, I stare out the glass with my mouth open as I look toward the path to the town where apple blossoms burst forth in pink and white in the vast orchards leading to the coast.

"Did… did *we* do this?" I whisper, my eyes flickering sideways to Blackwell's guards standing at attention at the end of the hallway. They stand in their usual places, but whisper to one another instead of focusing on the hallway and my door, intentionally avoiding making eye contact with me, their unease making it clear that *I* am the topic of their quiet words.

"I don't know, but I don't like it," Lennox murmurs. "I don't know if we're going to make it to Beltane, Nerissa. We already discussed it but we must hasten our plans if things like this keep happening. He's a tyrant, not an idiot. He'll figure it out. If not him, then Charleston."

"I need to be more amenable to him, distract him from these changes. I'll figure something out." Sundays are the day the townspeople are told to come to the cathedral to worship. Maybe if I show Blackwell that I can play nice he won't suspect my involvement with the blatant changes happening since my arrival. "I need to get dressed. Daniel, we should visit the church today to put on a good face with the priests on their holy day."

"Yes, my lady," Daniel answers more loudly for the benefit of the guards. "I would be honored to escort you to the cathedral when you're ready. Service begins in an hour."

"Wonderful. Thank you, Father," I reply, scurrying back to my chambers to dress.

Within a half-hour, Delphine, Lyra, and I are escorted to the cathedral with Daniel. Lennox waits outside under the newly leafed-out trees, casually running his dagger against a whetstone, while we enter the cathedral. At our appearance, the townspeople look confused, whispering fiercely to one another. It's as though they're eager to see me, to catch a glimpse of the future queen, but are unsure what to make of me being in the holy place, confirming my conversion to the worship of this strange God. I wonder how many have truly taken the priests' words to heart, and who is play-acting to save their skins. If the latter only knew how similar we are at this moment.

In my heart, even as I kneel, mimicking their behaviors as though I'm just as devout as they are, I know that this place is only sacred to the Goddess who ruled here first. It's to Her I now pray with my eyes closed. Thanking Her for the changes I witnessed this morning, and praying for what we might still bring forth in the weeks to come.

The old priest drones on about the blessings bestowed by their God, the prayers of their King answered by the lush growth on the trees, and I fear I'm going to have to drag Delphine from the building if she rolls her eyes once more.

"This is the final prayer," Daniel whispers to me as the room moves to kneel once again.

"Thank the Goddess," I murmur to myself, once again rising from my seat and sinking to my knees. My thoughts drift from the Head Priest's words, wondering how wide-spread the new growth is when I feel a subtle nudge from Daniel.

"My lady, I hadn't expected to see you here this morning. I would have attended to you myself had I known." Blackwell's voice forces me to open my eyes and look up at him from where I kneel at the end of our bench. Blackwell stands over me in the center aisle as the service ends, Charleston at his flank as usual. "I take it your Northman won't enter a holy place."

"I heeded Father Daniel's encouragement to attend. He reminded me that I needed to remember some of the teachings of the true God to adjust my temper," I reply, offering a shy smile while looking up through my lashes. "As far as my guard, he respects the rules of this house of worship. He waits outside for me since the priests made it very clear he wasn't welcome upon our first visit. Surely no harm could befall me in God's house. Although," I pause, tilting my head as though the idea just occurred to me, "I wonder, how do they expect anyone to feel safe or comfortable seeking guidance or exercising curiosity if they're so hostile? It was Father Daniel's gentleness that made me trust him enough to listen to his words."

Blackwell seems to straighten at my response, his chest puffing out, lips pulling into the semblance of a smile. Good. Perhaps a few gentle words of my own are all it will take to get him to forget any doubts that might have started to take root in his mind over me and my intentions.

"What do you make of the forest this morning, my lady?" he asks as if trying to imitate the demeanor I speak of. As though I could ever trust a man who keeps my mother's skull over his gates as a trophy.

"What do you mean? I was in such a rush to make it in time, I hadn't paid attention."

"The trees are blooming finally. It's been quite some

time since they were fertile; perhaps the cideries will be in operation again this year."

"Had they not been operational? You'll forgive me, I hadn't had the opportunity to consider the activities of the southern cideries in quite a while." I look down, almost as if I'm ashamed of my activities over the past years. As if it wasn't his doing that made me flee to the *House of Starlight* in the first place.

"The peasants cling to superstitious beliefs that the land was angry with me being king and that there was some kind of blight on their crops. I told them they needed to figure out their planting and pray to the true God to get their affairs in order. It seems they finally heeded my warnings," he sneers, studying me as I still crouch beside Lyra and Delphine. The other churchgoers have already scattered since the service ended, trying to avoid direct contact with their king.

"Join me for lunch today. Your ladies are welcome to attend or they can go back with your priest." The request isn't a question; my attendance is expected. Delphine looks at me, asking with her eyes whether I want her to come, but I simply smile and dip my head.

"I'd be honored. My ladies will go back to attend to things in their rooms. They have the rest of the afternoon off, as is proper for a sacred day."

"Very well, come along then." He offers a hand to help me up and I just manage to avoid cringing away when my skin touches his, allowing him to guide me to my feet. Charleston's hawk-like eyes never leave my face, always watching to catch a misstep. I wonder if he's already seen something that I wish he hadn't. Has he told Blackwell anything he might suspect?

When we walk out the door Lennox immediately falls in line beside me, mirroring Charleston's place by Blackwell. Today is the first day we've presented a united front like this to the townspeople since I arrived on the docks, and a hush falls over the crowd as we descend the steps toward the waiting carriages. Lyra and Delphine follow Daniel to the one we arrived in, while Blackwell leads me to the other royal chaise. Panic rises in my breast when I see Charleston step up to ride on a seat in the rear, his smirk making it clear my unease is obvious to him. The bastard even pats the seat next to him for Lennox to join him.

Bile rises in my throat as I stare at the carriage, and my vision tunnels on the open door, knowing there's no escape now. I must enter the close confines with Blackwell alone or it will be evident — both to him and those surreptitiously watching us — that I can't stand the man. Or that I fear him.

Exhaling, I once again take Blackwell's hand and climb into the carriage. Lennox's nostrils flare at the touch but he climbs up to sit next to Charleston for the short trip back to the castle grounds.

"How did our priests compare to the one you hold so dearly?" Blackwell asks once we're crowded in the carriage and the wheels begin to turn.

"The service was lovely," I lie, offering a sugary smile to distract from the fact that I've managed to scoot as far from him as possible. "I hadn't had the opportunity to attend a proper one since my conversion. I'm mainly taught by Father Daniel. Do you often attend alongside your subjects?"

"No. I prefer worship alone, but I thought it would be nice to visit with them on account of the blessing we woke to this morning."

I bet you do, I think, fighting to keep from rolling my eyes. I doubt Dargan Blackwell has worshipped anything besides his own ego in his entire life.

"Thanks be to God for answering their prayers," I say, making a small gesture like so many of the worshippers did today. "I hadn't heard of the trouble when I resided in Artemisia. Has the issue with the crops been concentrated to just Aphros?"

"No. It's island-wide. But I don't suppose a whore would need to be concerned with the state of farmland, would she?" He mocks me, dropping the air of kindness he wrapped himself in for the benefit of the people. As if they think he's anything but a despot and a monster.

Swallowing any retort, I whisper, "I did what was required of me to survive and have since repented my sinful past. Is God's forgiveness not enough?" I cast my eyes down, fearing my hatred will bleed through my gaze if I look at him directly.

"Ha!" Blackwell scoffs, then runs a finger over my cheek, dragging it down the side of my throat before using it to force my chin up to look at him square in his dark eyes. "I think your past will serve us both very well. I admit, I was shocked when you showed up with a priest and said you'd converted. Even more so to see you praying this morning in my church. But you were very pretty on your knees." He leans forward, his face mere inches from my skin and I fight back a shudder of revulsion as he says, "Do you really insist on waiting for our wedding night? I'm

God's favored ruler on this island. I can wipe away any sins you might think you're committing if you just give in."

My heart pounds in my chest as bitterness fills my mouth. His touch, his words, and the lust in his eyes all make me want to lash out. To strike him down now. To throw out any plans Lennox and the rest of us have formed just to be free of this man at last. But I manage to breathe through the panic, closing my eyes briefly as I sit farther back against the window.

"Dargan," I breathe, hoping the shakiness in my voice is mistaken for something other than fear. "We must not break the laws of the church. I won't be a hypocrite in my place as queen. I wish to be a bridge between you and the people, not a laughing stock. I'm not a whore any longer."

Blackwell draws even closer, his breath hot on my cheek as he leans down, and for a moment I think he's going to kiss me. Instead, he whispers against my ear, "Are you not? Offering your body in exchange for a title?"

Suddenly, I'm the young woman frightened and help-less in an army tent unable to get away, the woman trapped against the crates on the dock in Athene — my heart speeding in my breast, my breath too shallow — nowhere to hide, nowhere to escape. Even though I logically know I could fight him, I can't breathe as his scent fills my nostrils and tears burn behind my eyes. Thankfully, the carriage stops abruptly and the door flies open, Lennox holding it like a footman at the gates of the castle.

"My lady," he nearly shouts. "We are back at the castle."

"Obviously, you idiot," Blackwell answers, sitting back from me with an irritated huff. "She's dining with me in my study for lunch. We have no need of you."

"You may follow and stand with Charleston," I direct Lennox, my breathing evening out as I recover my senses, smoothing my skirts with trembling hands. Even if I'm trying to appease Blackwell I don't dare risk being completely alone with him. I don't trust myself to control my power if he tries anything more than what he did in the carriage.

"Please, I need to return to my chambers for a moment. I hadn't anticipated dining with you and I need to freshen up for a moment if that's agreeable?"

"Of course, Charleston will bring you to me when you're ready. Charleston, go with Lady Nerissa and her man and bring her to my study when you're finished," Blackwell orders, taking his leave without a look back. I silently curse that *this* is the moment he decides to have Charleston accompany me when I need distance from his watchful eyes the most.

We march silently through the halls, up the stairs, and to my room where I promptly shut the door in both Lennox and Charleston's faces as I enter my chambers. They can entertain one another for a moment while I prepare myself.

Sorting through my trunk, I find the nondescript box of herbs I brought along with me from the *Bartered Soul* and pull a small pouch free — foxglove. I can only hope I can slip it into the wine or another liquid without suspicion. Despite refusing him in the carriage, I fear that Blackwell won't continue to accept my protests much longer. I take a moment at the mirror to smooth my hair, making sure no strands hang free from the tight chignon at my nape, and dab a small amount of perfume at my wrists just for the sake of "freshening up".

Lennox and Charleston glare at one another in the hallway, one on either side of my door, when I open the door with a smile.

"I'm ready."

The muscle in Lennox's jaw flutters briefly, but he trails behind me obediently as Charleston leads the way to the King's study.

CHAPTER 43
BLACKWELL

Why the fuck am I pacing like a nervous boy courting his first conquest? I wonder, walking past the fireplace inset into the floor-to-ceiling shelves covered in books I've never bothered to open. I have no interest in the history of this land, but the sight of the shelves bare won't do either, so I've let them stay. This was once the library but, like most of the other portions of this wing, I've reconfigured it to suit my needs. A door between this space and the room I've made into the King's chambers makes it easy for me to move between the two.

Adelaide used this wing for formal meetings. She frequently made me wait in what is now my private dining room for her to grace me with her presence, always sending me away empty-handed. The memory of her careless smiles and silly laughter set me on edge. If I'm going to play nice with Nerissa today I need to tuck that memory away.

Nerissa seems subdued this morning, as though the yoke of her new religion has reminded her that she's beneath me, finally. Perhaps she'll become more obedient after all. A pity, really. Part of her appeal was how sharp her tongue is, how pleasing it would be to hear her grovel and plead instead of mutter orders and retorts.

I can tell Charleston still has his reservations, even if he can't take his eyes off of her most of the time. He hasn't offered whether it's because he finds her desirable or if it's because her resemblance to Adelaide is uncanny. Either way, he doesn't trust her.

He's repeated it often enough, but I still don't understand how he can think this woman could possibly be behind the issues we face from the foreigners on our coastlines. Charleston doesn't trust *anyone* easily; he didn't trust me when we first met on the streets in our youth, thinking I was simply another lord's son out to taunt the street urchins. Once I showed him he could trust me, and that *he* could do the taunting, that all changed. My brothers finally had to offer me some respect with the scrappy boy at my side, and we've grown up and fought together ever since.

As if summoned by my thoughts, Charleston knocks once, then enters the study, Nerissa and her Northman at his heels. Charleston and the man look like they'd be happy to rip one another to pieces, but Nerissa is calm as she steps forward. Her hair is smooth, all the tendrils that tempted me earlier tucked away into a knot at the base of her neck, and her gown is as frustratingly modest as ever. If I expected her to seduce me, I was wrong. If anything, she seems *less* sultry than ever before with her eyes cast toward the rug underfoot instead of meeting my gaze. What game is she playing?

"I wasn't sure where to expect him to bring me. You've converted this to your study then?" she asks, looking around at the shelves of books, dragging her fingertips over their spines with an almost loving caress.

"I did. I modified this entire wing for my purposes; it's why your chambers have been left untouched. My bed chamber is just through the new door and, of course, the dining room is on the other side," I answer as I approach. She smells of vanilla and herbs, sweet and clean, but she maintains a respectable distance by taking a step back. Infuriating woman.

"I'm thankful for my chambers. It eases the pain of the other changes," she mutters, the first time she's offered any softness. "You mentioned lunch? Forgive me for being forward but I'm famished. I was running behind this morning and didn't wish to be late for the service so I haven't eaten anything."

"Ah, of course." I had a light meal brought up for appearances but it seems she took my offer seriously. Gesturing to the small table in the corner where a pot of tea, decanter of wine, and plate of cheese, fruit, and cured meats wait, I allow her to brush past me and slip into one of the chairs with her back to me. She eagerly serves herself, pouring tea for us both and selecting several items to place on her own plate.

"May I serve you?" she asks, looking up through her lashes as I circle her and the table. Her eyes are the darkest blue I've ever seen, like night skies able to bewitch a man into getting lost in the darkness.

"Please. I'd like nothing more," I reply, my cock twitching at the blush that travels up her slender neck and pinks her cheeks. She's talented, I'll give her that. Whether it's from her time as one of the sacred priestess whores or her tenure in the Houses of Artemisia, she clearly knows how to make a man want her.

While she piles food on the extra dish, I take my seat and watch Charleston's wary expression. His brow is knit with a deep furrow as he stares at Nerissa, then glances at her silent sentinel to his right on the other side of the door. As she places my plate in front of me and moves to take a sip of her tea the Northman is in motion, causing Charleston to grip the hilt of his sword and step forward quickly as well.

"My lady," the man says, pulling her gaze upwards. The way she looks at him chafes, a combination of adoration and fierceness she only seems to express when he's near.

He must go. *Soon.*

"What is it?" she asks, confusion momentarily clouding her face.

"Your tea. I must taste it first. For your safety."

"Oh, of course," she replies, shaking her head as though in her rush to eat she'd forgotten the precaution. She hands him the cup, its fine gold edge and delicate design looking ridiculous in his savage grip. He sips the steaming contents, considers it for a moment making a face, then hands it back.

"It is too sweet for my liking, but we shall see in a moment if it is safe."

The clock on my desk ticks while we stare at one another in awkward silence, my irritation filling the space in lieu of conversation until the Northman nods and returns to his place. As if someone would dare poison her when I need her.

"Satisfied?" I snap, directing it at both her and the man now staring blankly ahead of him.

"It protects you too, Dargan," she says in a low tone. "We both drink from the same pot today. One can't be too cautious with the rumors of rebellion."

"What have you heard?" I ask, trying to mask the bite of my words and only mildly succeeding. I need to know if she has somehow gleaned anything that hasn't already reached me, anything that might be used against me. She shrinks slightly as she eats as if she wishes she hadn't mentioned anything.

"When I was at sea there were rumors that Selennia is in decline because of the destruction of the forests and temples. Some said it was because the Goddess wasn't being worshiped any longer. Then I saw the state of the city, and orchards and fields with my own eyes. The people I met at the crofts seemed hardworking, it can't just be sheer laziness that caused such struggles for them."

"Oh. That old refrain." I wave a hand dismissively. "It seems we've finally weeded out the weak, sacrilegious ones who still clung to the Old Ways, and have the correct balance in place now. Didn't you see the truth of it today? Did you not heed the priest's words? God will provide and all will be well. Nothing for you to concern yourself with," I add, glossing over the reality that no one knows how the new growth happened so suddenly, and steering her from the topic of Selennia's economic situation.

If she didn't know about the crops before she arrived, then she surely doesn't realize how the coffers dwindle and that the threat of rebellion persists partially because of the state of the economy.

Sipping the tea, I have to stop myself from making the same grimace as the Northman — it *is* too sweet — but

Nerissa seems to be giving in to me and I don't want to offend her. Not when the possibility to capture her fully looms large.

"I see. I think it does them good for me to visit them. It shows that we aren't unaware of their struggles and offers a softer touch than your soldiers. That *is* something I can focus on, even if the rest is beyond me. It will make them love us, and in turn, we will reap the benefits of their cooperation once more," she says, smiling over her cup as she drinks the last bit, and switches to wine.

To love *her*, she means.

It rankles me that she's already ingratiating herself with the commoners. Will that benefit me in the end? Or will they all merely love *her* and wish to rid Selennia of me even more vehemently? We eat in silence while I grow more irritable reflecting on her words. Would she be honest about those she spoke with or is she already trying to turn the tide against me?

Charleston's suspicions skip to the forefront of my mind as I study her from across the table, admiring how her wine-stained lips wrap around a fig. I can't decide if I'd rather throttle her or fuck her on the table right now. Perhaps both.

Could she really be responsible for the raids on the coasts?

Has she truly converted, or is this all a ploy?

"Did any of them mention the Old Ways?" I ask, hoping my irritation doesn't bleed into my question.

Her eyes widen as she studies her full wine glass. The dark liquid quivers, betraying whatever emotion I've drawn from her. "No. We all know that's forbidden." She drinks deeply and focuses on her plate.

Lies.

While I watch her, desire and doubt warring in my mind, I wait for her to relax with the wine she consumes. But, as I narrow my eyes, she seems to fidget and become more and more uncomfortable with each passing minute that ticks by on the blasted clock.

"Something the matter?" I ask more gruffly than I intend. So much for a gentle seduction.

"Um… I'm sorry. It's rather… indelicate, but I suddenly feel quite… *unwell.*" Nerissa swallows nervously with a grimace as she wiggles in her seat. "I'm afraid I *must* excuse myself. Thank you for the meal, but… I need privacy."

She stands quickly, one hand over her stomach as she turns to dash from the study. Her Northman looks alarmed, glancing at me and Charleston with panicked eyes, then follows swiftly behind her down the hallway. The echo of his deep voice shouts, "My lady! Wait!"

"What the hell was that about?" Charleston asks, strolling over to pop a piece of dried fruit in his mouth.

"I don't know. Nerves perhaps?" I laugh to cover the doubts flooding my mind, drinking the rest of the tea once I've added more from the pot to cut the sweetness.

"Nerves? She's shed her clothes for *how many* men? Why would bedding *you* be any different?" Charleston chuckles, knowing my intentions for the day.

My heart starts to race as he speaks. *Am I so desirous of her that nerves are taking over?* I wonder. But, I don't have time to respond before my own stomach flips uncomfortably. Suddenly, the room feels too hot, the neck of my tunic too tight, and I'm flushed with sweat as my bowels gripe.

"Dargan?" Charleston stands abruptly. "Are you well?"

"No. I'm not. I must retire to my chambers. Keep watch and make sure she stays where she is. See if the guard falls ill. And send men out to deal with any countryside commoners still talking about the fucking Goddess. If anyone shows any sign of the Old Ways, make room for new tenants."

"I'll send a physician to you," Charleston mutters as I walk away.

"Fuck the physician, take care of these rebels."

CHAPTER 44

I spend the rest of my afternoon hidden in my chambers feigning illness. I slipped the foxglove into Blackwell's tea when my back was to him without notice, a blessing I thank the Goddess for. Since Lennox hasn't fallen ill, and I've made it sound as though I've been vomiting most of the afternoon, the suspicion that I poisoned the King has waned. Charleston has stopped by more times than I care to count but seemed satisfied after the last time he arrived, when I was sweaty, wan, and shoved a chamberpot of vomit I'd forced myself to bring up under his nose with a hostile shriek to curb his curiosity. He muttered something about bad food as he escaped through the door under Lennox and Delphine's scathing gazes.

As the afternoon fades to evening I finally relax, pulling one of the books from the secret chamber into my lap while I recline on the pillows against the headboard of my bed. Lyra and Delphine keep quiet company with me by the fire, whispering and giggling together as they practice with their powers, causing the flames to rise and fall or coaxing dried plants to revive. For a moment, I relax into the comfort of the down pillows thinking I've gotten away with my scheme and have escaped Blackwell's attention for another day; all while assuring him that the people are on his side and that my joining with him will be what he needs to rule most effectively. Even if his outright question about the Old Ways gave me pause for a moment.

We don't have many more days to wait until Beltane when we can finally drop the farce and show the people their queen is back and ready to defend and serve them. I'm growing more confident that our ships will be in place, even if I haven't heard which ports and temples are under our command. I only know that Blackwell has cleared out so many of his men from the castle that taking Aphros shouldn't be too costly.

All of that confidence and calm dies when I hear brisk steps on the stone outside my door, followed by Lennox's rough voice and another man's speaking in rapid whispers. A sharp rap on the door has me shoving the book under the feather bed, Lyra grabbing a needlepoint project she'd discarded, and Delphine smoothing her skirts to answer.

"My lady is *sick* for the hundredth time, you—" Del's reprimand is cut short when Ciaran fills the doorway. His eyes are wild even as he tries to remain in control of himself, hands clutched tightly together in front of him as though pleading.

"Ciaran? What is it?" I ask, rising from the bed and pulling him inside the room. "Please, enter," I command Lennox, who shuts the door behind him, making sure we maintain the air of propriety needed for the sake of the guards at the end of the hall.

"Look, my lady," Ciaran pleads, striding across the room and throwing the shutters and window open as he points towards the forest and crofts beyond. A line of fire travels through the forest, bobbing along in the growing dark. Riders with torches.

"What's happening?" I ask softly.

"Charleston came to the barracks earlier to ask for volunteers. Blackwell has ordered the men to root out any rebels in the countryside who have been talking about the Goddess. It's happening again. I have to go to my sister, her farm is the first they'll come to. I can't just stay here. Will you help, my lady?" Ciaran begs, tears welling in his eyes. "Can you speak with him? Make him stand down the men?"

"He wouldn't listen. He's already suspicious of me as it is," I reply, my heart stumbling with fear. How is he ordering an attack when he should be sick in bed? Have I caused this?

"So you won't do anything? You'll let this continue?" Ciaran's voice is no longer soft or pleading, anger replacing any love toward me at his assumption of my refusal.

"I never said that."

"Nerissa, what do you mean?" Lennox drops all pretenses and grabs my hand, surprising Ciaran at the familiarity.

"Speaking with Blackwell will do us no good. I'll handle this. You and Ciaran must leave the room and act as though everything is normal. Ciaran, if they ask you at the end of the hallway tell them I'm still vomiting. Meet me at the stable as soon as you can. Have my horse ready and one for yourself."

"And one for me," Delphine adds.

"And me," Lyra chimes in.

"I'll ride out with you," Lennox interjects, his voice steady despite the wariness in his eyes.

"Not this time," I state, cupping his cheek gently to soften the blow. He looks as if he plans to argue, but I don't allow him to speak. "If you aren't outside the door, especially after Ciaran just visited in this state, rumors will fly that either we're conspiring in here together, or that we've somehow figured out how to escape without using the main entrance. If you both leave and you resume your place then no one will be wiser."

"Lyra, can you even ride?" Lennox asks his niece. Now that he mentions it, I haven't seen her on horseback.

"Well…" She trails off nervously.

"She'll ride with me. It'll be fine," Ciaran responds boldly, his gaze traveling swiftly between Del, Lyra, and me. "I'll have three horses ready. Sebastian can let us out the back gate to the pathway."

"I'll meet you in just a bit. And Ciaran—" I grab his arm to stop him. "If you do this, there's no changing sides. It means you are sworn to me. You'll fight with us from now on. Do you understand? No one can know what you see tonight."

"I was already going to fight with you, my lady," Ciaran replies, resting his hand over mine for a moment before departing my chambers at a brisk clip.

"Nerissa," Lennox starts, pulling me close. "I love you. I trust you. But, for fuck's sake, be careful. Come back to me, or else I'll have to fight my way through all of these men to get to you, and I don't want to do that tonight with only Daniel for backup."

I drag his face down to mine, kissing him deeply before he rests his forehead against mine for a moment. "This is not the end, Billy. I love you. We'll be back as soon as we can."

With one last kiss, Lennox turns and takes his place outside the door. I lock it behind him, both turning the key in the latch as well as pushing the table against it, just in case. Pulling my breeches and tunic from the trunk I change quickly, braiding all my hair back and tucking into my cloak. Even if the spring weather has begun to show, the night air is cool and I don't wish to risk anyone knowing for certain who I am, should there be survivors.

Delphine and Lyra both changed into similar ensembles and wait at the secret door beside my desk. Gripping the key, which I now have on a chain to wear around my neck, we push the door open, then close it behind us. My sigil lights the way down the stairs and into the chamber below until I cloak it to open the secret exit. Delphine, wrapped in darkness, peeks into the courtyard, but it's blessedly empty. With the soldiers being sent beyond the walls, fewer patrol this area than I've ever seen so far. Our plan of thinning the soldiers is working at least, scattering them across Selennia. Nevertheless, Del cloaks us all in shadows so we can close and lock the exit and dash to the stable undetected.

Ciaran cinches the girth of the third horse, while Sebastian bridles the others. I run my hand over my mare's gleaming neck, for once wishing she wasn't a grey since her coat will shine under the waning moonlight when Sebastian's grin catches my eye.

"Is something amusing?" I ask, confused by his excitement. He makes a motion toward me and the horse, then makes a few more signs at Ciaran who huffs a nervous laugh.

"He thinks it's a suitable coincidence that you've been given a grey mare. The priests' holy book says death rides a white horse," Ciaran explains, sending a ripple of gooseflesh over me, but whether it's from excitement or nerves I don't know.

"Let's hope it's death for the right people," Delphine murmurs, accepting a leg up from Sebastian.

Ciaran helps me mount, then gets Lyra settled in the saddle in front of him.

"Ready? Sebastian can open the gate in a few moments."

"There's no time. Let's go," I answer, turning the mare toward the exit and sending a blast of wind so strong the gates fly open. The few guards on the parapets shout and stumble in the heavy breeze as their vision is momentarily blinded by shadows. The heavy black mist muffles the thud of our hooves as we gallop from the castle grounds.

THE STEADY BEAT OF HOOVES AND RAPID BREATHS OF OUR horses is the only sound that accompanies us as we ride through the dark forest. Occasionally, the call of a lonely wolf reaches us on the breeze, making my heart swell with hope. The farther we get from the castle the closer and more numerous the howls become until the great she-wolf is running at my side. My mare shies for a moment but continues on as several more of the pack join us galloping through the woods.

The moon is still bright even as it wanes, and Ciaran's eyes grow wider with each addition. Lyra giggles and Delphine lets out a *whoop*, but all I can do is silently thank the Goddess at my side for Her help as we ride hard toward the crofts.

Smoke greets us, but thankfully it drifts from the already abandoned house we passed on the way to Caitriona's home. We can't be far behind the soldiers, but I push on at a hard pace, hoping the horses and wolves with us won't tire too badly before we can reach where we're needed.

Circling through the trees for cover, we enter the orchard at the front of the croft where Caitriona lives. The leaves fill the branches, casting shadows around us as we approach. Everything here is touched by the Goddess just like the trees near the castle. We're greeted by the wail of a baby and the panicked shouts of a child. Each cry sends a shard of ice through my heart as I hope we aren't too late.

From my vantage point in the treeline, Caitriona clutches her baby to her chest while her older daughter clings to her skirts in the front yard. Soldiers surround them, holding torches as the garden beside the home burns. One man stands close to the thatched roof, pointing to the flames and shouting at Caitriona to confess that she's been praying to the Goddess, but she stands quietly in response, her expression hard and full of hate.

I know that expression. I wore it myself as I was insulted by Crewes on the deck of the *Bartered Soul*, and as I allowed Blackwell and his priests to taunt me these past few weeks.

"Delphine, hide them when you can. Lyra, wait with Ciaran in case anyone needs you to heal them."

"And what about *you*? Shall I hide you as well?" Delphine whispers.

"No. I want them to see who comes for them." She nods, a vicious grin spreading across her pretty face.

I turn to the huge she-wolf still at my side. "Scare the piss out of them. I'll do the rest." She seems to smile, fangs gleaming in the moonlight as She and the pack drift through the woods, sending up a chorus of spine-tingling howls.

The sound causes some of the soldiers to look around, fear apparent in the wavering light of their torches.

"Alright, girl. Let's go," I whisper to my mare, confidence and power surging in my veins. Giving her a gentle squeeze, we walk beyond the cover of the trees.

"What is it you think you're doing?" I call out, silencing the little girl's crying and drawing the attention of all the soldiers. My mare gleams white in the moonlight combined with the *glow* of my sigil as we step closer to the men. Ten soldiers stand in the clearing staring with wide eyes and slack jaws at the sight of a cloaked woman suddenly appearing from the dark forest.

"Following the King's orders. Who the fuck are you?" The man holding the torch near the house regains his composure, moving toward the gate as I'd hoped.

I fold back my hood, revealing my face, my sigil, and the scrolling design across my brow.

"It's Blackwell's whore!" one of the soldiers scoffs.

Several of the men look at one another uneasily, afraid to take in my sigil directly but seemingly unable to look away.

I smile at the insult, lifting my hand casually and closing it into a fist, sucking all the flames from the torches and the garden in one motion. Now, the only light is that of the waning moon and the *glow* shimmering over my skin.

"What the fuck?" their leader seethes as he glances at the garden, then at his torches. Caitriona smiles, her teeth shining in the moonlight, then she bends down and grabs her older daughter, hoisting her to her unencumbered hip before darting between two of the shocked soldiers. Darkness wraps around them as they flee causing the soldiers to shout and gasp in confusion.

"I'm not *Blackwell's* anything," I offer over the cacophony of the men's voices. "I'm the fucking Queen."

As the words leave my mouth the wolves descend, tearing through the men as they scream and try to escape. A few manage to pull their short swords or daggers in an attempt to fight back, but I catch them before they can cause harm to the beasts, slicing through them with the *glow* with far more ease than I did in New Aphros. In the square, gripped by grief and fear, I struggled to control the *glow*. The power drained me and required nearly all my concentration, just as it did on the deck of the ship during the storm. But now, the bright light surges forth effortlessly and strikes down my enemies without faltering. The release of the power I've held such tight control over these past weeks in the castle is a relief.

Dismounting, I prowl toward the man who led the soldiers. He sits propped against the wattle fence, gut torn open by the sharp teeth of the pack, gasping for breath.

When I'm within his sight he flinches back but there's nowhere for him to retreat.

"Tell me, soldier. Did you enjoy tormenting these people?" I crouch down at his side, studying him, almost ashamed at the satisfaction his fear gives me. "Did you do it for your *God*? For love of your king? Or just because it made you feel big to frighten and abuse those who couldn't defend themselves?"

"Please," he stutters, hand over his gaping gut wound. "Please, I…"

"I have a healer. We could heal you if you just answer my question."

"It… for God. They're heathens. She openly worships the Goddess."

"They're *people*. Innocents trying to survive."

"Mercy, please," the man pleads, blood seeping between his fingers.

I offer him the same mercy he would have shown Caitriona and her children, slicing through his neck with the *glow* and leaving him to the wolves.

When I return to the others, Ciaran stares between me and the destruction with wide eyes. His lips part for a moment as though he would speak but no words escape before he closes them again. I hand the reins of my mare to Delphine, still sitting astride her horse, and approach Caitriona.

"Are you all right?" I ask gently, hoping I haven't frightened her or the children too badly. "My healer is here if you have any injuries."

"Nothing serious, my lady," she answers, dipping her head. Her older daughter steps from behind Caitriona's skirts and surprises me by wrapping her arms around my legs in a tight squeeze.

"You saved us. The Goddess saved us," the little girl cries against my waist.

Crouching down to eye level, I wrap my arms around her tiny shoulders, holding her tight as her tears drip onto the linen of my tunic.

"You'll need to hide somewhere safe for a bit. At least until things clear up," I tell Caitriona. "It won't do for the soldiers who come looking for them to find you here with their bodies all around and no explanation."

"I can go into town. My husband should be back from sea soon and there's a warehouse there that I can meet him at. It isn't unusual for us to meet him to take inventory after a voyage. I don't think anyone would question if I said I was already in town when these men arrived," she answers, looking at me from the side of her eye as she turns to Ciaran. "Will you be safe, brother?"

"Yes. I won't desert my Queen," Ciaran replies. His words draw my attention and when I turn to face him he takes a knee — the same way Jackson did at Johnny's tavern in New Aphros, crossing his arm across his chest in fealty. "Queen Nerissa. You are the rightful ruler of this land. I promise to devote my life to you and to protect you and your people until my dying breath."

Swallowing the tears that seem to well up every time someone makes an oath to me, I offer a smile, laying my palm on his shoulder. "I thank you for your loyalty and service, Ciaran. You are a brave soldier and a good man."

I wash my hands and face in the bucket Caitriona offers me, making sure I don't have blood stains or soot to draw suspicion on our way back to the castle while Lyra looks over the baby and little girl. Caitriona and her older daughter both have mild scrapes on their feet and knees from being roughly handled, but no lasting injuries. Once Lyra has healed them, they pack two bags and leave with their donkey to head into town. Their goat is missing, likely fled due to the wolves, and the chickens sleep in their coop undisturbed. I shudder at the thought of what we would have found if we had been slower, how many others they might have gotten to in the night.

After watering the horses, we gallop back to the castle, Delphine cloaking us as we near the gates. They're still open, the lock damaged from the sudden wind earlier, and we silently creep through without notice from the guard on duty thanks to Del's shadows. Ciaran stays behind with Sebastian to wipe down the horses while the three of us rush through the darkness to the secret entrance and back up the steps.

Del and Lyra retreat to their room exhausted from the hard ride. I pull off my clothing, hiding it under the bed until I can rinse the road dust and blood from it, then pull on a shift and open the door. Lennox stands at his post, turning immediately as the door opens.

"Please send for some water and food. I'm finally feeling better," I say, hoping the men at the end of the hall hear me.

"Of course, my lady," Lennox replies. We share a small smile and a wink before he leaves to do my bidding.

CHAPTER 45

"What the fuck do you mean they were attacked by wolves?" Charleston fumes in the courtyard while Lyra, Delphine, and I walk to take the air.

The morning dawned with a vivid red-stained sunrise, as though the blood of the men who died last night was rising into the sky. We've already circled the castle once, walked the dead garden, which has new growth sprouting as if shaking its fist in rebellion, and now linger by the stables to pat the horses and offer them little tidbits. In reality, I hope to gain any insight I can as to whatever gossip is spreading about the men who never returned from their mission to root out heretics.

"That's what one of the scouts said when he rode back this morning, Commander," Ciaran answers smoothly, wiping down a lathered black gelding. "He looked green in the face when he arrived and retreated to the barracks. Left me his horse."

"Superstitious bullshit," Charleston snaps, almost running into me as he turns to leave, muttering about a hunting party under his breath. "Wolves haven't been seen in these parts for nearly a decade."

I gasp, looking away as though he might harm me. "Excuse me, Commander."

His eyes narrow, raking over my body. "Hmph. *You* seem to be feeling just fine this morning."

"I began feeling better very early this morning, thanks be to God. How is the King? I hope he's been given some of Bridget's hearty broth. It made me feel much more lively once I could stomach it. I could bring him some later if he's agreeable to it. I feel bad about how our lunch ended," I reply, forcing a blush to rise to my cheeks as if I'm embarrassed over my own body.

"I think you've done plenty. I'll get him the broth." Charleston storms off, leaving me worried about his growing disdain and suspicion and wondering what steps I should take next.

***

"Guard, I require your assistance for a moment," I announce, opening my chamber door and addressing Lennox standing in the hallway. As he steps over the threshold his eyes drink in my ensemble with wariness.

This evening, I wear my cloak over one of the slim-fitting gowns I had made in New Aphros with my hair unbound down my back. Blackwell sent me a dinner invite this afternoon, obviously not as put out as Charleston over the way our lunch ended yesterday. I sensed his intentions to seduce me in the study, his needling about my past increasing with each meeting while his patience wears as thin as the veil covering the lust that emanates from him. So tonight, I bring something with me that I plan to use to quell his persistence while keeping up the illusion that I must put him off due to his own religion's rules. I hope I can keep up a more amicable attitude than usual, and that I can keep Lennox from finally breaking character.

While relieved by my success and safe return last night, it's becoming harder for Lennox to hide his feelings around Charleston and Blackwell, and each day I find him more on edge. If we don't proceed with our plans soon, I fear he will take matters into his own hands whether he intends to or not. I saw what happened in New Aphros when a drunk accosted me in the *Den of Sinful Delights*. I can't risk him losing control tonight.

"What is it, my Queen?" Lennox whispers, stepping closer and pushing the door almost closed.

I wish I could sink against him and hold him tightly or just escape down the secret passageway and retreat to the forest and never look back. But if we're caught, it would doom any plans we've worked toward and put everyone at risk.

"Remember what you told me the first day we arrived in New Aphros? Before we entered the Den?"

His golden brows pull together sharply as he studies me. "What part?"

"The part about it all being an act," I whisper.

His nostrils flare and his eyes narrow as I show him the leather strips I hold in my hand, pulled from the pocket of my gown. The ones I used on him in a much more enjoyable fashion in the aforementioned city.

"Remember our end goal. Remember this is all an act. I

love you, Billy. Hold it together tonight." I glance through the cracked doorway behind him, inspecting the empty hallway, then quickly press a kiss to his lips before stepping past him to lead the way to the dining room.

No one guards the doors of the dining room this evening and when we near the entrance raised voices reach us, both Blackwell's and Charleston's, as they hold a heated conversation.

"What do you mean they were killed by wolves? What are they saying?" Blackwell snaps.

"Just as I say, Dargan. The soldiers in the barracks were whispering about it when I was there earlier. About the wolves attacking to protect the people at the crofts with new growth. These are trees that have lain dormant for years and were thought to be dead. Fields that have been unable to produce suddenly have sprouted. The peasants are all saying it's a sign that the Goddess is returning. The men are starting to crack," Charleston answers, his voice strained with irritation. "They're afraid to go out again because they think they're going to draw down the wrath of Selennia itself. That the people *she* visited are blessed."

"I need to meet with the Head Priest. Send him and his priests into the fields to bless them and visit the people. Remind them this is God's doing, not some *whore's*! And what of the eastern coast?" The *clink* of a goblet slamming onto the tabletop echoes through the room as Lennox and I glance at one another.

"Should you be drinking that after not being able to keep anything down yesterday?"

"I don't need a fucking nursemaid, Russell! Answer me."

"No additional news from the east. I've had no correspondence from the messengers since we sent the contingent but rumors continue to tell of dark-skinned sailors moving through the Cybelene woods. It could be that the Delosians have landed and taken it, or they could be more ghost stories and superstitions. In the west, the remains of the ship we sent to Athene washed ashore. The only good news there is that pirates washed up alongside our men. Seems like they at least sunk one of the enemy's ships before going down. We won't know more than gossip unless we send more men though. "

I swallow at the news that one of our ships has washed up alongside one of the King's and meet Lennox's worried gaze as Blackwell continues to berate Charleston. Lennox's hand flexes over the hilt of his sword but he calms as we continue to eavesdrop.

"Then send them! I need to know what's happening!" Blackwell slurs, causing me to wonder just how much he's had to drink.

"We don't *have* any more men, Dargan! I've already told you that you've left us with too few as it is, and anyone we can hire from abroad won't make it in time."

Swallowing the unease that rises in my breast I reach up to knock, announcing our arrival, and ending their heated debate before Blackwell's temper heats any further.

The door swings open, held by one of the three soldiers who guard the interior of the room. Inside the torch and candlelit room, Blackwell waits at the head of the great table with a half-empty decanter of wine before him.

"You're late," Blackwell snaps at me, glaring at Lennox when he pulls my chair out.

"Already getting started? Without me? How are you feeling?" I purr, slowly unfastening the cloak and laying it across the empty chair next to mine before sinking into my seat at Blackwell's side. Lennox takes up a position behind me, back to the wall, eyes empty. Charleston stands in his place behind Blackwell, staring between the two of us with far more suspicion than usual.

"I've been waiting. What took you so long?" Slightly inebriated as he is, a hint of cruelty seeps into his words as he looks at Lennox over my shoulder. He then rakes his gaze over my body as I perch on the edge of the chair, a gleam of want leaching through the hazy focus.

I place a hand on his forearm, even though touching him makes my skin crawl, stroking my pale fingers along the dark fabric. "I wanted to look nice for you, Dargan. To boost your spirits after yesterday. Do you not like my gown?" Memories of the *House of Starlight* flash through my mind as I prepare to delude yet another lecherous fool.

His eyes travel from my collarbones, down to my breasts, and then to where I still touch his arm. He stops the motion by gripping my hand in his free one, gripping my fingers just tight enough to be uncomfortable. "I'd rather see it on my floor," he growls.

"Only a little longer until I'm officially your queen. You know what the priests say, no matter how *we* might feel. How would it look if we didn't have a proper ceremony when you outlawed the people from handfasting in the Old Way? When you shame them for laying with those they desire outside the bonds of marriage?" I know I should tread lightly, especially after hearing him in a rage, but I can't resist pushing him. His fingers dig into my hand harder and a boot heel echoes on the tiles as Lennox moves behind me, followed by the sound of one of the King's men taking a step forward. There cannot be a fight here tonight.

I hold up my free hand, signaling to Lennox that I'm all right before sliding it over Blackwell's cheek. "Perhaps I can offer you something… for your hospitality so far? To soothe your nerves?" I pitch my voice low as I disengage my fingers from his grip. His eyes glitter in the candlelight as I pull the leather straps from the concealed pocket of my gown.

"May I?" I ask, standing to circle behind him, forcing Charleston to step back as I drag a hand across Blackwell's chest over the lightweight tunic he wears.

"What is this?" Blackwell questions, watching me as I drop to a knee at his side, looping the leather around his wrist several times. Once it's tight, I tie it and move to his other side, kneeling before him and lifting my gaze to him in question.

"It's a surprise. I promise you won't be disappointed," I reply, fluttering my lashes as I tie the other wrist tightly to the arm of the chair. Once I'm certain he can't move his arms, and has no way to touch me, I stand before him. I look once at Lennox, pleading with my eyes that he understands and won't fall out of character. His mouth is a tight slash, but he looks straight ahead and never flinches beyond a slight tick in his jaw.

"I know how badly you want a taste of me, so I thought I would show you how good I can be," I whisper in Blackwell's ear, brushing against the shell of it with each breathy murmur.

He trembles and sighs as I brush my lips against his

neck, stepping back again. Glancing up through my lashes, I meet Charleston's amber eyes and allow a smile to ghost across my lips when he cocks his head. Blackwell grips the arms of the chair, the wood creaking loudly in the quiet room as I turn my back to him and sit in his lap, resting my head against his shoulder and grinding my hips against him. Whether he was hard before I started tying him, or whether the words I whispered aroused him, I don't know, but it's clear my proximity is enough to make him forget his need for control. I make sure I keep my face and neck far enough away from him so that he can't touch me with his lips as I grind my backside against him.

Once I hear a groan escape his lips, I turn to face him, lifting the edge of my gown enough to expose my legs up to my knees as I straddle him, placing my arms on the back of the chair to look him in the face. His dark eyes are wild as he rakes his gaze over me and I know I have him in a vulnerable spot as anticipated. I continue to roll my hips against his erection and lean forward slightly — allowing false whimpers and pants to fall from my lips, allowing him to think I desire this as well. I can feel him fighting the bonds at his wrists as he lifts his hips to grind against me.

Choking down the disgust I feel, I lean forward to whisper in his ear once more, this time making it sound breathy and desirous. "Once you've made me your queen, you can have me any way you like. When you're inside me you'll forget all about your God; you'll forget your own fucking name… Your Majesty." When I say the title I've refused to acknowledge since I stepped onto the docks I feel his hips jerk under me, shuddering as he moans with his release.

I step back quickly, pulling the dagger I've kept stored away in another deep pocket. Lennox and the guards all suck in a breath at the flash of steel, stepping forward in preparation to stop whatever I'm about to do, but I simply slice the leather bindings and step away from Blackwell.

"It seems as though you might wish to clean up. My appetite hasn't quite returned, so I'll retire to my room. Thank you for the dinner invitation, my King." I give a small dip of my head, not meeting Blackwell's eyes as I quickly depart the dining room.

Lennox's footsteps tap rapidly behind me on the marble floors as he follows me through the doors and down the hallway. As soon as we turn the corner to the wing where my chambers wait I speed my steps to reach my door, bursting through to immediately kneel and dry heave in the center of the room, holding my arms around myself as if I can hold the revulsion at bay. Lennox reaches my side and pulls me to his chest, stroking my hair as I tremble.

"Are you all right?" he whispers against my hair.

"No. But, I had to take matters into my own hands, on my own terms. I was afraid of what he might do if I kept flat-out denying him. I need him to let his guard down, to be distracted from everything else so we can finish this. Charleston is getting too suspicious. But..." I trail off as I cling to Lennox. "I can't have him touch me, Billy. I can't hide how I really feel much longer. We need to end this. Soon."

"We will, Nerissa. Do you want me to send the word to Erik now? The people already love you; you can see how nervous it makes Blackwell when you speak about them. We don't need him to declare you his queen when they'll accept you with open arms. Erik waits not far from the harbor; we can sink the ships that might hold him and the others off and make our move. You could take him down on your own, you know that." He holds me away from him to study my face. His expression is deadly serious, and I know he would walk back into that room right now and kill them all if I asked him to.

"We heard him say he's sending another contingent out this week to handle the raids in the east. Once he's done that, we strike, even if it's a few days earlier than Beltane. The ships we have hidden off the coast should be enough to handle his remaining troops whether he's declared me or not. I can't wait any longer." In response, Lennox holds me against his chest, stroking my hair gently.

Shivering once as my nerves begin to settle, I reach to tuck my cloak around me before realizing it's not there. "My cloak! I left it in the dining room."

"I'll fetch it. No need for you to return, or for him to have an excuse to visit you here," Lennox whispers, pressing a kiss to my brow before slipping back out the door. As the sound of his boots fades down the hallway, I close the door, sinking to sit with my back to its sturdy surface as I hold my head in my hands.

CHAPTER 46
LENNOX

I take a few moments down the hall from Nerissa's chambers to settle my temper, forcing myself to breathe deeply. Watching her with that asshole — touching him, whispering to him — was almost more than I could handle. He's old enough to be her father, how could he think he deserves to touch her?

This game is dangerous for all of us, but I could have slit his throat within moments and dealt with the repercussions from his guards afterward. I shake myself and begin the long walk back to the dining room to recover her cloak. As she'd reminded me before the dinner, it was all an act, but it doesn't erase the image of her writhing against him or the sounds of her whimpers from my mind.

The dining room door is cracked when I return and I pause at the sight. Voices rumble behind the wood once again, male and female this time, and I tilt my head closer to hear their words.

A nervous feminine giggle floats through, followed by Charleston's rasp.

"Will this one do for you?" Charleston asks.

"I don't care, just one of them to satisfy me tonight," Blackwell retorts harshly. The woman's giggles end and a small gasp sounds as footsteps carry through the space. "Take her to my room to wait for me."

"Are you sure you don't want to give us another show?" Charleston replies.

I straighten, surprised to hear Charleston provoking Blackwell like this.

"Watch yourself, Russell. You may be my friend but tread lightly." Blackwell's voice is light, even as he reprimands Charleston. The earlier stress of discussing lost troops is all but gone from their conversation.

"It really wasn't fair to put the other guards through that. I thought the younger ones were going to… well… *you* know." Charleston lets out a bark of a laugh. "She *is* something, Your Majesty."

"I will not have you or the men speaking of my future queen like a common whore, Charleston," Blackwell retorts, and for a brief moment, I think perhaps he's actually defending her. His next words chill me, though, when he begins to laugh along with the Commander. "You know I'll throw her your way as soon as I've gotten an heir out of her. Make sure the men know not to touch her until I give permission. Once she spits out a child or two you can take turns fucking her on the table in the barracks for all I care. It shouldn't be anything she, or the whores she keeps for handmaidens, aren't used to."

Charleston's laughter blends with the King's as he replies, "Oh, I don't know that I'll share this one, Your Majesty. I've come to admire her spirit. I might have to keep her for my own use when you're finished with her. Do you think that pretty white skin bruises easily?"

Rage surges through me and my hands shake as I push the door open and step into the room, casting my eyes over the two men. Charleston holds the upper arm of one of the kitchen girls as he drags her toward the room's second entrance toward Blackwell's bedchamber. Her doe-like eyes lock on mine, growing wider. Blackwell sits in his seat, still sipping the wine he started earlier in the night.

"What the hell are you doing in here, dog? Have you no manners?" Charleston snarls, the permanently scarred grimace deepening, the usual mocking tone harsh. I disregard his question and never stop as I cross the room to the chair where Nerissa's cloak rests, gathering it up.

"My Queen misplaced her cloak. I am retrieving it for her." I barely keep my voice from shaking with rage, but thankfully I remember to fake my Northern accent as I look over the scene. "Was she not enough to sate you tonight? Even *heathens* like myself know there is no pleasure in taking what is not offered freely." My words are dangerous and could very well land me in the dungeon, but I want to shame the coward who calls himself a king. I *want* to do worse, but I can't permit my rage to take over yet.

Blackwell stands abruptly, knocking over the dregs of his wine as he whirls on me but he has no weapon at hand. Even if he did, he wouldn't be able to touch me in the state I'm in. I *wish* the old fool would pull a blade so I could justify cutting him down where he stands. As he approaches me some of the fight seems to leave him, especially when he has to look up to stare into my eyes. Backing down, he orders, "Get out! Go sniff after that bitch like a good dog. You won't be around her much longer."

"Will you be all right?" I look away from Blackwell addressing the girl, the turn of my head angering him further if the flush on his cheeks is any indication. He can't stand that I show no fear in his presence.

The girl looks at her feet, then at me, before she nods. "Aye, I'll go willing to him." It doesn't take much to know she's only agreeing to do so to keep her position in the castle, to earn her wages, and not be cast into the streets or a brothel. It chafes knowing I can't pull her from Charleston's grip and help her, but additional guards have returned to the room drawn by the commotion and I can't risk leaving Nerissa alone for long. This will all be over soon. I give a curt nod to the girl, curl my lip at Blackwell, then spin on my heel and out the doors.

Rather than turning left to lead me back to Nerissa's chambers, I step back into a shadowed corner to watch the door. Within five minutes, Charleston closes the dining room doors behind him, spinning on his heel and starting down the hallway to the right. I quietly follow behind, down the stairwell and out into the courtyard where he heads toward the barracks.

The sound of soldiers' voices carries through the still night air when Charleston enters the building. I'm not sure how long to wait, but I've discovered he doesn't reside in the barracks himself, so I assume he'll return to the castle soon. My thoughts are cut short when after only ten minutes he appears silhouetted in the doorway once more, heading back toward the castle.

Rounding the corner ahead of him, I slip back into the

shadows of the destroyed hot house, near where he saw Nerissa and me the first night. When he reaches the same side he stops abruptly and whirls toward me, pulling his sword from its sheath.

"Didn't think I heard you, heathen?"

"Oh, I knew you would. I just wasn't sure you were man enough to confront me alone." I slide my blade from my hip, palming my dagger in the other as we begin to circle one another in the moonlit courtyard. Just like the night of the full moon, fewer guards are on watch tonight, and none man the back of the castle on the barracks side.

"Looking for help? My men won't come to your aid," Charleston taunts with his scarred smile.

"Merely wondering whether you had them removed so no one could report if something happens to Lady Nerissa, or whether you are afraid of your men seeing you get your ass beat," I return with a smile of my own. Killing the man in town was shamefully easy; it's been a while since I've had a good fight and Charleston seems to be itching to give me one.

"The King has had to send so many men out to deal with the piracy on the coastlines that I don't have enough to cover the walls. Wasn't that your plan all along? Hopefully, it doesn't inadvertently put your precious *Lady Nerissa* in danger." Charleston strikes, his sword singing as it meets my blade, nearly sparking as the steel rings through the courtyard.

"What is wrong, Commander?" I ignore his insinuating question as we circle. "Do you have so little confidence in your men's abilities at protecting the castle or defending Selennia? They cannot manage a few raids?" I swing, but Charleston is quick and parries, knocking me back.

"Oh, my men are good, but they're not savages like the ones reported on the coasts. I'm sure you're familiar with them. Captain Jackson on the *Selkie's Tears*, invaders from Delosia and the Northern Isles. At least Jackson and his crew are finally at the bottom of the sea where he belongs."

For a moment, I falter, unsure if he's baiting me with a lie about Jackson's death or if he speaks the truth.

"Why would I be familiar with those men, Charleston? Just because I am a Northman doesn't mean I know all who sail these seas." I meet his strike once again, but I'm rattled, my false accent failing as I take an unexpected blow to the cheek before he steps back.

"I assumed you'd be acquainted with the other pirates —" Charleston steps closer again, forcing me back until I realize the error in my distraction when my back bumps against the damaged hot house wall. Before I can change direction, Charleston's blade is pressed against my throat, the steel stinging where it bites into my flesh. "Especially Jackson, if rumors are to be believed. I thought he was something of a mentor to you."

His smile is cruel and satisfied as he leans closer and adds, "Come now, you can drop the accent for good. We both know you're no Northman, *Captain Lennox.* I already suspected but could tell by the way you watched her with him tonight. You love her, don't you?"

I bare my teeth as a trickle of blood slips down my skin from his blade, snarling at his words.

Charleston chuckles, confident in his victory, and lessens the pressure at my throat. "Don't worry about your pirate queen. I'll make sure Dargan doesn't handle her too roughly once I tell him my suspicions about your plans. I don't want her damaged before I get my chance with her. That would take all the fun out of it."

Rage thunders through me when he mentions Nerissa. Red hot anger combined with the shock of my name on his lips, devastation over the truth about Jackson, and the fact that he's slowly pieced together Nerissa's association with the raids gives me the surge of confidence I need to ignore the risk of him slitting my throat. A shiver in the shadows is the last boost I need to fake once more with my sword, drawing his eye for a mere moment as the shadows coalesce. The distraction is enough to allow Delphine to step from the darkness, sliding her slim knife into his shoulder. Charleston's blade skims down mine as he winces and looks toward Del in astonishment. The motion sends a jolt through the hilt and up my arm, but the moment is all I need. My dagger finds its place between his ribs, piercing his lungs as blood gurgles from his lips.

"Did you tell Blackwell?" I demand, catching Charleston as he falls, gripping his tunic as he slides to his knees. He coughs, blood splattering on my shirt and hands as he laughs at the panic on my face.

"I suppose you'll find out," he murmurs, choking as he laughs once more, then falls to the side.

I hadn't intended on killing Charleston and have no plan on what to do now, but even if Del hadn't come to my aid, I couldn't have let him live with this knowledge. Even if he couldn't prove it, the allegation alone would be enough to drag me from Nerissa and sentence one or both of us to death without warning.

If he hasn't already told Blackwell his suspicions.

Charleston hadn't mentioned Jackson by name when we overheard his report to Blackwell; perhaps he was saving it for a more opportune moment. A fresh wave of panic seizes me and my heart hammers wildly as I begin to unravel.

What if they already know and Nerissa is in danger?

What if Charleston was just a distraction?

"Well, it seems our life debt is almost even now," Delphine says softly, stepping around Charleston to stand at my side and forcing me to focus on the body cooling at our feet.

"We can call it paid if you help me get rid of him."

"Deal."

CHAPTER 47

I t takes far longer for Lennox to return with my cloak than I anticipated. I pace the floor of my chamber, pausing at any noise that could be mistaken for footsteps in the hallway, worrying about what could have detained him.

My mind spins wildly, hoping Blackwell or Charleston hasn't harmed him. I turn over the possibilities for over an hour until a door creaks, but the main door to my chamber remains sealed, the secret door opening slowly instead. Gripping my dagger, I wait for whoever might emerge to show themself.

"Del?" I gasp when blonde curls come into view. I knew she used the secret exit often, but didn't expect her to return through it tonight. I hadn't even realized she wasn't in her room with Lyra. My heart gallops and fear coats my skin when Lennox steps through the narrow opening behind her.

"Billy!" I rush toward him, expecting him to pull me close but he thrusts my cloak toward me instead of taking me in his arms. "Billy? What's happened?"

I cast my eyes over him from head to toe, taking inventory of any injuries that might explain the wild look in his eyes and his rumpled clothes. His hair is still contained in a tidy braid down the center, just as Erik always wears his, but his cheeks are flushed above his beard. One cheek has the beginning of a bruise discoloring it and a thin line of dried blood shows at his throat. His shirt is slightly untucked, and his boots are muddy. When I pull the cloak from his hands I reveal stains on his shirt, and his fingernails have crimson under them. Blood still streaks parts of his hands, as if he's rinsed them hastily. Sweat prickles under my arms and I shiver with adrenaline.

"Billy... what did you do?"

"Del, get Lyra and have her hide below, just in case. Then go to the caves and find Tom. We need to get word to the ships that things are in motion. Make sure they know the signal," Lennox orders, tugging his bloody shirt from his breeches and tossing it into the fireplace.

Delphine nods in response, brooking no argument for once, then disappears into the adjoining chamber. She and Lyra return within a few heartbeats and disappear into the doorway without another word.

"I'm sorry, Nerissa. I couldn't... I couldn't..." Lennox stumbles over his words, clutching me to him, cupping my face in his hands as though I might disappear.

Seeing him shaken like this is unnerving; he's usually the one to soothe me and stay calm. The memory of his violence in the salon of the Den rises to my mind — has he beaten someone?

"What did you *do*?" I demand when he still hasn't explained himself.

"I killed Charleston." His voice is flat as I pull away to look into his face.

"*What?*" I step away from him, still holding his hands though my heart thunders, urging me to gather my friends and run. "Explain."

"I walked in on their conversation when I retrieved your cloak. They were discussing *you*, among other things, and Blackwell had a servant girl pulled aside for his bed. We exchanged words, I grabbed your cloak, and then I left. I was still angry from the dinner, and more so after hearing them talk about using you in such ways. Charleston left a few minutes after I did and I trailed him down toward the barracks. He was baiting me. We fought. He called me *Lennox.* He'd figured out we were involved with the raids; he said Jackson and crew were lost. He had me pinned and Delphine intervened, but I just… I killed him. I couldn't risk him using it against us. If he hasn't already," Lennox blurts, his words running together as he paces the floor in front of the fireplace.

"What did you do with him? How did Delphine come to be with you?" I ask frantically, fingers twisting in my skirt as I try to decide what to do next, watching him as if he's a caged animal.

"She crept from the shadows. I don't know if she was following us or whether she was just in the right place, but she saw it all. When he had me pinned, she stabbed him to give me a chance to kill him, then she helped me pull his body outside the walls with the key. It's only a matter of time before his absence is noticed. We can only hope he gets dragged off by the wilderness, but we can't count on it."

"We must be ready then. We must strike—" My words

are cut off by the pounding of feet in the hallway. Lennox and I have only a moment to meet one another's eyes before a loud crack sounds through the wood.

Only a few blows are required to bust the single lock on my door, wood splintering as the door flies inward, so like the vision of Adelaide's final confrontation. Lennox unsheaths his sword, prepared to fight the soldiers who wait outside the entrance. We've been talking for less than an hour; it's still dark outside, the darkest part of the night before the dawn, illuminated by the waning moonlight. Not nearly enough time for Charleston's body to have been found if someone hadn't expected trouble. We've been watched far more closely than we suspected.

Four guards stomp into my chambers, followed by Blackwell and two more guards at his back. Terror shoots through me at the hatred on his face, all sense of his earlier drunkenness is gone, leaving only cruelty. It takes all the control I can muster to hold my power in check. My eyes flick between Blackwell and Lennox as my heart threatens to beat out of my ribs.

"Seize him!" Blackwell orders and three guards approach Lennox. He manages to slice into one of their arms before they twist the blade from his hands, forcing him to his knees. "You're charged with the murder of Commander Charleston, and for illicit relations with the future queen. Guards, take him to the dungeon. I'll hand down his sentence shortly."

"What do you mean? Unhand him!" I attempt to stand up to Blackwell, stepping forward in challenge.

"You think I'm a fool?" Blackwell sneers. "Do you think I don't know you've been fucking him this entire time? I suspected it from the beginning, and Charleston saw you sneaking out together on numerous occasions. Isn't that why you sent your lover to kill him? When Charleston didn't return to report back to me tonight about your movements, it was confirmed. Subdue him!" he snaps when Lennox continues to struggle against them. One of the guards kicks Lennox in the stomach, causing him to grunt at the impact.

"No! Billy!" I shriek, my composure seeming to fail in the face of Lennox being roughly handled by these men. It isn't all an act though. I'm bolstered by the fear that causes my heart to pound in my chest at the thought of Lennox being executed if Blackwell decrees it. Not that I would ever allow that to happen, no matter what he asked me to promise.

I stumble to my knees and throw my arms around Lennox's shoulders, burying my face in his neck. The guards pull at me, but I cling to him as tears run down my cheeks. "I can take them all," I whisper between overly exaggerated sobs.

"Not yet, Nerissa. Not yet. Del will get word to Tom. Follow the plan," he whispers into my ear as he nuzzles my cheek, arms still trapped behind him.

I give the barest nod in understanding, even if I don't want to see the sense in his words. I could kill everyone in this room if I unleashed myself, but it wouldn't be enough to fully take the castle. More would file in to replace them and, if they're loyal to Blackwell, then my actions could get both of us, as well as Lyra and Delphine, killed in the process.

"I'll be all right," he says louder, and Blackwell has the

nerve to laugh at him while the guards pull him away from me.

"And as for you—" Blackwell approaches me where I still kneel on the stone floor. He crouches down, gripping my chin painfully between his fingers, and forces me to look into his dark eyes, then turns my face to inspect my cheeks. "I knew you were a stupid slut just like Adelaide. Fucking a beast that's beneath your station."

"What the fuck are you talking about?" I grit through my teeth as he tightens his hold, bruising my jaw while his wine-soaked breath smothers me at this distance.

"He's half naked in your chambers and you have blood and dirt from his guilty hands on your face, yet you dare deny it?"

Realization dawns on me — the blood from Lennox's hands must show on my skin. We didn't take the time to wash them clean before he started explaining and we began our plotting. I curse myself for a fool at giving additional evidence to Blackwell that supports his theory.

"You will do what I tell you from now on or I will destroy him bit by bit while you watch. I'll even give you pieces as keepsakes. Do you understand?"

Anger rages through my body, overriding the fear I feel for Lennox's safety. Before I can stop myself, I spit in Blackwell's face. He rocks back on his heels, smiling as he wipes the spittle from his cheek, then backhands me so hard I'm knocked into the edge of the bed frame. Pain burns in my shoulder from the impact as I crumple on the stone floor.

Lennox struggles against the men when he sees Blackwell hit me, but he's trapped between them. "Nerissa!"

"Suit yourself," Blackwell says as he stands. He casually glances around my room searching for something, then picks up the heavy earthenware water pitcher from the table near the fireplace. Hefting it once, as if checking the weight, he looks over his shoulder at me with a cold smile before smashing it across Lennox's cheek.

"No!" I scream as Lennox goes limp between the two guards, finally subdued as blood trails down his already bruised cheek.

"Do you understand now?" Blackwell asks again, standing over me. "*That* is where you belong. On your knees. In submission. You *will* be tamed."

I drag ragged breaths through my teeth, seething with rage and sorrow as the soldiers drag Lennox through the door. Blackwell watches me as he backs out of the room, leaving me on my hands and knees on the slate. This time my tears are no act.

Lennox was right in telling me to wait. I must protect Lyra and give Delphine time to reach Tom to make sure our crews are in place. But at this moment, all I can do is hate myself for allowing them to take him. For pretending I'm as powerless as Blackwell believes me to be.

Alone in my room, I release a shriek of frustration and slam my fists on the floor where my mother bled all those years ago, sending pain radiating through my hands and arms. The castle seems to tremble with me as heavy sobs shake my body. The call of a wolf finds me from beyond the window and castle walls, the Goddess feeling my sorrow as keenly as if she were in the room with me.

How is this happening again? It happened to Her, then

to my mother. They both lost those they loved to evil men. Is our entire line cursed? Have I dragged us all to face death and merely sat back and allowed the monster to win? Why didn't Lennox and I flee when we had the chance in New Aphros?

The thoughts come fast and each one drags me deeper into my misery as I wrap my arms around myself, curled on my side in the center of the room.

"Nerissa?" Lyra's soft voice soothes me a short time later, a gentle hand resting on my shoulder. "Are you all right? Let me heal your injury."

"No." I jerk away from her touch. The thought of letting her soothe my minor hurts when who knows what I've allowed Blackwell to do to Lennox is enough to turn my stomach. I deserve to hurt.

"He won't kill him. At least not yet." Delphine's words snap my eyes to hers. I thought she had left to relay information to Tom, but she kneels on the floor next to Lyra, her jaw tight and lips set in a hard line. "Lennox is too valuable to use against you. Don't fall apart now. Don't waste it, Nerissa."

Don't waste it, Del had challenged shortly after Salome's death, referencing the power that was given to me. Here she is again, challenging me to focus, reminding me of the sacrifices we've all made already.

Salome's command to use my emotions rushes to the front of my mind, muffling the ache of hopelessness and the bitter taste of fear. I'll use both of those, plus the rage that courses through me. Like I told my mother, I have enough of it for all of us.

Another howl drifts on the wind, reminding me that the

Goddess didn't lay down and cry when her consort was killed. She tore out the man's throat who harmed her lover.

I will do the same.

Nodding to Delphine, I push myself up from the floor. With a steadying breath, I swallow my tears to prepare for what comes next.

CHAPTER 48
BLACKWELL

The heavy wooden door slams behind me, making the young guard standing sentry for Nerissa's chambers flinch. I can't remember his name — Charleston kept track of the soldiers — but he looks displeased at the sight of the man being dragged half-clothed through the hallway. The guard averts his eyes as a satisfied smile spreads across my face hearing the bitch's sobs through the splintered oak.

I'll break her yet. Even if it means breaking the man she loves to do so.

I should have taken him immediately on the docks and saved myself all this trouble in the first place. Losing Charleston is a wound I wasn't expecting would hurt so badly but I'll be certain they both pay for it in kind.

Turning to follow my soldiers as they drag her Northman away, I stumble when a guttural scream of rage ripples through the air, sending an involuntary shiver of fear down my spine. Swallowing, I swear it feels as though the entire castle shuddered along with me.

But that's impossible.

Taking a step forward I'm halted again when the sad call of a wolf sounds through one of the open panes of glass in the hallway. The men in front of me pause for a moment, nervously looking around and then back to me at the noise.

"Shut the window. Now!" I shout to the young guard. He dashes to do so, keeping his eyes downcast the entire time before returning to his post. The door across the hall opens and the bitch's priest steps out, bleary-eyed from sleep.

"What's happening here?" the priest asks, shock washing away all residual sleepiness when he notes the Northman being dragged through the hall.

"None of your concern. You'd best have the whore prepared for our wedding tomorrow, priest, unless you want to be held responsible for their actions, too."

"As you say, Your Majesty," he replies, glancing at the drooping Northman once more with pity before closing his door.

Met with no other interruptions my men quickly continue their march to the dungeon, dragging the limp figure along. It's time to have a bit of fun with the man who dared touch what has been promised to me. He was far too confident when he told her he'd be all right. Hopefully, he regains consciousness soon so we can commence my work.

As we reach the top of the stairs that lead down to the first floor, and then the lower levels where the makeshift dungeon cells were installed, the blond bastard stirs. Groaning, he begins to struggle against the soldiers who hold him, spitting blood and venom. He's a strong one, I'll give him that. At least he is for now.

It takes all the strength the two men holding him have to

keep him subdued enough to force him down the stone steps. Without his shirt, healed scars from previous lashings are visible across his back.

Perfect. Something he should fear.

More recent marks, fingernail scratches, run from his shoulders and down his back. From *her*.

"Shackle him and throw him in one of the empty cells. Whichever is closest; he won't be in there long," I command, fury igniting at the proof of their recent coupling.

I direct the faceless red and black uniforms to do my bidding. I'll need to get to know some of the officers better to determine who will replace my old friend soon, or else I'll need to learn their names. I'm not sure if it infuriates me more that this beast murdered Charleston, or that Charleston was weak enough to allow himself to be killed. After all these years, one would think he would have been able to see the brute coming for him. We probably should have chained him in the dining room when he dared challenge me, but I was so distracted by the thoughts of the harlot's smell and touch still lingering on me that I let him go.

Perhaps I'm most angry with myself. If I'd heeded Charleston's warnings from the beginning maybe he would still be here.

No matter, I'll channel that anger soon enough.

Removing my cloak and doublet, I roll the sleeves of my tunic up, flexing my fingers in preparation. I'll take pleasure in this punishment; I won't need one of the men to dole it out today. Gripping the lash that hangs on the wall next to other implements, I turn toward the cell the two soldiers guard, my boots echoing on the damp stone floors.

This used to be a store room for extra foodstuffs until I took over. I needed somewhere close to keep the few prisoners who didn't meet death immediately, and none of the queens who lived here previously had a proper dungeon set up.

Soft. Weak. Foolish.

I learned the proper way to deal with criminals from my father. I can prove that I'm just as capable of punishment as he and my brothers. Show that *I* am not soft, weak, nor foolish like he once believed.

When I'm finished, I have no doubt the whore will admit defeat and give me an heir, or anything else I desire, and it will be settled. I should have already taken her to ensure it. With this wretch out of the way and her more pliant, it will be done.

I don't know why I've held out this long: I'll have Molly take the wedding dress to her this morning. The ceremony can be arranged for tomorrow, and tomorrow night she'll be mine.

Shaking my head to clear the lust and distraction, I walk to the bars of the cell where the man waits. Blood slicks the side of his face from the blow earlier, his nose broken and dripping on the packed earth floor in front of him. He sits with his elbows on his bent knees, wrists chained. As I approach, his eyes track my movements, but there is no fear in them. He's like a wild animal chained and waiting for someone to get too close so it can strike, even if it's punished for the effort.

"Open the cell. Chain him."

The guards unlock the door and approach with caution, but the man's eyes never leave mine. He even stands of his own volition as they near. He's covered in tattoos, his arms and chest marked with symbols and sigils, both of the Goddess who once protected this island and of a seafaring life. Studying him, I ask, "Who are you, really?"

His expression remains motionless, lips tightly closed, green eyes hating. He simply extends his arms to the guards so they can pull him toward the center of the room where they loop the chain over a hook hanging from the ceiling, pulling his limbs overhead and exposing his back to me.

"You *will* speak. Your screams will be what I break her with," I egg him on, my anger becoming a living thing as he remains silent and those scratches on his back taunt me. I drag the leather of the lash across his scarred skin, letting him know what my plans are.

His only response is a huffed laugh, blurring my vision with rage at his disrespect.

"Do your worst, Blackwell."

The first lick of the leather across his skin leaves red streaks, his silence allowing the *crack* to fill the cold room.

CHAPTER 49

For the remainder of the day, my door remains barred with Ciaran posted outside. He'd been suspiciously removed from guarding my wing after our trip to the crofts, but with Charleston now gone no one has stopped him or questioned his presence at my door. When Ciaran opens it to pass a meal through, he refuses to meet my tear-swollen eyes, as if he's ashamed for not stopping Blackwell.

Lyra and Delphine are allowed to come and go — after all, what can a couple of young women possibly do to help me now? Thankfully, Blackwell underestimates us all.

Delphine returned just after dawn, confirming she was able to meet with Tom and deliver our message. She also confirmed that Charleston hadn't been bluffing — Jackson and the crew of the *Selkie's Tears* are gone.

"At least Salome will have Jackson to keep her company now," Del says quietly, taking a deep breath to hide the shimmer of tears in her eyes.

My mourning for Jackson is hindered by my worry for

Lennox and the living. There have been too many losses in too little time, numbing me to the news of more death.

Midday, Molly arrives, carrying a large box. She's been scarce since the first day she showed me to my chambers since I brought my own handmaidens, so having her here now is grating.

"What do you want?" Delphine snipes, opening the door to find the older woman waiting with a forced smile.

"I'm delivering a gift from King Dargan," she answers, pushing through the doorway with the parcel.

"Isn't it lovely, my lady?" she asks with a smile plastered across her face, opening the box to show me the gown within. "He's announced your wedding was moved up to tomorrow morning. Courtiers from the countryside are already beginning to arrive and word has been sent to the town for the common people to gather to celebrate."

My anger spikes, causing me to grind my teeth at the knowledge that Blackwell has arranged for our union to be held publicly as soon as possible now that he has Lennox in his clutches. Just as I knew he would, he'll use Lennox to get whatever he wants from me — our marriage will show the people that I accept him as the ruler of Selennia. It's what I'd planned, but I hope our crews will be in place on such short notice.

At my silence Molly's eyes soften, the false smile disappears, and her voice drops to nearly a whisper. "I'm sorry about your Northman, Lady Nerissa. I heard he was taken from you. I can try to get word to him for you or to find out his condition if you wish. I can find something to hide the bruise on your cheek for tomorrow, too."

"Please leave," I order, delicately touching my cheek at

her mention of where Blackwell struck it. I haven't looked in a mirror since they tore Lennox from my arms so I have no idea what state I might be in.

My words cause Molly's lips to turn down into a frown, but she dips her chin and closes the door silently behind her without another word, leaving me to stare at the contents of her delivery.

"Lady Nerissa," Daniel greets me with a deep bow when Ciaran opens the door for him shortly after Molly departs. "I'm sorry for your troubles as of late."

"Father," I reply respectfully as he enters the room and the door clicks shut behind him.

"Are you well, my lady?" Daniel asks, studying my face with concern.

"No," I answer honestly. "I'm surprised they let you in to see me."

"Well, I suggested one last confession before your marriage to Blackwell."

I can't hold in the bitter laugh that escapes me. As if any sin I might have committed in my life could remotely compare to those perpetrated by the monster who sits on the moonstone throne. Apparently, Blackwell and Charleston only suspected *Lennox* as being other than he seemed; no doubt they assumed a priest wouldn't stoop so low as to conspire against them.

"I'm glad you're here." Daniel offers a sad smile in response. "I need you to carry out a few tasks for me. Things must move swiftly now that Blackwell has decided our marriage is to be tomorrow."

He nods, proving yet again he's steadfast and courageous — from the moment I met him with a knife to his throat in New Aphros to today, he has never once shrunk from a task. I hastily whisper what I need him to do and he nods his understanding, retreating quickly from my chambers.

Lyra attempts to soothe me the rest of the day, but I can only lay in my bed, praying and promising revenge.

THAT EVENING, DANIEL RETURNS, SLIPPING INTO MY ROOM after making rounds to "pray for lost souls". In reality, he has visited the docks to pass messages to allies who wait outside the sight line of Blackwell's harbormasters under the protection of Del's shadows. He also made rounds in the dungeon to comfort those who might be suffering, namely Lennox.

Delphine and Lyra sit with me under the guise of readying me for the morning's festivities when he arrives, but in reality, we're preparing a small ceremony and prepping for battle.

"How is he?" I rush to Daniel as soon as the guards lock us in.

"He's..." Daniel begins, his sad eyes inspecting his boots. My breath hitches as panic wraps its fingers around my throat. *If he's dead, I will kill them all right now, even if it kills me,* the thought bears down on me unbidden and I feel my power surge with my fear. If Blackwell killed him, I will make this castle crumble around all of us.

"He's alive, my lady. They've taken the lash to him, but he breathes. It looks like he may have a broken rib or two, possibly a broken nose, as well. But he lives."

I choke on my tears as I grip the back of the chair I stand beside.

They flogged him. *Again.*

"Nerissa." Lyra takes my hand, holding my trembling fingers tightly in her warm caress. Although she has tears in her eyes for her uncle's plight, she remains steadfast. "If he's alive we can heal him. We just need to get through the morning. He's survived worse."

I was right to bring both Lyra and Delphine for this. Delphine is burning fury, but Lyra balances us both with her gentleness and positive outlook.

"You're right, Lyra. Thank you." I exhale as I slow my rapid thoughts and breath. "Daniel, has Tom returned? Are they ready?"

Daniel takes a seat on the floor next to Delphine, resting his cheek against her knee while Lyra and I pull chairs to join them, far from the door and any eavesdropping guards who might pass by. Delphine casually runs her fingers through his hair, but whether to comfort him or herself, is unclear. Lyra positions herself between me and Del so I can sit closest to Daniel to continue our whispered conversation.

"Yes." Daniel sits up slightly when he answers. "He had just returned from Captain Varangr. Erik estimates that the Delosians have had enough time to pass through the Cybelene woods. So we should expect their aid. Like you'd planned, the soldiers here in Aphros have dwindled. Tom's seen soldiers leaving on the roads to Athene, Cybele, and toward the mountains to the north for weeks. The numbers are in our favor."

As Daniel speaks I visualize a map of Selennia, checking

off the towns he lists and trying to calculate how far away the King's troops are. There's no way they can make it back to Aphros quick enough to put down a rebellion, as long as things move quickly tomorrow.

"They know to listen for the bell tower," Daniel states.

"And they know not to harm any of the women or children? Or any men who swear fealty and surrender?" I have no wish to follow in the footsteps of the usurper. These people are under his control against their will. If they offer no hostility, they will find none in return.

"Yes, it's been made clear. They know the penalty for disobeying."

"Good. I'll make sure the bell tolls. If for some reason I can't... Delphine, Lyra, you know what to do?" The younger women nod solemnly. Even if I don't manage to do my part, if Blackwell somehow anticipates our plan and ends me, he will *not* be King of Selennia after tomorrow morning.

We each drink some of the wine I have left over from the day before — I've refused to eat or drink anything that was brought to me today for fear that they might be poisoned or tainted in some way.

Together we light a small candle, say a quiet prayer to the Goddess, and place it in the center of my open window, where the moon and stars shine down upon us.

CHAPTER 50

The morning dawns, crisp and bright, but the barest hint of warmth beckons as spring finally creeps over Aphros. The new buds and pretty blossoms should make any bride feel elated for her wedding day, but I'm no ecstatic youth meeting her beloved at the altar.

Today, I dress for vengeance.

The gown Blackwell sent me is white and frothy but conveniently includes a full cloak to keep the morning chill off during my journey to the temple so early in the morning.

Instead of the wedding dress he expects underneath, I wrap myself in the cloth of silver robe that belonged to Anise Lennox, adding my circlet and choker with its body chain. The chain drapes over the bold blue ink of the tattoo on my breastbone which stands out starkly on my pale skin. Once dressed, I place the thick gold ring from Lennox on my middle finger and secure my gold bangle emblazoned with the name of his ship to my wrist. I've kept the engraved piece since the fateful night he placed it on me in

Celeste's office so many months ago — no longer a symbol of bondage, it's now a reminder of the support I have at my back and the family I belong to.

Before I cover myself with the cloak, Lyra and Delphine help me finish dressing, tightening laces on either side of the leather breastplate I wear over my robe. I view my reflection in the mirror, standing straight and proud. I've always looked like Adelaide, but today I'm a fiercer version of my mother. The version that Selennia needed when Blackwell stole her away from its people. A vision of the Goddess Herself — a wild thing who offered no mercy when She dispensed with the man who threatened Her home and took Her love from her centuries ago.

Swinging the full cloak over my shoulders, Lyra secures it to be sure it hides what lies beneath, so only a faint glimpse of pale fabric shows as I walk. When the bell tolls the hour, the door of my room slams open unceremoniously and an unfamiliar guard steps through the door.

"Who are you?" I demand, inspecting the large man wearing a disarming smile.

"I'm your guard this morning, *Your Majesty*," he answers, placing a fist over his heart in respect as he inclines his head in a bow. "My name is Velasco."

"Well, Velasco," I answer, studying his face more closely. His windburned cheeks and dark-tanned skin tell me this is no castle guard and I allow a smile to tug at the corners of my lips. "Lead the way."

Stepping into the hallway, Ciaran waits to accompany us. He bows his head and crosses one arm over his chest, fist on his heart, before taking his place on my other side, opposite Velasco.

Lyra, Delphine, Daniel, and I follow our guards through the hallways, past servants who avert their eyes as I walk by, down a private stairwell, and out into the main corridor. No one waits in the sun-bright hallway that leads to the front doors. The only thing lining these halls are Blackwell's tapestries and banners.

As we march toward the doors I raise my hands to the sides, palms up. A slow trickle of power escapes me and the tapestries begin to smolder, then burn, grey ash sifting to the floor to reveal the designs that cover the stone walls beneath. Carvings of night skies and the forests and mountains of Selennia shimmer in the bright sunlight.

Ciaran's eyes grow wide as the flames eat up the material and then extinguish just as quickly, the smoke wafting away on a phantom breeze. When he turns to look at me I meet his awe with a wicked smile before we step into the open courtyard beyond the castle door.

A carriage awaits me, carrying us from the castle, down the bridge, and around the edge of town to where the long pathway leads from Aphros to the Central Temple. Unlike my last visit to town, I *want* the attention of the towns-people lining the walkways. I want them to see us clearly as we parade through the street. Additional guards fall in line around us and walk at our backs for protection, but I have no way of knowing without a closer inspection as to whether they're my men or Blackwell's.

Even though the royal wedding was announced only yesterday, the entire population of the town seems to stand along the cobblestones, waving and cheering as I pass. I force a smile and wave to them, wondering if some were people I met these past few weeks when I ventured out, and hope they have the sense to hide when things begin.

Passing through the doors of the Central Temple, my eyes lock on Blackwell standing at the head of the room with the dour Head Priest. Blackwell is dressed in his full royal finery, including a smug expression on his lined face, a fur-lined cloak, and his crown. My mother's platinum crown rests on a velvet pillow near the priest awaiting the coronation to take place after the wedding ceremony.

The seats are filled with courtiers, nobility, and merchants, all dressed in their brightly colored spring finery, waiting expectantly for a happy union to be performed before their eyes. If they notice the stiffness of my posture, the set of my jaw, they don't show it, still tittering and smiling at one another in their excitement over a royal event.

Flowers line the aisle, their petals already falling onto the red carpet underfoot that leads to the dark man who waits for me. Their sweet scent and pleasant pops of white and pink clash with the red and black banners that still hang along the temple walls. Candles and torches illuminate the space, and only a few windows are open to let in the sun in favor of fire and shadow.

When I appeared in the doorway a violin began to play, but it doesn't bring joy to me like the music below deck on the *Bartered Soul*. I barely hear the gentle song over the angry sound of my blood rushing in my ears. Rolling my shoulders back, I prowl down the main aisle toward Blackwell, feeling the eyes of everyone in the room as I pass. Lyra and Delphine remain on either side of me as we walk toward the waiting men, wearing matching cloaks to hide their priestess robes.

When I reach the front of the room, Blackwell steps forward to take my hand, but I step to the side, keeping my hands tucked under my cloak as I take my place at the altar, ignoring him and avoiding his touch. Lyra and Del move to the side with eyes cast downward to wait as my attendants.

"Good morning, my dear Nerissa," Blackwell whispers through gritted teeth as my expression remains flat. "Need I remind you of your lover? Did you not see enough yesterday to subdue you?"

"Let's get this over with," I murmur, refusing to take his bait.

Anger flashes as his mask of contentment slips, he can't hide his emotions as well as I do, and I sense his irritation rising when I meet his hard stare.

As he turns to one of the guards at his back, I close my eyes and a sudden gale blows outside. The bell tower, once rung for warnings and celebrations alike, begins to chime unexpectedly from the force of the wind. The heavy shutters slam open, causing men and women inside the temple to scramble to hold on to hats and gloves that were just moments before casually resting on their laps in anticipation of the ceremony. Bright-colored blossoms and fresh spring leaves waft through the open lower windows, swirling around into the corners of the now brightly lit room alongside the petals from the decorations within. The torches and candles flicker, some now extinguished and smoking.

Blackwell turns back to me, seemingly unbothered by the wind as a cold smile spreads across his face. The guard he spoke with disappears and my heart skips when he returns with another — dragging Lennox between them.

He should have been freed from the dungeon by now, not having his misery being paraded in front of everyone. Tom was supposed to take a few men to take care of the task early this morning before first light. I swallow, taking in the sight of him shirtless and barefooted, still in the breeches he wore when he was taken from me yesterday, too weak to stand. The two guards haul him roughly by his arms as his feet try to propel him forward, but his toes scrape uselessly on the marble.

The courtiers in the pews gasp and pale at the beaten prisoner being paraded in front of them, the full sight of his wounds laid bare for them. Seeing his pain causes my stomach to flip and cold sweat coats my skin despite the warmth of the cloak I still wear. As they pull him past me, the lash marks that stripe his back come into view, raw skin and blood covering the scars he already bore. Dried blood soaks the fabric of his breeches. I sway on my feet as they turn him to face me in the middle of the aisle.

"Billy," I whisper as I reach my hand involuntarily toward him. Even the recognition of the guards who hold him does nothing to calm my distress over his wounds.

At the sound of my voice he struggles to lift his head, but when he does I see the extent of the beating — his broken nose and split lip. His green eyes meet mine gleaming savagely from within the blood crusted over his lips and staining his beard.

Blackwell watches me, a cruel smirk present now. He no longer needs to mask the contempt he truly feels for me and the man who posed as my guard. With his gaze locked on me, Blackwell never sees the small wink Lennox offers me. Once more, I close my eyes, steadying myself as I turn my focus back to Blackwell. The breeze picks up outside, rustling the new leaves of the trees as the bell tower chimes again.

Faintly, noise from the harbor drifts in with the leaves, but everyone in the temple is so focused on the standoff between Blackwell and me that most ignore it except a few of the nobility who nervously glance around at the muted *boom* of an explosion from the port.

"I'm here. I came to you without argument, agreeing to this union. Why are you parading a prisoner in front of these people and ruining our celebration?" I ask confidently, keeping Blackwell's attention focused on me. The guests shift in their seats and toy with their hats and reticules, whispering as they look between Lennox, the King, and myself.

"Oh, I think you know why, Nerissa." Blackwell takes a dagger from his belt and walks toward Lennox. "You need to be reminded of who is *actually* the ruler on this island."

The wind roars and the bell tower chimes once more. The heavy shutters slam in their displeasure as gusts of wind surge through the windows again, causing the guests to cry out as clothing rustles around and more candles wink out.

"Release him."

My voice is a cold command that carries through every inch of the temple hall, echoing with power. A gasp rises from the guests at my tone, daring to speak with such disrespect to their king.

Blackwell never turns as he stalks toward Lennox,

ignoring me to show his own power. "You stupid whore. You think you can command *me*?" he shouts over his shoulder, but his words are carried away on the wind. "I'll kill *this* guard the same way I killed the one your aunt was fucking. *Because I can.*"

His words burn through me when he finally admits he killed Adelaide's lover. My father.

"Release. Him." I take a step from the dais and unclasp my cloak, allowing it to fall behind me. "I command you, as your Queen, to release my consort — the Admiral of my Royal Navy."

"*Consort*? You foolish bitch! You are no queen! You have no power—" Blackwell's bitter words die as he finally spins on his heel to face me.

"My army says differently. *This* says differently."

I force my power upward with raised palms now illuminated by my *glow*, sending another vicious gust to shatter the black glass covering the ceiling and allowing the sunlight to shine down on us. The courtiers scream, but with a swipe of my hands, the same air forces the shards of glass to gather at the edges of the room instead of letting them rain down on us. Lifting my hands outward I send flames to engulf the red and black griffin banners along the walls. The smoke curls upward and out the now-open ceiling.

Drums and war chants drift in from the harbor, harmonizing with the howls of both men and beasts from the forest that echo through the temple on the breeze, and a smile curls across my face.

Finally, Dargan Blackwell knows what it is to feel fear.

CHAPTER 51
SIOBHAN

I roll my neck, trying to calm the tension in my shoulders as the sun rises over the harbor of Aphros. Erik braided my hair tight against my scalp in the candlelight of our room, making me look every bit like the warrior women of the north. The way our ancestors would have, or perhaps even the priestesses of Selennia did when they were responsible for defending these shores. Across the way, the *Hadriel* waits, Revna and Ulf standing on the deck while their crew mills about. Aisling stands apart, staring at the shore as I do.

After she roused me when I collapsed on the deck from igniting Blackwell's ship, we spent hours comparing our recent visions. Both of us have had more vivid dreams since reaching the waters closer to Selennia and, while many were still unfocused, some began to solidify and repeat — wolves and blood, warriors in battle, and blinding light recurring often.

It was during those hours that we determined we could work together from the decks of our respective vessels to begin this battle, to give our warriors an edge, even if neither of us are particularly battle-hardy.

Now, I mentally prepare to focus my power on the third ship that floats nearby. The *Kraken's Maw*.

So far, the messages from Delphine and Daniel have been followed to the letter. A portion of the crew from both ships is already on land, waiting for us to join them at Nerissa's signal. I can't promise a victory, but none of my visions have shown me defeat. So, despite the restlessness that shifts under my skin, I try to focus on Erik's steady comfort at my side and on the elements I control.

Erik has repeatedly told me he doesn't wish for me to come ashore, preferring that I stay on the ship.

"I need to be there for my Sisters, Erik. For *you*," I explained the final time, my tone brooking no further argument as he braided my hair this morning. I know he worries, but I will offer my aid in any way I can today. It's my duty to him and my friends.

As the sun crawls higher into the sky, Aisling strides to Ulf's side, her round belly growing larger by the day. She hugs her husband and he kisses her, caressing her stomach as they speak. After a beat, a vision of a bell tower flashes behind my eyes, causing me to suck in a sudden breath. At the same moment, Aisling looks to the shore, her lips moving. Revna and Ulf snap their attention between her and me.

Then, the great bell tolls.

A great gust of wind snaps in our sails as the metallic sound finds us.

One.

"Man the boats!" Erik shouts over the wind. The trip to

land will be short work for us as sailors climb the ropes down to the waiting longboats.

Taking a deep breath, I face the *Kraken's Maw* mimicking Aisling's posture. Together, we send wind to the deserted vessel, pushing it toward the harbor and Blackwell's remaining ships that now begin to unfurl their sails as men scurry like ants over the decks in response to the sight of our arrival. The sailors all stop to watch as the *Kraken* surges forth in the created wind, never slowing before crashing into the hulls of two waiting ships. Men shout and climb over one another as they try to flee the decks when Aisling and I once again send fire licking over the sacrificial ship.

Shortly after we begin, the powder ignites and explodes. The flares Morel left behind burst into colorful explosions to create chaos on the docks and provide a distraction that allows our allies on land to take their positions. Once the explosions begin, I climb quickly down the rope to join Erik on our trip to shore.

Minutes later, as we begin rowing, the bell chimes again, accompanied by another gust.

Two.

Shouts from those who remain on our ships in the harbor signal their readiness. Waiting for the final signal.

As our small boats touch the rocky beach the bell clangs louder, fury traveling through the breeze that forces its toll.

Three.

The final toll of the bell ends, and the deep chants of those on land join the drumming from the ships.

The war drums of the Northmen are not unique — similar ones were once used by the warriors of Selennia.

Regardless of who plays them, the purpose is the same — striking fear into opponents and bolstering the bravery of those they support. Today they will do both.

Voices raise in a chant from both the ships and those of us who have touched the beach, urging us on and warning those who stand in our way. I stumble up the beach behind the others, traveling up the rocky coast into town where we are joined by Morel and his crew.

"The militia from Delosia await in the forest," Morel relays to Erik, clasping his forearm in greeting.

Doors and windows slam shut as townspeople retreat from the celebration-turned-invasion. Nerissa was clear in her commands: our warriors are not to harm anyone who surrenders, leaving those who avoid the conflict to her. She will determine their loyalties when victory is ours.

"Quickly! Return to your homes," I tell the few lingering people who look at us with fear as we traverse the street. My sigil shines, showing everyone what I am — who returns.

"Priestess! What's happening?" one woman pleads, clutching my hand as we pass.

"The Queen returns," I answer, squeezing her hand. "Return to your homes until it's finished."

"Oh, great Goddess!" she gasps as I press on past her.

Soldiers wearing Blackwell's armor finally meet us as we make it to the center of town where a great fountain stands. These are the soldiers who should have stood as the first line of defense closer to shore, but they scattered from the shock of the explosion in the harbor. Now, they've regrouped and wait for us, swords at the ready. The sight of their red and black uniforms is overwhelming from where I stand on the edge of our motley army and fear momentarily shakes my confidence. A deep exhale of relief passes my lips when, on the signal from Ulf's horn, a portion of Blackwell's ranks break from their lines, turning on their supposed brothers — the men we sent ashore in the night doing their jobs in their stolen uniforms.

Those who fight against us now meet death from northern axes and Selennian swords in equal measure. Men's shouts, groans of death, and the song of steel are all that can be heard in the square. I stay pressed close to the fountain, the water soothing me as I focus on its sound instead and try to focus on the elements in case I can be of assistance. The breeze is gentle in the loose ends of my hair now, and I wonder how Nerissa and the others fare in the temple.

Suddenly, my vision blurs, the flash of fur making me stumble from the edge of the fountain to run to Erik's side. I grip his arm, directing his attention up the hill toward the Central Temple as the howls of wolves greet us.

Erik and I push through the streets toward the temple and I'm surprised to see it's relatively unblemished by Blackwell's takeover. After all the destruction he brought down on the other temples, to see this one still standing is a relief. His red and black griffin banners hang out front, as though it's him and not the priests' God worshiped here, but the red and black can't mask the serene beauty of the large white building. The sun glints off it, throwing shimmering rainbows across the trees and cobblestones out front. Buds from the trees and fresh leaves litter the ground, confetti forced from the branches on the unnatural wind gusts that called us forth from our ships to defend them.

Standing on the steps of the building are more of Blackwell's soldiers, fewer than there would normally be, but enough to challenge our passage. We knew we would face them here, even if we met little resistance in the town proper, and fear skitters over me at the violence I've already witnessed. If things are going to plan, Nerissa and Lennox should be inside with Blackwell now, taking her throne back from him, but we won't know until we can get through the men guarding the temple to join them.

Erik breathes deeply as he holds an axe in each hand, surveying the men on the steps and ours arrayed around us. Ulf and Revna stand at Erik's side, shields and axes ready to challenge the soldiers. I wait just behind them, gripping my dagger as I search the remaining forest behind the temple, looking for any hint of the vision that gripped me in the square. My eyes fill with tears as I take in the clear-cut field where sacred trees should stand, but my heart swells with relief at the sight of the great trees that still shield the far side.

As I watch, the Delosian militia melts into view from behind the church, but none of the armored soldiers seem to notice them. Studying the men, I'm overtaken by a surge of joy, clouding my mind with confusion. We're in the midst of battle, where does *joy* belong here?

But then, the howl from earlier rises once more, this time much closer, at our flanks. Tears escape my eyes, at odds with the smile now tugging at my lips, as I stare to our right.

"Siobhan? My love?" Erik whispers, glancing down at the sound of my gasp. He follows my line of sight toward the treeline, his mouth hanging slightly open.

"It's the Goddess," I reply, watching as a massive black she-wolf prowls out of the trees, a pack following behind. "Aisling and I both *Saw* wolves this whole time. And here they are. On our side."

With that, Erik extends his short-axe overhead, preparing to signal our crews. As he swings it down, a howl rises from both man and beast. Together, we move as one to take the exterior of the temple for our queen.

The Northmen lock their shields in the front line as we push forward. I stay back, unable to fight with my blade like the others who learned from a young age to do so. Revna fights next to her twin, her axe taking down nearly as many men as Ulf's. Erik bellows commands, both axes making contact with red and black as he towers above the enemy.

As the wolves descend on the soldiers, some of Blackwell's men cast aside their swords, fleeing away from the scene. Townspeople run from their homes and up the hill, carrying kitchen knives, rusty scythes, and other everyday items to aid our takeover.

The enemies who continue to fight do so with viciousness, and panic grips me as I wish for a vision to show that this will end in our favor. But that's not how my *Sight* works.

Erik throws his short-axe like I watched him do on the beach when he rescued me from Blackwell's men, and I send a gust of wind to aid it home when the man moves to dodge it. Erik's eyes meet mine, a proud smile on his lips. The small distraction is all the waiting soldier behind him needs.

"*Erik!*" Revna screams, throwing her own axe as he

turns. He raises his right hand, the one he holds his remaining weapon in, but both he and Revna are too slow.

It's as if time stands still as I watch things unfold, almost as if I'm *Seeing* a vision, not the reality of the scene in front of me.

The soldier's sharp broadsword slices through Erik's forearm and his axe falls uselessly to the ground. Revna's weapon finds its target in the man's shoulder, sending him reeling, but all I can see is Erik's face, white with pain.

No sounds reach me any longer.

Not the snarls of the wolves.

Not Erik's cry of pain.

Not Revna's shout for her twin to help.

Not my scream of denial.

All I hear is the rush of my blood in my veins as my *glow* flows from my hands. The sudden white light streams forth of its own volition to destroy those who would further harm those I love.

CHAPTER 52
LENNOX

I wish I was standing at Nerissa's side when Blackwell sees her. To see his face register who, and *what*, stands before him. The temple is bright from Nerissa's *glow* and the sun that now shines down from the broken skylight and open windows, but Delphine's flare for the dramatic casts black shadows that curl through the aisles and bracket Nerissa's slender frame draped in the robes of the High Priestess she is.

The dagger slips from Blackwell's grip, clattering to the ground as his head travels down and back up, really seeing *her* for the first time. My chest clenches at the sight of her, pride and love swelling under my broken ribs, overriding the pain my body feels.

My mother's silver robe shimmers in the bright *glow* that emanates from her brow. Boiled leather covers her chest, protecting her and preventing a wound like Salome suffered in New Aphros. Gold caresses her at her hands, wrist, neck, and brow. But the blazing sigil is what brings the guests in the pews to their knees.

Gasps of *"Our Queen"*, *"She's returned"*, and *"Goddess save us"* rise in the air as the war drums and chanting continue outside the building, moving through the streets and nearing the front of the building. The eerie howls of wolves and men carry on the winds surrounding the temple.

"Kill him! Seize her!" Blackwell stutters to his guards, his hand shaking as he points to Nerissa.

One steps forward toward Nerissa, but Ciaran is already there, sword ready to defend her from Blackwell's man.

"What are you thinking?" the soldier shouts at Ciaran, then glances toward the soldiers behind him that haven't moved from their posts along the walls. "This is treason!"

"I serve the rightful Queen," Ciaran replies, forcing the man back with a quick parry. "It's justice." The clash of their blades rings out through the temple while courtiers look on in horror at the other soldiers who do nothing to aid in stopping the fight.

Blackwell swings around to look at me, seething before he notices the men who flank me no longer hold my unshackled arms. Tom and Velasco smile standing at my sides, both holding their fist over their hearts and inclining their heads to Nerissa before drawing their weapons.

"You would do well to learn the names and faces of your soldiers, Dargan." Nerissa's voice is low and sends shivers over me at the icy tone. I meet her gaze and her feral smile matches my own while Blackwell opens and closes his mouth in confusion, swinging his head between her and the men he was depending on.

He looks around at the other *soldiers*: almost all are our men wearing stolen uniforms with fists over their hearts, but some are those who readily changed sides like Ciaran. Tom explained as he freed me from the dungeon that it was easy for the pirates to slip into the ranks unnoticed with the number of soldiers Charleston had recruited from overseas in the past, only having to dispatch a few who put up a fight.

Finally, Ciaran disarms his opponent, their chests heaving as the man kneels in defeat with Ciaran's blade at his throat. One more of Blackwell's forces steps forward, still loyal to the man. Foolishly, he draws his sword and steps toward Nerissa.

Her sapphire stare turns toward him and, with a simple swipe of her hand, his sword arm falls to the floor, cut by the blinding *glow* she wields. Guests shriek in response and Blackwell staggers back.

"*Impossible*! That's impossible!" Blackwell continues to bluster, frozen in place as Nerissa stalks toward him. "Even if you were training at the temples, no priestess can wield power like that."

"You need to learn your history, Dargan. I'm *the* High Priestess. And the rightful queen. This power is my birthright," she says clearly. The cowering guests all cross a hand over their bodies, resting their fists on their hearts in fealty. Delphine and Lyra stand on the dais watching Nerissa's back, their expressions stern and sigils shining. Deep shadows continue to flow dark and unchecked from Del's rage, caging in the guests in the pews.

"It was *you*. This whole time. The pirates, the raids. It was *YOU*!" The pieces of the puzzle seem to click into place for him as he looks between us, hemmed in on all sides now.

I smile at the tremor in his voice, the way his eyes dart about the room for some saving grace, but no one else rises to challenge the pirates surrounding the room. Chuckling, I gloat, "It's too bad Charleston died before he was able to tell you his theories. He even knew who I was in the end — I confess I'm a little shocked you didn't recognize Captain Lennox in the flesh after all the rumors you collected about me."

Blackwell risks a glance over his shoulder to glare at me but quickly jerks his head back to Nerissa when she moves.

"I could cut you in half with a mere thought, Blackwell," Nerissa murmurs, soft and low as she nears him, her eyes glittering with malice. With each step, the wood underfoot shudders. Golden light shines up from the gaps in the boards — the sigils of protection illuminated once again. As she presses closer, he flinches, almost stepping into where I now stand solidly at his back, not as broken as he thought. "You murdered my father. You broke my mother's heart. *You stole my life.*"

"Your father?" he stutters, not bothering to deny her claims. "What are you talking about?"

"Adelaide wasn't my aunt, you fool. She was my *mother*, and Gareth was my father." She presses so close to him he can't focus on anything but her face, her mouth whispering to him, distracting his eyes away from where her hand slips the dagger from its sheath at her thigh. "You stole her happiness, her love, her country, and then you desecrated her body. You won't do the same to me or him. But, I won't use my power to kill you."

Blackwell gasps as the dagger pierces his side, between the ribs Pike and I showed her to aim for. He staggers back, bumping into my chest as Nerissa whispers, "I could make this quick, but I want to feel your life bleed out. Your reign of terror is over, Dargan Blackwell, you're the King of Nothing."

Her eyes lock on mine at her final words, the same moment she twists the blade and pulls it free.

"Kneel before your Queen," I murmur as I knock Blackwell to his knees at Nerissa's feet. He gasps, looking even older than usual with fear and pain unguarded in his eyes, holding his side as blood runs from his wound and between his lips. Gripping his greying hair in my fingers, I pull his face up to look at hers, baring his neck as if he's a sacrifice for my Queen. My Goddess.

"My my, Blackwell, you do look *so pretty* on your knees, right where you belong," she remarks, nostrils flaring with rage.

Without hesitation, Nerissa slides the sharp blade across Blackwell's throat.

CHAPTER 53

Blackwell's blood on my palms does nothing to hinder me from gripping Lennox's face and pulling him to me with shaking hands. I step over Blackwell's corpse, forgetting him for a moment as I kiss Lennox, relief flooding me.

He's safe.

We've both survived so far.

My relief is short-lived when I hear his wheezing breath and see him wince. "Billy?" I pull back to look at him, but he gives a lopsided smile, then stumbles into me slightly. Daniel was right, his ribs are surely broken, not to mention the loss of blood he's suffered.

"Tom! Help him sit. Lyra! To me, quickly!" I bark orders as though I've been doing so for years. My adrenaline hones my attention and gives me the strength I need to hide the terror I feel and to choke down the tears that burn behind my eyes at the sight of Lennox bloodied and in pain. The sounds of battle surround the temple while the guests on the benches sit in stunned silence. Some clutch the hands of their neighbors, others rest their heads in their hands at the turn of the day's events. Expressions of both relief and fear flicker across the faces watching us, but I can't spare much attention for them while Lennox is still wounded.

Lennox groans as Tom lowers him to sit on the edge of one of the vacated benches. The former occupants sit pressed together with other remnants of nobility who stare at me as though *I'm* the savage one here. Lyra dashes to Lennox's side, running her hands over her uncle's skin as she determines what course of action to take.

"My Queen," a man's voice draws my attention away from my family to a familiar courtier kneeling behind me.

"Gavin, correct?"

"Yes, my Queen. Tell us how we can serve you." Gavin pitches his voice low, flicking his eyes to the corner where three priests huddle like rats in a larder. "It seems the battle continues and the priests are already plotting."

Delphine steps past where he still kneels to take her place at my side, a swirl of shadows drifting around our feet. She looks wary when she inspects the courtier, but he dips his head in respect, then pulls a pendant from where it was tucked under his tunic. The pendant is polished silver but looks ancient, with the phases of the moon carved into the surface. "You do not need to fear me. My family and I never lost faith in the Goddess. I took up the title of my wife's father once he was slaughtered in the siege but neither of our families ever wavered in their loyalty to Queen Adelaide. As I insinuated at court, we're relieved you've returned and will gladly defend you."

Looking from Gavin to the group behind him my eyes

land on his wife Tieve, speaking to a frightened group of courtiers. She bows deeply when she meets my gaze.

"Hmmph," Delphine snorts but says nothing further as I consider my next words.

"Keep watch over the priests. No one is permitted to leave, yet," I advise. "I must check on my consort, then address the room. Our allies will need us, but we must determine who in this room will stand beside me."

With that, Gavin dips his chin, rises, then strides off, grabbing another man by the arm to gather the priests. They guide them to one of the benches, then take places on the ends to block their escape.

"How is he, Lyra?" I ask, my eyes traveling over the people still in the temple and back to Lennox in turn. Velasco, Tom, and the other crew members wearing stolen uniforms guard the doors, looking as fearsome and imposing as any pirates I've ever seen.

"He's healing. The bleeding has stopped and his ribs have knitted."

"Stop," Lennox says, wiping a cloth across his face to clean the blood from his nose and mouth. "With my ribs healed, I'm fine. Lyra, don't waste any more power on me. We don't know who else might need it and I can't risk you draining yourself."

"He's right," I echo, even if I want him fully healed. "Remember, none of us are to drain ourselves today. We still have much to do."

Standing, I step over Blackwell's bloody body and take my place on the platform at the front of the room, where we were set to be wed. The crowd turns as one to me, expectant, even as fear hangs heavy in the temple.

"Everyone, I'm Nerissa Faelan, Queen Adelaide's daughter," I begin, holding a hand up to silence the whispers and gasps that run throughout the room. "I returned to Selennia to set things right, to take back my throne, and to be your queen. Dargan Blackwell has seeded hatred and misery during his reign, but I assure you, despite what you witnessed here, I'm *not* the same kind of ruler. If you stand with me and are able, prepare to fight any soldiers who may still support Blackwell. If you don't, remain here until the battle is over and I'll determine your fate."

"Heretical whore!" one of the priests held near the front of the room shouts even as Gavin shoves him back onto the bench. "You murdered God's King on this island and will be rewarded with plague and famine! Good people, do not listen to her devilry. Do not be seduced by her sinful ways! You saw the evil magic she wielded to cut down King Dargan. Do not be fool enough to think you aren't next!"

"Silence!" I order, pulling the air from the priest's lungs, then releasing it a moment later, leaving him gasping and clutching his chest. "We've all heard enough about your God and how He saves, yet the people of Selennia have suffered for *years* under your guidance."

Mumbles of agreement sift through the crowd and I turn back to Gavin. "Keep them here until the battle is done. Gag them if it suits you. And watch that one—" I point directly at Tiernan, the courtier who served on my mother's council, then defected to Blackwell's side, as he inches toward the end of the bench of courtiers he was seated on. "*He's* not to escape again," I coldly remark, then pull my dagger from its sheath once again and approach Blackwell's form. "I can't expend any more power right now, but someone needs to ring the bell to tell the town to gather."

Some of the courtiers turn away, gagging when they see my intentions as I hold the knife at Blackwell's neck. But if Blackwell has taught me anything, sometimes cruelty and brutality are the only language men respect, and I plan on showing anyone outside these doors who think to challenge me that I'm more than capable of it. I choke on my disgust as I slip the sharp steel through muscle and sinew. After a few moments I relent, sheathing my blade, and instead use my *glow* to sever Blackwell's head from his shoulders before I can change my mind.

When I stand, holding the black and silver hair in my fist, Lennox joins me, still shirtless, but no longer bleeding. We turn toward the door, ready to step out to view the battle beyond, but a woman's familiar scream pierces the shouts and steel that sound through the broken windows freezing me in place. A sudden blinding light flashes through the opening and I grip Blackwell's hair tighter in my bloody fingers, my stomach churning at the grisly trophy.

"Open the doors!" I cry, forcing myself to move.

Tom and Ciaran pull the oak doors wide, allowing the sun to fill the temple completely as we stare into the disarray before us. I thought to find a battle still in progress, but instead, numerous soldiers lay scattered over the ground, the scent of blood and ships burning from the explosions in the harbor mingling on the wind.

Any of Blackwell's troops that remained in or around Aphros have congregated around the Central Temple. Now, many appear to have been cut down with the *glow* I thought only I possessed.

Bewildered, I step from the safety of the doorway, drawing the startled gaze of Blackwell's remaining soldiers who stand between the temple and the town below. My own men and women are scattered throughout, breathing heavily in the interim. Upon seeing me, some kneel, others bow their heads, and as the bell tower tolls to draw the townspeople, the giant she-wolf bounds up the steps toward me.

Without hesitation, I hold Blackwell's head high, calling out, "It's done!"

The she-wolf howls and I toss Blackwell's head toward Her. She laps at the blood, the same blood that covers my hands and clothing, and takes her place at my side, greying muzzle coated in crimson as the remaining enemy soldiers drop their weapons.

The pirates take the remaining soldiers into custody with ease as they stare at me in confusion and fear. I scan the people, both living and slain, searching for our closest friends. Seeking out the source of the *glow* responsible for the casualties.

"Where are they?" I ask, my voice becoming more panicked as I search, my heart in my throat. "Who used the *glow*?"

"*Shit,*" Delphine hisses, pointing across the expanse to Pike. In his arms hangs Siobhan, her long copper hair is braided against her scalp, but the ends flow loose as her head lolls back with her eyes closed. Behind them, Ulf struggles alongside a shirtless Captain Morel to get Erik's haggard, unsteady frame up the path to the stairs. Tom,

Lennox, and Velasco all run down the steps to try to help Erik as Lyra holds her hand over her mouth in shock.

"Get inside. What happened?" I ask Pike when he reaches us. Turning on my heel I leave the she-wolf standing in the doorway, while the other wolves of the pack lounge on the steps guarding the sacred space, preventing any who would harm us from entering.

Delphine helps cradle Siobhan's head as Pike lowers her to the ground. Lyra already runs her hands over Siobhan's cheeks, brushing her hair from her freckled face while assessing her injuries. Siobhan's breaths are so shallow I have to press my hand to her chest to find her weak pulse and feel her chest rise.

"Erik was injured," Pike starts, pulling my attention from Siobhan to focus on Erik. His face is drained of nearly all color, and his eyes are barely cracked as he drifts in and out of consciousness. It's only then that I realize the severity of his wound. His right arm was severed just below the elbow joint and only hangs by a thin strip of muscle and flesh. My stomach flips at the sight of the brutal injury. Blood covers Erik and most of Morel from supporting him on the way to the temple.

"Lyra, go to Erik," I whisper. "Let me help Siobhan."

She swallows thickly when she sees the injury, turning the same shade of green as when she was seasick on our voyage to Delosia but nods and goes with Delphine to Erik's side. "Go on, Pike. What happened to Siobhan?"

"She killed them all."

I snap my attention to him, holding Siobhan's hand in mine. "*What*?"

He nods, his head bobbing as if he can't believe it.

"Siobhan screamed when she saw Erik wounded, a guttural, animal sound that stopped everyone in their tracks. When Blackwell's soldiers turned toward her she sliced through them with her power. The way you have. The *glow* spread from her in every direction and took down any of Blackwell's men that were near us like the power knew the enemy on its own." Pike sits back against one of the benches, exhaustion lining his face as he shakes his head in disbelief. "She crumpled to the ground right after, but she did it."

"Del, I need you," I call, drawing her back to my side while Lennox stays with Lyra.

"What is it?" she asks, kneeling beside me.

"I need you to channel some of my power to her. At least to bring her back to consciousness."

"Are you certain?" Delphine asks, hesitantly looking between Siobhan and me. "What if you need it?"

"She's too far gone to try to recover on her own. Just do it."

Breathing deeply, I close my eyes as Delphine takes my hand. My chest tightens as my power leaches from me, tingling through the hand she holds and into Siobhan. I can only hope she hasn't fully drained herself saving Erik, even if I would have done the same. As I begin to feel chilled and weak, I open my eyes.

"Come on, Sister. We need you. *Erik* needs you," I whisper.

I tremble as nausea begins to churn in my stomach, but I'm not sure if it's from the draining of my power or my growing fear at Siobhan's failure to wake. I can't allow

Delphine to continue much longer, or I might find myself in the same state.

My vision blurs with tears as Siobhan's lashes begin to flutter, her eyes moving quickly behind her lids as if she's dreaming. Just as I prepare to tell Delphine to stop, Siobhan's blue eyes pop open and she stares up at us. Del drops my hand immediately, studying my face with concern. I wave her off, fighting residual nausea, as Siobhan looks between each of us in confusion.

"Nerissa? Del?" Siobhan sits up abruptly, nearly pushing me over. "Erik! Where is he?"

"Siobhan, be careful," I hiss, weakly trying to grip her hand, but she's already crawling across the floor to where Lyra holds Morel's discarded shirt over the end of Erik's arm. Lyra's eyes are closed and sweat beads on her forehead as she works. Erik's eyelids twitch, his breathing shallow and rapid as Lennox holds his other hand for support, whispering something too low to make out.

"Erik! Erik!" Siobhan replaces Lennox, grabbing Erik's hand in hers and holding it against her chest. His eyes flutter open at her voice and he gives the barest smile.

"My love," he whispers.

"Erik, you'll be all right. Lyra and I can heal you."

"You both need a break," Delphine interrupts, her whole body stiff at the suggestion. "We can't let you drain all of your power. You were nearly at your end, Siobhan. We don't have any more to share."

Siobhan casts a glare over her shoulder but returns her attention to Erik. "You'll be fine."

"Even if I live, I am no longer the man I was. I cannot

defend you as I promised," Erik stutters, a flicker of shame on his face.

"I've seen you use both arms in battle with your axes. Your left is just as strong. And it doesn't matter. We don't have to fight any more battles. Your arm is so big you only need one to wrap around me. One to cradle our son," Siobhan whispers, tears dripping off her chin. "Please, Erik, stay with me."

"Our son?" Erik's eyes fill with tears and confusion.

"I've *Seen* it, Erik." Siobhan kisses his lips, then curls against him on the floor, holding onto him as though she can keep him here. "This isn't your end."

"I'm sorry. I can't do anymore," Lyra whispers, releasing her grip on Erik's wounded arm and sitting back. Pike helps her to her feet and walks her to one of the benches where Daniel brings her a drink.

I missed it, worrying over Siobhan, but someone removed the lower portion of Erik's arm. The severed limb lays wrapped in the discarded shirt used to staunch the bleeding. Even though Lyra is one of the most talented healers, she can't reattach an appendage. But, at least the grisly wound has ceased bleeding and is scabbed over enough to prevent more blood loss. Time will tell how it heals, but Lyra has saved him, and that's what matters at the moment.

"No, my love. You are right. This is not *our* end." Erik grimaces, then slowly wraps his left arm around her, holding her tight to him.

CHAPTER 54

"My Queen!" Daniel calls from the doors to the temple. One stands partially open so we can view the steps and pathway beyond, guarded by men and wolves alike. "Your people await you, as do your prisoners."

Despite the exhaustion tugging at me and the desire to comfort those closest to me, the burdens of my title begin now. I push to my feet, gathering my nerves as I look at my friends.

This single victory isn't enough to retake the island. I'll need to convene with the captains to know which temples and port cities we hold and which are still manned by Blackwell's remaining troops, but one step at a time. Now, I owe it to the people of Aphros to be their Queen, to answer their questions, to reassure them it's peace I bring.

Lennox peels away from where he sits at Erik's side to join me as I walk toward the doors, followed by Lyra and Delphine. Siobhan remains behind with Erik's head cradled in her lap humming softly to him, while Daniel and Tom guard the temple doors.

The remaining courtiers and priests who were held inside the temple are escorted by Pike and Velasco to stand at the foot of the stairs, greeted by the low growls of the wolves as they pass. Lennox and I stand at the top, him slightly behind me, while the great she-wolf sits on my right. Delphine and Lyra take up places a step down flanking us, sigils shining boldly.

"People of Aphros and all of Selennia!" I raise my voice over the crowd, rasping from unshed tears and fatigue. "You may have seen me arrive, a gift from a pirate to the craven *King*. But I assure you, I was never a gift. I was never a meek bride seeking safety in this stolen castle. This was my mother's castle. This is my birthright."

To punctuate my message, I now allow my entire sigil to shine, the larger mark something the people have never seen before, and set the remaining banners from Blackwell's reign ablaze against the shining front wall of the temple with a flick of my fingers. The action masks the fact that my power is as weak from helping Siobhan as it's been since I began training in New Aphros. A whisper travels through the crowd, but whether it's from awe or fear is unclear.

"This is your country and mine. Selennia is my home. I came to take it back in honor of the Goddess and our people. To right the wrongs that we have all suffered under the brutal rule of Dargan Blackwell after he stole it from Queen Adelaide. And today, I have begun."

A cheer rises from the Delosian militiamen, pirates, and the common people who fought with them in the streets. Some of the other townspeople join them, but several look hesitant or glance askance at the grisly sight of Blackwell's head still at the feet of the wolf by my side. Their fear is understandable. It would be arrogant of me to expect everyone to trust me so quickly, especially when many of them thought I was a myth. Change takes time, but I'm determined to do better for all of Selennia.

The thought of all I'll have to do to fix the damage Blackwell has done is daunting, but now is not the time to show weakness when Blackwell's supporters remain. The wolf on my right tilts her head up to howl, the others picking up the call, then the sailors do the same, lifting the hair on my neck at the eerie sound. Slowly, those in the crowd start to kneel, fists over their hearts. Lennox steps forward and takes a knee in front of me.

When Lennox raises his eyes to mine, the love and pride in them make my heart stutter. I have to force back the tears that threaten to continue speaking without my voice shaking. "Please rise. We have a long road ahead of us but know that I will not allow the soldiers Blackwell sent out to return here to reclaim this town or this castle. No one will take this land from us again," I add, earning a smattering of cheers from the townspeople. "I promise that together we will restore Selennia to peace and prosperity.

"As for those of you held prisoner now," I address the men still wearing the red and black of Dargan Blackwell. "You have two options: you can take the next ship leaving the harbor to return to the continent, never to return to these shores; or you can swear fealty to me and remain as a loyal subject. I know some of you took up arms for Blackwell under duress or because of his conscription — you had family to protect, or feared for your life. Fear is a strong motivator.

"I will not rule by fear. I do not demand your love. But I do hope to earn it. All I ask is for your respect: respect for my rule, respect for the Old Ways of this land and the Goddess who protects it, and respect for one another. In turn, I offer you fairness, justice, and safety. But, know this: just because I don't choose to rule by fear like he did, don't think it's because I'm incapable. I will protect my people from men like Blackwell. I am *not* my mother. I can easily speak the language of battle should it be the only one you comprehend. Make your choices and move accordingly. You have until tomorrow to decide."

The soldiers shuffle together, debating their choices and making decisions while my soldiers stand around to keep them in line, the din of voices rising in the air once again. I close my eyes and let the warm sunlight heat my cheeks, trying to forget the blood now dry on my fingers and covering the silver robe I wear. I doubt we'll be able to get the stains out this time.

"Daniel," I call to where he stands by the doors. "Please go with Tom and sort the dead. We'll need to have pyres built to honor them tomorrow."

With a dip of his chin, he walks down the stairs, shoulders squared to his task.

<hr>

THAT EVENING, I SIT IN FRONT OF THE FIRE IN MY CHAMBERS cleansed of all blood and violence, smelling of lemon balm and lavender. Lennox rests in a chair at my side, finally able to join me without keeping watch or fearing someone will catch us. He's clean-shaven again and, with his golden hair cut short, he looks like the rogue pirate captain once more, except for the Northern Isles tattoos peeking through his shorn hair. Lyra and Delphine retired to their room, resting for what's next, while Erik and Siobhan have taken up residence across the hallway together.

The sailors and militiamen who weren't completely exhausted agreed to take first watch tonight, some gathering around the castle, others at the port, while the townspeople gather driftwood and kindling for pyres.

"The losses are higher than I expected," I lament, pulling Lennox's gaze from the flames. He's been staring into them blankly as though he can see visions of his own in the red and gold, but perhaps he just sees memories. "I'm so sorry about Jackson."

"They are, but Del was right — Salome is surely sitting on Jackson's lap laughing in the Afterlife. That's what I tell myself at least. That they're with my parents, and with yours," he replies, his eyes glassy with tears in the firelight.

I blink my own tears back rapidly, sniffling slightly as I reach across to squeeze his hand in mine, nodding in agreement. "It will be good for the people to have the ceremonial pyres tomorrow, something they haven't been able to do for years."

Lennox hums his agreement as he shifts his grip to entwine our fingers, then leans back in his chair, sipping his whiskey. As my eyes drift closed, heavy with exhaustion, a brisk *tap tap tap* sounds on the oak of my door.

"What now?" Lennox mumbles, standing and ambling to the door on bare feet.

"Captain," Tom greets, dark curls pushed away from his face. "The Queen is needed. Scouts report that soldiers are on the move from the coasts."

"Which scouts?" I ask, circling the chairs as I wrap a cloak around me.

"Some of Morel's, and Trevino's ship has made it to the harbor with similar news. Troops from the north are returning to the castle. It seems they may have been told to reconvene before Beltane since that's when Blackwell expected your wedding to occur. Perhaps he was more suspicious than you thought and expected some kind of attack that day."

"Well, his eagerness to punish me served to end him more easily, didn't it? How far are they?"

"Perhaps two days due to their number and the slow march of their infantry. The scouts nearly killed their horses riding so hard to get us word."

"Very well. At least we have a little time. Tomorrow we pay our respects to the dead as planned. The next day we ride out to inform them this land has a new queen. Let's convene in the dining room to discuss the details."

CHAPTER 55

Driftwood smokes along the pebbled beaches of Aphros the morning after my successful recapture of the city. Townspeople huddle together as the sun rises to bid farewell to both their countrymen and those from across the sea who came to our aid. It's a ritual that was banned for years, but ushers in the beginning of change for Selennia and its people.

An empty pyre is lit in memory of those from the *Selkie's Tears*. Lennox lit this one with a torch instead of allowing me or my sister priestesses to ignite with our power. Standing at his side, I take the day to mourn, once again letting him hold me as tears run down our cheeks for our friends and allies like that winter morning in New Aphros.

We did it, Mother. We took it back. Now the work begins, I think as the pyre cradling Adelaide's silk-wrapped skull ignites. I had Ciaran remove it from the gates of the castle and placed it on the pyre myself at dawn before the crowds gathered.

After a few more moments and a shuddering breath, I

blink away my tears. Tomorrow we'll be forced to meet another round of Blackwell's troops, but hopefully, this will be our last pyre for some time.

<hr>

THE RED AND BLACK BANNER OF BLACKWELL'S RETURNING contingent catches my eye before the lead men are visible over the rise in the land. They have one more hill to top before the sight of an unfamiliar army welcomes them home.

I sit on my grey mare in the center of the front line. The dark Northern cloak Aisling gave me covers the same armor and robe that I wore in the temple two days prior. I've determined that perhaps the bloodstained robe is not something to discard, but something to be feared — as much a part of my battle attire as any other soldier's armor.

Lennox is mounted on Charleston's destrier at my right, a pleasant beast despite being trained for war, while Ciaran is astride his horse on my left. Delphine and Siobhan flank them, sigils shining bright in the early morning mist to match my own. The rest of the soldiers at my back are a mixture of pirates, Delosian militia, townspeople from Aphros, and soldiers who swore fealty to me in exchange for their lives. Each man had a tale similar to the next — threats to family, lack of other options, and fear for their life.

As the soldiers crest the next hill, a horn sounds, stopping their forward motion. Soon, three horses break from the front line, trotting toward us. Our position, with the rising sun at our backs, gives us a clear view of those who approach while blinding them between the fog and sunlight.

"I wasn't expecting a welcome party! Is the King so eager to—" The man riding in front's words stop as abruptly as his horse when he sees who waits for him. The horses the three men ride whinny and shuffle their feet as wolves wind their way through our troops to stand in a line before us.

"What the fuck is this? Where's our King, you witch?" His eyes dart to the men behind me, searching for familiar faces. I merely reach behind me to draw a linen sack from where it's been tied to my saddle, tossing it forward onto the dirt of the road. Silent.

"Dismount and see what it is," the leader tells the soldier to his left. The younger man does as he's ordered, flicking his gaze warily between the sack and us as he crouches, untying the laces.

"Dear God!" he cries when he finds Blackwell's head inside the bag. "What devilry is this? Where's Commander Charleston?"

Expecting this response I nod to Lennox who retrieves Charleston's helm from where he had it secured to his saddle, tossing it into the roadway the same way I did the bag. "At least Charleston put up a fight. Blackwell nearly pissed himself before she killed him." In his leather greatcoat, the pirate captain speaks today, not my lover or consort, sneering at the men's distress and sending pleasant shivers over me at his callous words.

"I'll give you the same option I gave the soldiers in town, then you can relay them to your troops. Swear fealty to me, or leave this island immediately," I advise in the silence that lingers. "Otherwise, you'll share Blackwell and Charleston's fate."

The third man looks toward his companions, then studies me before speaking, "So my eyes don't deceive me? You're truly the queen we've waited for? The heir returned?"

"What the fuck are you talking about?" the leader snaps, mouth agape at his companion's betrayal.

"I'm Nerissa Faelan, Adelaide's daughter. High Priestess and Queen of Selennia."

The man nods, crossing a hand over his chest before he rips the griffin from his tunic and tosses it into the dirt. He then urges his horse forward, through the line of wolves to join our side. "We've waited for too long for you, my Queen," he murmurs as he passes me to stand his mount next to Ciaran.

"I will not be ruled by some whore claiming a birthright!" the first man shouts, drawing his sword as if he plans to charge me. With a sweep of my hand, my *glow* easily slices through his arm, leaving him screaming as his sword lays in the dust, still held in a now useless grip.

"Threaten me again and you'll lose more than your arm," I reply calmly. "You," I address the remaining man, still standing next to the sack containing Blackwell's head with his mouth ajar. "Return to your soldiers; tell them what I've said. Should any wish to swear fealty, they may cross to do so. Take him as an example of what not to do should anyone think to challenge me."

He nods, mounting his horse and leading his superior's horse behind him while the other man holds his arm in shock.

It takes two more meetings with returning troops — each playing out similarly — before all those sent to the coasts have returned. A surprising number of men swear fealty, many originally Selennian who would rather live the way they grew up instead of fleeing to a continent where they're not welcome. Those who followed Blackwell, and who won't swear oaths to me, board the *Calypso* in the harbor of Aphros bound for the continent across the channel under the command of Captain Trevino. His safe return will signal the true end of this matter, as he carries a box for the remainder of Blackwell's family. The severed head, hands, and banner of the beast who stole my life are all tucked inside, along with a letter from the new Queen of Selennia. The reply from the Blackwells will determine whether we prepare for more bloodshed, or whether our peace can begin.

***

"Trevino's ship has been spotted," Lennox tells me as I finish my lunch. It's been less than a week since the *Calypso* departed to return Blackwell's remaining soldiers to their homelands, and my mother's — no, *my* desk — is scattered with scraps of parchment with notes and ideas for me to bring to the council meeting once the captains are all present.

"When he's docked, let him know we'll meet shortly. I want to discuss my proposals and convene with the representatives of the other towns soon now that they're all here."

Lennox nods, brushing a stray strand of hair from my

eyes before kissing me, studying my face briefly, and whispering, "Have no fear, my she-wolf. They'll all love you."

I smile at his reassurance, pressing my lips to his again before standing to ready myself.

Within two hours, the captains of the ships that aided our takeover, as well as my priestesses, and representatives from the main towns in Selennia have all gathered outside the throne room. Instead of waiting on my throne, as might be expected, I sit at the head of a long table that was carried in specifically for this meeting.

Shortly before the meeting starts, the doors open and Captain Trevino enters alone. After bowing, Trevino slips a folded parchment from his coat and hands it to me. The seal is a modified griffin in green, the symbol of the Blackwell family still residing on the continent. A reply to the gruesome delivery I sent with Trevino.

"How did they take it?" I ask the taciturn captain.

"Better than one would expect. It took very little time for them to pen that for you, Your Majesty."

Popping the seal, sharp script greets me:

Queen Nerissa,

Congratulations on your victory and upcoming coronation. I assure you the acts committed by my brother Dargan were not sanctioned, nor supported, by myself or my remaining siblings. My only regret is that I wasn't there to watch him brought to heel.

You will have no quarrel from the Blackwell family.

If anything, we owe you a debt of gratitude for ridding us of the foul reputation Dargan created in the wake of his misdeeds.

I'm sure he's currently trying to usurp the Devil in his final resting place.

Sincerely,

Cedric Blackwell

A DEEP SIGH OF RELIEF PASSES MY LIPS AS I READ THE FINAL lines. Time will tell if the Blackwells across the sea are trustworthy, but for now, we can focus on tasks other than battle.

"Thank you, Captain Trevino."

"Of course, Your Majesty." He dips his pale blond head once more, then takes a seat at the table. I hand the missive off to Lennox to read, then turn my attention to the doors in anticipation of the arrival of the rest of the attendees.

After another few minutes, the doors are opened and Morel and the Gunnarson twins enter, bowing to me, then shaking Lennox's hand before choosing seats, followed by Siobhan and Erik. They've been nearly inseparable since the battle, more so than usual, but Erik has healed cleanly thanks to Lyra's additional attention, and Siobhan has regained use of her power. The intensity of the *glow* she used to save Erik hasn't been evident since, but she can now wield it on a smaller scale — using it as a weapon when needed like the priestesses of the past. Lyra and Delphine take places next to Siobhan, Aisling joining them across from Ulf.

After the captains and priestesses, the Selennian representatives from the main cities cross the threshold, one from each main port town with a temple in place or to be rebuilt for defense — Aphros, Athene, Cybele, Murias, Airmedan.

Some look fearful, even though I've already met personally with each one to welcome them to the castle. Their eyes take in the rough men and women gathered around the table, the priestesses who slew men with a wave of their hands like in the stories we were raised hearing. Two seats remain vacant in honor of diMicios and Jackson.

When the doors close, all eyes turn to me at the head of the table, a tingle of energy flitting through the airy space.

"Welcome, everyone," I begin, taking a steadying breath as they watch me. Lennox cuts his emerald eyes to me, a smile twitching at the corner of his lips as he winks at me, reminding me of the rogue I met months ago. The warmth in his expression reminds me of the love I felt in these halls, the sacrifices made for this land, and the hope held in these hearts. As I exhale, my resolve solidifies and all doubt fades.

"Let's rebuild our country."

EPILOGUE

Twenty Years Later

"What are you doing?" one of the men, a boy really, hisses to the other as they step off the gangway onto the weathered wood of the dock in Aphros. He jerks his hand free of the other boy's grip, looking around fretfully as though they'll be arrested.

"I told you, you needn't worry here. That's why I chose this place. We don't have to hide anymore," the other boy insists, pulling his companion closer with a soft smile. Neither is watching where they walk and quickly bump into the broad back of the tall blond man supervising the loading of provisions on a neighboring vessel. From where I sit on top of a crate, I witness the fear in the young man as the tall captain turns to face him.

"I... I... I'm sorry, sir. Forgive me," the boy stutters, wrenching his hand from his friend.

"It's no trouble, son. No harm done," Lennox rumbles,

smiling at the teens, eyes sparkling in the early morning light glistening off the sea. "New to Selennia, I take it?"

"Yes, sir. Just came across from the continent," the more confident of the two answers as I push off the crate, approaching them from their backs as I listen. "Is it true what they say, sir? That the queen here is just? That she welcomes those who are… different?"

"She welcomes anyone who respects the land and those who live here, different or not," I answer, making the young men start and whirl to me as Lennox cocks his head with a grin.

"Oh! You… you're a woman!"

"I am." I smile at their nervousness. It will never cease to amuse me at the response when people see my sigil, even if it's only the one ordinary priestesses bear. I keep the mark of my title cloaked when I'm on the docks or traveling outside the castle for the most part. "Have you a place to go? Work lined up?"

"No, Mistress. We've just arrived. We have no family or friends here. Just… well, just each other," the bolder of the two answers again, wide-eyed as he studies my sigil, then looking away when I lift my brows and meet his gaze.

"I see. You should visit the pub on the corner. Ask for Tom or Daniel. They'll likely have work, or know someone who does. They can put you up for a night or two. Just tell them Andromeda sent you," I instruct, sending the boys on their way.

Lennox wraps an arm around my shoulders and the boys' whispers reach me on the breeze, "Do you think all the women are as brave as that one? Wearing men's clothing and lingering on the docks?"

"I don't know, but I hear the Queen and Princess are both beautiful and terrifying. That they can slice you in two with just a thought!"

"Maybe we'll see one of them here. It *is* the capital city!"

Their sudden excitement at being presented with an opportunity is contagious and I can't help but chuckle at their youth. "What do you think? Are the Queen and Princess so terrifying?" I ask Lennox.

"I don't know about Morgana being terrifying. *You* certainly can be." I feign dismay and playfully smack his shoulder, but before I can reply he continues, "But I can't deny that you're beautiful." He pulls me closer, kissing me deeply and raising a blush to my cheeks in the cool air, even after all these years. "Speaking of the Princess, where is our daughter? Erik and Siobhan should arrive soon and we need to be off."

"I saw her chatting with one of the crewmen. Have you heard the latest rumor?"

"Good Goddess, do I want to know?" Lennox replies, furrowing his brow.

"About the quartermaster of the new ship that's docked a few times now? The *Pale Queen*? Seems he's quite popular with the ladies in town, and, some say, with our dear daughter."

"I've seen the man — a tall, red-headed lad. Lewis? Lowell? No, Lovelace — that's his name." He sighs with a shake of his head. "I guess she comes by her affection for pirates honestly, though. I mean, look at her mother. Swept off her feet by a vicious captain so many years ago. But if she wants a red-headed sailor, I wish she'd pick the obvious choice," he adds with a jerk of his chin indicating one of the docking ships, resignation balanced with amusement.

Together we watch Morgana's dark hair reflecting the rising sun. She's turned toward the ship lowering its gangway and smiles broadly as a red-haired, heavily freckled sailor descends. He's as tall and broad as his father, even at only nineteen years old, and when he wraps her in a tight embrace his arms engulf her willowy frame.

"Trying to play matchmaker again, Admiral?" I tease as we head toward the ship. "Let's go see how the High Priestess of the Northern Temple and her man fared on the voyage. We can leave for Delosia as soon as their trunks are aboard."

"Sister!" Siobhan greets me with a warm embrace as soon as her feet hit the dock, still referring to me as though we are both priestesses of no rank instead of the Queen and one of her seconds. Erik carries a satchel in his left hand, likely containing Siobhan's collection of herbs and tonics for the voyage, but smiles warmly at us and then at his son and our daughter talking in low voices nearby. He and Lennox share a knowing smile while Siobhan and I roll our eyes.

"Morgana! Eriksson! It's time!" Lennox shouts, pulling them from their gossip and leading us to board the *Bartered Soul*.

"I can't wait to see Auntie Del and Lyra! Is Delosia really as beautiful as they say, Mother? Can we truly stopover in New Aphros, too?" Morgana asks, firing questions rapidly as her green eyes flash around to take in the activity on the decks, Lir Eriksson's long arm still draped over her shoulders.

"Hello, Lir. It's good to see you, and to have you joining us." I smile up at Siobhan and Erik's son before replying calmly to Morgana, "Yes, my love. We'll meet with Mistress Marie in Delosia to shore up the transfer of her leadership now that she's ready to retire. Lyra and Delphine will meet us there, then we'll escort Marie back with them to New Aphros. You'll get to see Aunt Celeste, too. I know it's been quite some time."

My daughter, so bright and happy like my mother was, grips me in a crushing embrace, then scurries off to chat with some of the crew, cutting glances at Eriksson all the while as he helps load items for his parents. At eighteen she's bright and happy, traits I don't think she'll ever outgrow. It pleases me, but I can only hope she'll be able to rule with firmness when the time comes.

We prepare to sail to Delosia to meet the new leader of the island, retrieving Marie to relocate her to New Aphros where Lyra and Del have lived for the past ten years alongside Celeste. This voyage also serves to introduce Morgana to the people we trade with across the sea, solidifying long-held relationships and forging new ones to ensure the prosperity we've enjoyed since I retook power twenty years ago continues.

Even now, after years of peace, I still find it hard to fully relax under the weight of my role as queen. Nightmares still wake me, leaving me clutching at Lennox in the darkness. Memories sometimes haunt my waking hours when the light hits just right, or smoke wafts past unexpectedly. But here, with the sea breeze in my hair and my friends and loved ones at my side, I breathe deeply and allow the worry to fall away completely.

Lennox wraps his arms around my waist, pulling my back against his solid chest as he nuzzles against my neck near the figurehead carved in my likeness. "Are you ready for our next adventure, my she-wolf?" he whispers against my skin.

"I'm ready for anything with you, Billy," I reply softly.

"Weigh anchors, crew! It's time to sail!" Lennox shouts, kissing my cheek and turning to give additional orders.

The crew moves swiftly, sails opening and ropes tossed from the dock. As the helmsman turns us to sea, a lupine howl from land reaches me on the breeze that whips my hair around my cheeks. The call is echoed by the crew of the *Bartered Soul*.

It's a reminder. All will be well until we return.

The priestesses stand watch once more.

The Goddess lives on.

THE END

AFTERWORD

Thank you so much for taking this journey with Andromeda and Lennox! I hope the conclusion of their story was everything you'd hoped.

If you enjoyed this book or any of the others in the series, please consider leaving a review on Amazon or Goodreads (or any of your other favorite review spots!)

Reviews and word of mouth are the best ways you can support your favorite indie authors, and I appreciate every review! The more people who read my stories, the more I can continue to write and share them with the world!

xo,

LB

Acknowledgments

It is so bittersweet to write these acknowledgments — if you would have told me a year and a half ago that I would be completing a trilogy right now I would have laughed at you, but here we are, saying 'goodbye' to my first book babies.

Matt & E: I love you both so much. Whether you know what I'm daydreaming about half the time or not, thank you for letting me escape into this little world of my own creation for hours at a time to create.

Aimee: Thank you for editing this from the beginning, you have helped shape this world with me and given me the tools to become a better writer book by book. Thanks for being on this journey with me!

Lauren P., Danielle, Rhiannon, Caity, Holly, and Kelly: You've each been a part of Book 3 in some way, shape, or form from the get-go. Thank you for taking time from your own works to read and offer feedback and reactions to mine. Sometimes your excited comments are all that pushed me through on the hard days.

The Daily Discord/Bookstagram/BookTok friends (you all know who you are because I'm in your DMs every day): Thank you for supporting this journey, whether it's writing-related, life-related, a funny reel, or just acknowledgment that I'm seen and heard, your input and friendship is invaluable and I love you all.

To my readers: Thank you so much for loving these characters with all their flaws with me, for supporting an indie author, and for joining me in this world for three whole books!

Easter Eggs in Book 3 brought to you by Aimee Vance (Ulf, Revna, and the *Hadriel*); Jess Perkinson (Ivan Trevino and the *Calypso*); and A.P. Walston (Lovelace and the *Pale Queen*) — IYKYK!

ABOUT THE AUTHOR

L.B. Benson is a native Texan and a lifelong reader. She formally immortalized her love of books by earning a Bachelor of Arts in English from the University of Texas. While she primarily writes romance, you can find her engrossed in almost any genre.

L.B. spends her spare time dreaming up stories in the Texas countryside where she lives with her family.

***

Stay up to date by following along at https://lbtheauthor.com or on social media (@lb_the_author).

instagram.com/lb_the_author